NUCLEAR

M. C. BLACKHEART

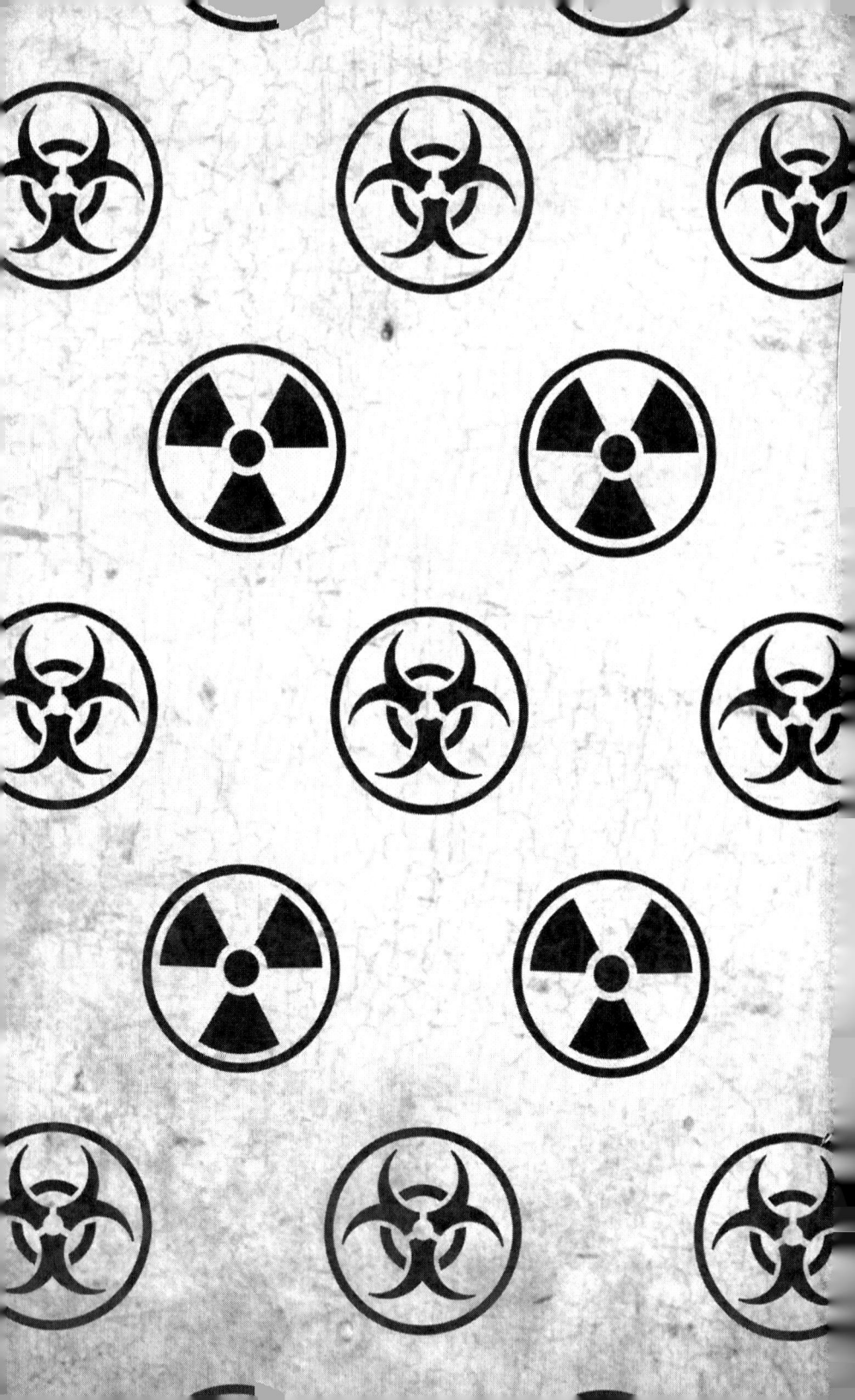

Content Warning

This is an adult romance horror novel that contains graphic and explicit content as well as serious mental health concerns. This book is intended for adults 18 and older. Reader discretion is advised. If you are sensitive to any of the following trigger warnings, this book may not be for you:

- Sexually explicit scenes
- Depression
- Suicidal ideation
- Self-harm
- Murder
- Death
- Blood and Gore Depiction
- Loss
- Grief
- Unprotected sex
- CNC
- Degradation
- Knife play
- Violence
- Death of a Parent
- Invasion of Privacy
- Home Invasion
- War
- Torture
- Kidnapping
- Stalking
- Physical Violence
- Explicit Death Scenes
- Rough Sex
- Morbid Humor
- Breath Play
- Alcohol Use
- Car accident (Remembered)
- Primal Play
- Mask Play
- Fear Play
- Strong Language

Copyright © 2024 by M.C. Blackheart

All rights reserved. No part of this publication may be reproduced, stored or transmitted in any form or by any means, electronic, mechanical, photocopying, recording, scanning, or otherwise without written permission from the publisher. It is illegal to copy this book, post it to a website, or distribute it by any other means without permission.

This novel is entirely a work of fiction. The names, characters and incidents portrayed in it are the work of the author's imagination. Any resemblance to actual persons, living or dead, events or localities is entirely coincidental.

M.C. Blackheart asserts the moral right to be identified as the author of this work.

Without limiting the author's exclusive rights, any unauthorized use of this publication to train generative artificial intelligence (AI) technologies is expressly prohibited.

Designations used by companies to distinguish their products are often claimed as trademarks. All brand names and product names used in this book and on its cover are trade names, service marks, trademarks and registered trademarks of their respective owners. The publishers and the book are not associated with any product or vendor mentioned in this book. None of the companies referenced within the book have endorsed the book.

Cover by the author

ISBN: 979-8-9904222-0-9

For anyone who has ever felt the overwhelming burden of being lonely, never feeling good enough, and not knowing their purpose. I hope you find comfort in knowing you aren't alone. Ryker sees your darkness, and he's waiting for you.

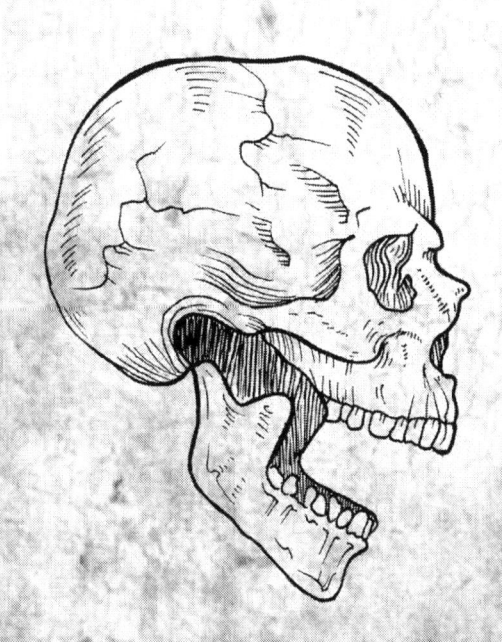

CONTENTS

PROLOGUE.. 9

1. THE PURSUIT...17
2. THE CAPTURE... 29
3. DECONTAMINATION... 39
4. CAPTIVITY.. 51
5. THE CONTAMINATION...................................... 58
6. THE NAIVE DECISION.. 71
7. WRAITHS... 88
8. EXTRACTION.. 99
9. THE LAST APARTMENT ON THE LEFT.......... 109
10. THE PRIVILEGE... 117
11. THE ONLY SURVIVOR....................................... 125
12. ESCAPE PLANS.. 131
13. OUT OF LOSS COMES OBSESSION................. 142
14. THE TWO-HEADED BEAST.............................. 148
15. HOME.. 156
16. INSTINCTS.. 163
17. THE STALKER.. 179
18. NEW FRIENDS... 188
19. THE BLADE... 197
20. THE ACCIDENT.. 213
21. CONFRONTATION... 221
22. MEMORY LANE.. 231
23. RAIDERS... 247

CONTENTS

24. TEAMWORK 265
25. EMOTIONS 282
26. I AM BROKEN, TOO 298
27. REDEMPTION 315
28. LOVE AND BLOOD 326
29. STRANGE GLOW 348
30. PREPARATION 369
31. CAT AND MOUSE 381
32. LILY 397
33. THE RECKONING 408

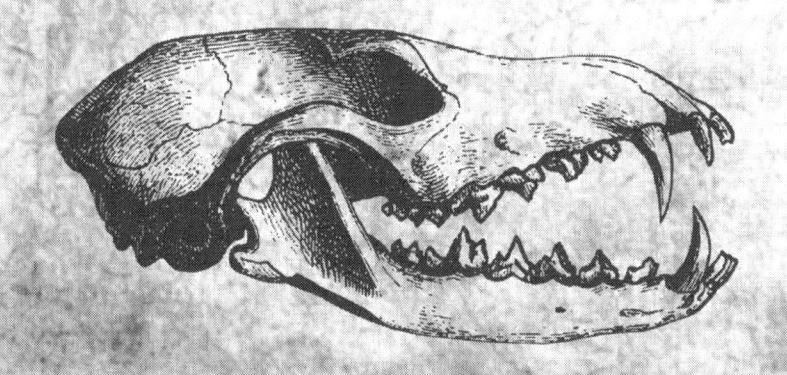

EPILOGUE 424

BOOK PLAYLIST

1. HANDLEBARS BY FLOBOTS
2. CLOSER BY KINGS OF LEON
3. CHEMICAL BY THE DEVIL WEARS PRADA
4. HOSPITAL FOR SOULS BY BRING ME THE HORIZON
5. THAT'S JUST LIFE BY MEMPHIS MAY FIRE
6. BLACK HOLE SUN BY SOUNDGARDEN
7. PROBLEMATIC. BY ARANKAI
8. IMMORTALITY BY PEARL JAM
9. NERVE ENDINGS BY TOO CLOSE TO TOUCH
10. DRIVEN UNDER BY SEETHER
11. ALKALINE BY SLEEP TOKEN
12. SEXTAPE BY DEFTONES
13. YOUR DECISION BY ALICE IN CHAINS
14. LOSING MY RELIGION BY THE WONDER YEARS
15. LONELY DAY BY SYSTEM OF A DOWN
16. SPACE ENOUGH TO GROW BY OF MICE AND MEN
17. CHOKEHOLD BY SLEEP TOKEN
18. TEAR YOU APART BY SHE WANTS REVENGE
19. THE DEATH OF PEACE OF MIND BY BAD OMENS
20. BLOODSTREAM BY STATELESS
21. END OF ME BY A DAY TO REMEMBER
22. TONIGHT THE WORLD DIES BY AVENGED SEVENFOLD

PROLOGUE

MAGGIE:

<u>*The world went to shit around a year ago.*</u>

The worldwide resources of natural gas were becoming harder and harder to find. Countries outside of America were dealing with overpopulation issues and were running out of viable land space for homes and crops.

Texas became the world's largest supplier of natural gas after an oil rig crew discovered one of the biggest oil and gas wells ever found. The issue was, everyone wanted a piece of it, but America wasn't willing to share.

In 2103, the United States suffered a cyber-attack that swept the nation in the worst way. Businesses were forced to close, precious government intel was leaked, and citizens were forced back into what seemed like the dark ages. The economy began to fall within a matter of hours.

Panicked by what could have been the end of the U.S., government officials reached out to China for help due to the financial arrangement already established for the trade system between the two entities. The American government proposed a plan that discussed buying technology from China that could help design an advanced AI-based cyber defense system, known as C.A.G.I.S. which stands for Cybernetic Advanced Guard and Intrusion Shield. China agreed to lend the money (all $914 billion of it) and equipment in exchange for access to the software in their own country, and the money to be repaid later. Within a week the U.S. was able to identify the threats and regain control over the national cyber network, resulting in a damaged, but recovering nation.

China offered to erase a significant portion of America's debt in exchange for access to the newly discovered oil wells in Texas. America declined the offer because they knew if China would make an offer, another country would likely offer higher payment to be an ally. This angered the Chinese government, and in their population crisis, they began to strengthen their allyship with Russia foreshadowing their attacks on the U.S. to gain not only oil and natural gas but also land to begin a new country under communist rule.

Russia and China fell off the grid for a few months. The government officials for these countries quit attending United Nations meetings and became hermits in their own countries. Representatives of India, Brazil, and South Africa soon followed. In response to their odd behavior, the U.S. began to set up underground bunkers and laboratories to create safe havens for the rich, and to prepare retaliation plans for possible attacks.

Nuclear

On July 26th, 2105, China's dictator issued one statement to America after months of silence, "This is your final chance to share resources with us."

Our president didn't respond.

Instead, he reached out to our military, preparing for war, and initiated the evacuation of all people who had reserved spots in the underground bunkers. One week later, China dropped a nuclear bomb on New York City, completely obliterating the city and its inhabitants. After the military had assessed the damage, the news channels fought over who would share the news that the weapon did the damage of what three nuclear bombs had done in the past.

It was the beginning of a nuclear wasteland. Within hours another bomb fell in Los Angeles. In response, America retaliated with the nukes we had, beginning with Shanghai and Hong Kong. Mass hysteria began to ensue as the American people were told to evacuate their homes and seek shelter in smaller cities and rural areas. In a matter of a couple weeks, the U.S. had regressed in environmental progress. Weapons we had only read about in books destroyed our hopes and dreams of a "free" world.

No amount of medical school could prepare my poker face for the carnage that stained the once peaceful streets. Any gunshot wound I had seen in my emergency rotation in the hospital did not prepare me for the way rapid fire bullets singe and tear through human flesh. No amount of training could prepare me to see a missile turn a person into a pile of webbed gore and twitching limbs. I truly believe that nothing in this world could've prepared me for the way it feels to get used to seeing people die brutal and agonizing deaths over, and over, and over again.

No weapons were excluded from the annihilation of the planet. You name a weapon, and I promise I've seen someone die from it.

Powerful individuals watched from their safe havens as hell unfolded on Earth, observing it all through satellite eyes. Even though America had collapsed, our government clung to a victimized and self-serving war, determined to persevere. It wasn't the way that any of us expected the apocalypse to begin.

Personally, I had my money on zombies. Speaking of which, the humans that were exposed to high levels of radiation did not survive or became mutated beyond the ability to function. Needless to say, zombies are not a part of this story. They sound like a cakewalk compared to what waits for us when we walk out of our front doors. At least zombies are predictable, but people? People are full of volatile thoughts and actions.

As a result of the war, there was a major illness that ravaged the people fighting to survive. Radiation sickness was killing people rapidly as the human body could not withstand the intensity of Grade X radiation. In response to this, a large pharmaceutical company called Radical Inc. began to develop a medication that could temporarily relieve the symptoms of radiation poisoning. This antidote was called RADBLOCK. Tiny vials of the potent blue liquid were bottled and dispersed quickly, and they even made sure the elixir had a good flavor so people would be more compliant with taking it.

However, in typical American fashion, they came at a cost. They would let people in poverty die before they would give a dose away. Even at the end of our world, greed still sinks its teeth deep into our country's flesh.

The military depleted resources and soldiers over the first eleven months of the war. When they realized they had killed off a large portion of the soldiers and they did not have enough people to fuel their fight, the US initiated an emergency draft. The slogan was "You may not be interested in the war, but the war is interested in you. It's time to give your all for your country."

Innovative Readiness Training or IRT was a pushed propaganda to expedite the soldiers who at least somewhat qualified to fight the war. The mascot for the campaign was a retro clock cartoon character who represented the crucial aspect of time in the grand scheme of the war. The cartoon was used in multiple advertisements to try and downplay the severity of our world's current demise while pushing the government's agenda. "Tick-Tock Teddy" became the spokesperson for mass genocide.

Anyone between 18-30 was to be drafted, preferably voluntarily, but they made sure to take you involuntarily if they had to. Anything to maintain a "whose dick is bigger" contest between the people in power fueling the war.

Lucky me, I'm 29.

People started disappearing rapidly. One day you'd see someone, and the next, they were gone without a trace. Large military vehicles and helicopters would raid urban and suburban areas to find warm bodies to serve. We were never told of what awaited us on the other side of kidnapping, but you would never see the victims again once they were taken. The rumor was that the government was trying to develop a super soldier that could withstand the harsh conditions that the high levels of radiation created, but nothing was ever confirmed.

TV and news radio stations stopped broadcasting after the first week of the bombings. The final sign off was from America Today news which ended with "May God be with you all, and may you find comfort in knowing that your soul will rest with him no matter the outcome of the apocalypse." After living post-apocalypse, I'm certain that God can't exist and if he does, this world we live in has to be a fucked-up version of the rapture. God took his people and left the rest of us to suffer in the flames of this hell.

The radiation did not only affect people, but it also affected the wildlife across the nation. Radioactive rays began to disassemble animal DNA which mutated even the humblest of creatures into feral beasts. The tiniest of animals became some of the most feared, while larger ones just became more dangerous than anyone could've predicted. The food chain became rearranged, and humans reached the bottom.

Ironically, these creatures are the things I fear the least. It's a wasteland of everyone for themselves, and people will torture you, kill you, or even sell you for their own personal gain. America has just become a ruthless barter system.

Humanity is on the brink of extinction, and hope is nothing but a four-letter word.

Regardless of all these things, one primal instinct is still prominent in the human mindset: survival, and that's what I plan to do, no matter the cost.

YOU MAY NOT BE INTERESTED IN THE WAR, BUT THE WAR IS INTERESTED IN

YOU!

IT'S TIME TO GIVE YOUR ALL FOR YOUR COUNTRY.

THIS IS A PAID ADVERTISEMENT OF THE U.S.A. MILITARY

1

MAGGIE (8 MONTHS AGO):

THE PURSUIT

Bang!

Snap.

Well shit, that was my last bullet. I stare at my empty pistol in frustration, never slowing my pace as I sprint. I pull on the slide, praying that it's just jammed. The chamber is empty and my heart sinks when I eject the clip only to discover that I'm now unarmed.

All I can do is run.

I feel like running is the only thing I know how to do anymore. Trying to remain a ghost hidden away in a wasteland is almost impossible when you are always running from someone or something.

Keep going. I tell myself, feeling my ankles quiver with every step I take.

Faster.

Exhaustion screams from my muscles while adrenaline and fear flood into my veins like a broken damn, supporting my momentum. I'm sprinting with as much speed as my legs can produce despite being weighed down by my thick anti-radiation suit, belt, and boots, but they are much faster than I am.

My breathing is heavy, and I do my best to inhale through my nose and exhale out of my mouth to maintain some kind of pace and composure.

I try to ignore the feeling of smothering as my respirator resists my desperate attempts to breathe. The warmer air inside the mask seems to choke me as I continue to circulate my own humidity.

I've successfully avoided the soldiers twice, so surely the third time is the charm, right? The only advantage I have is that I know this town better than they do.

The city is small, and the roads are full of sharp twists and turns. I quickly veer off to the turn on my right.

"Don't lose her!" a coarse male voice yells from behind me. There is no indication of fatigue in his tone.

I take an immediate left into a hidden entrance driveway and make my way to the house at the end of it, never turning back to see how close they tail behind me.

Nuclear

I won't stand a chance at getting away if I hesitate, even for a second.

Sweat runs into my eyes as I grab the front doorknob. I take a deep breath followed by a small prayer that this door is unlocked, as I turn the tarnished metal knob.

Click.

The door swings open forcefully, and I can't tell if it's from my desperate push or from loose hinges, but either way, I'm in.

I throw myself through the threshold and slam the door behind me, making sure to lock it. Three locks are on the door and I make sure to engage the knob, deadbolt, and the sliding lock at the top for safe measure.

I lean my back against the door.

My heart throbs in my skull, and my legs feel like gelatin as I do my best to not collapse. I can't get my respirator off fast enough as I unfasten the straps in the back, tossing it to the ground not caring about the radiation exposure.

Hyperventilation comes naturally as I try to restore oxygen in my body. The air is rigid and cold, much like the prison my brain has found itself in with the anxiety coursing through me. My eyes ping pong in every direction making sure that I am safe for the moment. Silent tears stain my cheeks and blur my vision as I try to discern my surroundings. I stifle my breathing and suppress the sobs threatening to escape as I press my ear against the splintering wooden door. No heavy footsteps or gruff voices can be heard, and I release a quiet sigh of relief.

That was close.

Too close.

   A dusty staircase is directly in front of me, indicating it hasn't been used in a while. A very outdated dining room is on my right, with an antique cherry wood table in the center. Six chairs with intricate scroll work surround it. A large window decorated in sheer curtains casts the filtered afternoon sunlight into the dim room illuminating the heavy blanket of dust on everything. A large china cabinet sits in the back of the room, old and stoic in stature. I pull back a curtain and peer out.

No sign of the unflavored pop tarts anywhere.

   Unflavored pop tarts being the big, angry men that were chasing me. I figure it's a fitting term because they are all the same and lack personality.

   I make my way over to the china cabinet that is full of stringy cobwebs. A series of drawers are just below the main cabinet, two of which have locks. I rummage through the others without much luck of finding anything. I jiggle the locked drawers, but they don't budge. I'm in serious need of a weapon.

   I walk into the kitchen, careful to take hurried but quiet steps. The room is spacious and is joined with the living room. It would've been a great asset to house parties.

   I dig through drawers looking for anything small enough to pick those tiny locks, because my gut is screaming that in an abandoned house, anything with a lock on it must be worth getting open. No sign of a key, but the third drawer I opened appeared to be a junk drawer.

Thank God for junk drawers.

After pulling everything out, I manage to find the world's thinnest Allen wrench and a Bobby pin.

Perfect.

Lock picking is something I've only seen in movies, but I'm willing to try my luck. It's pretty much the same concept as after seven seasons of medical shows, you are pretty much a doctor.

I hurry back into the dining room and kneel to make the drawers eye level. For the first drawer, I line the Allen wrench up to the bottom side of the lock. I wiggle my makeshift tension wrench through the keyway, feeling each pin inside the lock give until the wrench won't advance anymore. Taking the bobby pin, I bend the flat side back so I can use the end with the hook to engage the pins in the lock. I slowly pass the bobby pin into the lock, trying to imagine the layout in my mind. Five pins stand between me and this drawer's contents. I start to apply pressure to the pins in order.

Click.

Click.

Click.

Click.

My breathing hitches as I can't get the fifth pin to engage. I dig in the lock trying to not break its delicate interior. I push with more pressure, taking the risk and hoping I don't damage it.

Click.

I turn the lock to the right agonizingly slow to avoid messing up my hard work. The lock stops at a 45-degree angle. I release the Allen wrench and try the drawer.

Pop.

The drawer slides open shakily as if its wheels aren't on its tracks correctly.

It's empty.

I put my hand in and feel every corner of the drawer. Panic sets in as I realize how much time I've wasted. I look over my shoulder through the large pane window, but still see nothing other than decayed greenery. The sun is low in the sky, inching closer and closer to dusk. No figures linger in the botched landscape, making a small bubble of hope that I lost my pursuers rise in my chest.

My hand continues to blindly search until I feel it. A small key is taped to the backside of the drawer front just below the handle screws. I pick the tape with my thumb nail until it releases. It hits the wooden bottom with a "plink." The key is oxidized and aged as if it was a relic from World War II. I wipe it off on my pants to get rid of the residue. It's small in size, but

Nuclear

not small enough to fit the other drawer. This has to go to something important, why else would it be locked up?

Before I have time to begin searching for locks in this abandoned and hollow home, an overwhelming feeling of nausea chips away at my insides much like a chisel does to stone.

Vertigo sets in as the room spins, and my brain forgets how to control my body. I stumble into a small closet sized bathroom located right next to the kitchen. I reach the toilet just in time before vomit spews from my mouth.

Supporting myself against the deteriorating porcelain bowl, I dry heave uncontrollably. The sickly green color of bile stains the shallow, murky water wading in the bowl. I'm surprised there is anything to throw up considering the fact that I can't remember the last time I ate.

This is a feeling I'm all too familiar with.

Radiation sickness.

I unzip the upper part of my suit and reach into my bra. The tremors in my hands are so severe I find it hard to grip onto anything. I manage to secure my index finger and thumb around a small vial resting against the support wire. I take a deep breath trying to calm the sudden onset of symptoms. If I pass out, I'm done for.

The vial is no bigger than an inch, and is filled with a thin, blue liquid. I place the metal pop top of the vial between my teeth until I hear the "clink," and I spit it to the side with an excess amount of saliva leaving my mouth with it.

I throw back the liquid like a shot of tequila. The taste of sweet cotton candy dances across my taste buds as I wait for the radiation protective medication to disperse through my cells. I concentrate on breathing as the high tide of nausea starts to fade out of my system. Slumping against the cool wall of the interior bathroom, I realize that was my last dose. It'll buy me at least another week out here.

(Word to the wise: while trying to survive the nuclear apocalypse, I learned very quickly to hide the important things in my bra. No one thinks to look there, and most attackers who get close enough to rob you, won't have the chance to search you that thoroughly).

As I wait to feel the sickness dissipate, my mind wonders to the place it always does when I have time to think.

Stevie.

That last night replays over and over in my head.

It was never supposed to be this way.

"Maggie, are you okay? You just seem kind of off today."

I glance down to check that the thick manila envelope, packed with all the documents, isn't sticking out of my work bag as I head to the kitchen. I don't have the heart to explain it to her, and she would try to stop everything. It'll be so much easier for her to find the note with my explanation tomorrow.

Nuclear

I smile, a true one for the first time in months.

"I'm fine. I feel the best I have in a while actually."

I know tonight everything ends. No more pain, no more meds, no more numbness, and most importantly, I never have to be alone again.

Tonight is the last night Stevie will be in the house, the last time she will rely on me as her older sister. I look to the beautiful blue sapphire ring on her hand.

She has James now and I'm so happy for her.

She is all grown up, and she has a full life ahead of her. Even though she's my foster sister, she's become my closest family. I remember when I filed for her adoption from the state ten years ago. We are six years apart so she was twelve when I turned eighteen, and I couldn't let her stay in the home we had spent the last three years in, not with our creepy foster dad always watching us, especially with the way he looked at Stevie.

I had to always sleep in her room because I was afraid he would do God only knows what to her when I wasn't around. I missed out on so many things in my teenage years to protect her, and she would continually validate that nothing ever happened, so it was worth it to me.

For so long she has been my only purpose, but now there is nothing left for me. The depression has slowly eaten at me for years, eroding me into an empty shell. She was the last thing that made me not ache so much.

"I got the last few boxes moved to the truck this morning. Did your night at the hospital go okay? It's a little later than usual for you to be coming home," Stevie inquires with concern.

"Yeah, my last patient coded right before shift change so I got held up a little longer than I would've liked."

The lie rolls easily off my tongue.

I went to see my attorney this morning to sign over my house, my bank accounts, and everything I own that can help her and James start their life together.

"A residency student's work is never done, huh?" She shakes her head with a small chuckle.

I nod with a laugh.

"Hey, thanks for letting me stay one more night. James says the bed frame is coming tomorrow and personally I just don't want to sleep on the floor," she remarks.

"Girl, you know you are always welcome here," I respond before grabbing some coffee from the pot she's already made.

"It would mean a lot to me if you could come over tomorrow and see the place! I just know you'd love it," she states excitedly, practically jumping up and down.

"There's nowhere else I'd rather be," I affirm with a smile, knowing that for me there won't be a tomorrow.

Nuclear

That evening, she turns in for bed before sunset, saying that she was absolutely wiped from the day. I took her out for a massage and mani pedis one last time and overall, the day was everything I wanted it to be.

I laid the large envelope on the counter with a small white envelope containing my final letter. I write her name on the back of the smaller envelope, before grabbing my bottle of Xanax and heading out the door.

Little did I know that I wouldn't even get to take the pills and still I'd never see her again.

I planned to end my life at one of my favorite places when I was a kid. The Cobweb Waterfall is an enormous waterfall that spills into a small river. If you sit at the top, you can see almost the whole city from the outskirts of town.

The bombs started to fall right as I dumped the pills in my hand to take. The mushroom clouds started to blend with the oranges and reds of the sky as the impact of the bombs vibrated the earth.

In that moment, all I wanted was to see Stevie.

I just needed to know she was okay.

When I was able to return to our home a few days later after I got my hands on an anti-radiation suit, it was completely annihilated. All that remained of the small, cozy home was silver ash and smoky char. Tears filled my eyes, and sobs overwhelmed me as I knelt beside the remnants of what was once my life.

I wish she was here.

I wish I could keep her safe again.

2

MAGGIE (8 MONTHS AGO):

THE CAPTURE

The symptoms of radiation sickness fade within a matter of five minutes. Although it took the sickness away, the tiredness still aches heavy in my bones.

I catch glimpse of myself in the aged mirror of the bathroom and quickly recite my mantra of, "You are good enough. There's a purpose for you here. Keep going." I started the affirmation after I lost Stevie because I know that's what she would tell me.

I shake off the feelings and fatigue before focusing back on the task at hand. I search the entire first level of the house, unable to find anything that has a lock.

Making my way upstairs, I create an audible squeak with every step. The hallway at the top of the stairs is long and leads to the left. Four doors line the walls along with the words "It's Over" written messily in black paint. The carpet lining the hallway appears to be a different color than what it should be from all of the dust that is piled on top of it.

I make my way through the three bedrooms and one bathroom. I'll never get used to the creepiness of abandoned houses that appear to be stuck in time and slowly rotting.

The last bedroom I walk into appears to be the master. I scan the room until my gaze locks on the answer to my prayers. A dusty, worn gun safe rests next to the closet of the room with a big, beautiful padlock on it.

Jackpot, baby.

I hurry over and try the key, a sigh of relief escapes me as it slides in with no resistance. The lock pops as I turn it, and I quickly slide it out of the securement loop and toss it to the floor. The door swings open to expose four beautiful guns including a sawed-off shotgun, a twenty gauge, a forty-five, and a Glock 19. A small but ample supply of ammo rests in the bottom of the safe.

Slipping the Glock into my hand, I eject the mag and it's as empty as my stomach. I reach to grab the ammo when I hear a sound that makes my heart jump into hysteria.

A gunshot echoes through the barren house from outside.

Fuck.

I load the mag as fast as I can, counting the bullets as I go. I struggle to get all fifteen rounds in because my hands have started shaking like a shirt in a hurricane. Loud and aggressive voices start to become audible.

I grip the slide of the Glock and pull back, hearing the bullet load into the chamber before looking out the upstairs window that faces the front yard. Three large men in camouflage uniforms emerge from the thick trees. Tactical vests cling tightly to their chests. Skull shaped half masks cover the upper parts of their faces while the lower part is coated with black war paint. White teeth shine from their mouths as they talk and search.

"She had to have gone this way," a skinnier man says to the largest one. "This is the only house we haven't cleared."

I swallow hard, and kiss the side of the Glock, hoping it'll help with an outcome in my favor.

Aiming out the window and trying to remain out of sight, I catch one in my crosshairs. My finger rests on the trigger and hovers there as I weigh the option of taking a life.

"I bet with the way she fights, she's a hell of a fuck." The tallest smirks.

Okay, thanks for making the decision for me.

He will be the first to go.

I pull the trigger and fire a bullet directly through his throat. I was aiming for his head, but it'll do.

Blood spurts from his neck as he grabs it. Falling to his knees, he coughs and chokes as the deep red liquid comes out of his mouth and nose. Crimson streams engulf every color of his clothing. The other two begin to search the windows, looking for me, completely ignoring their comrade.

Without thinking, I point the weapon at the second tallest man, but my hands are shaking from the lightning bolt of adrenaline igniting every nerve in my body. I pull the trigger regardless because a wounded enemy is better than an unwounded one. The man yells in anger and pain,

"Motherfucker! When I find you, you are a dead bitch!"

Blood trails down his arm indicating that I hit his bicep. I line up for another wobbly shot, and fire.

Snap.

I try to shoot again.

Snap.

Great, it's jammed, and they have reached the front door. The reverberation of the door slamming open shakes the floor beneath my feet. I rush into the closet with bi-fold doors. The door squeals across aged metal tracks, and I wince at how loud it is. The door is missing a knob, so the screw hole is my only way of viewing outward.

I kneel watching through my peephole and listening to the men angrily tear the house apart, looking for me. Standing on the ungodly shoe pile across the closet floor, I try my best to maintain my balance. I feverishly pull over and over at the slide on the Glock.

No dice.

I should've picked the forty-five.

I put my hand over my mouth to smother the sound of my breathing. The bedroom door opens, and hefty boots drag through the dirty carpet.

"Come out, come out, wherever you are," the larger man teases. "You aren't leaving this room, naughty bird. I can smell you."

Smell me? What the fuck?

The smaller man motions toward the closet. I sink further into the disheveled clothes, trying to avoid getting a shoe stuck up my ass. He sticks his finger through the knob hole; and cracks the door just enough for his fingers to slide in the side.

I'm trapped.

Absolutely defenseless.

The door squeaks open as the old closet door track screams from rust and wear.

Their confident gazes meet my terror filled eyes.

Before I can react, the larger man lands a blow to the left side of my face. Stars bloom in my vision as pain spreads like wildfire across my face. The metallic smell of copper overwhelms me, as blood droplets trail down my chin.

"That's for the bullet wound, you stupid whore," the large man spits in my direction.

"Get the fuck up," he commands, as his calloused hands try to pull me to my feet. My vision is blurred from the force of his hit, so I can't get a good look at either of their faces. Before I can react to my situation, a bag is quickly placed over my head, rendering my sight futile. A stale smell of cigarettes and old canvas invades my nose as the material rubs harshly against my face.

My hands reach up and scratch at the fabric with dubious intent, but my arms are forced down and behind my back with a robust grip that my strength cannot even remotely match.

Thin but sturdy plastic is placed around my wrists which I quickly discern is a zip tie. I flip through the memory of a self-defense class I took a couple years ago which discussed that if you are ever bound with a zip tie, ensure that you present your hands to your captor with clenched fists and palms facing downward. The angle is awkward behind my back, but I manage to rest the thumb sides of my hands together using the width of my wrists to my advantage before I'm bound tight.

I kick and thrash, hoping to get free, but the two men in this room who now hold me are much stronger than I am. They carry me carelessly down the stairs. I bump into the handrail and the opposite wall, as I continue to try and wiggle free from their grasp.

Nuclear

"Stop moving!" one guy yells, but it just makes me want to squirm more violently.

"I will knock your ass out if I have to. Stop. Moving," the larger man orders, and as much as I hate to listen to a man, I need to be awake. They carry me for at least a mile, before stopping and whispering words to each other that I can't understand.

The men throw me forcefully into the back seat of a car, and the slamming door makes my ears ring. Once I'm sure that they don't plan on reopening my door, I start to wiggle my wrists against the tether that binds them. I gradually twist my wrists until they're parallel, leaving just enough slack for one hand to slip through.

I'm out of restraints, but I'm definitely not strong enough to take on these two men. My brain starts to run through scenarios of attacking one of the men from the backseat, but none of them end well for me. I cannot guarantee I would survive a car crash if I attack the driver, and I'm not strong enough to head lock either of them effectively. At least I know when we get to our destination, they need me alive because if they didn't, they would've already killed me.

I run my fingers across my surroundings. The seat below me consists of cracked leather and exposed foam. The car or van is clearly in run-down condition. A smell of body odor mixed with old whiskey permeates through the canvas sack on my head. I do my best to suppress the vomit rising in my throat.

The driver's door opens first, and the car rocks back and forth when the driver takes his seat. The passenger seat opens shortly after, but the car doesn't rock nearly as hard when he enters the vehicle. The imbalance of the car tells me the driver has to be the larger of the two men.

I know better than to panic and ask questions; it'll just get me a black eye or a concussion. If I ever want to regain some form of freedom, I must stay vigilant and take in all the information I can.

I fight the urge to fidget with the broken pieces of leather that protrude from the seat into the underpart of my thighs. I sit back and listen despite the tears building in my eyes.

"Next stop, Fort Hamby," the larger man's husky voice states sarcastically. Another male voice perks up excitedly from the passenger seat,

"That would give me one hour in the backseat with her."

His voice is significantly more nasal than the other man's voice. A loud slap sound rings through the air, followed by the other guy saying,

"Listen here, you horny fucker; the lieutenant says she's worth a lot. If we get there and she's tarnished in any way, they'll cut your dick off and feed it to you, understand?"

I assume the other guy nodded because the man followed with, "Good, now adjust your junk and shut the fuck up."

Okay, well, at least I'm worth enough not to get raped. The nasally voiced man mumbles under his breath, "When we get where we are going, someone will make her their bitch anyway." Heavy metal music fills the car as if the other man is trying to tune him out.

Great, it's the end of the world, and I get to be someone's bitch.

Rad the Atom Says:

> Don't Forget Your Weekly Dose of
>
> RADBLOCK!

THIS IS A PAID ADVERTISEMENT BY RADICAL INC.

3

MAGGIE (8 MONTHS AGO):

DECONTAMINATION

The car comes to a sudden stop. My body jerks forward, and I brace myself on the seat in front of me. The vehicle is so old it likely doesn't have seat belts, or if it does, my kidnappers simply don't care about my safety.

It's ironic considering I'm "worth" so much.

Both the driver and passenger doors open simultaneously with a loud squeak. My guts start to churn as my fear heightens. I feel like a child in a storm, lost and anxious.

I wait for the click of my door opening, and I push with everything I have. I hear one of their bodies slam into the door, but I don't waste time to inspect what happened. I get the bag off my head and run, not looking at any of my surroundings but the lush greenery in front of me.

Footsteps are on my heels within seconds, and they are fast.

Too fast.

Faster than I could ever go, but I keep going.

A strong arm wraps around my waist and lifts me off the ground, but my feet are still moving.

Still trying to get me to the safety of the trees.

I know how to hide; I just have to get there. I scratch, dig, and bite at the arms that hold me desperate for any give.

But there isn't any. I'm captured again and tears fill my eyes in defeat. I don't stop trying to get free, and the man just laughs.

"Persistent, aren't we?" he inquires. I can't see his face, but I can hear his smirk.

The nausea of anxiety comes creeping back as he one handedly puts the bag back on my head and holds me against him with the other.

The other man grabs my hands again, but this time, they are in front of me. I fight until I hear the zip tie teeth slide through the locking mechanism.

I'm caught for now, but at least with my hands in the front I can always try to slam them toward my abdomen in an effort to break the bonds, which was an option I didn't have when my

Nuclear

wrists were bound behind me. I just hope I get the opportunity to use it.

Two strong hands wrap around my waist and throw me head-first over a hefty shoulder. I imagine he's the guy who was in the driver's seat because I feel like I was just thrown onto a brick wall. I lay limp against him, because my arms are stuck under my body weight and above his large frame. There is no fighting I can do in this position that won't just waste my energy.

Dizziness blurs my vision like a bird who flew too hard into a window as blood rushes to my head. His sweat bleeds into my clothes making me want to gag from the sensation and the odor.

It can't be that hard to find some damn deodorant.

After a few minutes of what feels like eternity, he stops, slings me to my feet, and pushes me forward.

"Move along princess, we don't have all day," he scoffs at me before laughing with his creepy friend. The bag still fits snug over my face, but I do my best to guide myself ahead.

As I take two steps forward, an earsplitting squeal fills the air. The automated doorway opens so slowly that it only intensifies the dreadful noise, and you can practically hear the rust scraping off the old metal.

When the sound stops, I take cautious steps inside, unsure of what nightmare awaits. The room I walk into echoes my footsteps boasting its size. Little peep holes through my burlap sack move into my view and let through minimal light from ancient fluorescents as they flicker in and out. I'm able to make out a few random things like flipped couches and damaged desks. Shadows and blurry images of a doctor's office lobby in disarray stain the back of my retinas.

Their footsteps boom and overshadow mine as they try to get in front of me. I hear the sound of a button being pushed, followed by a ringing bell. Large doors slide open indicating that there is an elevator that has just arrived to the floor. Straining my eyes through the tiniest hole in the burlap sack, I try to make out anything to help me figure out where I am, but it's impossible to focus my vision on anything useful.

Hefty hands push me from behind. The fact that these men have stopped talking makes my anxiety begin to eat at my composure. My stomach drops as the elevator begins to descend, beeping with each floor it passes.

I count twenty-eight beeps before the elevator comes to a shaky stop, knocking me off balance. I'm pretty sure if someone jumped, the elevator suspension system would snap, and we would fall to our deaths.

The doors open and the smell of bleach fills the small lift. I begin to walk forward slowly; before someone tries to make me move again.

"Well, well, what have you all brought today?" a loud female voice asks. The way she talks reminds me of an infomercial, happy and obnoxious.

Like is she going to sell me a ShamWow or????

I try to visualize her face, but she is too far out of view of my peep hole.

"We found the girl. The one that Dr. Hyde says has the GTM46 mutation."

The what???

"Ah, he will be so pleased. Take her to intake lab four please," she directs.

"Not so fast, lady, there is a huge bounty on this girl's head, and we intend to fully collect on it."

Absolute silence falls around me, and the fangs of fear pierce into my gut exacerbated by the fact that I can't see what's happening.

"Does she have any other marks on her other than the bruising on the left side of her face that you mentioned?" the lady asks with a slice of disappointment in her voice.

"No, ma'am. I assure you; she did more damage to us than we did to her." The large man's voice is tainted with nervousness.

I jump at the touch of what I think is the lady's hands. She chuckles before saying, "Calm down. I'm not the person that you need to be afraid of." Her voice is all but calming and it makes my stomach flip.

Another beat of silence follows, and I can feel myself trembling with trepidation.

"Okay, you will be paid before your departure." I can hear the lady writing something on a wooden surface.

"Here, take this to financial on your way back up. It'll be on floor eight, you can't miss the big double doors."

I'm escorted down a hall and the further we walk, the worse the bleach smell is. I'm stopped by a grip on my right arm after about five minutes of walking. I hear the swipe of a badge followed by a beep and a click as the door in front of me opens.

I'm placed in an unsteady chair and the nuisance of a bag is finally removed from my head.

The walls are such a bright white, and I have been in darkness for so long that my eyes struggle to adjust. A door slams behind me, and I assume my kidnappers have left me alone to collect their bounty.

Fucking assholes.

When I can see with some clarity, I realize I'm in some sort of auditorium with a large projector screen directly in front of me. The only thing on the screen is Radical's logo, which pulses in and out, as if waiting for instructions.

Two soldiers circle the room as to intimidate us. My gaze carries from side to side revealing twelve other people who seem to be just as confused as myself. Scared eyes all around the room try to avoid eye contact.

"Remove your clothing and head through the decontamination chamber on your left," an automated voice directs through a loudspeaker from above.

Mixed emotions of fear, anxiety, and dread become visible on the twelve faces that surround me, and my own feelings bubble to the surface as terror strikes me like a baseball bat to the chest.

Solemnly, we all do as it says, understanding our fate and that running will only result in death. I remove my top, leaving my bra unless someone tells me otherwise. After observing I've received no attention for my action, I unbutton my pants and slide them down as I remove my tattered shoes.

I picked one hell of a day to wear a red lace thong.

I stand cold and exposed, and as much as I want to curl into a ball, I refuse to give them the satisfaction. I hold my head high and focus on my breathing as my curves are on display for everyone to see. I glance around and see the look of defeat on a few others' faces, a clear sign that I'm not the only one struggling with this.

Panic smears itself onto the face of a man to my right. It's as if I can see his intrusive thoughts telling him that he can escape. His fingers fumble with the laces of his shoes, clearly taking as long as possible to untie them. His gaze darts feverishly between his laces and the unmarked door on the other side of the room.

Every fiber of my being wants to discourage his actions, but there's no time. His muscles are already flexed in his arms as he lunges into a sprint. Half-way through it, a soldier swings at him with a baton.

The weapon hits the man in the small of his back and discharges a shock of blue and white electricity that brings him to the ground. The jolt renders him immediately unconscious.

"Anybody else?" the soldier asks sardonically.

"I didn't think so."

Every person in the room is either fully undressed or scrambling to do so to avoid the possibility of being hit with a personalized surge of electricity. The other soldier begins to lift the large screen which reveals a huge entrance with no door. He points his baton toward the doorway wanting us to all move forward. Everyone rises cautiously from their seats, and makes their way into a single file line, treading with apprehension.

We file into a room with metal walls covered in dripping rust. The air is sterile, like the smell of a hospital. An alarm blares so loud that I have to cover my ears. Thick iron doors fall slowly from the ceiling, closing off the exits.

A powerful mist sprays on us from above through an extensive sprinkler system, and it begins to accumulate on my skin. The substance appears to be oily as it adheres to my flesh. It becomes warmer, which turns my skin pink from the heat. I lift my hand toward the light and watch as steam begins to rise in irregular shaped clouds.

Nuclear

The sensation takes me back to a time at the beginning of the war. The world grew cold when the nuclear fallout blocked the atmosphere and prevented the sunlight from reaching the earth's surface. I remember getting into the shower during one of the early weeks and letting the hot water help me escape from the nightmare I was in. When I emerged, steam rose from my skin like I was a smoldering fire at the end of its life.

Before fear can sink into my bones as the heat starts to be scalding, a shower of cold water falls to remove the oil build-up.

As quickly as it appeared, it was gone. The water feels calming not only to my skin but to my anxiety as well. The cold shower helps me keep my sanity as it becomes the only thing I can focus on. Fat drops as icy as snow sprinkle onto my skin relieving the sensation of overstimulation and lead my thoughts back to an escape plan.

I begin to take in my surroundings, checking for exits or poorly defended areas of the chamber. All my eyes find are sorrowful and confused victims, locked in behind iron doors with no escape.

After the water stops abruptly, my skin is red and irritated, similar to what you'd experience with a sunburn. It's uncomfortable and sore but tolerable. A large fan begins to run, removing the toxins and residue from the air around us. The force of the fan makes the room feel like a wind tunnel. The alarm sounds again as the metal doors begin to rise from where they came.

Everything and everyone are silent for a beat. We look to each other for any reaction, but only the same emotions from earlier resurface. The automated voice commands from overhead, "Please exit through the left doorway; in that room, you will find uniforms with your names on them and your assigned experiment numbers. Please place the articles of clothing on and return to your designated area."

I am one of the first to venture into the next room. I move slowly but with purpose. Upon crossing the door's threshold, the room seems to transport me back to high school.

The high school experience for me was broadly defined by nervous expressions, awkward situations, and the general terror of being shoved into a locker for someone else's enjoyment.

So far, this place has checked all but one of those boxes for me.

Lockers are strewn in a similar pattern on each wall. In front of each of them are benches with stacked piles of clothes on top. I walk to the first bench, examining each card I pass for my name. When I make my way halfway down the third bench, a small index card houses my name. "Maggie Compton, experiment 416," reads the card on top of my clothes. I look over to examine everyone else's attire and cards. The uniforms are all the same. Women get white tank tops and cargo pants, while the men have similar pants and white T-shirts. We all have the same combat boots beside our designated clothes pile.

Nuclear

One of the cards of the girl next to me catches my eye. Hers does not list an experiment number, but instead says, "Organ Donor."

I quickly get dressed as dread settles in the pit of my stomach.

I am being reduced to a number.

My identity is being stolen from me right in front of my eyes, and there's not a damn thing I can do about it. I take a deep breath and hold back the tears that are trying to fall from my eyes. I keep my head down and make my way to the last door to accept my fate.

RADICAL INC.

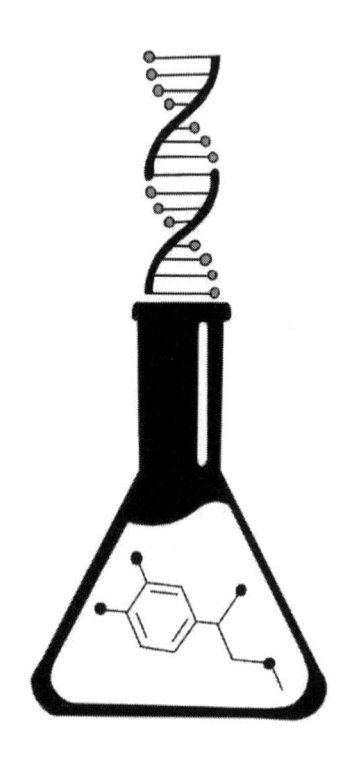

BETTERING THE

NEW WORLD

4

MAGGIE (8 MONTHS AGO):

CAPTIVITY

After crossing into the next room, a feeling of disgust mixed with anguish washes over me when I see them.

Cages.

Human-sized iron bar cages circle the room before us. No furniture resides in any cell. The only things I can see are one pillow, one blanket, and a toilet at the far end of the cells. The faces that I see behind the bars are angry, sad, and numb. Empty cages sprinkle throughout the large room, and they haunt me as if patiently waiting to consume me whole.

They are going to imprison us like animals while we endure whatever they want to do to us. I ball my fists, trying to keep my cool and bite back the words that threaten to escape me. The wounds on my tongue will take forever to heal at the rate that I keep biting it.

My pace is steady in walking to my prison. The room is a large octagon. I count twenty-eight cages, but only seven of them are empty. Guards line the two entrances that I am able to locate on opposite sides of the room. There is a large desk to the north of the room, which houses a giant control panel. I go to stand in front of the cage labeled "416."

I stare at the number as if I'm a dead woman walking who has just found her tomb.

My mouth goes dry, and I lock every muscle I have to keep from trembling.

A large man walks over to me with no emotion in his eyes. "Trackers first and brand second," he states in a raspy, monotone voice. He pulls out what looks like a tag gun I used when I worked in a retail store. It's handheld, black, and has a single trigger. There is a long two-inch needle that protrudes from the top part of the gun, which makes dread kick me in the stomach.

I swallow hard but refuse to give off any sign of distress. He loads a small pellet into the gun and looks at me, his dead eyes hollow and jaded.

"Deep breath," he demands as he slides the long needle of the gun at a 30-degree angle just under my skin. When the needle has reached the hilt, he pulls the trigger.

Pain surges through my body, and I feel my breathing become erratic. I grab onto my forearm, but no amount of pressure that I apply to it dulls the cauterizing sensation. It's as if I can feel the tracker welding itself into my tissue. It is singeing and marking me from the inside out. Tears sting along the waterlines of my eyes, and I am unable to control them as they trail down my cheeks.

He removes a band-aid from his pocket and places it over the entrance wound. It's not just any band aid, though. On the small white bandage is Whiskerkins, a cartoon cat from around 2085, playing with a ball of yarn.

Really?

A fucking band-aid?

What am I? Five?

"Sorry about the child's print. Band-aids are no longer in circulation since the war began, so we take what we can get," the man says nonchalantly.

I do my best to suppress the anger that threatens to force itself out. It's like a slap in the face after already inflicting so much pain. I've never really been good at fighting back words, and typically, I'd spew some profanities, but I know it'll only end badly for me.

I'm outspoken, but I'm not stupid.

He then motions for me to sit inside the threshold of the cage and closes the door in my face with no remorse. He grabs a tattoo gun from a small rolling table beside him and sits in a chair in front of the cage door.

"Give me your wrist," he dictates sternly. I slide my hand through the metal bars. The cool metal that grazes my skin makes me shiver in the most disgusting way.

He grabs my wrist aggressively and rests it on his knee. Dipping the gun in ink, he begins to carve the tattoo needle through my flesh. Shocks of pain elicit from my tender skin as he randomly strikes and avoids nerves.

The pain is annoying, but it's nothing compared to the tracker that he implanted in my forearm. He finishes his work within five minutes.

The line work is scratchy and poorly executed, a disgrace to all of us who have paid good money for top tier tattoos. I glance quickly at the good art that trails from my shoulder down to my wrist, grateful that I was able to get good art before the war, because it's looking like the art of tattooing may be lost forever. If he does this all the time, you'd think he'd be good at it. He places a piece of sticky, stretchy plastic material over the new tattoo.

"You can remove that in twenty-four hours," he says with a spiteful emotion in his tone, almost like he could hear my hateful thoughts. He pushes my hand into the cage and moves to the next person.

Five people without cages stand in the center of the room, their faces marked by absolute horror. They tremble not just from the cold but also from their fear. A man in a scrub-like jumpsuit directs them to a door across the room from my cage that is labeled "Organ Donor Storage."

Nuclear

The thought of what is behind that door makes me physically ill.

I slowly inch towards the back of the cage, sit down on the cold floor, and release the bottled-up emotions that have been afflicting my insides for the last hour. Hot tears fall uncontrollably from my eyes, and sobs force their way out of me. My hand over my mouth does very little to dampen the sorrowful sounds. I do my best to quiet them and avoid drawing attention to myself.

A small TV screen descends from the top of my cage. It's nothing more than just a screen. No buttons are visible for volume control or channel variability. A black and white Radical logo blinks on the screen as if loading, just like on the big screen in the first room I was in.

Static consumes the little television until switching to a man in a lab coat. The man is tall and lanky with a very flat affect. He has large square glasses that seem too bulky for his face, and a slender nose. He appears well kept and put together, but his hair seems out of place. Messy hair curls back out of his face, but there are a few tendrils that refuse to be tamed. Audio comes through the screen, but I miss the introduction of himself.

"Hello. Welcome to Radical Laboratory 102. You are probably wondering why you are here. To answer that question, we must review a little history. As you know, China and America became locked in a nuclear war beginning in 2105. The war not only resulted in a radioactive wasteland in almost every city in the US, but also depleted a large portion of America's resources including soldiers."

He pauses and slides his glasses up the bridge of his nose with one finger before flipping through a spiral bond notebook. The more I listen to this, the more it sounds like a presentation for a company desperately seeking investors.

He reads from a page as he continues, "After studying the effects of the high levels of radiation on the human body, we have found that the basic genetic makeup of humans will not sustain the war. Since the war is still ongoing, the government and military powers had to put their heads together, thus the idea came along of how do we make people resistant to the toxic conditions? We began with offering radiation resistant suits, followed by a serum that can cure radiation sickness for a short period of time."

My heart lurches in my chest. I'm out of RADBLOCK, and I've been so distracted with all of this, it totally slipped my mind. I only have a few days until I'll need more.

Wouldn't it be my luck that I would die from radiation poisoning that is totally preventable before they had a chance to kill me with whatever their plans are.

"However, despite those things, people would still fall victim to the harsh conditions. Then, one day, our chief scientist, Dr. Hyde, offered a solution that we are so excited for you to be a part of." Breathing feels impossible as I wait for him to finish his statement.

Nuclear

"Genetic altering experimentation."

I try to swallow, but my mouth has become dryer than the Sahara Desert. My heart races roughly in my chest from fear as I realize what they are actually doing to people.

The rumors were true.

I'm nothing more than a lab rat, a pawn for important people to use.

"You now belong to Laboratory 102. We reviewed your genetic DNA from a previous sample for lineage testing you had submitted, and we have high hopes that you will be a showcase example of what we can turn humanity into. Thank you for your cooperation 416."

My stomach drops and all I want to do is puke, cry, and scream. God forbid I submit my DNA to see if I have any family left in the world. I look around at everyone else freshly trapped in their kennels.

I'm not the only one panicking. People are shouting pleas of mercy, some are pacing the expanse of their space for escape options, and others have already given up as they sit on the ground and await their fate.

The tears come heavier and with uncontrollable sobs, that make my body ache and twitch from their force. The screen retracts into the ceiling as quickly as it descended.

I'm left alone with my thoughts, desperately trying to avoid considering what happens next.

5

MAGGIE (8 MONTHS AGO):

THE CONTAMINATION

I must've fallen asleep as I'm awoken by a loud, demanding voice, "Get up, 416. The Doc is ready to see you."

Already?

How long did I sleep for?

I guess when there's a nuclear war going on, they don't have time to waste. I swallow hard, even though there's hardly any saliva in my mouth. I can't remember the last time I had a drink of anything, and they aren't exactly eager to help you out here.

"Now, 416! Don't make me make you get up."

Nuclear

I stand on my feet, still a little shaky from my slumber. I rub sleep from my eyes as I walk to the door. My gaze hardens on a man in a tan uniform with a square face and scarred skin. The scars look to be the remnants of knife wounds as the edges are clean and precise. His eyes flame with so much evil that his irises are practically red. My gaze catches a badge listed on the left side of his uniform which just says "Lieutenant." No last name or other identifying words are legible on his suit.

A voice as hateful and aggressive as his eyes threatens- "Don't try anything stupid. There are guards around every entrance, and none of them care if you live or die." Adrenaline overwhelms my system as he looks into the bio-lock of the cage. The door opens with a buzz.

I'll have to keep in mind that they use retinal scanners.

The lieutenant's warm, sweaty palm grips the back of my neck harshly, and he ushers me forward, unfazed as I stumble from his force. He has a baton in his other hand pressed firmly against the small of my back. Sweat begins to form on my brow as my anxiety starts to think of all the cruel things that await me.

A pager buzzes relentlessly in the man's pocket after we cross the threshold of the door across the room from my cage. Frustrated groans and huffs come from behind me.

"I must attend to something. I need you to stay right here. Don't do anything stupid. I'll make sure it hurts if I have to chase you. There's no escape this far underground, sweetheart."

He laughs, obviously proud of himself. I roll my eyes and shake my head at his pride.

He fumbles with the handcuffs in his back pocket while I begin to take in the scene through the big window on my left. He slaps the cuffs on and hooks me to large metal piping protruding from the wall.

"I'll be right back, enjoy the show," he remarks with a wink that makes my blood boil.

The girl that was beside me in the locker room is strapped to a large metal table. Her eyes are dilated and full of sheer terror.

She kicks and thrashes against the binds, but she is not strong enough to get free. The man in the lab coat from the video I watched stands behind her with a large needle. He jams it into the outside of her arm, and she goes limp within seconds. His assistant moves into my line of sight to help the man in the lab coat adjust the woman to a more practical position. Her eyes continue to dart back and forth in unfiltered fear despite her medication induced cataplexy. Screams fill her gaze, but only garbled sounds escape her lips.

Next to her table, a row of small, empty tables with wires protruding from them stretches out. Clear cloches cover the tables, sealing off their interiors from the outside world.

I know I need to try and escape, but I can't tear my eyes away. The man in the lab coat raises the largest scalpel I've ever seen and begins to cut through the woman's abdominal tissue. Blood pours from her wound, and the man does not try and stop it. Scarlet streams coat the pristinely clean white floor, and my stomach jumps to my feet with unease.

He digs around in her abdominal cavity and begins to slowly unspool her intestines outside of her body until he locates the spleen. He clamps the artery supplying the organ and removes it quickly and with precision. The assistant lifts the cloche off the first table. The "doctor," I'm assuming, begins to hook the organ up to the wires that protrude from the table in disarray. I'm unable to see what he's doing, but when he steps back toward the woman, the spleen lays there on the table beating with a pulse. Wires are pierced through the organ in a systemic pattern around its edges.

My jaw drops in horror as he goes back to search for more organs. The victim's eyes have become dilated pits of agony and panic, but her expression remains blank.

She can feel everything that's happening to her.

The realization hits me like a derailed train.

"Kidneys next, right?" the assistant inquires, excited for the next step in their organ harvest.

"No, Kevin. Kidneys are removed after the heart, to avoid any toxin build up in the body. If you remove the kidneys next, the other organs could be subject to contamination. The order is as follows: spleen, pancreas, bone marrow, stem cells, heart, lungs, brain, kidneys, and liver. Then we will begin tissue harvest for veins and skin."

Kevin nods in understanding. The "doctor" begins to remove the pancreas in the same fashion he used with the spleen.

Clamp, cut, table, wires, and cloche cover.

"Can you please grab the bone saw and marrow suction?"

Kevin turns to grab the saw. Terror churns my stomach like butter while I take in the nightmare fuel in front of me. The scrawny assistant hands it back to the "doctor," and watches with determined concentration as he activates the motor on the saw and swoons. Kevin has a look of absolute bewitchment as he watches the saw chip into bone.

My stomach has taken all it can, and I vomit everything I have into the floor beside me. Like the ground beneath me suddenly gave way, dizziness causes me to stumble. My brain tries to make me hyperventilate, but I do my best to slow my breathing to prevent the panic attack I feel coming on. After I get my bearings, I frantically scratch and pull at my restraints to get free.

"Well, well, didn't enjoy the free show?" the Lieutenant asks as he looks at the puke cascading across the floor.

"You all are nothing but a bunch of sick fucks!" I sneer, trying to maintain my composure and not show weakness, but damn am I totally unnerved and terrified.

If they did that to her, then what the fuck are they going to do to me?

"Oh darling, you don't know the half of it."

He chuckles as he removes my restraints and keeps ushering me toward the end of the hall with a firm grip on the back of my neck.

"But you will soon."

He forces me into a room with metal cabinets against the walls full of bright-colored vials and large warning labels. A metal table sits directly in the center of the room. It has four-point leather restraints and a waist belt. Surgical-type spotlights hang above the table, creating an insidious ambiance. A lump forms in my throat as fear clouds my thoughts, and I can't shake the image of the girl's spleen glistening under the sterile surgical lights, twitching for the final time.

A man in a long white lab coat, khaki dress pants, and round metal glasses that are too big for his face approaches. The man gripping my neck throws me forward at the exam table. I try to catch myself on the edge of the table, but the wheels on it roll in front of me, causing me almost to fall as I try to regain my footing.

"Hi, 416, my name is Dr. Hyde. Please hop up on this table and lie flat on your back," he commands calmly, nodding toward metal workspace as he rolls it back to its original location.

"I don't lie on my back for any man unless he earns that from me," I mutter through gritted teeth.

His assistant rears his arm back without hesitation making the familiar feeling of a right hook ache in my face. A sharp pain pulses through my right cheek, and a metallic taste begins to fill my mouth.

"I take what I want," Dr. Hyde responds.

"Fortunately, or unfortunately for you, however you want to look at it, it's not sexual in nature."

He winks as I spit blood in his direction. The crimson liquid splatters on the floor at his feet.

"I will ask again, and if you don't comply, Seth here will force you up." My face throbs as I can feel blood pooling around my eye. I sit up on the table and lay back begrudgingly. They strap me down, and I wonder if I even have circulation to my extremities with how tightly I'm bound. Dr. Hyde pulls out a tape recorder as he gathers his equipment.

"Experiment 416. Date 6/26/2105, plan to test chemical 1837 by intrajugular injection."

He grabs a vial from the cabinet that has a bright yellow warning logo that reads "corrosive," followed by a syringe with a large needle before popping the plastic tab off the metal top of the vial.

It's something straight out of a Frankenstein film when he begins to extract the neon purple fluid into the syringe.

Nuclear

I suck in a deep breath and hold in the tears that I'm struggling to keep at bay. My mind continues to flash the traumatic images of the girl on the table and her organs that were definitely on the wrong side of her.

The syringe is similar to the one used on her, but the liquid is a different color. If that syringe paralyzed her, then what is this one going to do to me?

I know I'm worth something, according to the disgusting men who brought me here anyway, so I'm most likely not going to die here, but there's always a possibility that everything I think I know is a lie.

For all I know, the only part of me leaving this room will be my organs.

I will not show fear to them.

I will *not* give them the satisfaction.

"Alright, sweetheart, this is going to hurt… a lot." A wide, creepy smile manifests on his face.

I close my eyes.

I can do this… but what if I can't?

The large needle rips through the tender flesh of my neck, and I hiss through my teeth, trying to maintain my dignity. The pain that takes over my body is excruciating. My veins begin to glow a sickly purple beneath my reddened skin, and I clench my teeth so tightly that I fear I might break one. I refuse to black out from pain.

I will not let these fuckers do anything to me that I can't witness.

My heart is pounding so hard and fast; it's the only thing I can hear. My vision begins to turn yellow, making my surroundings turn from appearing sterile to being contaminated.

Dr. Hyde speaks into the recorder as I thrash on the table, "416 has survived two minutes after the injection of chemical 1837; living through the bonding process is looking promising for her." Hateful words build up my throat, but I'm unable to let them out as I no longer have control over my convulsing body. It feels like an eternity goes by as the pain shocks my muscles.

"At five minutes, the reaction is slowing, which is an interesting finding." My vision has started to return to normal colors; however, my veins are still glowing beneath my skin. My body begins to be still, and the pain becomes bearable.

"416 has successfully merged with Chemical 1837. This is a first. We will monitor for deterioration over the next twenty-four hours. Hopefully, 416 will continue maintaining a stable body and chemical makeup," Dr. Hyde beams into the recorder.

"Seth, take her back to her cage and set her up with monitors. Keep her hydrated. If any vitals are abnormal, alert me immediately." He removes his gloves and tosses them to the side, a slapping sound filling the air. Seth undoes my restraints, and I give him a sour look.

"Come on, buttercup, back to your kennel." His tone is mocking like what I just experienced is normal. I sit up on the edge of the table, hair and clothes sopping wet from sweat. I can see my pulse in the electric purple lines streaming through my arms.

Am I always going to glow purple now?

Am I supposed to be a superhero now or something?

Seth shoves me in my cage like a dog who just got lost on the street and is now being forced into a confined cage at the pound. He has me stand in the cage's opening while he grabs two large AED-like patches. He puts one on the left side of my chest and the other on the right. The gooey material on the back side of the patches doesn't stick well because of how sweaty I am.

No shit, asshole, I could've told you Wet + Sticky = not compatible.

"Do you have a towel?" I ask, annoyed and still out of breath from what my body just experienced. He grabs a hand towel from his "branding" cart that holds the tattoo gun. I tremble from the painful memory and the feeling of my identity being flushed down the toilet.

He hands it to me, and I dry my chest until it no longer glistens in the light. I hand the towel back to him, a scowl cast across my face. He goes to put the same pads back on, and the sarcasm slips out of my mouth before I can think about it. I shake my head and remark, "You're going to need some new ones if you want them to stick appropriately."

This is just sad at this point.

He pulls another set out and gets them to stick.

"Good job! Gold star for Seth!" I cheer sarcastically. His eyebrows furrow as he realizes I'm mocking him, and a flair of anger rises in his eyes. His jaw clenches as he rears his hand back to slap me.

"I wouldn't do that if I were you. You may piss off the ol' Doc. According to what he was saying, I'm pretty valuable." I wink at him, and the sarcasm gets heavier in my voice as the comprehension that he can't touch me without being reprimanded since I now house Chemical 1837 clicks in my mind.

He grips his fists tight and does not respond as he turns on the monitor. The machine is definitely higher quality than I've ever seen in a hospital. To be honest, the equipment is the fanciest technology I've seen since the world fell apart. It monitors my heart rate, respiratory rate, temperature, blood pressure, and oxygen levels. It's interesting that it even monitors my blood pressure without needing a cuff. Everything is elevated from my usual on the monitor display, but the craziest thing is my temperature.

My body temperature is reading 105.2 degrees.

Nuclear

How can I feel okay when I have a temperature that could kill a typical human? I feel completely normal regarding my body temperature minus being thirstier and sweatier than usual. I guess I run hot now as this chemical ravages my system or whatever the hell it's doing to me. He slams the metal barred door in my face in frustration.

I lay on the cold tile floor beneath me, embracing the way it cools my skin even if it doesn't last that long as my body heat disperses along the slick stones. It's then that I notice something.

My senses are more intense. I hear a "thud-thud" and look around for the source. I can't pin it, but it starts to quicken as Seth approaches the next cage, which is about ten feet from mine.

Holy shit, I'm hearing the guy's heart racing as he prepares for his fate. Then, a sterile smell starts to attack my nose. It almost burns it as I discover that it's isopropyl alcohol. The alcohol is located at least ten feet away on the "brand" cart that Seth uses to assign our numbers to our bodies. It feels like the alcohol is right under my nose.

My fingertips start to tingle, and I look down at them. I run my fingers along the metal bars on the cage, and I can feel every minuscule dent and scratch in the material. I look across the room and can read every word on a guard's cell phone over twenty feet away.

I spent my whole life being nothing more than a disappointment to myself and others. If I ever escape this place, hopefully my newfound powers can help me be something other than ordinary.

6

RYKER (6 MONTHS AGO):

THE NAIVE DECISION

I wake up with blurry vision.

My head pounds, and the light makes my eyes ache. The cold floor beneath me leaves me covered in goosebumps. I bring my hand up to the back of my head and feel the knot on the back of my skull.

After the room stops spinning, the image of iron bars around me comes into view.

I'm trapped in a cage.

Like the violent winds of a hurricane, it all comes rushing back.

I decided to go willingly because I thought it would make my escape plan much easier. I ventured to a local recruitment facility clothed in my cumbersome anti-radiation suit and respirator. The people I initially met were very kind and welcoming; however, just below the surface lay their real intentions.

"Hello!" a very enthusiastic voice booms from the front desk.

"Hi, my name is Ryker Evans- I'm here to volunteer for the draft."

A cute, tiny, redheaded girl with freckles sprinkled on her face nods at my statement. She displays a robotic smile that gives me the creeps. Her suit is gray with yellow accents whereas mine is black with orange details. I'm sure hers is far superior in protection against radiation if hers is government grade.

"Yes, sir. How old are you?"

"I'm 29," I respond.

"That's the perfect age for our draft!" She giggles. To be working for the government at the end of the world, she's pretty damn bubbly.

"Okay, I've got all of your info pulled up here. Did you bring a bag? We plan to deploy you to your designated location at this time. It looks like they are in need of soldiers in the Appalachia area." I hold up my bag and shake it, indicating that I came prepared.

Nuclear

The bag contains everything I have left. A few changes of clothes, five vials of RADBLOCK, two rolls of toilet paper, and a toothbrush. I have two daggers, one pistol, and three full mags holstered snugly onto my hips, ribs, and ankles. Only a fool would leave weapons in a bag someone could easily steal, and I do not intend on disclosing that I'm armed unless I'm forced to.

Her eyes dilate to the size of black saucers, consuming every ounce of green hue in her irises. I tense as I watch her expression freeze. An unsettling sense of dread erupts in my stomach like grotesque fireworks. Her head tilts to the left, and her dark eyes scan up and down my body.

Like a ton of bricks, it hits me that she is indeed a humanoid robot. Robots have become more and more common especially since the war began. They are not as sensitive to radiation exposure as humans and tend to be more reliable.

I've only met one other before, and it was sent to try and kidnap me. I shudder at the way it chased me, and all the dark promises it made before I successfully avoided it.

The most important thing to remember about robots of any kind, is that someone is ALWAYS watching. Robots rarely have their own agenda, so if they are after you, it's at the will of someone else. A robot is NEVER your friend unless you created it, and even then, it's still debatable if they can be trusted.

Even though I know this, I'm tired of running. I have yet to be able to find a secluded rural area to hide in that isn't already festering with people waiting to rob, eat, or kill you. At least this way, if I volunteer and fake loyalty, I will have plenty of opportunities to "die" in the field, and hopefully find a new home in the rural mountains as a ghost. I guarantee there's some unoccupied space out in the Appalachian wilderness.

After her eyes meet my feet, her gaze returns to mine and the black orbs begin to shrink, exposing the artificial green they had once shown. The expression on her face unlocks and she returns to the bubbly character she portrayed before.

"Please disarm your weapons on the counter before we proceed." She continues smiling, but her tone is stern.

Of course, she has a metal detecting gaze.

I give a tight frustrated smile before I unsheathe the dagger at my ribs and lay it on the counter. I slide my hands into my radiation suit pockets.

Her eyebrows raise before she responds, "The pistol and magazines also, Mr. Evans." I breathe in a long sigh trying to keep my cool, but I unholster the gun from my hip as well as the three magazines. She quickly opens a compartment in her metal skeletal frame, and dumps the weapons in. Anger burns in my chest, but at least my steel toe boots hid the dagger at my ankle.

"Excellent," she says. "Please step through this way."

Hesitation eats at my demeanor. My feet feel heavy, as if they're anchoring me to the spot where I stand. She guides me to a black door behind the check-in counter, before opening the door and encouraging me through.

The room is large and hushed. I guess it's quiet because they don't have anyone to recruit, and I'm the only dumb ass willing to surrender. No normal person in their right mind would do what I'm doing right now.

She walks me over to a burly man sitting in a chair beside a medical phlebotomy chair. Her movements are shockingly human, and the only give away that she isn't alive is that with every movement from walking to gesturing with her hands, there is a sound much like little motors all working together at once.

"Please have a seat," the robot insists, pointing to the chair next to the man. I place my bag down beside me and do as she says.

"My name is Simon; I'll be completing your intake today," he states, not displaying much emotion.

"I need to place a tracker and your military ID number. This room is safe against radiation. Please remove your glove and roll up your sleeve." I nod, moving slowly trying to avoid the inevitable. He pulls out a trigger-looking gun with a large needle attached to the hilt, and my eyes widen.

"This is a tracker so we can find you if you go missing in areas that are foreign to us."

"These are removable after our time is served, right?" I ask, uncertainty striking my nerves.

"Yes, sir, they sure are, but most people never need to remove them."

The comment is dark in nature, and I'm unsure if that means I'll die before I get the chance or if I'll be held hostage.

I guess only time will tell.

Anxiety starts to crawl under my skin as the insinuations become clear. He grabs a thick, short, needle-like syringe, attaches it to the gun-like object, and slides the tip under my flesh. I grit my teeth as he pulls the trigger, eliciting shocks of pain through my arm.

"Fuck, man, couldn't have numbed that?" I inquire with a scowl. The pain is overwhelming, but I do my best to breathe through it.

"No. It makes this process longer than it needs to be."

He lies the gun-shaped device down and picks up a tiny tattoo gun. His large hands almost make it comical how small the device is.

"Give me your wrist," he demands while holding his hand out. Reluctance weighs solid in my mind. I lay my arm down on the side table of the chair. He dips the gun in black ink before rubbing my skin with alcohol.

"This will be quick," he affirms, confident in his abilities. He applies traction to my skin, pulling it down firmly with his thumb, and begins etching the needle into the complex layers of my derma. Sharp pinpricks dance across my flesh as waves of pain make their way down into my hand. He doesn't waste time, and within three minutes, he's finished. I look down at my wrist, which now reads "830."

Great, now I'm fucking livestock.

He stands up and snaps his gloves off.

"Follow me," he dictates, nodding toward a door behind me. We almost reach the threshold when he reaches for the handcuffs in his pocket.

I stop, my consternation freezing me in place. I'm here willingly.

Why would he need handcuffs?

Unless I'm not going where I had volunteered to go. He notices my change in pace and hesitation.

"Don't make this hard." He sighs, looking back at me.

"I only go in handcuffs for pretty girls, and I hate to break it to you, bud, but you aren't a pretty girl." I scoff at him.

Before he can do anything, I get a left hook into his nose.

"Fuck you!" he howls in anger, snarling his words. He looks up, and blood begins to trail from his nose and bottom lip. He lunges for me, but I'm faster than him. I dodge his attempt to grab me and kick him in the back, throwing him forward.

His body slams into the concrete flooring. While he's on his hands and knees, I kick him in the ribs, knocking him to the side.

A wheeze of escaping breath is forced from his lungs. He reaches for my ankle in an effort to pull me down, but instead, I lift my heel just slightly until one of his fingers rolls under it. I put all of my weight on my heel, feeling his bones crack under me.

He screams, "What the fuck?" While he's still spiraling from his now shattered finger, I punt him harder, feeling a few ribs break from the blow.

Rage digs in its claws, and I begin to throw my fist into his face over and over again. I feel the skin of my knuckles tear as our bones collide.

His face has turned into an unrecognizable abstract canvas of gore. I pull back for one last hit, but a sharp pain strikes the back of my head, and everything goes black.

I guess I got fucking pistol-whipped by one of the other henchmen in the facility. I look around and take in my surroundings.

I'm in a cage that's over-sized for any kind of domesticated animal, and I'm not the only one. There are multiple other large metal barred cages around me.

A zoo of imprisoned people.

Nuclear

Most of the occupants appear to be men. Guards surround the exit door, and a few others make rounds, constantly watching the caged men, including myself.

"Psst."

I hear, slowly turning my head to not draw attention to myself. My head throbs with the simple movement.

Damn, the lighting in here is cruel to my eyes.

In the cage closest to me, a man with curly black hair, olive skin, and light blue eyes is desperately trying to get my attention. I ignore his attempt for recognition, but I do make eye contact.

"You've been out for a couple of days. I was starting to think you were dead. The name is Cairo, or if you're feeling politically correct, I'm experiment 828," he whispers just loud enough for me to hear and shows me his wrist, displaying his number.

"Experiment?" I say, keeping my voice as quiet as possible.

"Yeah, man, you might as well forget everything you know. Your body belongs to the government now." He shrugs, obviously having accepted his fate.

I say half-heartedly, "I'm Ryker, number 830." I glance at my wrist disgusted by the permanent mark.

He nods. "Just do your best to lay low and don't draw attention to yourself. It'll make your time here a lot easier and a lot less painful." I bar my teeth.

How long HAS he been here?

"What the hell does that mean?" I ask, trying to maintain my volume level.

Before he can respond, a man walks in through the doorway. Cairo backs away from the bars of the cage and sits toward the back of his enclosure, picking feverishly at his fingernails. His expression betrays fear as he tries to avoid making eye contact with the man, and his body stiffens, as if to keep himself from trembling.

"Ah, 830. Good to see you have finally joined us in the world of the living." The man chuckles.

He's a giant, tall and stocky. His face is very square and has multiple stages of scarring on it. The scars line his face in mostly longitudinal lengths, which I would assume were knife inflicted. His tan suit does not flatter his frame; however it is kept pristine. A name badge reads "Lieutenant," but no other identifying words or patches are noticeable. Why would someone have that many scars on his face from the same weapon?

"Lucky for you, your services are not needed today."

A sardonic smirk curls at the edge of his lip. I don't acknowledge him as much as it pains my pride to bite my tongue, but I have to remember that I am not in a place of having the upper hand.

In fact, I'm currently captured like a naive animal who has walked into a hunter's trap.

The large man lifts a finger tauntingly, points to Cairo's cage, and goes down the line of cages as he spouts, "Eenie, meenie, miney," he hastily points to a cage and confidently says, "mo! Come on down, 819; it's your turn to fulfill your duty to your country."

The poor soul in the cage swallows hard and begins to step backward until he hits the back of his cage. I can see the sweat on his brow from here. I watch intently as the large man walks over and unlocks the bio scan lock with his retina. The lock pops open, and the man is forcefully pulled from his prison.

He's begging, "Please, Lieutenant, please, don't do this." The lieutenant laughs and responds, "What's the fun in that?" A wicked grin crawls up his face as he pushes the man forward with a taser baton pressed firmly into his back. My heart sinks for the guy. After they leave the room, the atmosphere turns back to how it was before the lieutenant entered the room to begin with. I keep reminding myself to focus and take in as much information as possible. The guards' actions and break times, passwords, how locking mechanisms work in the room, and, of course, things that I can use as weapons.

My gaze rakes over a guard as he paces throughout the lab. He has a taser baton which he seems to carry specifically on his right side. His military grade vest has nine pockets which I would bet contain weapons or at least useful equipment. A gun rests at his hip glimmering in the bright luminescent light. I catch a glimpse of exposed wires from the control panel which conveniently are just long enough to wrap around someone's neck, even the large neck of the lieutenant. If I can take down a guard, I can get out of here with the weapons at my disposal. It just has to be timed right.

"What the hell was that?" I whisper to Cairo.

"It's his turn for initial chemical inoculation. The government's goal and the reason we are here is to genetically alter us to sustain harsh radioactive environments and maybe develop superhuman capabilities."

"So, we are fucking guinea pigs until the government is happy with us?" I conclude in disbelief.

He nods.

"Just do your best to survive. If you can, I will get you out of here with me when the time is right. Keep your eyes peeled, and do not let your pride overtake you. It will only get you killed here. Make them think you want to be here and that you are cooperative. It'll result in a better chance of you getting to keep your own mind. They can turn off your humanity, so don't give them a reason to."

I cock my head to the side, processing his words. A guard on his hourly rounds is making his way toward us, so Cairo and I drop each other's attention and pretend to do anything but communicate. My gaze drops to my hand, and I drag my fingers across my bruised and bloodied knuckles, remembering how good it felt beating that asshole's face in. I can guarantee you that he was the first of many in my path as soon as I return myself to a vantage point.

A thought quickly passes into my mind, and I pretend to adjust my boot.

Please let me still have a weapon.

The dagger that was supposed to be strapped around my left ankle is gone. For the first time since the war began, I'm completely unarmed.

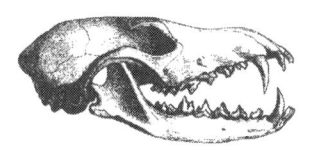

I crack my knuckles, sitting here pissed off in my fucking dog cage. Today, it's my turn to experience chemical inoculation. The lieutenant walks through the door and beelines to my cage.

"Well, well, 830, it looks like your luck has run out."

I roll my eyes and try not to gag at the bad ass he tries to be. He was 100% one of those ROTC kids in high school who followed the rules. He unlocks my cage and grabs my wrist, yanking me to my feet. I look at Cairo, making sure to hide my emotions. He nods at me as if wishing me luck, and I nod back.

I need to stay conscious to gather as much information as possible to help Cairo with our escape plan. The door slides open, and for the first time in over a week, I step out of the sterile lab rat dungeon.

The room I walk into is much smaller than the one I left. The smell of acids, like cleaning products, fills the air. I can specifically pick out the smell of bleach, but it's mixed with something that I can't discern. A man in a lab coat and business casual clothing stands next to a metal table.

"Based on your genetics, 830, you will be a huge success for us," the man says proudly.

"My name is Dr. Billings, and together, you and I are going to achieve greatness." I stare blankly ahead, pushing down the rage and hatred threatening to spew from my mouth.

"Quiet one, isn't he?" Dr. Billings taunts.

"Chemical 6571 will change all that." A malicious smile forms on his face, and I realize I truly am fucked.

"This is going to hurt... a lot," Dr. Billings says confidentially.

His assistants have already strapped my wrists and ankles in leather restraints. The straps are worn down, and you can tell I was not the first to try to escape their hold. I grit my teeth as one assistant wraps a final restraint around my waist, pulling it snugly to my skin.

"We must alter your DNA to something more primal to elicit the response we are looking for. We will use an acid that

Nuclear

will strip your cells of a certain protein and hopefully rewire your RNA with a new transcription."

My eyes dilate with fear.

The adrenaline in my system makes my heart beat so hard that I can no longer hear any other words except, "This has to be directly injected into cardiac tissue."

I swallow hard and every muscle in my body tenses. He lifts a long syringe with a blue opaque liquid and a sizable, beveled needle above my chest. I close my eyes and feel the needle tear through muscle and scrape bone as it enters my heart.

I scream and let out a whimper as I feel the liquid sting all four chambers of my heart and make its way through my arteries and veins. It feels like lava as the thick liquid burns me from the inside out. I lay in agony as the acid tears me a part, destroying every cell I have.

The pain becomes overwhelming, and I lose consciousness.

Everything is fuzzy as I return to the world of the living, except for the throbbing pain in my muscles and bones. Even though my body feels like I got ran over by a truck twice, I can tell something about me is different. I can't quite put my finger on it yet.

Flashes of Dr. Billing's face as he looms over me fill my head as his smile seems to grow wider and wider. The way he's enjoying my suffering makes anger bubble under my skin like a geyser about to blow.

I've never felt this out of control with my emotions.

The rage I feel is like an abyss that I'm trying to pull myself out of, but my footing keeps slipping.

I will not be a victim anymore.

I snap the restraints off my wrists and ankles in one swift motion, before grabbing the belt on my waist and ripping it in half with ease. I turn around and use every bit of anger I have to knock Dr. Billings clear across the lab with one punch to his chest. I feel his sternum crack from the impact.

His head rebounds off the glass cabinets containing all the vials of chemicals, knocking him unconscious. The two assistants that were helping him experiment on me stare at each other. One swallows hard and the other trembles as I look in their direction before they run out of the lab.

Fucking cowards. They can dish it out but can't fucking take it.

I take long but patient strides towards Dr. Billings. Every fiber of my being demands for me to decapitate the bastard and kill him quickly, but that's not the way I want him to die. I want it to be drawn out. I want him to fucking drown in agony and beg me to stop like countless other people have asked from him in the past.

Nuclear

I want him to *pay* for his sins.

A breach alarm echoes through the disheveled room. I grip onto his shirt, pulling him roughly upward. His body too easy to manipulate in my superhuman grip. A pale green mist emits from the sprinkler system above me. Within seconds, sleep threatens the very fiber of my being, but revenge is so close.

Revenge is literally in my hands; all I have to do is stay awake and take it.

Numerous footsteps echo in the room, and I try to shift my gaze to the sounds, but my eyes close and my thoughts start to slip away.

7

RYKER (4 MONTHS AGO):

WRAITHS

Cairo has been missing for three days.

Since I've been trapped in my cage, all I can think about is that he's probably dead. After two months of him quietly coaching me through the iron bars, loneliness is beginning to engulf my thoughts.

The lieutenant came to get him that morning, which was odd because based on rotation, it wasn't his turn to go. The thought makes nausea slam into my gut.

He's dead, isn't he?

Based on the rotation I track it should be 826's turn. The white, metal door of the room's only exit opens harshly as the lieutenant makes his way through it. It's hard to hide my emotions when I'm as upset as I am, but I manage it. His gaze locks on me, and I stand sturdy in my position waiting for him.

"Ah 830, there's something I have waiting for you right behind those doors," he teases.

I don't respond, but inside I'm screaming with trepidation.

The bio lock buzzes and clicks as it scans his retina.

I step out of the cage after my door swings open and step out into the open, waiting for the usual press of the taser baton against my back.
"Wow, you are such a star student. You've come so far in being cooperative." He chuckles as he ushers me forward.

The only thing keeping me from ripping him apart is that Cairo might still be alive, and I'm probably being taken to wherever he was.

My strides are long and paced. I refuse to look rushed or concerned. I'm not afraid of this man anymore. I know I could take him in a fight, but I don't want to risk leaving Cairo in limbo.

We walk down the long hallway, farther than I've ever been before. We pass windows of large empty labs, and doors with not only retinal scan locks, but palm print scanners as well.

When we reach the end of the hall, we stand in front of a double doorway. The doors are white with tarnished silver handles.

Like the other doors we passed, both types of locks are positioned above the right door handle. The flickering luminescent bulb overhead creates an insidious ambiance. My heart rate picks up as fear begins to sink its teeth into me.

From my right side, the lieutenant keeps the baton in the same hard-pressed position it has been in for our entire walk. He scans his retina and then his right palm.

An earsplitting buzz sounds from a speaker directly above us as the doors open inward. My hands cover my ears.

"After you," he says when the alarm stops and gestures through the doorway.

The room comes into full view, and I walk in, revealing a large circular room with a cathedral ceiling. There are four cameras that I can see in random places across the walls. The room is bright white and once I get to the center of it, a large, mirrored window, which is obviously a two-way mirror, is directly next to the doorway we came in through.

The lieutenant laughs as he removes the baton from my back. I look at him in confusion.

"You see these scars on my face?" he asks as he gestures to the longest one that runs across his cheek.

"I got them all in this very room. I was one of the first experiments to be a part of the war. This is a sparring room. We used to practice hand to hand combat with just one dagger. Sure, I wasn't great at first, but you get better as you take slice after slice."

I mean with the way his face looks, I'm willing to bet he was a terrible fighter, and probably still is.

"So, I'm going to fight you?" I ask skeptically.

He laughs hard to the point that his face turns red.

"Oh no. With your acquired abilities, that wouldn't be a fair fight. We typically would have you spar someone with your caliber of strength, but we can't afford to give up any of our good soldiers, so we... improvised." The smile that curves his lip makes dread pool in my stomach.

"We saw you the day you were injected with the chemical, and how you acted, but we have yet to see you perform to your full potential." He crosses his arms.

"This room will either determine your place among the ranks of the military or it will become your tomb. Your choice. Good luck, you're going to need it," he remarks, shaking his head as he walks out the door from where we came.

I panic and dash for the door as soon as he's out of sight, but I'm not fast enough—the door locks shut. I tug desperately at the handle, praying for it to budge, but it remains unmoving. I have not been able to channel the power that consumed me the day of the injection, but right now would be the perfect time for my power to manifest.

A door opens from the ceiling and a dagger hits the concrete floor with a thud. I pause unsure of why I need a dagger if I'm not fighting anyone.

Unless I'm fighting something that isn't human.

The realization grips me hard, and I dart across the room to grab the blade.

It feels so good to be armed again.

A soon as I fist the dagger, another alarm sounds, this one more like an emergency alert, followed by the lights in the room turning red. The scarlet cascade of light sets a treacherous tone to the once bright room.

A large rectangular exit roughly the size of a garage door reveals itself from the blank wall directly across from me as it opens upward.

Cold-blooded snarls echo louder and louder through the room as the door continues to rise slowly. Once the door is fully ajar, a deep and guttural growl reverberates around me as the beast begins to enter the room.

I shake off the horror that fills my chest and kicks my heart into overdrive. A large wolf the size of a healthy bear stands before me. Its grey fur is thinning as radiation burns decorate its body. It has six legs total, but two sets are front legs, all appearing to work in sync with each other as it paces. It has a third eye that sits between the other eyes, and its face is covered in necrotic and weeping wounds, with an ear that's had a bite taken out of it.

Adrenaline surges through me, helping to dissolve the fear that has me frozen in a chokehold.

Its gums pull back exposing a mouth with too many vicious teeth causing it not to close properly. It begins to foam at the mouth as it snaps its jaws in my direction. Frothy saliva flings into the air around it.

Oh fuck, oh fuck, oh fuck.

It lunges for me, covering the space between us within seconds. I dodge it as I slide to the right. It comes to a skittering halt as it realizes it missed me and it turns back, its tail flicking back and forth as it fixes its fiery eyes back on me.

I don't want to kill this beast, but I'm starting to think that I don't have an option. It's me or the monster and I refuse to die today.

I get into a fighting stance with my hands up, clinging to the dagger in my left hand. It snorts as foamy saliva drips onto the ground below it, creating a puddle at its front paws.

The beast charges at me, and I swing my blade, slicing through the tissue on its face and neck before it knocks me to the ground. I land about ten feet from where we collided. It howls in pain as the wind is knocked out of my lungs.

Before I can stand back up, it pounces for me again. I have just enough time to roll onto my stomach to the left side. Its left paw lands right between my shoulders pinning me to the concrete. It's at this moment I realize my mistake.

I will never turn my back on an enemy *ever* again.

It rests all its weight in its paw making it nearly impossible to draw in a breath. Intense burning pain radiates from my back as it rips its claws through my flesh from my shoulders to my tailbone.

The pain ignites a rage that I have never felt before. The feeling that I can't seem to control returns. My body trembles from other worldly pain as I scream. Its hot, rotten breath sends chills through me as it huffs hungrily at the back of my neck. I feel it rear back, preparing to tear me apart.

I force myself upward, knocking the creature off balance. It catches itself as I rise to my feet. The red-light ambience hides the crimson color of the blood pooling at my feet making it appear more black than red, and the feeling of blood rushing down my legs makes me cringe.

I snarl my lip up as if to mimic the beast.

It doesn't back down as it continues to growl menacingly and drool as its mouth hangs open. We simultaneously lunge for each other, but this time, I'm ready for the fight.

I've never been more ready for something.

My hands grip onto its neck and we lock into a brawl as we wrestle and roll across the cold concrete floor. It continues to try and snap at my face as it attempts to keep me pinned. Hot puffs of putrid air threaten to make me gag as my robust grip keeps the creature just centimeters away from my face.

Its strength can compete with mine, but I'm stronger. I roll us back to where I am in control and straddle the beast.

It's a vicious thing and it continues to fight, even though I plunge the dagger into its chest with such force that its ribs crack under my hand. It howls in agony but doesn't falter in its attack.

I hadn't truly felt just how strong I really am until this moment, as its bones continue to break while I jab the knife in over and over until the creature stops fighting and goes limp. Black tarry blood sprays over me with every stab. A whimper of defeat echoes through the room as it takes its last breath. I pull the dagger out of its ribs with a squelch.

I feel dizzy as I rise to my feet. The adrenaline is starting to come down and the blood loss isn't helping. My hands tremble as my body shifts from fight mode into recovery mode.

My eyes stare into the glass window, praying that I catch the eyes of the person behind it before throwing the knife with everything I have into it.

The blade pierces through what I'm assuming is bulletproof glass but stops when it reaches the hilt. Micro cracks trail from the point of entry creating a network as intricate as a spider's web. I raise both middle fingers to the cowards behind the glass.

My breathing is heavy as another door opens from the wall beside me. The lieutenant stands in the doorway, waiting for me to approach.

"Welcome to Apparition Ops," he cheers with what I think is pride in his eyes.

Fucking asshole.

I want to kill him so bad right now as my rage still seethes under my skin, but I'm losing so much blood, there's no way I'll escape before I pass out.

The lieutenant yells into a hallway that I can't see from the other side of the door, "We need a medic."

Nuclear

"Come on, 830, I'll show you to your new home," he gestures for me to walk through the threshold. I hesitate, but honestly, my body feels like it could give out at any second.

My new cell is an adjoined room with bunk beds. The entrance door still has a retinal scan lock, but the room is significantly nicer than my previous cage.

There's a bathroom with a door, a mini fridge with waters, and actual comforters on the bed. I notice there is a label next to my door that reads "828 and 830."

Excitement overwhelms my fatigue, as Cairo's number is displayed in conjunction with mine.

Is Cairo here? Is this where he's been?

The lieutenant lists off a bunch of rules that I am too distracted to listen to before ushering me forward and closing the door behind me.

Honestly, it's nice not having a baton pressed into my back, and I don't feel like I have to walk on eggshells even though I'm still locked in.

The top bunk is not made, which gives me hope that Cairo is alive.

As if he's listening to my thoughts, the lock on the door buzzes, and a familiar face with black curly hair and bright blue eyes walks in, carrying a medical kit and a cautery.

I don't even hesitate; I limp over and give him a one-armed hug.

"I thought you were dead," I whisper, keeping my voice low because you never know who's listening.

He lifts his shirt, revealing two amateurly stitched gashes across his abdomen.

"I almost was," he responds, his voice at full volume for the first time since we met.

8

RYKER (2 MONTHS AGO):

EXTRACTION

Desolation radiates from our environment as the Humvee comes to a stop. I grab a cigarette from my front vest pocket and light it up with a cheap gas station lighter I found on our last "extraction." As I step out of the vehicle, I suppress my emotions and let a coldness devour me inside and out.

When I look at Cairo, he's already done the same. To stay alive and stay sane, we need to hide our humanity, and the scientists in the lab know how to take it away.

Fortunately, our squadron wears half masks that cover from the nose up, so we can easily hide the emotions in our eyes without trying. The masks are skull shaped with black fabric hoods attached to hold them in place. They are very complex despite their simple appearance.

The imitation ivory bone mask is constructed of a bulletproof acrylic material which covers my forehead to right below my nose. The design is as intricate as a real skull, featuring sutures and bony prominences throughout. The material molds to my face, fitting perfectly against my cheekbones and nasal structure. Black tinted acrylic lines the eye sockets of the mask. The interior of the right eye will display maps, thermal imaging, and help with rear view, meaning it can identify incoming threats from behind to help improve my chances of survival. My mouth and chin are the only parts of my face exposed. I cover them with black war paint when wearing the mask to integrate in my surroundings better.

Six more men with expressionless faces exit the Humvee and begin to split up. Knoxville, Tennessee is a lot more depressing than I remember it. I visited often when I was in my teens. One of my aunts lived here most of her life, and we would visit every Fourth of July. The fireworks would always light the sky over the big oak trees in her backyard. The memory is pleasant, but it feels like a past life.

Most buildings are just heaps of rubble cascading down cracked and cluttered streets. A thick haze lingers in the air and sets low on the horizon, blurring everything behind it. Power lines hang haphazardly from decaying power poles as cracks zigzag through the carnage of botched asphalt and cement. The once colorful streets now only display shades of white and ash. Warped and jagged metal frames protrude from the remnants of hollow structures lining the ambiguous roadways.

Nuclear

The only thing still beautiful about Tennessee is the lush greenery in the mountains that remains untouched by warfare. I'm honestly not sure why they put me here, but I'm glad I'm here instead of dealing with the creatures AND the heat back in Arizona.

I hold my cigarette between my lips and crack my knuckles as I prepare to be "bad" at extracting possible soldiers. Cairo and I split off from the group of men and head into downtown to evacuate apartment buildings. The government wants people between 18-30, but honestly, they will settle for anyone since they are desperate and running low on viable draftees.

I discharge the clip from my pistol and verify that all twelve rounds are in it. Snapping it back in, I cock the gun, hearing the audible click of a bullet in the chamber. It's music to my ears.

"What's your plan?" Cairo whispers to me.

"Save as many as we can, kill whoever gets in the way, and don't get caught," I respond.

"Ryker, this is serious, man. We can't get caught. They will kill us," he retorts with fear looming in his eyes.

"I promise we won't get caught, and if we do, I'll take care of it. Just trust me," I swear with sincerity.

"Now hush and follow my lead."

Cairo shakes his head, but he would know if I were worried.

A large apartment building towers abandoned streets and businesses. Cairo grips the handle of the entrance door, and I hold my gun up, ready to attack if needed. I'm grateful my mask comes stocked with thermal imaging, so I'll be able to easily identify survivors. Cairo quickly opens the door, and I step inside, swaying side to side to clear the room.

Not a soul is in sight in the lobby.

Vegetation has started to grow over the furniture, and a heavy layer of dust covers every visible flat surface. I look up to see a dirty glass chandelier hanging by loose cords from a severely cracked ceiling. Fissures trail up the walls around us and suggest that the building is close to collapse.

I motion toward the steps, and Cairo and I quickly but quietly tread to the second floor of the building. The stairs are metal and rusty, making it hard to take hushed steps. I take a deep breath as we reach the emergency exit door separating the stairwell from the individual apartments.

Sweat beads are on my brow as the anticipation of what lies on the other side eats at my insides. Cairo swings the door open, and I cross the threshold to find an empty hallway with outdated carpet. Nine doors line the hallway, five on one side and four on the other. The doors are staggered, so if you were in an apartment, you couldn't see into another one directly. We start on the left side and work our way through the doors. I kick in the door labeled 201. The door is rotted and gives in easily, breaking in the middle across the wooden grain lines.

Nuclear

A loud scream pierces the air as a raccoon-sized rat runs between Cairo and I. Cairo jumps to the side, aiming his gun wildly.

The thing is covered in brown fur which blends into the bald patches of rotting flesh scattered throughout its body length. Two large, rounded ears are deformed as if something had been chewing on them. Its nose comes to a distinct point at the center of its face despite large front teeth causing its mouth to hang open. Its feet are a grotesque mixture of paws and finger like phalanges with long claws that echo off the floors as it runs. A two-foot skinny, tail brushes my legs as it passes between us, and I can't help but notice the way the creases in it look like deeply defined lines on a human palm. Chunks of tissue are missing from the gruesome appendage, and it makes my blood chill.

"Stop, don't shoot," I command, giving Cai a serious stare.

"You'll attract the rest of the squadron, and we won't be able to save anyone," I whisper harshly. The rat runs into the stairwell from which we came.

As we enter the room, sweeping for threats, supplies, or people, a hissing sound can be heard from the bathroom. I pocket the pistol I'm holding before drawing my blade.

Whatever's inside is definitely not human, and I don't want to draw attention to us. I open the door to find a group of massive cockroaches climbing over each other, desperate to escape.

As soon as they see us, they immediately turn to charge through the doorway. There are four of them, all the size of a large house cat. Their bodies are oval in shape, covered in a sienna-brown exoskeleton. Six legs protrude from each one appearing too long for their bodies, and sharp spines the size of small daggers are sporadically placed throughout their length. Buzzing wings pulse in shades of gray from the backsides of the repulsive insects. Lengthy setaceous antennae twitch wildly from glowing sickly green head capsules with massive black compound eyes. Instead of normal mouth parts, the bugs have an upper and lower jaw from which giant tusk-like mandibles that have razor sharp teeth project from. They look like they are used to grip a meal before pushing it into the depths of dark orifices.

Unsure of what they are capable of, I stab the one closest to me through its head. I meet resistance from the insect's armor, but in the end, it is no match for my strength.

One of the remaining three jumps at Cairo with its mandibles open. It snaps at him, just grazing his forearm. He manages to get it into a choke hold between his torso and bicep. The sound of a cracking exoskeleton is all that can be heard as his blade cuts through the little monster like butter.

Two more angry insects try a run and go, exposing their useless wings as they attempt to glide toward us. I'm able to land a blow to the thorax of one, throwing it backward, and cracking the filthy toilet on the back wall of the bathroom. It stumbles as it rolls back to its feet.

Head shaking, it hisses, ready to strike at me again. It snaps at my hand, but it's jaws clamp around the length of my blade, preventing the very close loss of my extremity. The blade sinks further and further into its shelled mandibles, until the bottom of the right one breaks off.

I rip my knife from it in its moment of weakness and slam my weapon through its head. I stab it repeatedly, until the thing goes limp. Breathing intensely, I pull it from the creature's skull and turn my attention back to Cai.

The insect charges him one last time before he lands his blade into its upper thorax midair. A high-pitched squeal echoes through the small bathroom as it stops moving.

He throws his hand up trying to initiate a high five. I walk over and lazily slap his hand. The earthy smell of rot and decay fills the air around us. A bright green goo pours from their wounds and begins to run through the grout lines of the tile floor. The substance starts to steam as it slowly erodes the tiles that it surrounds.

We back out of the room trying to avoid contact with whatever that shit is, but not before I notice a box of menthols on the counter. I haven't had a menthol in over six months, so obviously, I have to go back for them. The only cigs I have are ones I find on extractions, so I pocket what I can.

Cairo stays out in the hallway while I fight him from trying to stop me from reentering. I shake off his grip and give him a hard stare. He puts his hands up and backs away in surrender. I rush in and excitedly grab the cigarettes from where they lay, quickly opening them to see how many I just bet my life on.

Seven.

There are seven perfectly untouched and stale menthol cigarettes in the worn paper box. I gesture to Cairo offering him one, but he waves me off with a relieved but anxious expression.

While I bask in my success, I notice movement from under the counter. Another cockroach, much bigger than the others, hisses loudly and opens its mouth, trying to snap at me. The motherfucker has teeth the size of toothpicks. I lift my foot high and come down on its head, avoiding its mouth altogether.

Of course, you can't crush a cockroach even with super strength.

The bitches just won't die.

As I do my best to hold it under my foot, I grab my knife from its unlatched sheath on my belt. It thrashes under my grip, with a buck so hard it launches me backward. My knife flies just out of my grasp.

The gruesome insect jumps onto me as I lay flat on my back. It snaps erratically, trying to do as much damage as it can. I hold it by the side of its mouth, keeping it inches from my face.

Cairo whistles some annoying tune, which distracts my assailant long enough for me to secure the thing under my

Nuclear

weight and regain the upper hand. I place both of my knees on the back of its thorax, stretching as far as I can until my fingertips graze my knife.

I grip it as if it's the last glass of water in the desert.

It takes three jabs for the creature to stop trying to escape from under me. Green goo begins to seep from the longitudinal wounds, just like egg whites running out of a freshly cracked egg.

When the bug stops moving, I slowly stand up, but quickly remove my hand to avoid an acid burn. I wipe my knife across the rug, which is already starting to steam, and then pocket it once I'm sure it won't burn a hole through my pants.

The creature hisses and turns back for one last snap at me, but I stomp its head in, feeling the crunch of its exoskeleton underneath my weight.

Green goo sprays upward, but thankfully only covers my boots and a couple other things in the living room. Steam begins to rise from them, but I hastily wipe the acid onto the dusty rug in front of the couch to avoid further damage to them. Melted rubber from the soles of my boots web from the rug as I pull my feet away.

The thing begins to tremble erratically as its nerves try to send pointless signals. Its legs twitch and shake just like you'd expect a freshly squashed bug's extremities to. Trying to catch my breath, I look out at Cairo, who asks,

"Was it fucking worth it?"

I open the box and sniff the cancer sticks, releasing a satisfied sigh.

"You bet your ass it was, Cai." I smirk and pocket my treasure.

9

RYKER (2 MONTHS AGO): THE LAST APARTMENT ON THE LEFT

We quickly clear every room on the floor except for room 209. Cairo and I have come up empty-handed but try not to let our guard down. I kick in the door with a pistol in hand, and what I see breaks my heart. Three college-aged girls cower in the living room. Fear fuels their wide eyes and quivering bodies. Their clothes are tattered and falling apart at the seams.

I look at Cai, and he is just as speechless as myself. As if we are on the same brainwave, disbelief plasters itself on our faces. It's been a long time since he and I have actually found people to rescue.

Just as I open my mouth to speak words of peace, a loud gunshot from the bathroom on our left makes my ears ring.

The hot metal of a freshly discharged bullet burns through the flesh on my upper bicep as it grazes me. Pain pings through my nerve endings, causing anger to rise in my chest.

When I turn to my left, I'm face to face with a slender man dressed similarly to the girls. His scared eyes widen as he prepares for my backlash when he realizes he misses.

"You have no idea what you've just done," I announce through gritted teeth. One thing I know for sure is that the only thing the military hates more than losing a soldier is having one of their soldiers kill people who could potentially fuel the war in our ranks.

If the others stumble upon this situation, we would be exposed. They always assume the worst when hearing a gunshot, so they won't hesitate to investigate what happened immediately.

"I—I'm sorry. Please don't take them. Take me instead," the man pleads.

I swallow my irritation with him as I acknowledge our time is now limited. I narrow my gaze on him, inspecting his thin frame for more weapons. Absolute fright beams from his eyes as he cowers with his hands up next to his head.

"Do you have any other weapons?" I ask, torn between leaving them here and trusting that he doesn't try to kill me again.

"N— No, sir," the man says trying to look me in the eye.

Nuclear

"We are the good guys," Cairo reassures from behind me.

"But the sound from your gunshot will attract the bad guys. It won't take them long to get here." One girl's mouth trembles as she states, "You are the bad guys. Look at your uniforms." She gestures toward my attire.

"It's a long story, and if you want to live, I don't have time to explain," I retort, trying to regain the sympathetic demeanor I had previously by softening my gaze and dropping my arms to my sides.

"We've got to leave now, or we risk being exposed." Cairo quakes as anxiety heightens in his voice. I nod in agreeance. I glance quickly at my bicep and note that it will likely need to be wrapped to stanch the bleeding, but the wound is superficial. I'll deal with it when these people are safe.

"C'mon, they'll be coming any minute," I insist, motioning the girls and man into the hallway. We don't have time for pleasantries, so I'm unsure of their names. They are hesitant, but after a few glances toward each other, they agree to follow us. I lead out of the apartment, and Cairo trails behind the others to cover them from attacks from behind.

We creep through the hallway and make our way to the stairwell door that Cairo and I used to gain access up here. We tread lightly and remain quiet to avoid drawing attention to ourselves. The girls' breathing increases behind me as unease seems to fill their minds about what decision they should make.

Before I can turn around to calm their minds, the door in front of us flies open. My heart kicks into overdrive as adrenaline pulses through me. I keep my gun raised. Pearson walks through the door with his gun pointing at me. I take a deep breath as I lower my gun and try to put on a facade.

"I heard a gunshot and came as soon as I could. Ryker, is anyone wounded?" Pearson asks, addressing me with blank emotion, as he lowers his gun almost robotically. Part of the government stripping you of humanity is that every emotion you used to display no longer exists. Concern does not fall on his eyes; it's just an empty stare following orders. I blankly look at my arm as blood is still trickling down it.

"I got grazed, but I'm fine. We found three in the last apartment on the left. We were just heading back to load them up now," I respond, trying not to look at the girls behind me.

"You fucking liar!" the man behind me loses his composure and lunges for me. Without hesitation, Pearson raises his gun and fires a single shot to the man's shoulder. He falls to the ground, whimpering in pain.

"What did you lie about?" Pearson inquires. There's no time for logical thought and reason. I quickly aim and pull the trigger without a second thought.

"Ryker?!" Cairo yells from behind me.

"What else was I supposed to do?" I snarl back to him. Pearson lays on the ground before me with a single bullet entrance wound in his forehead.

"Do you believe me now?" I ask the man lying behind me, gripping his shoulder and trying to hold back tears.

I press the barrel of my gun to his forehead.

"You are a real pain in my ass. If you want to die, you are on the right track!"

The man swallows hard and locks a tear-filled gaze with the girls before nodding to them in acceptance. His eyes squeeze shut as he waits for death.

I remove my gun and end the scare tactic by extending my hand to help him up.

"Get up, we have to go, now! I don't want to hear another word from any of you," I exclaim in frustration. They nod and follow closely behind me. I descend the staircase, making sure to listen for footsteps down below. We make our way to the front exit, but three more of our squadron are heading up the sidewalk toward the building.

"Hide them," I look at Cairo and state the command.

"Follow me," he whispers, ushering them all behind the front counter.

"Do not make a sound. Do you understand?" Cairo looks at the girls, and they nod in understanding. Their eyes ping pong between us, obviously questioning what they should do. Their gazes move from us to their surroundings desperately searching for exits, but if they run, we can't help them, and they know that.

"We will get you all out of here, but you have to trust us," he promises as he heads back toward me. As he gets halfway back to my side, the others come through the door. Blank expressions haunt their faces and give an eerie feeling as my hand remains on my gun.

"We heard a couple of gunshots. Is everything okay? Where's Pearson? He announced to us that he was the first responder," Rick, one of the soldiers, asks.

"Cairo and I just cleared the first floor. We were just about to head upstairs to continue looking. We haven't seen anything yet," I lie through my teeth.

The men move directly toward the staircase, and as they cross the threshold, Cairo and I rush to the front counter.

"We have to go now!" I warn, sliding over the counter and grabbing the wrist of one girl. We head for the front door and round the corner of the building to find a small alleyway.

"Run towards the graveyard around a half mile from here. There's a funeral home building with multiple caskets in the showroom. We saw it on our way in. Pick a casket and hide in it until nightfall. We will be gone by then. We can't help you if you get caught. Be careful," I order quickly, ushering them forward.

"Thank you," the girl who appears to be the oldest whispers as she leans up and kisses my cheek before disappearing at the edge of the alley. It was sweet, but it's not why I do what I do. I do this because I couldn't live with myself if I bring people into this life. Cairo and I make our way back to the building entrance.

"How are we getting out of this one?" Cairo asks, brow raised with curiosity.

"Follow my lead," I say as I open the building door.

"Is it too late to bum one of those cigarettes?" Cai inquires as he breathes a sigh of relief.

I chuckle as I pull the pack out and hand it to him.

"For you, brother? Never."

WRAITH COMBAT MASK, 2105.

10

MAGGIE (6 MONTHS AGO):

THE PRIVILEGE

After two months of painful experiments and testing, I have been deemed a sufficient soldier. I suffered through sixty days of chemical after chemical and needle after needle. They think they have broken my will, but it's all an act. Given the opportunity, I will escape. Only four out of the original thirteen of us survived the torture inflicted upon us over the last two months.

The majority of the ones who didn't make it failed to merge with the chemical they were injected with. Some did not survive the sparring challenges, and others were either killed for organs or insubordination. This place is a game of fake loyalty, intelligence, and luck.

"You're up, 416," the Lieutenant says as he enters the room. He looks into the bio-lock to open my cage. A red laser scans his retina from top to bottom, followed by a buzz as the lock opens. I step out with relaxed body language and a blank expression on my face even though my insides are screaming.

"Your first extraction starts today. It's time for you to recruit for us. We are sending you and six others to Nashville, TN, to retrieve viable potential soldiers. It's about a one-hour flight. Good luck," he states as he walks me to the helipad. He hands me a pack with gear as I'm the last to load into the aircraft. We should fly over rural Appalachia, which I hope is as beautiful as it used to be.

Even two months later, my core temperature remains elevated, typically ranging between 103 and 106 degrees, depending on my stress levels or strong emotions.

The purple glow has faded from me, but I can feel the chemical's heat traveling through my veins. I've started to gain more control of my heightened senses, but sometimes they can still be overwhelming. The Lieutenant's footsteps boom as they hit the ground as he paces impatiently, waiting for the aircraft to take off. His aftershave scent was so strong that it still lingers in my nose, and it reminds me of something an old fart would wear.

Suits him perfectly.

I still am unsure what the point of that injection was, and if we're being totally honest, I don't think anyone else knows what it's supposed to do either. All I know is that my body accepted it, I didn't die, and I'm no longer a purple glow stick.

Nuclear

My heart burns with anger as my ears pop from the altitude change. I'm physically on this aircraft, but mentally, my mind is reeling, trying to figure out a way to save the people that I'm being forced to kidnap. It makes me sick to think that to stay alive and survive, I have to take someone else's freedom away.

A sharp ache of empathy stabs at my chest as memories of my own abduction flood back. Every day, I replay what I could've done differently, and now I'm expected to inflict the same pain on someone else. I'm supposed to just be grateful that I'm trusted to do it. I scoff silently to myself.

And yeah, maybe I don't have to be the one to do it, but I still have to let it happen, and that's bad enough.

Dr. Hyde thinks he turned my humanity "switch" off by prodding around in my brain, but out of the five times he's tried, none were successful; however, on his last attempt, I pretended that he had completed his task. Pretending to feel numb and unbothered with emotions has been a hard act to keep up, and if I return with no prisoners of my own, they will know that I still feel.

I still have the one thing that if I let go, my chances of escaping and helping others vanish.

I'm no angel, but I don't believe in what the agenda is taking from people. I don't know how, and I don't know when, but I will take them down. The government and illegal experimentation will fall because of me. I will claim retribution for what has been stolen from me.

"Do you ever wonder if people we love are still alive?" Marcie asks from beside me. Her shrill voice makes me want to gag. She's the worst kind of person because she WANTS to be here. Her blonde hair curls behind her ear as she twists a thick strand repeatedly.

What little bit of humanity that comes naturally to Marcie is still intact. Every soldier that can be used as a weapon, refuses to abide by orders, or has too many irrational emotions, has to experience the humanity switch flip. There is a part of the brain, which is usually in the frontal lobe, that controls our ability to feel, to empathize, and to make us human. If that is poked and prodded enough, a soldier's humanity can be turned off.

Marcie didn't have to experience the switch flip because she proved her loyalty through a series of lie detectors, and she WANTS to be here.

Honestly, I'm not convinced that she hasn't been sucking the Lieutenants dick for favoritism.

I've heard her repeatedly talk about the difference we make and how important it is to give our all for our country. Her repulsive opinion makes my ears burn hot from anger, and it takes every bit of self-control I have to not knock her teeth down her throat. I clench my fists, doing my best to maintain my composure and not blow my cover. She isn't worth it, but I can't wait for karma to catch up with her.

"Honestly, I try not to think about any of it. It would just make it harder to be here," I respond. I've been unable to establish trust with anyone, and I'd like to keep it that way if I stand a chance of escaping this hell. The aircraft's cabin descends into an awkward silence as everyone avoids eye contact. Marcie's smile fades, but there is still a light expression on her face that is unfazed by my response.

The helicopter is small but functional. There is a cockpit with two seats for two pilots; however, today we just have one. Two slender open doors let roaring air tunnel through the cabin. The environment is loud and overwhelming.

Part of me debates jumping with or without a parachute, like a high stakes Russian Roulette.

In the main cabin of the aircraft are two benches, just long enough to seat six people. Three people on one side and three people on the other. We are packed in like sardines, and I can see into the pilot's quarters to watch the sonar. Military grade weapons hang above us for quick retrieval, and our necessity packs sit under the benches.

The sonar begins to alarm from the pilot's quarters, catching us all off guard. The pilot pulls out his radio and announces to the cabin, "Please arm yourselves with weapons and brace for impact. We have an incoming object."

I lift my AK-47 from the securement hooks above me. Grabbing a magazine from my left lower cargo pocket, I check that it's full before loading it into the gun. Clicking the safety off, I pull back the loading lever as a bullet snaps into the chamber.

I walk over to the opening on the left side of the craft and position myself in a sturdy stance before setting my scope. When I am happy with my projected vision range, I wait, taking in my surroundings. The gun's rear rests comfortably on my shoulder as I wait for the target to appear in my sights.

The aggressive wind funneling through the door feels good as it chills my skin. The others are fumbling with their guns, and frustration emits from them as I realize this is everyone's first time on a mission, and none of them know how to use a military-grade weapon.

Fucking perfect.

We are fucked.

I focus back through my scope, acknowledging that I have to look out for myself because none of these idiots have the capability to have my back.

The monster fast approaching is a giant. Its wingspan is at least twenty feet, and a blue hue shines from the creature. The closer it gets, the more deformities I can see.

It has four feet and exposed red and yellowing flesh on its face, body, and wings. Its eyes are solid black, and its beak is broken in multiple places resulting in jagged edges and a malformed alignment. Big blue disheveled feathers cover almost every inch of the creature. My eyes widen as I discern the thing is a mutated blue jay.

Blue jays are known to be aggressive and territorial birds, so we are most likely in for a battle. I locate the beast between the cross hairs of my scope and suspire before pulling the trigger. The gun vibrates and kicks back as the semi-automatic mode assists me in rapid fire. The beast takes multiple hits before screeching. Its flight falters a little, but it levels back out rapidly.

Honestly, the gunfire and bullets just seem to piss it off more. It flies faster until it rams into the side of the aircraft. The aircraft rebounds as the pilot tries to return it to a steady position, only to be hit by the creature on the opposite side.

It knocks Marcie's footing loose. She falls and slides to the opening of the aircraft. She holds on to the edge of the opening while her body dangles above the tree canopies below. I go to reach for her trying to maintain my balance, but before I can get to her, the helicopter is struck again, and she loses her grip. Her fear filled scream begins to dampen as she disappears into the greenery below.

I didn't know I had karma on speed dial.

I turn around and notice there are only three of us left. The thing is circling, and I don't have time to have emotions. I crawl through the hatch at the top of the aircraft with my AK in tow. Pulling myself through and ensuring my stance, I aim the gun upwards. Small wounds pepper the bird from its wings to its abdomen. Its flying lopsided, but still pursuing us at a hasty speed.

I wait until the moment is perfect, and the creature's abdomen is right above me. Without hesitation, I pull the trigger and let the semi-automatic do its job.

The beast lets out an earth-shattering scream as it loops back around, prepared to strike. Inky black blood covers me and the top of the craft. When the bird returns for one final swoop, I drop back through the opening as it nose dives through the top of the aircraft, crushing the metal into the cabin. Its beak stops inches from my face as I lay as flat as I can against the cold metal floor. The pilot shouts words that I can't understand as the aircraft descends rapidly due to the dead weight the bird has inflicted on our plane.

All I can feel is the sensation of my stomach dropping as we fall out of the sky. I slide out from under the beak and brace myself for a violent impact. Oxygen masks descend from what's left of the cabin's ceiling. However, we are way past those being helpful.

I cover my head with my forearms and wait for the inevitable, and then everything disappears as I hear the metal crashing and people screaming.

11

MAGGIE (6 MONTHS AGO):

THE ONLY SURVIVOR

I wake up in a daze.

My head is busting, and I'm not sure where I am until my vision starts to clear.

"Hello? Can anyone hear me?" I yell for anyone, but no one responds. I go to stand, but with my AK on my back, I'm pinned between crunched metal. I take the strap off and pull myself to my feet.

My muscles ache to the point that I have to force myself to move. Smoke clouds my vision as I discover the aircraft is on fire, and I discern I'm in a race against time before the plane explodes. God only knows how long I was out for.

I cough as I try to control my breathing. If I breathe in too much of the jet fuel tainted smoke, I'll pass out. My pack is wedged between two smashed pieces of metal. I steady my weight and yank the bag. It doesn't budge as I pull with all my strength despite my bones quivering inside me.

I look to my left and find a straggling, long, and thin piece of metal. The thickness of it seems sturdy enough to work as a pry bar. I shove the bar in between the metal and my pack. It takes every bit of force I have to move the metal, but it eventually moves a few centimeters.

As I pull, I can feel the metal slice through my palms. The pain of the wounds barely registers as my fight or flight response has completely taken over.

I drop the metal bar next to my feet, before feverishly digging through my pack when it's free. Small flames burst up from the melting cabin floor and my veins burn hot as I dig.

Where is it?

Sweat beads on my forehead from the mix of heat, anxiety, and fear.

Come on, it has to be here.

The silver casing flashes, and I bring the zippo to my lips and kiss it in appreciation before placing it back in the pocket of the pack, making sure it zips all the way.

When the people in power at the lab begin to trust you, they reward your service by returning some of your precious belongings. The zippo was my dad's and it's the only thing I have left of my biological family. I finally got it back after last week's sparing challenge, and I'm not about to lose it again.

Nuclear

The floor starts to bubble and warp, and I refocus on getting the hell out of here.

Crimson droplets from my hands trail my path as I navigate through the clouds of dense smoke and the pulverized metal of the interior of the aircraft. My eyes frantically scan side to side as I desperately search for an exit. I can feel the oxygen decreasing around me as fumes burn the inside of my lungs. Coughing only temporarily alleviates the sting.

There is one window slightly cracked in the back of the aircraft. I swiftly grab onto the support bar above me and swing into the window feet first. It doesn't budge even a little.

Again, I kick, and the crack elongates. Four more blows to the window, and it finally gives. The sound of shattering glass echoes through the crumpled aircraft cabin.

Shards splinter my flesh, and tiny pain signals overwhelm my nervous system as I crawl out of the window. I slice my forearm on a serrated piece of glass, but my adrenaline is so high I'm starting to become numb.

I jump to the ground, feeling the reverberation of my landing in my ankles. I'm slightly wobbly and off balance due to smoke inhalation and possible concussion.

I don't have time to diagnose myself.

I gather my thoughts and make sure I can run as I haul ass to find some kind of safe haven that's far away from here.

All I know is that I'm in rural Appalachia, so at least exposure to radiation and creatures will be limited for now. Most of the nuclear fallout surrounds major metropolitan areas, so most heavily rural areas are unaffected from direct radiation; however, that doesn't mean that something can't wonder from heavily radiated areas and expose everything in its path. The only threat I have to be concerned about right now is this aircraft exploding.

Avoid the explosion now, worry about radiation exposure later is what I keep telling myself.

An earth-shattering boom sounds within minutes. The noise makes my stomach churn as the ground vibrates beneath my feet. I turn to see flames erupting in the sky, followed by bellowing plumes of opaque smoke that reach so far into the clouds that I can no longer distinguish what is sky and what is fumes.

My aircraft and crew are gone.

It's just me.

It's only me now.

After the shock settles in my shaking body, I can't help but be excited. This is my opportunity to escape and start over. My heart aches for the others who have just lost their lives, but who's to say they wouldn't have turned on me?

I grab my knife from my bootstrap and sigh. If I'm going to get away, I'm going to have to remove my tracker. I undo my

Nuclear

belt and put it between my teeth, so I have something to bite down on. I line up the knife with the bruised and excoriated skin of my forearm before noticing the glass inflicted laceration is bleeding steadily and is in the exact location where my tracker should be.

This is going to fucking hurt.

I expertly carve through muscle and tissue to remove the glass shards embedded in my skin and the deep wound. As I dig deeper, I locate a tiny metal object in my arm. I know I'll need stitches, but I won't suture it until I can clean it as best as I can.

The last thing I need is to die from an infection after surviving everything I've been through.

Crimson ropes stream down my arm and off my fingertips. I hold back tears and a yelp as I extract the object. When close enough to the entrance of the gnarly wound, I grab it between my index finger and thumb. The tracker is only about one millimeter, explaining why it wasn't palpable under the skin. A small flashing green light catches my eye.

It's still active.

I drop it to the ground and dig the toe of my boot as hard as possible into the dirt until I see no flashing light. I tear off the wide hem of my right pant leg and wrap it around the wound tightly to stanch the bleeding until I can better assess it.

For the first time in 2 months, I'm free. A weight lifts off my shoulders, and I feel like I'm breathing easier.

M.C. Blackheart

Now, all I have to do is ensure they never find me.

12

RYKER (CURRENT DAY):

ESCAPE PLANS

"Are you ready to go?" Cairo asks as he pats my shoulder.

"Yeah, man, I just finished packing my bag." I throw my pack over my shoulder and follow behind him as we head toward the loading bay. Four other large men dressed in military uniforms are waiting there for us. Chad stands with his arms folded across his chest.

"It's about time. We don't have time for you all to jerk each other off."

I roll my eyes before giving him the middle finger. He's not even worth a verbal response. He'll just keep on with his snide comments because he always has to have the last word.

A typical Chad if you ask me.

Cairo responds, "Just get in the vehicle like your other friends already have." I make my way to the driver's door, while Cai has already seated himself in the passenger seat. Chad finally loads into the back of the Humvee, slamming the door behind him like a child.

Our mission is somewhere in rural Appalachia. Our goal is to journey to the designated coordinates, retrieve the target, and return within 24 hours. We were given a bare minimum description of the target as it is highly classified information. The target is a weapon for the U.S. military and is of the utmost importance to return alive, indicating that they are a person rather than an animal or object.

Cairo and I have spent much of our time in the "military" together. We were brought in together along with sixteen others. My initiation process was fighting the giant wolf in the sparring room. The sixteen of us were to be tested to be a part of an elite group of soldiers known as Apparition Ops. The trials were nearly impossible to survive, but I feel mine and Cai's chemical induced abilities saved us. All members of the unit have special abilities from genetic experimentation.

Cairo has become the closest thing to a brother I've ever had, even though he can be a nuisance sometimes. He's a worrier, and it can chap my ass, but his intentions are always pure. His anxiety is beaming from him like it always does when we are on assignments.

It's strange to me that he's a genetically altered soldier and a trained assassin, yet he still gets nervous. I think it's because

Cai and I are the only ones who still maintain our humanity, and he's afraid of blowing his cover. Dr. Billings has made multiple attempts to strip us of our humanity, but we've only gotten better at hiding it.

To the people in charge, we are only weapons, and they will do anything to make their weapons function to their benefit regardless of the cost.

"Cai, stop shaking your leg. You're acting like a teenage boy who's about to get laid for the first time."

"Fuck off, you know I can't help it." I reach into my pocket, pull out a cigarette, and offer it in his direction.

"You know that shit isn't good for you, man." I roll my eyes and remind him, "We kill and kidnap people for a living. I don't think puffing a cigarette is going to be what would disappoint your mom at this point." He snatches the cigarette out of my hand with a scowl.

"As if I'll ever get to tell her about my choices." He grabs a lighter from the console while I pull another cigarette from my pocket. He lights it up with a puff of smoke releasing into the air. I slide the filter of mine between my lips. He hands me the lighter, and I light the cigarette one-handed with my other hand still on the wheel.

This particular pack of cigarettes came from the shirt pocket of a deceased man in Asheville, NC. He must've just bought it because there were all twenty in that bad boy.

We were sent on an extraction of a hotel, and when Cairo and I arrived at the penthouse after clearing most of the rooms, there was a tall back suede chair facing the large pane window. It was impossible to see anything from behind the chair. We carefully approached the person in the seat, only to find the man had taken his own life with a shotgun.

Dried gore covered the man's shirt, the chair, and the ceiling as he lay in decay, fortunately more in the mummification phase rather than the rotting phase. You would think that we would have noticed all the blood on the ceiling, but age and dirt had made it blend into the deteriorating room.

My eyes caught on the sealed cigarette box, and it may be wrong, but cigarettes are too scarce to past them up when the opportunity arises. I got to listen to Cai lecture me about my morals for two hours that day, and I would do it again.

I breathe deeply, feeling the carcinogens penetrate my lung tissue. The nicotine immediately brings a calm to the anger swelling inside me. The anger of being forced to do the government's dirty work and losing my free will to be a person rather than a slave. I breathe out with a cloud of smoke rising to the ceiling of the Humvee.

Cairo looks at me with curiosity in his eyes and inquires, "Do you think we will ever get the chance to escape?" I stop for a second and tap the steering wheel with both thumbs, contemplating the question.

"If we ever stand a chance, we probably shouldn't discuss it around witnesses," I sneer, moving my eyes toward the rest of our squadron in the back. Cairo nods in understanding.

I love the guy, but Jesus, he can be so mindless sometimes.

I take another long drag on the cigarette, feeling the toxins burn as they diffuse through my airway. Cancer is the least of my worries since I've been a fucking lab rat injected with poison for the last few months. I grip the wheel harder causing it to bend.

"Ryker!" Cairo slaps my arm, which releases a shot of adrenaline into my bloodstream as his smack catches me off guard. The chemicals inside me make it hard to regulate my anger. Any slight frustrating thing can turn to rage in a second.

I'm working on trying to control it.

"Calm down; otherwise, we may get stranded out here." I shoot him a glaring look, and he swallows hard. He is afraid of the rage inside me, even though he's probably one of the only people who could somewhat take me in a fight.

I release my grip on the wheel and take another drag on the cigarette, finishing it off and flicking the butt out the window. I turn the volume knob up as the early 2000s divorced dad rock fills the car. I look to Cairo and keep my voice soft, "Today is the day. Our service is done as far as I'm concerned. We will be free by the end of the day." Cairo's eyes widen with a mix of fear and skepticism. I smirk, acknowledging his emotions and reiterating my words.

"Our day has come."

As we near the coordinates given, the air begins to still. The once vocal creatures are silent. The leaves on the trees don't even rustle. Goosebumps creep up my arms, and I get the nauseating feeling that this is the calm before a storm.

But what storm?

I look to Cairo and whisper,

"Something is wrong, man."

Just as the words leave my lips, an enormous creature emerges from the thick green brush on the left side of the Humvee.

Its face is horrifying, and I can't help but stare.

Its skin is sloughing off its bones as they protrude outward. The creature is tattered and scarred, like it has endured many fights. It has an extra set of legs and paws located just behind its front set. The paws are large and necrotic looking, and the claws are exposed through frayed flesh.

My eyes gaze upward to its face through the rear-view mirror. Almost barren of skin, its face is something from a nightmare. Its eyes are white with no color projecting, and it has deer-like antlers that have at least four points on each one. Moss has begun to scale up the antlers and hang off in certain places. It was, at one point, a black bear, given its stature and tufts of black fur, but now it's a mutated beast. A large, jagged scar runs from the top of its forehead through its right eye and onto its neck.

"Oh fuck," Cairo mutters from the passenger seat.

"Hold on," I remark as I press the gas pedal as far down as possible. As we jet off, the creature follows suit, not trailing far from our bumper. I swerve, trying to avoid contact with the creature and everything else in our path. The thing reaches out a paw with claws the size of a small child, harshly knocking the bumper off the Humvee. The other men in the back watch intently through the windows.

Not even absolute nightmare worthy horror can break their emotionless demeanors.

"Come on, man, you've gotta go faster!" Cairo screams from beside me.

"You're not helping," I respond through barred teeth. I turn sharply to the left, trying to throw the creature off, but it follows closely unfazed by the attempt, trailing us by mere inches. It hits the rear again with such force that it sends the vehicle into a tailspin.

"Brace yourselves!" I shout, anticipating the next action before it happens. In the midst of the car swaying violently from side to side, the creature abruptly hits a rear tire, causing it to blow. The Humvee swerves harder and more uncontrollably. A tree is fast approaching the front end of the vehicle, so I make a split-second decision and turn the wheel quickly. The Humvee flips three times as it tumbles down an embankment on our right. The sounds of crunching metal and shattering glass penetrate my surroundings until it's deafening. Everything feels like slow motion when the vehicle comes to a stop.

We are suspended upside down. I look to Cairo but can't quite hear what he's saying at first because the ringing in my ears is thunderous. Dizziness comes on at an alarming rate as the blood rushes to my head.

"Come on, man, stay with me. Don't pass out; we have to get out of here now!" He shakes me out of the daze I was in.

"You're always the one with the plan," Cairo says with a shaky voice.

"Do you have room to get out?" I ask, desperately looking for an exit. Loud paws make their way down the embankment towards us.

Everything is so blurry and no matter how many times I blink, I'm unable to clear my vision. Wooziness threatens to take me under, but Cai's voice is the only thing that keeps my head above water.

I look behind me squinting for visual clarity and discern Cairo and I are the only people still alive in the vehicle. The window on my side is completely smashed shut. After inspecting the passenger side window, Cairo finally responds, "I think I can get out this way."

Nuclear

"Good, because I'm blocked in, and I am not at a good angle to create an opening with my hands," I say, struggling to maintain my calm attitude. Cairo brushes as much glass from the window frame as possible before pushing his arms through and pulling his body halfway out.

The booming footsteps creep closer.

Cairo starts to panic as he notices his right boot is stuck between two pieces of frayed metal. I try to help him out of it as quickly as I can. The footsteps grow disturbingly closer, followed by low pitched growls that make my skin crawl. Massive claws scrape through the carnage of smashed alloy, and it's a sound that I hope I never hear again.

"Cai, just get back—" a scream bellows from Cairo's throat as he is violently ripped from the vehicle, leaving his boot and large pieces of flesh behind as the crushed metal avulses his calf and ankle.

I reach to grab him, but I'm pinned. I do my best to use my strength to get myself out quickly, but I know it's already too late.

His body quickly falls to the ground. Cairo's eyes are full of terror but also peace, like he knows he doesn't have to suffer through any more torture, but this just wasn't the way he wanted to go. As soon as the emotions pass through his eyes, they're gone, and so is he. The light that used to be so bright in those blue eyes fades as if it were ice melting away in the summer's heat.

The creature rips through his tissue aggressively as if trying to pull him apart. I drive my fist into the windshield, only eliciting mere cracks. It takes three more punches to shatter the military grade glass which splinters into my knuckles. I look and make sure the creature is still distracted.

After seeing its gaze and concentration was unaffected, I pull myself through the windshield. The ache of bruises and wounds is barely noticeable because adrenaline, fear, and grief burn hot inside me. When I get myself out of the vehicle, only one thought remains…. Run.

I dash into the thick greenery, sprinting for what feels like miles until I'm sure I've lost the monster chasing me. I duck behind the trunk of a massive oak tree to catch my breath, then slide my back against the rough bark and drop to the ground. Hot tears collect in my eyes as my failure tugs at my heart. The goal was for us both to get out alive, not just me.

The emotional dam that I have built breaks, and my body wracks with an onslaught of sobs and tears. Cairo is all I had, and he's gone. I try to breathe past the lump in my throat to get control of myself, but more tears come until I find myself punching a hole so deep in the grass below me that dirt flakes off every crevice on my hand when I raise it to do it again.

"I'm so sorry, Cairo. I will miss you, brother," I whisper, before taking a deep breath, trying to pull myself back together. As much as I need to mourn my friend, I don't have time right now.

Nuclear

This is my chance to escape. This is what Cai would want.

I grab my knife from my belt and begin to dig out my tracking device. It's in my forearm, but unfortunately, I have to go in blind as it isn't palpable under the skin. My teeth gnash as the blade maneuvers through layers of flesh. Blood pools in the wound before flowing over my arm in little streams. It blocks my view as I blindly poke through my tissue for the tracker.

After a few minutes, a metal bead pops to the surface. I pull it out and toss it to the ground, stomping it until I see that it's in minuscule pieces. I rip off the sleeves of my shirt and tear them down the center, turning them into two rectangles. Tying them together, I ensure that the knot rests on the backside of my forearm so that the thickest part will lay flush to the wound. The fabric crosses and I pull one end taut with my teeth and the other with my free hand until enough pressure is against the wound. The bleeding slows, but still oozes through the cotton. My eyes fixate on the vast thicket of trees that stands before me.

This is freedom. Now, all I have to do is survive.

13

RYKER (CURRENT DAY): OUT OF LOSS COMES OBSESSION

Dinner doesn't come easy out here in these woods. I have my pistol and my dagger, but I've found that avoiding the gun is the best thing.

I want to avoid drawing any unnecessary attention to myself. You never know who or what might be out here listening, and I have no intention of getting captured again. With my ammo running low, avoiding confrontation is my best option for now.

I've had to practice my knife throwing skills for food. This afternoon, I was able to land a rabbit that is roughly the size of a raccoon. It has tall ears that are too long for its head, and light brown fur that fades to patchy white under

Nuclear

its belly. Its front teeth are too long and hang below its bottom jaw, while its eyes are solid red with no pupil in the center.

It'll make for at least two days' worth of food depending on how much meat I can salvage.

Some of the more radiated animals have a disgusting burned taste that I can't get past no matter how hungry I am. Fortunately, this little guy doesn't appear to be too affected. I pull my knife out and slide it through the skin of it. The sharp edge slides through it like butter, and blood begins to trail down my hands. It's definitely not the worst thing I've done, but it feels a little unfair to these creatures, given the current state their bodies are in.

All I know is that I'm somewhere in Appalachia. I've only been here for a few weeks, but I've not been able to establish a place to stay. I feel like a nomad as I find a new tree to call home every night.

On my weekly patrol out for water, I avoided conflict with as many creatures as possible. The day-to-day survival makes it hard to devise a great plan of what happens now. I honestly figured Cai and I would escape together, and that he would have a plan, but for now, surviving is better than being trapped. Maybe I'll get lucky and find some kind of shelter in the next few days so I can stop sleeping in tangled branches of ancient trees for safety. Mundane is my new normal, and I'd like to keep it as consistent as possible.

Noises of a struggle catch my attention, and my curiosity gets the best of me. I perch low in some overgrown vegetation that runs the expanse of the lake. My eyes get caught up in the scene before me, and I find myself frozen and unable to control my body.

A ten foot long, horse sized, sickly orange colored salamander thrashes and snaps its enormous teeth at a woman balancing between its shoulder blades. Black spots appear to be necrotic as they trail up the thing's sides, but my eyes can only focus on her.

She is absolutely magnificent.

Her jet-black hair is pulled back in a long ponytail with thick curls that cascade the expanse of her dainty shoulders. Sun kissed skin glows with every movement she makes. Black and gray tattoos entangle into each other as they run the expanse of her entire right arm. Siren eyes hypnotize me where I stand and could make any man bow to her. She has one blue eye that looks like it is made from the sky and one eye that is red with flames that circle in it. Her eyes are an accurate depiction of heaven and hell, and it makes her all the more enticing. If she is a mix of heaven and hell, maybe this is purgatory and she is the angel meant to purify my soul, or maybe I'm the demon meant to drag her to hell.

Only time will tell.

Her lips are full, pink, and house white, straight teeth. She is dressed in a white tank top and camouflage cargo pants. If I didn't know any better, I'd say she was auditioning for the next

Tomb Raider movie. I take in her curvy, hourglass figure, struggling to inhale.

For a split second, I think about intervening to help her, but honestly, she doesn't need saving. She is entirely unphased and unafraid of the beast before her. She fights with grace and experience.

It's as if she does this every day.

The creature doesn't stand a chance against her skills, despite its size. I'm finding myself having to adjust my cock to a more comfortable position from the sight of her. She blows out a breath as its tail whips her in the back as she grips onto what I imagine are slimy scales. Her grip begins to slip, so she reaches behind her to grab one of her arrows from her quiver so fast that if I would've blinked, I would've missed it.

She scoots as far up the salamander as she can, wraps her thighs around its neck, and double fists the length of the arrow before slamming it through its skull. Its movements stall, and she releases the grip with her thighs and slides down its back, dismounting while the creature is still standing. A loud thud echoes across the lake when the monster collapses.

She walks toward its head with its lifeless eyes staring through her, and wraps her hand around the arrow, pulling it from its skull with a small moan of effort.

A gush of rotten blood spurts from the injury, splattering her clothes and boots. She continues to hold the sticky arrow, not placing it back in its quiver.

She steals the breath from my lungs.

Now that I've seen heaven, I can't live life without more of it.

She wades into the water just barely above her ankles and watches. She is so still I can't tell if she's breathing as she studies the water. In a swift motion, she plunges the arrow into the water and pulls up a giant bass. Once the fish stops flailing, she removes it from the quill.

"Cerberus, time to go," she shouts with a smile.

Fuck.

Her voice is pure seduction. It's sultry with hints of raspiness, and it could damn near send me into an orgasm here and now.

I bite my lower lip as I imagine her saying my name over and over. I've fucked a lot of women in the past, but I have never had a woman make me want to fall to my knees like this. One look and she has me addicted like a moth to a flame.

She puts the fish in her pack and loads the arrow into her weapon as she walks back into the lush greenery from which she came.

Like a little fox, she treads alone, ready for anything. Careful, cunning, and intelligent.

Nuclear

Her thick black hair swings behind her with every step she takes. The two-headed wolf follows closely behind her. I've always wondered what people mean when they say, "love at first sight," but I think I finally understand the concept.

I have to know her.

I'm obsessed and I will make her mine.

No, scratch that.

She is mine.

She doesn't know the mistake she made just by being out at the lake today.

I won't stop until I have her.

I quickly follow behind her into the greenery from where she disappeared.

Every demon inside me was quiet when I saw her, and that's a feeling I will crave for eternity. I will gladly set the world on fire if it means she belongs to me. Even if I have to make her mine, she will never be alone again.

14

MAGGIE (6 MONTHS AGO):

THE TWO-HEADED BEAST

After the crash, it felt like I ran for miles. I haven't had a chance to really assess my injuries, but I can tell that I have a sprained ankle, a concussion, and some bruised ribs. My breathing is restricted to shallow inhales from the pain of lung expansion, my head aches from the sunlight, and I have a slight limp as I try to keep my left ankle from rolling while keeping a steady pace.

There are a couple rips in my pants that hover over lacerations. The longer I look at myself, the more wounds and bruises I find. Little cuts and scrapes decorate my chest and arms in a kaleidoscope of blood, bruises, and soot.

I'd hate to know what my face looks like.

The farther I can get from the explosion, the less likely they will be able to find me. I'm hoping they just think I fell out of the plane instead of Marcie, or maybe that I was so

Nuclear

close to the initial impact of the detonation that nothing remains of me.

A ghost is all I want to be.

The sun is starting to set, and more and more noises are filling the forest around me. The nocturnal creatures must be waking, and I have no desire to meet any of them. I look at the cloudy sky and notice a storm is rolling in, and that I need to find shelter soon before the cold droplets descend on my wounds.

I trek for a little longer as a sprinkle of rain breaks through the dark clouds. Up ahead, on my right, is a cave. I increase my pace, trying to avoid the monsoon sure to come.

When I arrive at the entrance, I assess for animals that already reside there. It seems to be empty. The air inside is heavy with humidity, and the musty smell of dense earth fills my nose. The walls are covered in mismatched rocks, and the only sound resonating from the stone walls is the stalactites dripping water from overhead. The light tapers off through the length of the cave until only darkness remains. I sit down and lean against the side of the cavern wall so I can see out, but no one can see me.

The sky breaks loose, and the rain splatters loudly on the dirt and mud in front of the cave, creating cloudy pools of water.

Lightning follows as well as roaring thunder. The air becomes pressing as moisture begins to hang in the air, making it hard to breathe at times, or maybe that's just my anxiety.

Another roar of thunder sounds, and I hear a whimper from deeper inside the cave. I reach behind me and unholster my pistol from the side of my pack. I breathe in to steady my shaking hands as I question my ability to fight with exhaustion chattering my bones. The first bullet clicks into place as I pull the slide of the small handgun. Fear washes over me in icy waves making me shiver as it courses through me. My heart pounds in my throat like a drummer who is lost in his solo.

"Is—" My voice comes out croaky and cuts off before I can ask the question.

I clear my throat and inhale sharply before trying to ask again, "Is someone there? You don't have to be afraid. I'm just passing through and waiting out the storm."

Two sets of small eyes glow in the darkness, slowly moving toward me. Another bright flash of lightning illuminates further into the cavern, revealing a two-headed wolf puppy.

She's scared, alone, and can't be older than a few weeks. One set of eyes is bright blue, and the other set is a golden yellow. The pup's fur is black, thick, and silky. She is roughly double the size of what a normal puppy size would be, but her size is somewhat normal compared to creatures I have seen in the past.

The little wolf puts a paw on my thigh and cocks both heads to the side. I raise my hand to pet both of her heads. Moving her paw, I lie down on my side. I do a quick once over of the wounds from the crash, and miraculously none of them will need stitches except for the one I had to exacerbate to remove my tracker, but the lighting in this rock cavern is only decent when a blinding bolt of lightning illuminates it. So, I remove an ace bandage from my pack and wrap it securely to protect the wound until I can find a better time and place to tend to it.

A deep pitched growl echoes from the dark depths of the cave, definitely more menacing than the whimper from the sweet pup. I grab my pistol from my pack, before securing the puppy under my left arm, praying that I don't startle her into biting me. I leave my gun drawn and aimed in my right hand towards whatever the hell is in the back of the cave.

The ground shakes as large footsteps pound into the moist earth. Loud huffs of air blow toward me, forcing my hair to blow back over my shoulder. The flap of large wings follows the now increasing breathing.

I feel like I can't inhale with my heart ramming against my rib cage. I keep my steps light, trying to escape this place without drawing any more attention to myself. When I meet the mouth of the ancient cavern, a bolt of lightning shines into the cave once more.

Oh shit. Oh shit. Oh shit.

Did I just kidnap this puppy from its mother?

A gut-wrenching roar rips through the air, and my stomach hits my feet. A massive hunchbacked creature continues hurriedly toward me. A large mouth with lengthy canines breathes hot air while the rest of its face is wrinkled up in a snarl. Its eyes are black as sin. There are two sets of ears, with the ones on the top of its head being the longest. They twist and twitch looking for sound. Huge hairy arms creep closer to me. Four claws splay from each hand across the damp ground. Webbed wings extend from the monster's forearms to the sides of its abdomen, indicating they are only good for gliding. Hair is everywhere on the animal, displayed in shades of grays and purples.

I quickly come to the assumption that I'm not getting out of this without a fight.

Well, the good news is that it's not a scorned mother wolf, it's just a bat that's had too much radiation exposure.

If I'm going to keep running into beasts like this, I'm going to have to give them names.

I swallow hard as I throw my pack totally on my shoulders. As I start to run in the opposite direction, I forget to keep thinking about my steps and I roll my ankle. Pain surges up my shin and a yelp escapes my throat. Every fast step I take echoes in throbs in my leg, but if I slow down, I'm this thing's dinner.

I turn my upper body aiming my weapon at it, thinking about my footwork to avoid any faltering, and fire the gun just as the creature reaches its gruesome claws for me. It rears back, howling into the sky in pain. My hands tremble as I start to run, but it's on my heels within seconds. Fear burns in my chest as I force my legs to go faster. I somehow manage to dodge swipe after swipe of the monster's attempts to grasp me. I never change my pace and continue blindly aiming *hoping* to hit

Nuclear

anything. Another bellowing scream pierces the air, and the thing stops, running its massive paws over its chest.

I JUST WANTED TO TAKE A NAP!

While it stopped to grab at its pain, I dove behind some greenery off to the side of my path. My pack on my back rests against the damp bark of an oak tree as I lean into it, trying to make myself as small as possible. The wolf settles between my abdomen and thighs as I pull my knees closer to myself. I throw my left hand over my mouth. My gaze settles on the puppy, silently pleading for it to stay quiet for the next few minutes. The head with the blue eyes bumps into the golden-eyed one, and before I can react, the golden-eyed puppy nips at the other, eliciting a tiny whine.

The massive creature roars before turning in our direction. I sit the pup on the ground as I stand up and round the tree back into the path of the beast.

Maybe it's the dangerous concoction of anger and fear flooding my system, but I'm tired of running.

I'm tired of other things controlling my sanity.

I step back out from the pine, just behind the creature. Whistling through my fingers, I catch its attention.

"You want me? Come and fucking get me."

It turns around with talons raised, but I don't let it lunge at me. I empty every round left in my pistol directly into its head. A purple aura emits from my hands as I pull the trigger relentlessly, but it's gone within seconds as if I imagined it.

I scream, letting my feelings finally escape with every bullet ejected from the weapon. Tears stream my cheeks as every emotion I've had over the last few months bleeds from me.

After the last bullet, the monster sways side to side before falling to the ground. The sound echoes even through the pouring rain. It reaches out for me one final time, but it isn't close enough to grasp me. A loud puff of air is the last sound that it makes.

My heart wrenches in my chest and the hollow burning pain of sorrow grips me with sharp claws. I fall to my knees and sob uncontrollably, chest heaving as my body shakes with emotional agony. Tears, saliva, rain, and snot run down my face.

I need the storm to wash this ache, this pain, this emptiness away.

I punch the ground with my gun still in tow over and over until a small whimper catches my attention.

The pup walks calmly toward me despite the heavy rain blurring our surroundings. I pick her up and squeeze her in my arms, and both of the pup's heads lean up to lick at my unrelenting tears.

For the first time in a very long time, I feel a connection to something. I wipe my face with my palms before holstering the gun. Standing up, I still sniffle as my muscles protest the movement.

Nuclear

"Let's go take a nap," I whisper with a shaky voice. The rain has soaked both of us, but it doesn't seem to matter. We tread back to the cave (now that it's empty) and settle against the cavern wall once more. I pull her close as I get as comfy as one can on rigid, wet earth.

I have a feeling this is the first time in a long time that we will both have a peaceful night's sleep.

I look outside the cave opening and focus on the rain that continues to fall.

After the emotions in my mind begin to calm, my thoughts wonder to what I'm going to name that thing that I killed because "batlike creature" is not cool enough.

"Duskwinger," I whisper under my breath.

I slayed a Duskwinger.

15

MAGGIE (6 MONTHS AGO):

HOME

I wake up and immediately look for my new friend. She must sense my distress and raises both heads to look at me, concern in her eyes. I reach down and rub her heads in assurance that everything is okay. I stretch and feel the tension leave my muscles. For the first time, I don't wake up afraid.

I sit up and state, "Well, you'll have to have a name." My thoughts wonder as I think of the possibilities. Different cute generic names run through my mind, but she's no "Oreo."

She deserves a commanding name.

Cerberus pops into my thoughts, and I immediately settle on it. I feel like it's very fitting, given the mythology behind that name; even if she is a girl, it's still badass. "Cerberus. That's your new name," I announce confidently, nodding in self-approval. Cerberus wags her tail excitedly as if happy to hear her name for the first time. I pick her up and dust myself off. The sun is shining bright, and it feels so surreal to feel the sunlight warming my skin. I can't remember the last time I was able to appreciate the little things like this. I continue to walk and take in the scenery that surrounds me.

"It's just you and I, Cerberus. Let's start our new life."

After hours of hiking, we stumble upon a small quaint cabin. The outside appears neglected, but hopefully, the inside is functional. I tread lightly, observing the area and ensuring we are safe. Cerberus mirrors my footwork and is able to navigate behind me quietly. She does so well, I have to turn around to make sure she really is following me.

Peering through the windows, I notice nothing significant. Surprisingly, the inside of the cabin looks untouched and pristine. I walk through the front door and am immediately in the front room of the home. The interior is outdated but houses a comfortable and cozy atmosphere. I flip the lights on, and to my surprise, they work. After studying the room, I notice a medium sized generator sitting in the far corner of the room.

That's why there's still power in the house that doesn't seem to flicker.

Walking into the kitchen, I head straight for the sink. The lever has some resistance as I turn it right to left. Rusty brown water sputters as the air filters from the faucet. It takes a few minutes for the lines to run clean. Both temperatures flow well, which to me is a success. I look at Cerberus who has already found the couch and made herself at home.

"Welcome home, sweet girl." She barks in approval. I make my way through the rest of the house, scanning the rooms for weapons and threats. The layout of the home consists of two bedrooms and two bathrooms.

I walk into the master bedroom and sit on the bed. I run my fingers over the cheap cotton sheets realizing that I can't remember the last time I slept in a clean bed. A queen mattress with a box spring and sheets feels like being a part of an "elite" society.

Sleep weighs on my eyes. Now that my body isn't constantly flooded with cortisol and adrenaline, it craves rest, and I plan to indulge that need. Here, simply existing doesn't feel like a burden; in the lab, I felt like I was walking on eggshells, where one wrong word or action could lead to death. I lock the door and have Cerberus cuddle up with me. The next task after this nap is to find food.

Can I even eat the meat of the animals out here? I've never had the problem of eating radioactive meat, but there aren't many options, and I'm starving. Anything is better than the freeze-dried shit they have been forcing down my throat for months. I found a crossbow in the cellar, and honestly, I have no idea how to use one, but when I figure this out, I'm pretty sure this will be my weapon of choice. Guns are great and effective, but my goal is to not draw any unnecessary attention to us.

Cerberus and I sit below tall blades of grass. She's like a sponge; she absorbs everything and takes in every action I make. She can read my body language and understand what it means, sometimes faster than I can process what I'm feeling.

Even though she's one creature, her heads seem to have different personalities. Blue Eyes is always happy and panting, while Golden Eyes is always observing me and our surroundings with her head cocked to the side.

I load an arrow into the crossbow, studying the band strength. We wait for anything, silence stilling the grass we lay in. A squirrel comes into my sight. The animal searches through decaying blades of grass, looking for its next snack. I aim and breathe out before releasing an arrow which pins it by its tail.

Damn, the sights are off.

I quickly try to set it so I can put this poor thing out of its misery. As if reading my mind while I'm fumbling to reload, Cerberus springs into action. She pounces on the squirrel, breaking its neck in one swift motion. She turns to me with a now deceased squirrel in one of her mouths and attempts to trot back to me. The arrow lodged in the squirrel's tail has it stuck to the ground. Cerberus falls backward, and I can't help but laugh at how cute she is. She gets up, confused but excited, as I walk towards her to release the squirrel. "Good job," I praise, patting her heads. We return to our grass beds and wait for more game as a tiny squirrel won't fill up two starving animals.

Our hunt ended with four squirrels of different shapes and sizes. We return to the cabin and head to the fire pit behind our new home. The pit is located on a concrete patio, surrounded with makeshift benches constructed from cinder blocks and repurposed lumber. It's composed of random rocks cemented together in four rows, standing about two feet tall. High enough to contain a small fire, but also the perfect height for roasting meat.

I grab my knife and begin preparing the carcasses for cooking. The squirrels are mutated in size as they have more muscle and meat than pre-radiation squirrels. They are roughly the size of large rabbits, and their eyes are white and glazed over. Other than that, they don't differ much from what you'd expect.

Honestly, I doubt that tree limbs could support their weight now. That's probably why I typically see them scurrying the ground, rather than the canopies above us.

The skin of the squirrels separates from the muscle fairly easy, making it simple to render as much meat as possible. Each creature had its minor deformities, but surprisingly, there wasn't anything super off about each one, so prepping them was relatively simple.

After I've collected all I can, I walk over and start a fire. Thankfully, there were a few pans in the kitchen, and whoever lived here before us had the perfect setup to cook down here. I take out a cast iron skillet, rest it on a makeshift grate suspended above our contained fire, and let the flames lick at the bottom of the pan until it's hot enough to sear the meat. I lay the meat in piece by piece, with the pan hissing and sizzling from the cool flesh hitting the hot iron. Cerberus licks her lips,

Nuclear

and I find excitement in eating actual food, even if it is contaminated. I'm sure ingesting radioactive material is the least of my concerns, given that I am likely either radioactive or radiation resistant. Either way, I'm ready to eat, and so is my girl. I shake the pan around, making sure the meat cooks all the way through.

When it's all done, I lay half on a plate for myself and evenly split the rest between two plates for Cerberus. We both eat like rabid animals. Our meal is gone within a few minutes. I sit here satisfied for a while before snuffing the fire and gathering all the supplies. I leave the cast iron skillet to cool.

Dusk is beginning to fall, and I'm not entirely comfortable being out here in the dark yet. I may have night vision, but that doesn't mean there aren't things lurking in the shadows.

I look at Cerberus and say, "Come on, girl. Let's get ready for bed." She rushes ahead of me, and I chase after her. It sparks excitement in her, and I feel like a kid again playing tag for just a moment. The memory comes and goes before I have time to genuinely reflect on it. I try not to dwell too much on memories from the past. They usually just come with heartache and tears, as that life is long gone. It feels like a dream, even though it all happened in this lifetime.

I miss the people. My parents, my foster sister, and my friends were all stripped away so fast. I try to block the memories out.

M.C. Blackheart

The last thing I need is for my depression to come back, especially in a world where there are no antidepressants. I sigh to myself as I walk into the house and kick my boots off.

Maybe this could be a forever home. It's not perfect, but it's much better than where I just came from. It'll never replace the memories or the people, but at least it's safe, and I'm not alone.

16

MAGGIE (CURRENT DAY): INSTINCTS

"We scored big today, girlfriend!" I belt excitedly to Cerberus. She has become the closest thing to a best friend I think I've ever had. I never imagined my "familiar," as they used to call them, would be a two-headed wolf. It feels like I have one of those wizardry pets.

We walk outside to the fire pit, and I reach down before holding my zippo lighter to the fire starter I had in my pocket. I'm so grateful that you get some of your belongings back after the military supervisors start to trust you. My zippo was my dad's, and he had it custom-made. It's silver with a beautiful etching of a wolf's face and a detailed engraving on the back that says, "Feed the wolf you want to win." This is a reference to the old Native American story of two wolves that live inside us: one evil and one good. When you live your life, you choose the one you feed. He always told me to choose the good wolf. I try daily to remember that, but I'm not sure it matters which wolf I pick anymore.

I smile as my gaze leaves the zippo and focuses in on my two headed girl. Coincidentally, despite the wolves that live in us and their constant battle of good and evil, her heads always interact in harmony and never have conflict with one another.

It brings a sense of peace over me.

It's fall in Appalachia, so a cool breeze is always present. However, this evening it's different. It feels darker and lingering. My gut tells me Cerberus can feel it as well because she is pacing more than usual. She's always on guard, but tonight there's more intent. I feel like I'm being watched and can't quite discern why. The last person I saw was months ago, and unfortunately for him, he had to die. He wanted everything I have built here, including myself, but in a belligerent man kind of way.

Men are so entitled, so stupid.

Even in the apocalypse, they think they are still superior. He was obviously thinking with the wrong head until I pulled my knife out of his abdomen. He fell to his knees with a look of disbelief and betrayal, even though I owed him nothing.

I love it when men underestimate women. It's something I could get off on, especially when you see the defeat in their eyes. After falling to his hands and knees, Cerberus finished him off. I watched the life leave his eyes and felt no remorse as his last breath escaped his lungs. He's not the first person I've killed, but he was the first I killed with a knife. Blood is much cooler to the touch than you would think. In movies, they portray it as a hot liquid, but it's actually just lukewarm, metallic, and sticky.

Tonight, though, I feel someone's eyes on me, and I feel vulnerable for the first time in a few months. There's a stillness in the air that is normally consumed by the creatures of the woods. I breathe deeper and try to open my senses. I search the tree line expecting to catch the eyes or movement of anything, but there's nothing.

Nothing but a haunting *knowing* that is gnawing at my sanity.

I stalk back into the house to do a sweep of the rooms just to try and ease my growing anxiety. I tread silently through the outdated cabin with my handgun raised, ready to shoot. My heart beats wildly as I turn the corner into my bedroom. I blow out a controlled breath as I make my way to the closet. The bifold door slams open from the force of the nervousness in my hand before I aim my weapon into stagnant clothing. I slide the clothes back and forth.

Nothing.

I click the safety on the gun and slide it back into its holster at my waist before turning to head back outside. The hairs on the back of my neck are still raised, despite me turning up empty handed. A tinge of doubt about my abilities creeps into my mind.

Am I just paranoid?

I walk into the kitchen and grab my hoodie, a cutting board, and a chef's knife. The people who owned this cabin may not have had a lot of money, but they did have good taste. I skin the fish and filet it appropriately.

The knife slowly glides between the fish's skin and the tender meat beneath it. I remove the tiny rib bones that protrude from the filets before placing the prepared meat in a cast iron pan and letting it roast over the fire.

A rustle in the trees snaps me out of my flashback. Cerberus goes quiet and studies her surroundings. The hair on the back of her neck is standing erect, and her body language shows her cautiousness. Something I admire about her is that you won't hear her until she strikes, despite having quadrupled in size over the last few months. She stands at roughly four foot tall on all fours, but on her hind legs, she's just as tall if not taller than me. It's uncanny how she is so quiet with her size, but I'm grateful for it. We waited but only silence resonates from the forest, although I could've sworn I saw a human skull from behind the tree canopy.

I grab a tennis ball that I found in the cellar off the ground and toss it for Cerberus to go get. She loves to run but won't go far. Maybe it's because we saved each other. At this point in my life, I need her most. She is a companion and the only constant in my life, and I haven't had continuity in a very long time. I hope the radiation she was exposed to gives her fifty years to spend with me.

Nuclear

She runs eagerly after the ball and puts it directly in my hand when she returns. Both heads pant in excitement as she waits for my next pitch. I chuck the ball as hard as I can, and it takes her seconds to find and return it to me.

"Good girl," I say as I pet both of her heads while her tongues flop to either side, creating an adorable site.

If only I had a camera.

I play fetch with her until she sits down and curls up beside my feet. I grab my water bottle and pour some into the two bowls next to the fire pit. She drinks fast, panting in between each lap of water. I pat her side.

Her blue-eyed head continues to focus on me and when she'll get her next pet, while the other remains torn between watching me and monitoring the tree line for intruders.

I toss the ball down the hallway one last time for the evening just because I love how excited Cerberus gets. The ball bounces repetitively against the aged carpet until it rebounds off a baseboard and into my room. Cerberus takes off and I start to put the cutlery and cutting board away in the kitchen. The house goes silent for a beat, which is odd because she should've brought me the ball back by now.

A symphony of whimpers and whines comes from the bedroom. I make my way down the hall and turn the corner with trepidation. Cerberus sits at the side of the bed with the ball in front of her paws.

"What's wrong, girl?" I ask quietly, unsure of the circumstances. She turns to stand on her hind legs and snuffles my pillowcase.

What. The. Fuck?

"I knew it."

I look at Cerberus and shake my head, and both of her heads cock to the side.

"We were being watched." My heart sinks to my feet as I see the passionflower on my pillow.

Someone is here and watching.

I run my fingers across the petals of the flower despite my disgust and fear. It's large in circumference, with dense, silky lavender shaded petals that provide a backdrop for thin and deep purple petals toward the center of the flower. It's beautiful, but it was left with malicious intent. A lump of anxiety forms in my throat as I realize someone was here without my knowledge.

"We are going to have to be more vigilant." I reach down and pet her heads loosely.

Obviously, someone is trying to scare me.

The problem is that it's working.

Nuclear

I've had many people come through these woods and try to push their agendas on me, but I've never had someone stalk me from the forest. I shudder at the thought of someone watching my every move.

They've probably seen me naked and that gives me the heebie-jeebies.

I guess I'm going to have to start changing in the bathroom down the hall that has no windows.

Ugh, I just want to exist in a world where I don't have to wear pants if I don't want to, but men have to ruin everything good.

I dig through the closet for anything that I can use as makeshift curtains. I gather up a few men's sized jackets and begin to line every window I can in the bedroom. I stretch the jackets until they are taut across the windowpane, but there is still a sliver of the window that I can't get covered no matter how I arrange the coats.

Frustration settles between my brows, until I finally accept that the one sliver will just have to remain exposed. My eyes sting as I come to terms with the fact that even though he can't see me, he still knows how to get in. The most unsettling fact is that even though I can put up a good fight, I am not the one in control of this situation.

Someone is learning about me, and I can't tell if it's romantic or threatening. Part of me screams to toss the flower, but another part can't give up something so beautiful in this ugly world. I lay it on my nightstand and grab my knife from the top drawer. I place it under my pillow in its leather quick-release sheath. At least if he sneaks up on me, he'll be met with a weapon of some sort. I tuck myself in, and Cerberus curls up on the foot of the bed. My mind is sent into a tailspin as I feel myself losing control; however, there's nothing I can do to change it. That thought alone makes a vice squeeze around my heart.

For the first time in six months, I'm helpless and it scares the shit out of me.

I wake up in the early morning hours from a nightmare. They are a common occurrence and tend to be worse when I experience stress, but truthfully, they never seem to get better.

I run my hand across the back of my neck, warming it from the cold sweat pooling on my skin. My clothes are stuck to me and my hairline is damp. I walk to the shower, and flashes of the dreams from the past invade my thoughts. Every damn time I close my eyes, another trauma-filled memory clouds my head. The images of needles that filled my veins with excruciating poison over and over, pushing me so close to death I could taste it, exasperate my sanity.

I can still feel the leather wrist straps restraining me to a cold, rigid, metal table. The cruel, sterile smell of the lab I was "reborn" in makes my chest tighten as it overwhelms me. I can feel the ungodly amounts of potassium iodide moving through my tissues causing my heart to pump painfully slow. Dizziness

Nuclear

and fatigue were immediate symptoms, followed by air hunger and dissociating thoughts of confusion.

This particular nightmare was about when they gave me a drug cocktail that had a volatile reaction with the excessive amounts of potassium in my system that began to erode parts of my bones. I laid for hours while doctors observed and took notes of my reaction to the cocktail that ravaged my system. I consider myself half bionic because, after that experiment, I earned myself some steel bone replacements.

Five ribs, six vertebrae, my right humerus, left femur, and right tibia were almost completely dissolved after the chemicals tore through my body. They literally called the drugs they used "The Swiss Cheese Cocktail" because, on X-ray, that's exactly what my affected bones looked like.

I snap back to reality and find myself curled up in the bottom of the shower. I look down at the tattoo on my wrist that reads "416." A constant depressing reminder that my body was not mine for two months of my life.

Experiment 416.

That was my name and my identity for two whole months. All I can think about is how many people let things happen to me. How people robbed me of so much.

My name, my life, my autonomy, and my fucking eye color.

My mind flashes back to when they did an experiment where they had decided they could make our vision nocturnal. Like night vision goggles without the goggles. Dr. Hyde was so proud of what he had discovered and the possibility of creating a new kaleidoscope for "human" vision.

"Now 416, I need you to hold extremely still so I don't leave you totally blind," Dr. Hyde said as he reached over and grabbed a massive needle with a syringe full of a red viscous liquid. I later found out that substance was isotopes attained from a mix of chemicals and the retinas of barn owls.

"We are playing in your occipital lobe today, which affects your vision. If you lose vision at any point, I need to know." The way he said "playing" like he wasn't probing my brain makes disgust churn my stomach.

The sound of an electric razor buzzes from behind me as one of his assistants lifts my hair and shaves a spot on the back of my head. The next sound is one that still makes my chest heavy. A bone saw begins to grind into my skull, removing a small chunk of bone so Dr. Hyde can access my brain.

They never used any kind of anesthetic so they could study our full threshold of pain. I felt every agonizing buzz and movement of that saw through my bone, and I was expected to hold still. If I moved or gave into pain, it would be my fault if I lost my vision. I wince at the memory of the sensation of that needle penetrating my cerebral tissue. The cold chill that rushes my spine makes me almost jump out of my skin with the thought.

After the pain and the worst headache I have ever had faded, so did the blue pigment from my left eye. However, the project was only partially successful. My right eye remained unaffected, but my left eye is keen on night vision. Excellent for war and hunting, however useless otherwise. It makes the unknown monsters in the dark a lot less scary, but my own personal monsters are a different story. My eye color is a constant reminder that I am only half-good during the day, and half-good with my skills at night, but I'm never good as a whole.

I wipe the tears from my eyes and turn the water off. I reach for the towel on the hook next to the shower door. The cold air makes goosebumps rise on my skin. Wrapping the towel around me, I walk back into the bedroom. Cerberus perks her head up as if asking if I'm okay.

"I'm alright."

I gaze into her mismatched eyes, which mirror my own, finding comfort in our shared solidarity before her heads rest back on their paws.

I sit on the bed and wonder if my life could ever be on the path to some normalcy.

Not likely.

I have always had darkness inside me. It has gnashed and clawed at my insides for years. Through depression, a suicide attempt, and being a government experiment, it has only swelled and integrated itself into my personality. It's created an interesting fascination with death. Death is no longer a fate that I fear. When my time comes, I feel comfort in knowing that the afterlife, whatever that is, can't be worse than this life. I look forward to blissful, dark nonexistence.

I've been pushed so close to that line multiple times in my lifetime that I feel like death has become a friend that I walk hand in hand with. A friend that takes and takes and leaves nothing. My parents, life, and the person I used to be, have all fallen through my hands like sand. With the reaper's hand on my shoulder, I will continue to walk alone… well, with Cerberus on my other side, of course.

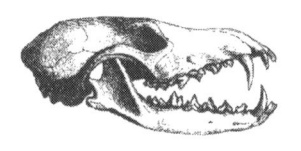

"Come on, Cerberus!" I yell from the front door. I'm restless today. The anxiety of a new stalker is eating at me, and I need to blow off some steam.

I need to get out and walk, run, or fight.

Anything is fine at this point.

She greets me at the front door with excitement shining in her eyes. I double-check my weapons as I toss my crossbow over my shoulder. My pistol feels cool against the small of my back as I tuck it into my waistband. I slide my knife into its designated sheath inside my right boot. We walk out into the crisp fall air. I breathe it in, and as it settles in my lungs, it brings a sense of peace. Fall has always been my favorite season, and although the leaves on the trees have not fully begun to change color, the smell of autumn has sunk into the air.

We walk farther into the brush, detangling branches and creating our path as we go. I take in everything and keep my senses keen. It's been good practice going into the silent woods and searching for anything. The skill is something I feel I should keep just in case they come looking for me. I don't hear anything other than the usual small creatures that inhabit this part of the forest.

Cerberus looks at me for approval to run ahead of me, and I nod to her. She takes off with both tongues hanging out of her mouth. I keep a steady pace behind her.

The cool autumn breeze feels rejuvenating to my face. The wind blows my hair over my shoulder, and I can feel how it caresses each strand. My feet move fast but stay silent as they hit the rigid earth below me. Cerberus skillfully avoids branch after branch, her agility no match for the forest we reside in. The trees begin to thin as we enter the clearing where the lake is located. Cerberus slows down and waits at the threshold of the tree line for me to give the okay to be out in the open. I approach and stand beside her, listening through the whistling wind and rustling leaves.

All I can hear is the call of a blue-winged warbler and the sound of clacking tree branches.

We walk through the tree line to the beautiful body of water. Light fog has descended in the air just above the lake. The trees seem to disappear as the fog thickens in the distance. I walk to the water's edge onto its little shore. Like the ocean meeting land, this area is calm, and the earth under my feet trails seamlessly into the clear water. I dip my toes in, feeling the refreshing water rush over my skin. Colorful rocks dance beneath my feet as I shift my weight, while silver minnows dart by, gone in the blink of an eye. Cerberus gets excited and chases them deeper into the water, trying her best to snap one into her mouths. She strikes but comes up empty-handed. She blows water from her nose and looks at me before a dramatic sneeze leaves her. The golden eyed head sniffs the blue eyed one concernedly. I roll my eyes and can't help but laugh.

She's just so damn cute.

She tracks more fish through the water, and I sit on the dry sand, submerging my feet. I lean my head back and braid my hair into one long French braid. It gets on my nerves when my hair hangs down in my face. The strands of hair graze each finger, but I notice something odd.

My fingertips are numb.

Just the pads of my fingers don't elicit any sensation. No matter how much pressure I apply to them, I can't feel anything. I slide my right hand into the water, and it creeps up my skin feeling like little pinpricks. I pull my hand out and try my finger pads again, hoping just to wash away the feeling. Surprisingly, I see a slight purple aura radiating from them. I continue to rub my thumb over my finger pads, and just as quickly as it happens, the purple aura fades, and my sensation returns.

Fear fills my chest as I question what I'm turning into, but I do my best to suppress the thoughts. An image of Stevie pops into my head and I hold onto the peace that comes with it to avoid tumbling into unrelenting worry.

The truth is, I won't know until it happens. Worrying about it just makes me more vulnerable.

As if sensing my inner struggle, Cerberus resurfaces from the lake, soaking wet. She trots over to me with a small minnow in one of her mouths. Victory and pride diffuse from her, but she approaches me with caution. She walks up and licks my cheek with one of her mouths while the other refuses to give up the trophy. I lean forward and pet her.

"I'm okay. Thank you for checking." She walks a couple of feet away at my statement and then shakes herself off. The water from her coat soaks just about everything nearby. The head that had the minnow quickly devours the tiny fish whole. She looks back at me like a child asking permission for something. I nod and reassure her, "Go on and play; we have all afternoon." I smile as she turns to run. She chases small dragonflies that fly around us, without a care in the world. My gaze fixed on my hand in confusion, running my thumb over my fingertips several more times.

All sensation is intact, and no purple haze trails from my fingers.

M.C. Blackheart

I shrug it off and dig my toes into the round stones beneath the water's surface as I watch Cerberus chase small dragonflies that hover just above the lake's surface.

17

RYKER (CURRENT DAY):

THE STALKER

Dammit.

I almost blew my cover.

The tree that I currently reside in is old and starting to decay. I didn't realize how weak the branches were. One of my arms was resting on a branch above me, and my stance was as if I stood in a doorway, holding onto the door frame. After a few minutes of constant pressure, the branch snapped without any warning, and the sound caught the attention of my sweet little fox. I froze as I watched her study her surroundings. Part of me hoped she would investigate the sound, but another part wanted to watch panic settle in her.

A smile curls at the edge of my lips as I discern that I'm already a part of her life. Her mind is reeling in thoughts of who I am, and the pleasure of knowing that I've already caught her attention has me beaming.

She makes me so vulnerable because I forget to survey my surroundings when I see her.

Hell, I forget everything.

Her presence is demanding and overshadows everything in my brain, including rational thoughts. I want to be her madness and watch her come undone as her mind is consumed by the thought who I am. I found some passionflowers in a field this morning before I saw her. I went back and picked one to leave for her. The petals are a silvery lavender with smaller petals growing darker in color as the recurve into the center.

This little hiccup has exposed one possible problem though.

Her wolf is about the size of a lion, and without earning its trust, getting my little fox alone will be nearly impossible since they are inseparable. I can handle her alone, but with her wolf? I'll be a dead man.

I sneak through the brush, treading lightly to not draw attention to myself. When I arrive at the front entrance, I test the door for squeaks and creaks by slowly turning the knob and pulling the door open. Even though the door appears aged, it still functions as if recently installed as no sounds leave the hinges. Slipping through the threshold of the door, I listen to make sure my girl and her wolf are still by the fire pit.

"Good girl." I hear her appealing voice praise from a distance.

One day, she will beg me to give her the same affirmation.

I make sure to gently close the door behind me to avoid it slamming shut and blowing my cover. The shag carpet compresses under my boots as it dulls the sound of my footsteps. I make my way through the rooms, studying the house's layout until I find her bedroom. It's very plain and outdated. The walls are tan and boring with an obnoxious floral wallpaper border haunting the edges of the ceiling meeting the wall.

I cross the threshold into her room.

I can tell it's hers because the bed is the only one that has been used and is unkempt.

I can't help myself.

I run my fingers over her sheets feeling the wrinkles caused by her restless sleep.

I lift her pillow to my nose and breathe in my little fox. Her scent is hypnotizing as notes of vanilla and sandalwood invade my nose. She smells as good as she looks, and I can't wait to see if her taste is up to par as well. My heart pounds a little bit harder against my rib cage. I kiss the passionflower and gently lay it on her pillow. The petals caress my lips like I imagine she would, soft but firm.

As I turn to exit the room, my eyes lock onto a small, pocket-sized, black, leather-bound book on the nightstand. The binding shows minimal wear, but it was obvious that it has been used frequently.

A journal? Could this be my girl's diary?

Anticipation squeezes my heart as I run my fingers over it, just taking in that I am so close to seeing into her mind. It's like my little fox left this here for me to find. She wants me to see what lurks behind those mismatched eyes.

I undo the band that holds the book closed, and I'm practically shaking with excitement as I open the cover to the first page.

"What in the hell did I fight today?" is written in bold, jagged manuscript across the cream paper.

I flip the pages slowly taking in every stroke of graphite as they entangle to reveal sketches of…. monsters?

So much for a diary of her inner thoughts.

Underneath each sketch is a made-up word like Duskwinger or Skyscreamer followed by a short description of weaknesses and how she has killed each one.

When I get to the last sketch, recognition slaps me in the face as I study the repetitive markings. It's the salamander beast I saw her fight the day I laid eyes on her. Underneath the image was the word "Scalderith."

Nuclear

My girl is creating an encyclopedia of the new monsters that plague the earth.

Clever.

Really fucking clever.

I take one last look through the pages making sure I had seen all its contents, before carefully binding the book back together with the band and placing it softly back on the bedside table.

After I get my fix of my new favorite drug, I leave quietly without leaving any other sign I had been there. I hope the flower makes her keenly aware someone is here wanting her, craving her, and needing her.

I'm used to being quiet and disappearing without a trace. The United States military literally trained me for this. Not only am I a genetically enhanced soldier, but due to the abilities I acquired through experimentation, I was deemed worthy of being a part of an elite group of super soldiers called Apparition Ops. Think like navy seals, but scarier and better. Mostly, everyone just referred to us as the Wraiths. Essentially, to do the government's dirty work without drawing attention back to them. We had unique uniforms and were required to wear masks that helped us become more proficient at our duties. I still wear my mask while hunting, but that's usually the only time anymore. I look down at my wrist, and the image of the "830" still scars me.

In this moment, trauma overwhelms the obsession I crave and my mind flashes back to the crude experimentation laboratory. The imagery of the human-sized cage comes rushing back.

"Oh, 830, we have big plans for you." My muscles tense as I see Dr. Billings with multiple vials in his hand with labels that read "corrosive," "toxic," or "do not ingest." I backed away from the cold metal barred door until I hit the other side of the cage.

"Now, now, 830, you know what happens to people who aren't cooperative," he taunts with a wicked grin.

He looks to his left and nods at a guard behind a large control panel. The guard flips a switch, and immediate unfiltered electricity ravages my body from the iron bars that my back is resting against.

The pain sends me seizing and renders me useless to a fight. I swear, when looking at my fingertips at that moment, I saw streams of electricity leave my hands, just like a plasma lamp I used to have as a kid, except a million times more painful.

The guard flips the switch back, and I fall face-first onto my hands and knees. Realizing I have been beaten, I crawl forward to the door, unable to stand. Dr. Billings unlocks the bio-lock with his retinal scan, and my heart sinks to my feet as two guards carry me from my cage to a suspension contraption.

They lock my wrists and ankles in separate metal cuffs. Dr. Billings nods to someone, at what point the contraption spreads to suspend me in the air in four-point restraints. My heart beats against my rib cage like a bird trying to escape its enclosure. The smell of sterile death lingers in the air. Dr. Billings pulls out a massive needle and smiles as he pulls the "corrosive" vial into a syringe. The liquid is a sickly opaque green, which makes my stomach flip. I look up and pray to whatever God is out there, if there is a God left. I understand that I will probably die where I hang, and I welcome death with open arms.

Even black oblivion has to be better than the hell I'm in.

I just wish my death didn't have to be this painful. He stabs the needle into my neck as he calmly says, "Breathe, 830; it'll be over soon."

Except it wasn't over, my life anyway.

The chemical wreaked havoc on my system and set my veins on fire. I screamed and thrashed until the pain caused me to blackout. To this day, I have no idea what that chemical was, but I imagine it had something to do with radiation resistance.

I snap back to the show in front of me, shaking off the traumatic reminder. I can see just into her bedroom window as she and her wolf enter. Her eyes narrow on the flower, and her skin begins to redden with uneasiness. She's mumbling unclear words, but she's clearly scared based on her body language, and I feed off that.

I thought she was sexy, but when she's afraid, it sends my body into overdrive. She hastily runs to the closet and brings back a towering pile of jackets and coats so she can cover the window.

The best part is watching her try to pick up a trace of me. She's good, but I'm better at this game than her. She's in the dark about the situation and has no puzzle pieces to connect. I chuckle to myself as she tries desperately to cover every inch of the windows but struggles with one sliver. That one gap in fabric is the epitome of luck as I can still see where she sleeps.

Damn, I wish I had some popcorn to watch her unravel.

I'm not a good man, and I've never claimed to be, but I can tell you that she will love all the things I do to her. No one will ever be able to hurt or scare my little fox except for me.

The moon light shines through the uncovered crevice of the window, and I'm able to see the entirety of the bed if I move throughout the branches I'm perched in. She's sleeping and watching the calm slow rise and fall of her chest makes me wish I could feel her against me.

Feel her breathe me in.

Her wolf is curled up beside her, both heads resting on her arm.

I'm jealous of a fucking dog right now.

What I wouldn't give to be in her bed and be her security blanket.

In due time, I remind myself. I look down at the wound where I removed my tracker and examine it. It appears to be healing nicely, but it will definitely scar.

Nuclear

Oh well, I guess there will be one more for the collection. I'm full of scars and tattoos, each with their own story. I imagine that when I move into the afterlife, none of those will carry with me into my new being.

The trauma, the stories, and the chemicals will be left behind.

I'm sure I'll find plenty more trouble to add to my soul in hell.

But one thing is certain: the only thing I plan to drag to hell with me is my sweet new obsession. Even in hell, I'll protect her from her demons and the ones that manifest to tear us apart. I smile at the thought of flames behind her. It would match the fire and wrath visible in her scarlet eye. She is the Persephone to my Hades, and I will stop at nothing to have her by my side.

I climb through branches and down the trunk of the tree I'm in. Since she is fast asleep and resting well for the moment, I think it's time to make friends with her wolf. If I'm going to do this, I'm going to need to find some "treats."

18

RYKER:

NEW FRIENDS

I pull my dagger out and track the sound of mice through the tall grass of the forest. I manage to rack up four within thirty minutes. I'm getting pretty good at my knife hunting skills if I do say so myself. These will make for a very happy wolf.

I keep my pace controlled and steps soft as I approach the front door of the cabin. I dig through my vest pockets just hoping that my military ID is still in one of them. The doorknob lock looks to be pretty ancient, so I'm hoping it is loose or poorly installed.

I balance on the balls of my feet and squat to bring the knob to eye level. After checking six pockets, I finally find the card and carefully slide it between the door and the frame. Excruciatingly slow, I begin to glide the card between the latch bolt.

Nuclear

The card stops and meets resistance. I let go and inhale deeply before continuing.

I cannot break this card off in the door.

The key here is despite my excitement, I must remain composed and collected to avoid my strength ruining this plan. I grip the card firmly and push with moderate pressure, until the card releases from where it was stuck and begins to slide again.

Click.

My heart skips as the door slowly swings open.

The chain lock on the inside of the door jingles, and I briskly step to the side of the door as to not be seen in case one of them awoke.

I wait and wait until it feels like an eternity has gone by.

I hear nothing except the midnight chirps of crickets. I blow out the breath I've been holding for at least a minute. There's no doubt about it; that was luck that I didn't just get charged by a pissed-off woman and her man-eating wolf.

I very carefully reach through the door frame and slide the chain lock off the door track, making sure to gently guide it to hang loosely to avoid making more noise. The door continues to creep open.

Phase one of my plan is complete.

Cerberus will come straight for me when I get her attention. Since she won't have to wait for my little fox to hear her to open the door, it should give me enough time to make friends and have her back before she notices the wolf was ever gone. My mask is off, and my face is bare of makeup to look less menacing.

I find the biggest branch lying next to the tree line and snap it over my knee. The crack of splitting wood echoes through the backyard, louder than I had expected it to be.

Within seconds, I hear growling and heavy paws as the black creature emerges from the house. Both heads scan their surroundings, and I make sure I'm within their sight. She sprints toward me at a speed so fast that I almost don't have time to react. This brings back the worst feeling of déjà vu.

"Easy, Cerberus," I whisper with my palms up and facing outward.

She stops just a few feet shy of me with confusion in her eyes as if unsure how I know her name. Both sets of eyes narrow on me as her gums lift to expose teeth so vicious that fear sends a shiver down my spine.

I drop to my knees with both hands still raised to look submissive to a wolf I know is the alpha here.

"Hey, girl, I've got something for you." I stay relaxed and smile as genuinely as my adrenaline will let me. I slowly take my left hand and reach behind my back and the golden eyed

Nuclear

head snaps at me as foam begins to form at the corners of its mouth. I take a mouse from my back pocket and lightly toss the dead animal between us.

The blue-eyed head sniffs the air, before taking another step closer. My mind screams in trepidation, but I refuse to show it. Golden Eyes breaks eye contact, but still snarls at me. Blue Eyes picks the mouse up and takes a step back dropping it at a huge set of paws. Golden Eyes leans down and sniffs and seems to nod at Blue Eyes.

Blue Eyes picks the rodent up and begins to chew. Splintering bones echo on the outside of her mouth and for a split second, I actually relax.

"Atta girl," I praise, with a quick sigh of relief.

"I have more, all you have to do is trust me."

I toss another mouse and let it land in the same spot as the first. Golden Eyes picks this one up and devours it much like the other head did. The narrow eyes of both heads focus on me, but their mouths begin to soften.

"You are gorgeous, you know that?" I ask, hoping flattery will help my situation. "I can tell you are such a good girl. I've got two more for you if you want them." I pull out the other two mice and hold one in each hand.

"If you want these, you are going to have to come to me to get them."

Her heads look to one another as if truly contemplating their options. She creeps forward, neither head taking its eyes off me. When she is within inches of me, both heads steal the mice from my hands, but to my surprise, she doesn't retreat.

Golden Eyes leans in and sniffs my palms before trailing up my arms, to my face. Intimidation grows in my chest as the realization that one of her heads could easily decapitate me crosses my mind. She gives one final puff of dog breath into my face before sitting in front of me, as if giving me a few minutes to plead my case.

I scoot closer, making sure to stay on my knees.

"I just want to be friends," I say, reaching my hand out to scratch under her chins. Over the head petting will get your hands bitten off as it can feel threatening to dogs. My fingertips encounter silky fur, and I scratch them both softly.

Blue Eyes's tongue hangs to the side while Golden Eyes watches me calmly but intently.

"You are such a good girl. Thank you for letting me pet you." Blue Eyes leans in hard against my hand.

"Let's get you home before Mama notices you're gone." I stand and raise my palms again before walking past her. She growls a soft but firm warning insinuating something like "try anything, and you'll die."

After I've past, she follows behind me and I encourage her through the front door when we arrive to the porch. She crosses the threshold and stands in the doorway as if to let me know I'm not allowed any further. I nod at her before closing the door quietly.

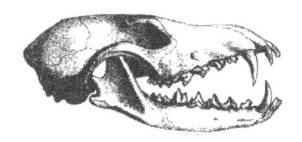

My little fox and her friend have decided to trek back to the lake today. I swiftly get to my feet and follow them, remaining as quiet as I can. When your prey has super hearing, it makes the stalking part a little more complicated.

She weaves through the greenery with impressive speed, navigating obstacles with ease. My little fox has been facing her own monsters lately, and I'm not ready to give her another to worry about.

I may be a bad guy, but I'm not evil.

Something is plaguing her, though. The nightmares have been more frequent for her as the days go on. Her panic and stress will worsen now that she knows I'm out here, burning for her.

I follow her closely, but not close enough for her to pick up on me. I watch Cerberus run into the clearing where the lake is. My girl follows behind. She's breathing slowly, and despite being outside in the open, she isn't afraid. She lets her feet submerge in the water, but she only goes far enough in to still sit on the dry shore at the water's edge. Her eyes follow

Cerberus as she swims and enjoys the expanse of the water. I watch my fox closely.

She's acting out of character today.

I'm used to my anxious little fox, but today, she seems angry with the emotions and feelings that wage war inside her.

I notice something when she touches the water with her hand. It's almost like she sends energy through the lake. A slight purple glow radiates from the clear water while her hand is submerged. I wouldn't have noticed it without studying her so closely. I think she sees it, too, because she pulls her hand out and quickly runs her thumb over her fingers.

My mind starts to wonder as to what that purple aura could be. The thought of her being from the military briefly crosses my mind, but I've never seen a woman survive the chemicals, let alone seen someone glow purple from them. Maybe her glow is radiation exposure induced. The possibilities are endless.

I'm seriously debating introducing myself to her sooner rather than later. After all, I'm sure the government will be coming for me once they realize I was not at the scene of the attack. I hope they think the beast that mauled my team ate me and moved on. But with the extensive testing I endured and my high price tag, they'll ensure their bases are covered. They believe I'm still a zombie. It's been a difficult facade to keep up over the last couple of months, but it was my only way of knowing I would eventually get out. I pretended for months to serve them and go on their stupid missions, but this mission that led me here showed me my purpose.

She is my purpose.

I know I'm the villain in this story because I would destroy the whole world and everyone in it for her. A hero would sacrifice her to save the world.

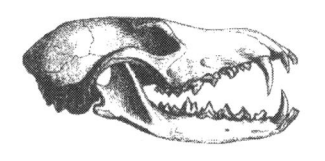

Another two weeks have passed since I left my beautiful little fox that passionflower. I've been watching her from the thick cover of the tree canopies and abundant brush. She's only going out if she must, as she is nervous about what lurks in the trees.

She should be.

I want to break her down into a million pieces and fit them into my own shattered self. To show her how to ride the line between life and death. I want nothing more than to worship her and own her simultaneously.

I don't know her yet, but my soul longs for her.

I want her touch, her love, her soul, and her pain.

Cerberus and I have been continuing our nightly routine of midnight snacks and pets and last night was the first time she let me scratch behind her ears. I even got her to sniff my mask before putting it on. She growled for a few seconds, but after I continued petting her, she accepted my attire.

We've made so much progress in the last couple weeks, that I feel she won't attack me unless my little fox commands it of her. With Cerberus on my side, the confidence of meeting her has bloomed tenaciously.

I watch her through my small window of bliss. She tosses and turns, never attaining sleep.

She misses me, I can tell.

I've tried to give her some space because as the saying goes, "absence makes the heart grow fonder," but maybe I've been a bit too busy focusing on my relationship with Cerberus and not giving my girl the attention she deserves.

She gets up and starts to put clothes on, and I can't help but wonder if maybe she needs a distraction. I know where she's going. There is only one place she goes to clear her head.

I pluck the passionflower from my pocket that I found this morning. I was planning on having a date with a wolf tonight but turns out I actually have a blind date with a fox.

19

MAGGIE:

THE BLADE

Sleep evades me like a shadow at dusk, always just out of reach when I need it most. I toss and turn in the bed trying to find a comfortable position, but my thoughts won't stop racing.

It's been two weeks with no new flowers or interaction. I can't figure out what he wants from me, but it feels like he's playing mind games. I'm constantly on edge, and if his goal was to keep me uneasy, he's already won. I throw a pillow over my face and huff into it with frustration before rising from the mattress.

Cerberus perks up as I slide into actual clothes. Her eyes squint at me as if to say, "Do you have any idea what time it is?"

"Yes, ma'am, I'm aware it's late or early depending on how you look at it, but I can't sleep," I remark as I pull my boots on. "I need some fresh air. Do you want to come?"

She stretches dramatically engulfing the entire king-sized bed. When she curls up, she takes up a third of it, but sprawled out, it's as if the bed is too small for her. She hops off the bed with an echoing thud and we head to the fire pit.

The bright full moon light illuminates a passionflower on the large stones of the fire pit, along with a note and a fire starter. My heart is racing so fast that I can feel it in my throat, and my hands tremble as I unfold the wrinkled piece of paper.

I can forget about any sleep tonight.

"You've lit a fire inside me, so I think it's only fair to return the favor. See you soon, little fox." My throat feels like it's constricting with anxiety. The thin piece of paper sticks to my sweaty fingertips.

Little fox?

Surely, he isn't addressing me. But who else would he be talking about? I close my eyes and try to regain control of my shaking body. I can tell with the silence around me that someone is here. Everything is too quiet. There are no cicadas, no crickets, and not even a breeze dares to rustle the leaves.

The silence before a storm. I feel like I've just walked into a trap.

Stupid sleep deprivation has severely altered my decision-making skills.

Nuclear

He is here. Cerberus is scanning the tree line's brush, which tells me she feels it, too.

There is movement in the trees to my left, and my heart feels like it's going to come out of my chest as it hammers erratically inside me.

Cerberus growls, a low pitch snarling growl that makes the hairs on the back of my neck stand up. I draw my knife from my boot into my right hand, the blade end resting against my forearm. The knife's blade is around eight inches long with a hook at the end of it, and the handle is big enough to fill my palm. It has a rounded end and a slender finished wooden handle that leads to a gold hilt at the base of the blade.

It is truly a beautiful piece of work.

It was clearly used as a gutting knife for game previously, and I plan to use it for exactly that right now. It's one of my favorite things I found in the rustic old cabin I call home. Blade drawn; I move toward the still leaves that were once rustling. Before I can reach the threshold, a hand grabs my right wrist, rendering my weapon useless.

Sometimes, I wish I was ambidextrous.

It's strong, and it takes everything I have to put up a fight. As I pull the man (attached to the hand that has me in a bruising grip) out of the thick greenery beneath me, I'm stricken with awe.

He is large (at least 6'5"), and his muscles are notably huge and remarkable with how his shirt hugs his body. His veins are visible and pop out dramatically from under his skin. They rope from his neck down through his arms. He is dressed in all black clothing, with a canvas vest that has multiple pockets on his chest. It looks to be bulletproof, so obviously he came prepared for a fight with me. His face is hidden behind a half mask. The mask is in the shape of a skull, but it doesn't take away from his sharp jawline that could cut gemstones. Bright green eyes peer from the depths of the mask's sockets and are not diminished by the tint on the acrylic in the eye openings of the mask. The rest of his exposed face is covered in black war paint, including his lips. The mask immediately strikes a memory for me, and I know what he is.

He's a wraith.

Dread kicks me hard in the gut.

He's here to take me back. They found me.

The power struggle between us continues despite my epiphany, and I deliver a sharp kick to his abdomen. Unfazed, he gets me to drop my knife by applying strong force to a pressure point in my wrist that I didn't even know I had. The pain sears in my hand and I feel heat burn through my arm. Tiny tendrils of purple electricity pulse from my hand but disappear as quickly as they manifested.

I yelp in pain. Cerberus growls, waiting for my command. "Stay," I say through gritted teeth as Cerberus lies down and continues watching intently.

Nuclear

This is my fight.

It's my revenge to seek for the fear he has instilled in me over the last few weeks. Cerberus is here for reinforcement purposes only.

I hook my foot into the pit of his knee, sending him lurching forward onto his knees. He releases my wrist to catch himself, leaving a perfect white imprint where his hand once was, a testament to how tightly he had gripped me.

I don't give him time to think as I throw my fist into his right cheek. My hand aches as if I had just hit pure steel, and I shake out the sensation before returning it to a fist. Blood drips from an open wound on one of my knuckles as I prepare to deliver another blow. He doesn't waiver from his stance, and slowly turns his head back to me. A sinister smile spreads the expanse of the lower half of his face as he spits blood to the side. White teeth with scarlet outlines shine from his dark lips, and my heart sprints as panic builds inside my chest. Like a dam overwhelmed by raging water, I tremble as fear begins to choke me.

I'm probably going to regret that, but, damn, it felt good.

Like a predator that has cornered its prey, he pounces at me, grabbing my ankle with a robust grip. Before I can react, he pulls my feet out from under me. I see stars from how hard my head hits the unforgiving earth. He drags me to him despite my spastic kicking, hopelessly trying to free myself. He fits both of my wrists into his large palm and slams them to the ground above my head. His grasp is that of a starving python, strong and desperate. Anger seats itself on my tongue. Cerberus whines and inches forward, eager for my command.

"I had a feeling you wouldn't be easy to talk to," he says with a smirk as he straddles me and holds my wrists steady, tying them together with frayed rope that he pulls from his pocket.

His voice is like absolute fucking nirvana, and he smells like leather and mint, intoxicating and consuming. I furrow my brows in frustration as I try to think of a creative way to get out of this.

"I will bite," I threaten.

"Oh baby, I promise, you'll do more than that."

My teeth click, and he laughs at how tongue-tied I am. The intensity in his eyes seems to disconnect my brain from my nerves, as it's screaming at me to do something, but my body is paralyzed under him. He wraps the rope around his hand, ensuring that I can't wiggle free. Little pinpricks irritate my wrists as untamed twine rubs against my skin. I thrash against the knot and finally say in a snarky tone, "In your dreams," I attempt to spit at him, but before it can leave my lips, he grabs my cheeks hard with his free hand and says, "If you only knew how right you were. You haunt my dreams, my thoughts, and my soul."

Wait, I thought he was here to kidnap me.

His hand keeps my lips parted as he nods to them and asks, "Do you really want to start this off by being a bad girl?"

"I—" I struggle to find the right words.

Hell, I struggle to find *any* words.

"That's what I thought," he says, with a malicious smile. His calloused hand leaves my face, but his eyes trail the expanse of my upper body.

"What do you want from me? Do you want my house, my food, or my supplies?" I ask, not quite sure how this is going to play out. He lets out a dark laugh that resonates deep in my chest, and I'm sure it will find its way into my nightmares later. He leans down to my right side, and his lips ever so gently trace the edge of my ear, as he whispers,

"I. Want. You."

I'm taken aback and the intensity in his eyes scalds me like wildfire. It feels impossible to breathe in, but not because of his body pressed against mine. Those three little words sucked the air from my lungs.

"What if I don't want this? What if I don't want you?" I inquire in a small voice. His eyes darken and he growls,

"You will crave me like I crave you." Despite my instinct to run from this man, I bite my lip as he continues to breathe hot air into my ear. I feel my heart sink into my stomach, but my body shivers as he drags his lips down my neck. "I— rape isn't a kink of mine," I say, terrified of his response. I can feel him smiling against my tender flesh.

"I have no plans for that little fox. If I'm going to fuck you, you are going to beg me for it, but I can worship you in other ways."

He raises up just slightly to look me in the eyes, his lips just mere centimeters from mine. Astonishment and desire swirl in his bright green pools, and I can feel my panties starting to dampen.

How is it possible to feel hate, fear, and desire all at the same time?

It's like my body, brain, and heart are just as confused as I am. He's serious; he wants me but not to take advantage of me. My stubbornness gets the best of me, though, because fuck the patriarchy. I've fought hard to create a safe haven here, a home in this wasteland, and this man thinks he can just waltz in and take it from me?

Hell no.

"Cer—" Cerberus stands to her feet, ready to attack despite that her full name didn't leave my mouth. He presses my knife to my lips before I can finish. The blade slices just below the surface of my bottom lip, and the metallic taste slowly creeps onto my tongue.

"Let's save this fight for the humans, okay?" He winks and smiles at me.

"Then let me go," I mutter under the blade, sensing his slight fear of Cerberus and flashing a mocking smile.

"Why, little fox? Are you afraid?" he asks as he pulls down my bottom lip, sliding the knife down my chin.

"Yes," I whimper as a tear trails down my cheek. He bites his lip at my response and traces the sharp edge down the length of my torso until he reaches the hem of my shirt. I do my best to stay still and hide the fear that's rattling my bones, but I am failing miserably. The blade catches a loose stitch in the fabric, and he pulls it up towards my chest. He glides his tongue over his bottom lip as he unwraps me like I'm a gift to die for. He runs the knife over my exposed abdomen with just enough pressure to leave pink marks but not enough to break my skin. My body trembles beneath him as the realization of how easy it would be for him to kill me right now sets in.

"I'll make a deal with you, love."

The tip of the knife rests at the button of my cargo pants, and he spins the knife slowly eroding the cheap metal.

"If I slide these pants off and that pussy isn't dripping with excitement for what I have in store for you, I'll untie you and be on my way."

He looks up at me with a devious grin that makes my pulse audible. I feel a bead of sweat make its appearance on my forehead.

Oh fuck, as much as I want to sit here and say that I know for a fact that I'm definitely not aroused right now, my traitorous vagina is the exact opposite.

"I— I don't think that's fair," I argue breathlessly.

"Well," he says, "if you are just so disgusted with the situation you're in, like you say you are, then there shouldn't be an issue. But I think my little fox is *enjoying* being pinned and scared."

I look at the knot that he has my hands tied in and thrash against it again.

"Well, you're going to be disappointed because that's the last thing you'll find! Why would I get turned on by being afraid of you?" He laughs and smirks. "We'll see."

With that, adrenaline jump starts me. Why can't I look to Cerberus and say anything? She could take him down in one go.

My brain definitely doesn't want this, but my body is shaking with anticipation. I don't even know what his face looks like, and I'm going to let him slide my pants down?

Maybe it's the loneliness from the last few months or the fact that his touch makes me vibrate, but other than verbal protest, no other fight escapes me.

He ties the rope to a tree trunk beside me, securing it tightly so my wrists are still above my head. His body weight on top of mine keeps me pinned to the ground below me. Even if I wanted to try to roll, there is not enough space between us for me to move even an inch.

He glides his body against mine, and his muscular frame fits to my curves almost perfectly. He slides my pants off slowly, waiting for me to respond, to fight, to do anything. He tosses them to the side. His left arm wraps around the underside of my right thigh, and his bulky bicep forms a vice grip, holding me in place, making my hope of rolling over to my stomach as an escape plan null and void.

He supports his weight hovering his head over the apex of my thighs. A coldness washes over my torso from his absent body heat.

He runs the blade of the knife under the front of my black lace thong with his right hand, and I freeze.

"Sorry, love, these are just in the way," he remarks as he swiftly cuts my thong off and throws it to the side.

Before I can object, I feel the cold metal blade pressed against my clit. "What are you doing?" I ask as my fear heightens to dangerous levels.

He pulls the blade from me and looks into my eyes as he presses the flat side of it to his tongue and licks it, never breaking eye contact with me. His eyes roll as he says,

"To be so bad, you taste so fucking good."

My mouth drops, and I can feel my arousal trailing its way down my thighs.

"I think you're a liar, little fox." He drops the knife beside my left thigh and gently glides his fingers over my slit.

"Lying is what bad girls do, but I'm going to let it slide just this once because I want you to see what a real man can do. I want you to know how I can make you feel if you behave for me. You can tell me to stop at any point, but there's a catch."

I raise my eyebrows inquisitively.

"You have to mean the words you say." He smiles and slides one finger inside me. I instantly get wetter as much as I try to deter my mind. Why am I so turned on? I don't know this man. He literally just grabbed me from the brush, and I'm just going to let him have me? I don't even know his name.

I have to stop this.

"St—" My speech is disrupted by the sensation of another large finger making its way through my entrance.

"Sorry, love, I didn't quite catch that," he whispers tauntingly. Before I can gather my thoughts to process the word stop, he curls his fingers inside me right on that sensitive spot that makes thinking futile.

An orgasm begins to form low in my stomach. Am I really going to let this man make me orgasm? I need him to stop before I can't ask him to.

"Stop," I whimper uselessly.

"Sorry, you're going to have to be more convincing." I'm edging so close to an orgasm that the trees are starting to spin.

"Stop," I say with no force behind it.

"Little fox, I don't believe you. You're as wet as the ocean kissing the shore at high tide." I get ready to muster the strength to tell him to stop, but before I can, his tongue softly licks my clit.

"Fuck," I mumble breathlessly, followed by a small moan. I start to buck his face as my orgasm threatens my entire being. He quickly withdraws his fingers, never coming up for air, but he slides something different inside me. I feel my face pale.

This motherfucker has the handle of my knife inside me. I prepare to spew vial words, but he tilts the knife to find that spot again, and it takes my breath. He continues licking me with just the right amount of pressure, and feasts on me like I'm the last thing he will ever taste. My vision blurs, and the sky above dims as my orgasm approaches, sending me into near convulsions. I clamp my thighs around his head, arching my back, convinced this might be the closest to heaven I'll ever get.

As I come back to earth, he gently backs the knife handle out of me. I lay there satisfied but also so ashamed.

This feels like a fever dream.

He kisses my pubic bone as he finally leaves my clit. He leans up and grabs my pants from beside me. Very carefully, he places my feet through the leg holes before sliding my pants all the way back up.

"I'm going to untie you. Don't do something stupid," he whispers the command. I debate punching him in the face again, but I don't. My body is too stunned to do anything except sit here.

He unties the knot and lays my hands on my lap before he runs his fingers over the marks on my wrists and leans down to lightly kiss them. Faint black lip marks stain my skin. His attention directs back to the soaking wet knife in his hand, and he slowly licks it clean.

"Can't let something so good go to waste," he says as he hands me my knife. I see blood on the blade side and notice the deep cut on his palm. He shrugs as he sees me staring at his wound.

"A scar I'll proudly wear. It'll remind me what heaven tastes like."

He turns to walk away and states, "I'll be seeing you, little fox."

He reaches over to pet Cerberus's heads, and she *lets* him?

Today is so fucking weird.

Nuclear

"Never again," I promise, spent and ashamed, still dumbfounded on the ground.

"I don't even know your name."

"You can call me Ryker, Maggie." He smiles and winks at me before disappearing into the dense brush.

"How does he know my name?" I whisper under my breath to myself.

I have no idea what just happened.

I don't think I liked it, or did I? I've never been fucked with an inanimate object; however, apparently, I can come on one.

What have I done?

Now he'll just come back. At least he wasn't selfish, or was he?

The confusion and mixed feelings weigh heavy on my mind as I stand up, pull myself together, and walk away with Cerberus by my side. Cerberus cocks both heads to the side as if to ask, "Are you okay?" Hot tears pool in my eyes and I'm not able to verbalize an answer. I reach down and softly pat each of her heads, trying to keep the tears at bay. I let it happen, so why am I so upset?

"Don't look at me like that," I beg, looking at a judgmental Cerberus. She's an animal, but I swear her mannerisms and facial expressions are exceptionally human, or maybe it's because it's only been her and I for so long. My mind is spinning with emotions and thoughts that seem to make breathing a difficult task. I try not to cry as the disappointment in myself plagues me.

   I walk to the bathroom and slide my pants off my legs in one swift motion. I'm now down by one sexy thong, and I think I only have three or four left. (It's hard to find sexy underwear during the apocalypse.)

   I pull my shirt over my head and reach into the shower to turn the water faucet on. I look down and notice black marks all over my pubic area and inner thighs, and my mind whips back to the painted lower half of his face.

   His black lip marks as he kissed my skin, *his* black smudges of painted scruff as he tried to devour me deeper, and *his* black streaks staining my skin with shameful bliss.

   The smears bring back the memory of his tongue gently sweeping over my clit. A cold chill makes its way down my spine, followed by a shiver of pleasure. I step in the shower, let the water run down my body, and cleanse me of whatever the hell just happened to me.

20

RYKER:

THE ACCIDENT

The days seem to get longer when you ache for someone.

Another two weeks have passed since I got to taste my little fox. My cock jumps in my pants as the thought lingers in my mind. Her body begged for me, but the look of confusion and shame on her face after her orgasm told me that I needed to stop.

My selfishness and excitement faded into care and concern for her emotions. I want her to need this like I do, not be regretful of the way I make her feel. She will admit she wants me like I need her eventually, but that is going to take time.

I walk towards an open field with tall grass. The blades alternate between shades of green and brown. Their thickness varies, and I can feel the more mature and thick patches scrape the fabric of my pants. This has been a good hunting ground for small animals like rabbits and mice. I could go to the lake to fish, but unlike my little fox, I am not as talented.

I carefully scan the field, trying to distinguish prey from the vibrant autumn colors surrounding me.

A rabbit moves in the clearing around ten feet in front of me. It doesn't see me, as its gaze is focused on the fresh green foliage in front of it. Its body language is relaxed and calm. I grab my knife from my bootstrap and quietly usher myself forward, leaving no sound as I creep up to the animal. The blade reflects the sunlight as I get the knife in the position I want it.

When I am within inches of the rabbit, I raise my dagger and quickly stab through its flesh, making sure to end its life quickly. The knife glides through its neck so easily that I had to double-check that I struck the creature. The rabbit does not seem to be too affected by radiation exposure. It's larger than a pre-radiation rabbit but does not house any deformities that I can notice right off.

"Thank you," I say under my breath. It's important to me to thank the creatures that contribute to my survival out here.

After I skin and prepare the little animal for cooking, I walk back to my "bed" made of thick leaves and brush. I sit down, feeling the leaves beneath me crunch and flake apart from the force of my weight. I created a small roasting pit from mismatched rocks I had found in the area over the last couple

Nuclear

of weeks and place dried-out leaves into the center of the ring of stones.

Grasping my knife tightly, I strike it against a piece of flint I had found a few days earlier down at the lake. It takes a few strikes before I can ignite a spark against the leaves. The flicker jumps to one leaf and burns up its veins as it slowly infects the next one. Quickly, the chain reaction elicits a choreography of chaotic flames.

Taking the skinned rabbit carcass, I wrap the extremities around a slender branch, securing them with dried-out vines from the tree above me. A roasting frame is easy to assemble for the branch to rest on and rotate the rabbit, cooking the meat evenly.

I glance at my hands and see blood from the rabbit's muscle tissue pooled in the crevices around my nails. I start picking at them, trying to remove the slowly coagulating liquid.

As my hands move mindlessly, my gaze moves onto the small but mighty glow before me. I feel the reflection of the fire in my eyes, and my mind can't help but wonder to *her*.

Tiny devils flicker through her eyes as they carelessly strike matches in her soul. I've never seen a fire so pretty than the chaos behind her eyes. I want so badly for her demons to teach mine how to play with fire, instead of just letting it consume them. If only she knew the flames that lick at the edges of my being for her. She is kerosene to the raging inferno that lives in my chest, burning through my veins and nerves like lava trailing down a freshly erupted volcano. The feelings smolder and linger as the idea of her burns in the back of my mind like a cattle brand. Desire fills me, as I picture myself carving a home inside her heart, inside her soul. Now that I know the feel of her, the way she tastes, and how beautiful her little moans can be, the longing for her is more intense, and I find myself having to physically restrain myself from marching right into her room and taking her. Ideas of what I would do to her, given the chance, flash through my mind until the rest of my thoughts disappear.

She's slowly driving me mad.

My surroundings begin to dim as I watch the sun start to set. The sky is a masterpiece of purples, oranges, and reds, all swirling together like a Bob Ross painting. Half of the sun is visible just above the horizon. This scenery is beautiful, but it still pales in comparison to my girl. Even when there is amazing art in front of me, all I can see is her.

The smell of charred meat rises through the air as I continue to roast the rabbit, but the sound of crackling fire has faded away as my eyes close and the image of Maggie getting off consumes every sense I have. A stillness settles in the air, as no sound resonates from the environment around me.

The earth below where I'm sitting begins to vibrate. My heart rate increases as I search my environment for the cause of the disturbance. I get to my feet and try to focus on how far away the threat is. The shaking of the earth comes in waves, and when it stops, the air becomes silent once again.

Nuclear

The calm before the storm that I'm all too familiar with.

The vibrating was previously a tremble, but this time, it comes back, nearly shaking me until I lose my balance.

Just as I get ready to run in the opposite direction, the ground to my right erupts violently. Dirt and grass fly into the air as long, thin claws break through the soil.

Two sets of claws become visible, each with six vicious blades that are black and sickly looking. Two massive paws reveal themselves as the ground is pulled apart to each side. The paws balance the creature as it rises from the depths of the earth. A massive, animalistic head protrudes from the ground. Half of the creature's face is exposed skull with a deep empty socket where its eye used to be, while the other half is covered with dirty and thin brown fur with a milky white eye. Its nose comes into an abrupt point, clearly used for sniffing the air for prey without having to penetrate the ground's surface completely.

The mouth is large and gaping. It has two large top canines disproportionate to its lower jaw, causing its mouth not to close properly. The large teeth are yellow and rotting, but their sharpness and size could still do some damage. So many other teeth shadow behind the longest ones.

This thing before me used to be a tunneling ground mole, but now, I'm not sure what you would call it. Realizing that it's blind, I do my best to brace myself on the base of an old oak tree, making sure never to waive my eyes from the beast. I slow my breathing and try to decrease my adrenaline levels to quiet my heart aggressively thumping against my rib cage. The tree bark scratches against my palms as I steady myself with an unwavering grip, tearing through the bark of the tree, straight into the meat of the wood.

Its large nose takes in the air as it sniffs for its next meal, which could be the rabbit or me. The silence around me becomes stale as it continues searching. Just as I think it's going to return to the underground fortress, which it calls home, a squirrel rustles in the tree above me.

Well, fuck.

A loud screech leaves its creepy mouth, and I take off into thick brush and overgrown branches. It chases after me, harshly pounding the ground as it trails not far behind me. Its long, slender tongue protrudes from its mouth as its mismatched jaws hang open.

I hide behind a decaying tree stump as the creature runs at least twenty feet ahead of me. I don't wait for it to try to sniff me out again. I quickly begin to climb the tree overshadowing the rotting wood, shuffling fast up the branches and not having time to have a second thought about their sturdiness.

My heart is pounding in my throat as I grab branch after branch, until one breaks under my weight. It throws me off balance, and I find myself suspended at least fifteen feet from the ground. I tighten my grasp around the only branch within reach.

Nuclear

My breathing escalates as panic settles in my chest. The acidic taste of fear coats my tongue. Fear is something I haven't felt since the day Cai died. I do my best to keep a level head, but then I notice the creature is no longer on the surface where it once stood.

In its previous spot is a giant hole, indicating it has tunneled back underground. I try to pull myself higher in the tree as I feel it starting to vibrate from the velocity of the tunneling mole headed right toward me.

The branch starts to quiver, and I realize that if I pull myself up, the branch will likely break, sending me crashing to the dirt, which would make me mole food. My very creative imagination paints a very gory picture of what those teeth would feel like as the thing consumes me.

The vibrations worsen as I hear the sound of roots splitting and ripping from the earth. The thing is tunneling under the tree, trying to give me no choice but to descend from the canopy. The threads of the branch begin to snap one by one from the force of giant mutant claws beating the ancient wood of the oak.

Well, this isn't how I thought I would go out, but at least I can die knowing I satisfied my little fox at least once. I hold the degrading branch for as long as I can. The tree begins to slant as the roots holding it up are now only on one side. My heart plummets into my stomach as the feeling of impending doom creeps into my mind. I close my eyes, and a couple more threads of the branch break.

A loud crack splits the air around me, and I'm not able to discern if it was a gunshot or a tree branch breaking before the limb I'm clinging to snaps.

I grab the trunk of the tree and try to hold on, but my grip is not wide enough to maintain a steady hold, and I find myself falling to the ground and probably my death.

I suck in a sharp breath of air and brace for impact as another crack echoes through the air around me. My body slams into the ground, and when my head meets the grass below me, my vision blackens, moving from the edges of my periphery until everything I can see is absorbed by darkness.

21

RYKER: CONFRONTATION

"Wakey, wakey," a voice calls.

It sounds so close, but yet so far away.

The stars I see on the inside of my eyelids start to spin as I come back to consciousness. A wave of nausea crashes in my stomach like a tsunami into an abandoned city. My muscles ache like every single one has been stretched and overworked. My hands are trapped and suspended above my head.

When my eyes open, light burns my sensitive corneas until I can focus. Her silhouette becomes clear, and I'm stunned under her gaze. She is straddled across my lower abdomen with a murderous blade in her hand that is pressing firmly against my throat. I can feel my pulse rebounding off the sharp steel edge, threatening the tender flesh of my neck. Her angry eyes flicker with flames as I meet her gaze.

Fuck.

She is immaculate.

The way she feels on top of me, even with the threat of the knife, makes my cock twitch in my pants. Her warm thighs wrap around my waist, which is too high. I would give anything to have my hips line up with hers, so she could feel every inch of me.

My hands are pinned, otherwise I would show her what this little stunt is doing to me. I'll let her have her moment, mainly because I don't think I could put up a fight due to the concussion I'm pretty sure I have. She lets out a giggle before she says, "That's the funny thing about those damn tables, they always fucking turn." She nods to the knife, referencing her current place of power.

Before I can say anything, she demands, "So this is how this is going to go. I'm going to ask questions, and then you will answer them. There's a catch, though."

"And what's that, my sweet fox?"

"You have to tell the truth. Sound familiar?" She raises her eyebrows.

Damn, I guess the tables really have turned, haven't they. A smile creeps across my lips, and I can't help it. I nod.

Nuclear

"Otherwise, I'll kill you where you lie. Got it?"

"Got it," I mumble, my eyes never leaving hers.

"Who are you? How long have you been here? And why did you do what you did to me?" she asks with urgency. I answer the rapid fire of questions in the order they were given to me.

"My name is Ryker Evans. We've met before, and it sounds like you remember our first encounter well." I smile widely. "I saw you down at the lake when I went to get water a few weeks ago, and I watched you slay that Stephen King version of a salamander. I found myself becoming totally and utterly enthralled by you. I followed you in the trees to see how many of you there were. To my astonishment, it's only you and a two-headed wolf just out here surviving. I've been here for a little over a month I think. A violent creature attacked my squadron and I'm the only survivor." I feel her hand tremble, holding the knife when I say that. It's almost like being a lone survivor tugged at something inside her.

I weigh my answer options for the last question, making sure they're good enough to satisfy the human lie detector with a blade at my throat.

"Finally, I did what I did because you wanted it, little fox, and you deserved it. You deserve to be treated like a queen, and I intend to give you that unless, of course, you want to kill me now. I'll gladly die at your hands, but I guarantee you that you'll regret it. Based on how hard you came on that knife and my mouth; I would bet that no one has ever made you have an earth-shattering orgasm like that. You may not regret killing me but tell me you wouldn't regret ever climaxing like that again." I look at her with a smile that I can't hide, knowing damn well that what I said was the truth. She sucks her bottom lip between her teeth in acknowledgment of the statement but refuses to give me the satisfaction of telling me I'm right. A red heat flushes her cheeks, and the sight of her biting her bottom lip could bring me to my knees if I was standing. Before I can make a remark about it, she deflects with more interrogating questions.

"What are your intentions here? Are you just passing through or planning to stay?" I interrupt her before she can ask all the questions swirling in her mind.

"Is that an invitation?" I taunt, laughing to myself and licking my bottom lip. Her eyes narrow, and she presses the knife harder into my neck until I can feel my pulse rebound off it. I smile, she's so cute when she tries to keep the upper hand.

"I'd gladly stay and keep you company." I look her up and down. She rolls her eyes before she removes the knife from my throat and lands a punch to the left side of my face.

"Remember the rules. I will not hesitate to kill you," she snarls.

Ironic because she's done that twice now. Once, the night when I got to taste her, and upon finding me. She isn't going to kill me, she's too intrigued by me.

I laugh as my lip begins to bleed.

"Is that all you got?" I ask, running my tongue over the fresh wound.

Her eyes fill with frustration, and I am loving it.

"You haven't seen half of what I'm capable of."

Oh, I can only imagine what she can do.

The unforgiving edge of the blade presses back into my neck so hard I can feel it slowly slicing through the layers of my skin.

"Answers now," she demands.

"Fine. I was planning to leave and find my new future. However, I discovered you, and now you are all I want. Your presence consumes my thoughts, and all I can think about is giving my newfound freedom to you. I will gladly let you tie me up and enslave me. I crave you, even if it's just to be near you. I know you feel it too, little fox." A sinister smirk plasters itself on my face.

"I promise I could pose a threat to some of the best parts of you if you wanted. But I'll only do that if you beg." She rolls her eyes again.

"You must just be starving for pussy, huh? Poor boy," she jokes and laughs. "That's unfortunate. I'm sure there's some insecure girl you'll come across who's just desperate enough for the likes of you." She slides the knife from my throat and rests it just below my chin, forcing my head to look upwards at her.

"Let's get one thing clear now: I belong to no one. You don't know what I want or how I feel; hell, you don't even know me." She huffs and removes the knife from my chin.

"Maybe for now, but soon I'll be the reason you breathe," I reply with confidence.

"Yeah, yeah, that's what they all say," she retorts deliberately expressionless, completely unimpressed with my words. She wipes my sweat and blood from the blade onto her pants before asking, "Last question, why 'little fox?'" She makes sure to put air quotes around her nickname.

"Foxes are solitary creatures. They don't function in packs like wolves or coyotes do. They are also known to be clever, cunning, wise, and creative, which I feel suits you well after watching you for weeks. There is an Inuit fable that tells of an argument between the raven and the fox as they decide which would dominate the new world after the creation of light. The raven hunts during the day, and the fox hunts at night. To compromise, they split every day up into two parts so each creature could survive." I pause to see her eyes studying me closely. "The fox was willing to give up all light for happiness in the darkness. That's how I feel about you. I would give up the world, the fireflies, the sun, the moon, everything, whatever you asked me to in exchange for your love. I would gladly live in the darkness with you and watch the magic of our demons dancing as deep devotion devours us. If you prefer, female foxes are called vixens. I will happily call you my little vixen instead." I offer with desire, followed by a wink.

"I'll just stay a fox," she mutters, clenching her jaw and rolling her eyes for the third time.

"Oh, and one other thing about foxes, love. They are monogamous and typically only have one mate in their entire lifetime, and when I get you to your breaking point, I'll be all you'll ever need. I don't fucking share, and if any man breathes in your direction the wrong way, he will die." She narrows her eyes at me as I continue.

"I will cross every line you lay before me, because you make me feel something other than the rage, hate, and numbness that boils under my skin. You make me feel desire, tenderness, and hope, and for the first time in a very fucking long time, the lava rushing under my skin is cooled. I will do anything to keep that feeling. You might as well accept it, my sweet fox, you are mine." She does her best to maintain a poker face, but she slips up for a split-second as desire flashes in her eyes.

Although I would've missed it had I blinked, it's all I need to solidify she thinks about me more than she leads on.

"I am nobody's," she whispers with dark eyes.

She slides off me, landing on the floor, and pockets the large knife back into its sheath in her belt loop.

"I'm going to untie you now. Try to keep your hands to yourself." She starts with my ankles, sliding the rope off them and dropping the course twine onto the floor.

When she gets to my wrists, I can't help but wish she'd leave them on and show me what she is capable of. Her restraint is a mixture of two knots. She has a handcuff knot tied initially on my wrists, and then she has secured that knot with a double overhand knot.

Simple, clever, and effective. I can't help but appreciate the thoroughness of the restraint.

"The shower is in the master bathroom. There are some extra clothes in the dresser over there. You can stay for a while, as long as you respect my space and keep your hands off me. This will be your room, and please, for the love of God, be respectful and don't do anything stupid. I will kill you and not think twice about it." Her tone is bitter. I nod at her and say, "Thank you." My voice is soft and sincere.

She turns her back to leave, and I jump up quickly wrapping my hand around her throat, not as a threat but to catch her attention. I squeeze in on the sides, pull her back, and bring her shoulders into my chest. She gasps, and I lean in, grazing her ear with my lips as I whisper, "This is your empire, baby, and I will gladly serve you from my knees if it means you are mine." I feel the heat trail from her neck to her cheeks, and she does her best to suppress a shiver as goosebumps prickle up her arms. Before she can panic, I release her, knowing one day she will beg me to squeeze harder.

On her way out the door she avoids eye contact with me and says, "If you are going to stay for a while, please make yourself useful and help with tasks and food. I don't care to share; just hold up your responsibilities. You're not a kid, and I won't pick up after you like one." I nod again, and she goes across the hall to her room. One thing is for sure, I may not be a kid, but I'd make a mess just to call her mommy.

I walk towards the bathroom. I was so distracted by her that I didn't notice the splitting headache I have. I reach up to grab my forehead and realize there's something bumpy across my skin. When I get to the bathroom mirror, I lean forward and observe the eight perfectly executed square knot stitches.

She did a damn good job.

I probably won't even have a noticeable scar with how she put the skin together.

A thought crosses my mind as I take my clothes off. I wonder if she looked me over for more injuries. The idea of her fingers running over my skin sends a chill through me.

I wonder if she just took a little peep at what I had to offer. A smirk curls the corner of my lip, and I silently chuckle to myself. My hand wraps around my length, and I contemplate touching myself and thinking about all the ways I could make her scream my name.

I stop myself.

I'm going to wait until she can't hide it anymore. I've only known about her for a couple weeks, but it was in her eyes.

Why else would she let me live?

She doesn't strike me as the merciful type. I glimpsed the cruel, unforgiving woman lurking beneath the surface when she held me at knife point; she can be just as sinister as I am.

I grab both sides of my shirt and pull it over my head, feeling the splinters from the tree bark graze my skin as they fall from the fabric. I reach over and turn the water on as hot as I can stand because I can't handle that warm water bullshit. I step into the shower, but my thoughts never stray from the way she trembled, holding that knife to my throat. I can't wait to see her ride me, holding that knife there, screaming for me to take her closer to heaven.

22

MAGGIE:

MEMORY LANE

I'd be lying if I said I didn't think about him yesterday. I'd also be lying if I said my pussy didn't start dripping while I was on top of him with that knife to his throat. I'm chalking up my horniness to the fact that I've not gotten laid in over a year. I snap out of my daze and focus my distracted thoughts on anything other than him.

I get up, walk over to the kitchen, and reach in the upper part of the cupboard. I've got to admit I'm so grateful that whoever lived here loved coffee and hoarded it. There's so much that I think I could have a cup every day for the rest of my life if I stay here. The only downside is I have to make it by the pot. I try not to be wasteful and save what I'm able to so I can reheat it for later.

I grab a filter and line the strainer part of the coffee maker. The paper is so thin and fragile. It reminds me of the girl I once was. The callous I built over her through the war and all the loss in my life has smothered her.

So much fucking loss.

All the demons I possess helped place brick after brick in the wall that has thickened the skin over the heart I used to wear on my sleeve. Sometimes, I even wonder if my heart could ever feel anything other than numb.

It feels like she is a different person.

Like someone I knew but can't seem to remember fully.

I grieved that girl like I lost my best friend. Had I known what the world would become, would I have pulled the trigger back then? Would I have taken those pills that I stared at for hours?

I pour some ground coffee beans into the coffee filter, close the lid, and hit the red "brew" LED switch. The earthy smell of the crushed beans teases my nose. I look at the scars on my thighs and remember when I was so numb I couldn't feel the razor slide into my skin. To bleed was the only thing I could feel. I run my fingers over the tattoo covering that part of my life.

The tattoo is of a wolf, reminding me of which one to choose.

It's quiet in the house. Either our guest is still asleep, or he left. My gut clenches as I hope he left with plans of returning, as much as I hate to admit it.

I would never let him see that, though.

Nuclear

I peek in the guest room. The bed is made, and he is nowhere in sight. Cerberus perks up off the couch when she notices I'm searching. I walk over and pet her heads. "I was just curious," I reassure.

"It never hurts to have company. Especially if he's actually a decent human being." She seems to nod with both heads in agreement. I open the porch door, step onto the patio, and breathe in the cool autumn breeze. The morning haze of fog lies close to the ground, but you can still see the tree line.

The greenery starts to tremble and shake as he emerges, pulling a deer behind him. I walk inside to put some pants on instead of just a long shirt. By the time I return, he's already reached the door.

"Ah, found you a 'not deer', I see," I state confidently. His head cocks slightly to the side, and I can tell he didn't get the reference.

"You aren't originally from these parts of the woods, are you?" I ask as I let out a playful laugh.

"Not deer are Appalachian lore. They are cryptids, as the kids call them. It's essentially a creature that is highly predatory. They mimic other, more innocent creatures so they can get close enough to you to attack. The best way to identify one is by looking at its characteristics. They appear like deer, however, there's just something wrong or off with them. There's no typical presentation of one; it could have an elongated snout full of teeth similar to a coyote, or maybe it walks on two feet instead of four," I continue explaining, not really looking at him. My gaze fixes on the trees behind him.

"To me, the radiation exposure caused them to be real. I always believed they were real, but now it confirms the myth. The deformities are all different across every creature. The radiation war was a nightmare itself, but now the creatures it has created are the monsters of my childhood."

I lean down to examine his kill: a ten-pointer with three eyes on each side, totaling six. The main eyes are endless black pits piercing through rotting skin, while the smaller ones are a sickly yellow with black centers, wide and wild even in death. The deer has an abnormal, almost camel-like hump. Along its ribs are hairless patches that look like radiation burns. He is a creepy one, for sure.

I look back at him. His response was simple, "Where I'm from, we call those types of creatures..." he mouths the word, "skin walkers." My stomach sinks. I'm all too familiar with the myth from all the creepypasta I used to read.

I shake my head and say, "Let's avoid that word if we can." He nods in agreement. When it comes to summoning a skin walker, all you have to do is say the word. Given the current state of the world and the unknown, we definitely don't need to bring one of those into the picture.

I help him hang the deformed deer from a tree.

Nuclear

"Can I have that knife, please?" he asks, motioning toward the knife I have on my belt.

"Only if you promise not to kill me with it."

He solemnly swears, "I promise no malicious intent... this time." He winks at me. I roll my eyes, pull out the knife, and hand it to him. So far, I'm impressed because with the cabin's freezer, we will be set on food for a while.

"I have been hunting these woods for weeks now, and I have yet to get a kill like this. Typically, it has only been rabbits and squirrels. You must be my lucky charm," he chimes with a soft smile. It tugs at my heart a little, but I stay stone faced.

"Maybe you are just getting better at hunting," I retort with a shrug.

Ryker punctures through the deer's chest on its underside and drags it down through its abdomen. Before responding, "Yeah, maybe you're right."

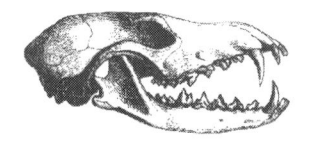

This evening, the stars are so bright. The sky doesn't even look real. It looks like something made up on a movie TV set. I grab a sweatshirt and lazily throw it on. I reach into the cabinet under the sink and take the whiskey out. Good old jack, he's been there for me on my worst days. I walk out to the porch door in the direction of the fire pit.

"Not going to invite me?" his voice chimes from the kitchen.

"That depends," I say.

"Can you hold your liquor? I'm not a great babysitter," I joke. He laughs. "I promise not to inconvenience you, little fox." The way it rolled off his lips made my nipples pebble up.

It left me speechless, honestly.

I flick my zippo, and a steady blue tinged flame emits. I lean down and hold it to a small piece of wood until embers creep and jump up its length. I sit beside the fire, and Cerberus curls up next to me, both heads on my thigh. He sits across from me.

"Well," he starts. "Is it possible for us to talk and get to know each other? It's hard to find good human interaction these days."

My thoughts swirl as I contemplate if we could even have a normal conversation after me threatening his life with a knife.

"Sure, I say, but prepare to be very depressed or very bored because I'm nothing to brag about. My life has been a mess since the beginning of my existence. Honestly, this time in the cabin has been the best part of my life."

There's an emotion on his face that I can't determine. I tried to laugh it off, but I was serious. He replies, "How long have you been here, and how did you get here?" The haunting images and remnants of memories from the aircraft crashing come in waves.

"My team and I were flying to Nashville. A massive mutated blue jay attacked us. No exaggeration, but I would estimate the creature was the size of what a pterodactyl would be. We all just braced ourselves for impact. The aircraft crashed into the mountain just over that ridge." I point loosely to the scenery to our right.

"The crash knocked me out. I woke up to the smell of smoke and the metallic taste of blood. My head was splitting, hence the scar on my face." I run my index and middle finger softly down the right side of my temple to my mandible. "I sutured it myself when I found this cozy place. When I awoke on the aircraft, I was so shaky. I honestly don't know how I got out of there before the explosion happened. There were seven of us on the craft. I checked pulses on members of my team that were not mangled by metal." I shiver noticeably at the memory. His eyes study me with rapt attention.

"Unfortunately, they were all long gone. They most likely died on impact. When I got off the craft, I hiked up to the woods. I sought shelter for hours until I came across a small cave not too far from here. The sky was black with streaks of lightning. I knew the storm would be impossible to weather. That's when I saw her, a baby wolf pup." I motion toward Cerberus beside me. "I decided to stay in the cave that night, however, I ran into a little problem. Apparently, a giant bat like monster had already taken up residence in the cavern, and it was not happy that I tried to have a sleepover. It chased me back out of the cave, but I ended up killing the creepy thing.

After that, exhaustion screamed from my body, so I decided to go back into the cave for a nap.

"I was so tired; it didn't matter that I was soaking wet from the rain. Thankfully, I had my pack with me and used it as a pillow. Trees fell, and animal screeches could be heard in the distance. She cuddled into me, and we laid there and watched the world crash around us through the cave's opening." I look down at Cerberus and smile.

My eyes catch his. He is staring intently and studying every word I say like I'm telling him a secret gospel of a religion he worships. A look of sadness crosses his face, but he forces a smile to encourage me to continue.

"In the morning, when we awoke, the forest around us had been destroyed by the violent winds and heavy rain. We trekked through all of it and encountered multiple... creatures along the way here. I initially came in to look for supplies, but the place was stocked and well taken care of. I had nowhere to go and no plans of wanting to get back to the military. As far as they are concerned, I died with the others, and I'd like to keep it that way. I want to stay a ghost. Cerberus and I plan to live out our time here, whether that's months or years. We have been here almost three months and have made the most of it." I nod with a soft smile crossing my face. He pauses and says, "That's amazing that you have done this alone for so long. I'm not underestimating you by any means, but if you've seen the creatures I've seen, you know that they are savage and unforgiving." His tone is warm and genuine, with a raspy, smoky quality that captivates me. I could listen to him talk for hours.

It's fucking intoxicating.

He's intoxicating.

"Out here, you have to do what you must to survive. It's not all bad, though. There is some peace here. Most creatures pass through, but on the other hand, there are always the few that want to fight. Those are the only ones we kill if we must." I lean back on my palms. The ground feels cold and rigid beneath my hands. Before he says another word, I cut him off and say, "Okay, my turn." He nods, encouraging me to continue. The look in his eyes tells me he wants to ask for more from me, but he understands that I need more from him first.

"What gave you those scars across your back?"

"I had a feeling you stripped me down and looked me over. Did you find anything else you liked?" he asks with a smirk.

"I—uh, I promise I only looked you over for injuries. I didn't impose on, well, you know." Red heat flushes my cheeks, and I feel him smiling at me.

"I wouldn't blame you if you did," he purrs. Without missing a beat, he jumped back in to answer my original question.

"As you know, not all the animals of each species responded the same to radiation exposure. For example, you ended up with a friendly wolf. However, the wolf that attacked me was all but inviting. He was grey and radiation wounds weaved throughout his thinning fur. He was very shabby-looking and had two extra front legs, making him all the more dangerous.

"His face was scarred and brutal, and his left ear looked as if something large had taken a bite out of it. He had an extra eye in the center of his forehead surrounded by open, necrotic, and weeping wounds. His mouth was larger than it should be, and he had too many teeth for it to close. I would estimate he was the size of a bear. Like a normal pre-radiation warfare bear."

He laughs as he does his best to describe his assailant. His breathing shallows a little, and it makes me wonder if he's not totally comfortable with telling the story. His description of the creature is very blunt, but I don't press for more information.

"Did you ever have to spar in the facility you were in?" he asks.

"Yeah, a few times. Mostly knife fights with people who didn't know what the hell they were doing," I respond.

"Well, after I obtained my abilities from the lab, they felt regular sparring wasn't enough to test me. So, to get into Apparition Ops, I was forced to spare with that massive wolf with only a knife. It caught me in a moment of weakness and a mistake in my fighting stance and was able to sink its claws in deep."

I stare in disbelief. "That's insane. I'm so sorry they did all of that to you."

"It's okay, I survived. I had Cairo who became like a brother to me. Fighting that creature got me one step closer to what was supposed to be our freedom. However, he died in our run-in with the bear a few weeks ago, which just leaves me." His face hardens. There's an emotion he doesn't want to show, and he looks down to his boots and avoids my gaze.

"I'm sorry. I am all too familiar with loss," I respond. I lift the bottle of Jack to my lips and take a drink. The alcohol warms my throat as it travels down my esophagus. I pass the bottle over, and he takes a shot as well.

"So, tell me what happened to that creature that almost killed me the other day. I heard gun shots, but the last thing I remember is the branch breaking and me falling." I laugh before responding.

"Between you and that thing, there was so much noise that astronauts could've heard you all in space." He chuckles before I continue.

"Well, I guess it started when Cerberus began growling and pacing by the door. Honestly, I thought you were trying to get in or something, so I grabbed my pistol."

"Oh, so you were going to kill me?" he asks, shaking his head. A glint of pride is in his eyes.

"If I had to," I reply and shrug.

"You wouldn't be the first man I have killed out here, and I'm sure you wouldn't be the last." We both laugh.

"Anyway, as I slid my boots on, the ground started to shake, and I lost my balance. My brain couldn't process that we were having an 'earthquake,' I say with air quotes.

"It's already the apocalypse, so I was beginning to wonder if Satan himself would come up from the depths of the Earth. I opened the front door, and that's when I heard the sounds of branches breaking, which I thought was odd. How silly of me to make my way into the forest during an earthquake." I say with a hint of sarcasm.

"Cerberus found you before I did. Both of her heads howled in a harmonious sound that drug my attention to what she had found. When I saw you, that thing had you dangling from a sideways tree. I began to pop rounds off into the ground as the creature resurfaced to eat you. It took six bullets to even get it to slow down. By that point, you were already knocked out. After I unloaded my entire mag, it finally succumbed to its wounds. Its claws had just ripped back through the dirt. So be mindful of the giant claws protruding from the ground if you go that way." I shake my head. I deliberately leave out the part where I was terrified I might find him dead. There's no sense in blowing up this man's ego just yet.

"I don't know what you did, but you pissed that monster off. It wasn't going to stop until you were dead."

He sighs and scratches his forehead.

"Honestly, I have no idea what I did either, I was just existing and trying to cook myself a rabbit." I shrug again before responding, "I guess it just didn't like you. It must be a good judge of character."

"Better watch your tone, little fox. I'd hate to prove how wrong you are."

I roll my eyes.

"I'm not afraid of you anymore." I stick my tongue out at him before picking at my nails.

"We'll see about that, but first you need to finish your story. What did you do when you found me?" He smirks as the words pass his lips.

"I checked your pulse to make sure you were alive, and when I discerned that you were, I drug you by your wrists until I could get you into the guest bed. I tied you up just in case you woke up and were violent or something." He interrupts me with, "Definitely the 'or something.'"

I ignore him and continue.

"I sutured the gash on your forehead before looking you over for other injuries. Other than some scrapes and massive bruises, you were fine. At that point, it was just waiting for you to wake up." He nods and opens his mouth to say something sexual in nature, I'm sure.

"You did a fantastic job with the sutures. I don't think the wound will scar," he compliments about my work.

"Honestly, it's not a big deal. Anyone could do it," I respond before tucking my hair behind my ear and focusing my gaze on my black leather boots.

"Can I ask you a more personal question?" he asks with a slight hint of need in his voice, like he is aching to know whatever is on the tip of his tongue.

"No, I will not sleep with you." A hint of a smile tugs at my lips.

He chuckles. "Not that kind of question. A deeper question, one that will make you think. I feel like it's a crime to not have cozy conversations around a bonfire."

The thought of a deep personal question scares me more than any other question he could ask.

"Sure," I respond, trying to keep my voice level.

"If I asked you to name off all the things you loved, how long would it take for you to name yourself?"

"I feel like if I think too hard on that one, I'm going to hurt my own feelings." I half smile and scratch my forehead, not able to bring my eyes to his.

We sit in silence for a beat as he waits for me to answer and I try to find the lie in my brain, because the truth is, I don't think my name would ever appear on my list.

The lie never surfaces.

Nuclear

"Honestly, I don't think my name would ever end up on my list." I sigh before taking another fiery shot of whiskey.

"Isn't it so damn fascinating that the list of things I love would only consist of you?" he asks, and overwhelming emotions beat violently in my chest.

"But why?" I inquire, genuinely so confused as to how someone could be so interested in me.

"Because you make me feel things I didn't know I was capable of feeling. The idea of you has wrapped itself into every fiber of my brain until all that's left is obsession. Like a summer storm, it's powerful and uncontrollable. It overrides every thought and every decision I make. A wound that never heals unless I'm in your presence. I need you close, even if you don't need me. I will always be in your shadows. It scares me how much control you have over me, and I am at your mercy."

His eyes bore into mine like he is trying to grab my soul and shake me to make me understand.

He whispers, "I will never stop chasing you. There is nothing in this world I desire more than you."

Apprehension begins to slide through my thoughts, slowly forming a lump in my throat. My heart swells in my chest, and speech is no longer something that comes naturally.

My mouth dries, and trepidation creeps up my spine with a slow agonizing chill.

Afraid.

I am so terrified by the way he looks at me.

I drop his gaze before rising to my feet. Cerberus stands and nudges Ryker's hand for one last pet before following suit.

It's odd to me that she seems to have some kind of connection with him, despite the threat he could pose to us.

"I'm headed to bed," I mumble, avoiding his feelings. It's the only thing I can think of to get out of this conversation.

"I'll do the same," he says without any argument. Cerberus and I walk ahead of him, and not another word is said between any of us.

23

MAGGIE:

RAIDERS

I wake to the sound of a loud rumble and realize that Cerberus is growling, staring intently at the doorway. It's the scariest sound I've ever heard her make.

The room is inky black with moonlight creeping through the window in pale streaks, giving minimal light to assess what is happening. Her eyes are fixed and unwavering and her lips curl up over her gums, exposing vicious teeth. Her ears are set back low as if she's ready to attack. My heart burns in my chest as the familiar taste of adrenaline overwhelms my senses.

I press my ear against the wooden door and listen for Ryker across the hallway, but all I hear is silence echoing through the house.

As I open the bedroom door, Cerberus darts past me into the living room, her heavy paws silent on the outdated maroon shag carpet. Loud growls and snarls echo from the room, signaling that Cerberus has not found a threat in the house.

    Being cautious of what I might find, I grab my knife and pistol and holster them in my waistband. Ryker has only been here for a few days, and I don't totally trust him yet. He says a lot of things about his obsession with me, but what if it's all a cover-up for him to kill me and take everything I have here?

    The only reason I didn't kill him is because I truly don't think he would hurt me, but I'd be lying if I said he isn't still alive because he's attractive. Something about those green eyes has me in a damn choke hold.

    But honestly, I don't believe in murdering just to murder. When I kill someone, it's a consequence of their actions. I guess I'm about to learn whether I can actually read people since I haven't been around a human being in months, or if my naivety got the best of me this time.

    Before following Cerberus, I peek in the guest bedroom across the hall. Ryker is nowhere in sight. However, his bed is unkempt, which is unlike him. Typically, if he leaves, he always makes his bed. From what I've seen, he's very organized and clean, so the bedroom in any kind of disarray is concerning. I fill my lungs to capacity and hold the still air until I turn the corner, treading lightly, calculating each step before it's made. Drawing my blade from my waist band, I position it forward as I walk through the dark hallway. My night vision indicates a clear path.

Nuclear

Just as I reach the door's threshold, a large, calloused hand reaches from around the corner and covers my mouth. Almost simultaneously with the first, a second hand grabs my waist and pulls me toward the wall.

As I lift my knife to stab the rough hand gripping my cheeks, a deep, raspy voice catches the helix of my ear. "You've got raiders in the yard currently scoping the place out. There must be at least eight of them from the flashlights I've seen and voices I can hear."

The scent of leather overwhelms my nose as I realize I'm in *his* grip. I relax into him as his hand on my waist tightens.

My brain screams not to trust him, but my body aches for him despite my desperate rational thoughts of rejection. When he feels my body language change, he removes his hand from my mouth, and as much as I hate to admit it, I wish he had kept it there.

"Have you ever had to fight raiders before?" he asks with concern. I whisper back without turning around, "A few times, but never that many people. Usually, two or three of them get lost out here in the woods and stumble onto the cabin." The scruff on his jaw drags across the side of my neck as he stays close to my ear, and the heat of his breath on my skin makes delectable goosebumps rise on my arms. A twinge of desire ignites in me, despite all the hateful thoughts I keep circling in my head about him.

Before I let myself give into his touch, I push off of him and slide to the wall beside him.

"What's wrong, love? Not liking the things you're starting to feel for me?" he asks, followed by a hushed laugh and lust creeping into his eyes.

"I feel nothing for you. You've done nothing but give me anxiety since you got here. You're just another mouth to feed," I retort with a scowl.

"If you feel that way, then why didn't you kill me when you had the chance?" I feel my cheeks turning pink, so I turn to the windows, avoiding his question.

"Can we do this later? I've got some people to kill," I say, scanning our opposition through the fogged windowpanes. Cerberus is still growling and staring through the window, waiting for the go-ahead.

"You ready?" I look at Ryker, and he nods in approval. All three of us stealthily move to the back door, since no people appear to be around the fire pit area. We sneak to the tree line, treading lightly to avoid the sound of crunching grass under our feet. I hold my gun securely in front of me with my finger resting beside the trigger. Cerberus goes slightly ahead, hitting the threshold of the tree line first, and Ryker and I follow quickly behind.

Fortunately for us, raiders are just normal people who survived the nuclear war. They have no special skills, so avoiding their attention is very easy. As we circle back to the front of the house, we count eleven raiders. They are all

Nuclear

dressed in weathered and frayed clothing and have an array of weapons ranging from guns to whips.

Seriously, one guy has a cattle whip on his belt. Their faces are all tattooed, and most of the men have long beards full of matted and dirty hair.

There is one man who is more ominous than the rest, and I'm willing to bet that he is in charge. He has a dirty white tank top with a brown set of distressed coveralls on. A sash of bullets crosses his front side, and he carries a baseball bat with nails and barbwire decorating it. A tattered black leather mask is fit over his head with hazy goggles that appear to be sewn into it. One man refers to him as "Executioner."

That tells me he is probably going to be a problem.

All of the raiders are men except for two women. The women are currently trying to pick the front door lock while the men are impatiently threatening them. One girl turns around, flips them off, and they laugh at her idle threat.

We've been isolated for a while, but I feel like the raiders have upped their game compared to what I had seen previously. Their weapons make them stronger, but I feel Ryker and I have seen worse threats in our time in the military.

Without speaking, Ryker and I agree on a plan. He raises his pistol, and I follow in sync. Before firing simultaneously, he winks at me, releasing vicious butterflies in my stomach.

Two bullets fly from the small barrels of our handguns and into two of the men's skulls directly in front of us. The bullets strike the men in the back of the head, and bloody brain matter sprays the men standing before them.

They turn and shake off the gore from them before they all turn to charge in our direction. We are able to pop off two more shots, resulting in two more direct blows to the head, except this time, the hot bullets pierce through the front of their skulls. The one I hit freezes in his tracks as the bullet pierces through his forehead and into his cerebral tissue. A single trail of blood begins to descend his face before he falls to the ground.

As they cross into the tree line where we hide, Cerberus attacks one, quickly knocking the man off his feet. The man fights for his life as Cerberus begins to tear through his muscles, all the way to the bone. One head rips his throat out in one fatal bite, while the other gnaws through his arm. As the man screams louder and louder, Cerberus digs deeper and deeper until a human humerus lands a few feet from me.

I forgot how fast she can tear someone apart.

The man begins to choke on his own blood as his breathing labors. Two of the men attempt to corner Ryker with knives drawn, and he fights back, dodging almost every move they have. He knows their moves before they act and has their skulls cracking into each other within seconds.

SNAP!

Nuclear

The sound grips my full attention. As I turn, I see the man with the cattle whip standing before me. The whip barely missed me. He's a rugged man, but in the worst way.

His skin is dirty and his clothes are torn and weathered as if he left them on a clothesline during a storm. His hair and beard are matted and disheveled. The expression on his face is mean and vile, and I have no doubt that he will do his worst if I don't stay one step ahead of him.

He winds his wrist up and sends the whip at me, I don't hesitate, but I'm not faster than the braided leather. I pull the trigger of my pistol, barely noticing the kickback. The whip grazes my arm, and my skin breaks open with a gruesome pop, like when you leave a hot dog in the microwave too long. The pain sears into my flesh, but I refuse to acknowledge it. My bullet landed off target, and it pierced through his shoulder.

Well, shit.

"Fucking bitch. You're going to die for that," he threatens through gritted teeth as he mindlessly clutches his shoulder, He lunges in my direction but misses, and lands face-first in the dewy grass.

As I prepare myself to take another shot, I'm put into a choke hold from behind.

"Aw, what's wrong, sweetheart? It seems like you are at a loss for words," a croaky voice taunts close to my ear. Bullets press into my back, and even through my shirt I can feel how cold the metal is.

I am in the grip of the Executioner.

He laughs as he squeezes my neck harder. The smell of stale sweat pierces my nose with the little air I'm able to inhale. His breath on me is nauseating.

With his other hand, he explores my curves, making sure to grab my ass. He runs his hand down my thigh and says,

"Whenever you go out, I'm going to have to see how you feel. I bet that pussy is so tight." His hardening cock presses into my back as vomit rises in my throat.

Adrenaline surges through my veins like hot acid as I struggle to break free from his grip. I claw at his large arm, my nails digging into his skin. My lungs burn, begging for air, and stars explode across my vision, followed by a black haze as Cerberus attacks the guy I shot in the shoulder. She gets him from behind, forcing him back to face down in the grass. Her claws slash across his skin as she holds her weight steady in place. Both heads latch onto his shoulders and begin to rip violently, eliciting cries of agony from the man. The bright purple aura glows from my fingers against his flesh, but like a flame in the wind, it fades quickly as my brain demands a breath.

Just as the world starts to fade, the guy holding me starts gasping as he drops me to the ground.

I land on my hands and knees in the cool grass below me. Drool leaves my lips as I aggressively cough trying to regain

Nuclear

precious oxygen. My breathing is heavy and erratic while I try to focus on what's happening and not just my air hungry lungs.

Ryker has the man in a chokehold. He kicks the executioner's knees forward until the man lands on them. Ryker adjusts his stance just enough to tease the man with minimal air.

"Apologize," Ryker says sternly.

"For what?" the guy asks with unfiltered hate, frustrated because he can't see Ryker behind him. Ryker rips the man's mask off, revealing a face with half sun damage and wrinkles, and half radiation burns.

The seared flesh looks like large blisters that have popped and span the length of thinning hair down to his collarbone. Sloughing and scorched tissue hangs aimlessly from his face, while new pink flesh tries to heal the massive, webbed craters. The eye on the burned side is cloudy and distorted indicating severe ocular damage.

If I wasn't so out of breath, I'd probably gasp.

Ryker pulls his knife from his belt and presses it at the base of the guy's eye socket. The blade immediately draws blood from the sheer pressure of Ryker's anger.

"This isn't a game of twenty fucking questions. Apologize to her for putting your disgusting hands on her, or I'll pluck your good eye out and feed it to you."

He squeezes harder into the man's neck, and I can see bruising start to form under his grip. The guy is silent for a moment, but Ryker follows with,

"Have you ever pulled out an eyeball before?"

He twists the knife making little cuts as his anger and impatience move the blade closer to the man's waterline.

"You can literally just reach your fingers around it as if you were plucking a grape from a vine and pull it out until you rip the optic nerve in half."

Ryker shrugs as he lets out an *evil* laugh.

A laugh that should repulse me, but it doesn't.

In fact, it makes me want him more.

It makes me admit to myself how much I want this man, even though I shouldn't.

The guy hisses through his teeth, saying, "I— I'm sorry." A grimace forms on his face as he rolls his eyes back to the knife threatening his eyesight.

"Here's the thing, that beautiful girl that you were strangling is mine. That heart is mine, her body is mine, and her soul is mine, and when you touch what's mine, I hurt you. It's a very easy concept to grasp."

The man struggles under Ryker's grip, refusing to make eye contact with me. "Come on, man, she's just some pussy. You can have her, and we can all walk away from this," the man's voice trembles with terror, trying to bargain his way out of dying.

"Just some pussy, huh?"

A rage flashes through Ryker that I've never seen in any human's eyes. He looks at me with a vicious gaze.

"Where did he touch you? I want to know every place his hands touched on you."

I swallow hard, still trying to catch my breath.

"He— He touched my shoulder first," I manage to get out through my hyperventilation even though my voice is rough. I cough again, trying to maintain some kind of a voice, even if it is a small one.

The man lets out a scream as Ryker dislocates his shoulder in one swift motion. The sound of the bone sliding past its socket makes me wince. The guy's arm dangles uselessly as he breathes heavily.

"Where else, Maggie?"

Ryker's fury seethes in his eyes. The guy sobs as he looks to me for mercy. I hold his gaze knowing that what is about to happen is my fault.

"My ribs," I say, watching the show unfold in front of me. Ryker grabs the guy's side and looks me in the eye as he breaks the guy's ribs one by one with just his hand.

Crack.

Crack.

Crack.

I hadn't been able to comprehend the degree of his superhuman strength until now.

Crack.

Crack.

Crack.

The guy screams in pain and is on the verge of passing out.

Crack.

Crack.

Crack.

After the audible crack of nine ribs, Ryker taunts, "Oh buddy, don't go yet; we haven't even gotten to the best parts." He pats his face mockingly. The guy mumbles incoherent pleas for mercy as his breathing labors. I'm pretty sure he has a collapsed lung from the force of the ribs turning into his chest abnormally.

Ryker drops his chokehold on the man as the Executioner's pain has become his restraint.

"Maggie?" He looks at me, waiting for me to fuel his fire, and I fully intend to oblige.

"He grabbed my ass and told me he'd have fun with my unconscious body." Flames light up his green eyes, and his nostrils flare. Through locked teeth, he looks at me and states,

"Well, I can't exactly break his ass, but I have a better idea."

Ryker lifts his right leg and stomps harshly on the guy's right femur. The loud snap of the bone resonates through the trees. The guy screams and cries, but Ryker doesn't give him a break. He lifts his leg again and stomps the guy's left femur.

The sound makes my bones quiver in my skin.

He drops his grip on the man, as he can't walk in his condition now. The raider's head hangs as blood drips out of his mouth, and his femurs are in compound fractures, as the bones protrude from the bottom of his thighs.

Like a broken doll, his body is limp and misshapen.

Ryker grabs the guy's hands in each of his and simultaneously breaks them with just a simple motion. The man's screams have just turned to harder sobs.

"Now you can't touch or try and fuck things that aren't yours. You disgust me." Ryker spits on him and kicks one of the man's fractured legs.

The man blows out a breath, trying to contain his misery. He is shaking in agony as he avoids eye contact with both of us. He mumbles words that I can't understand, but the way he says them sound familiar. It sounds like he's praying.

"Pray all you want, my guy, but there's only one goddess in charge of your fate right now, and you just threatened to rape her. Maybe you should try praying to her instead."

The man's barely conscious gaze catches my eyes searching for any kind of reprieve. I just give him a cold, hard smile.

Ryker's gaze fixes upon me.

"Where's the last place he touched you?" He knows the answer, but he wants me to say it. The man looks at me with begging eyes.

"My neck."

I am curious as to what his next move is. He has a lot of options, but he always seems to keep me guessing. Ryker's eyes lock on mine, like he's waiting for my orders. He wants my order for the execution of the Executioner. Ironic, isn't it?

"Personally, I don't take threats of rape lightly, and honestly, after you healed up from the damage Ryker just inflicted on you, I think you would just try and take advantage of some other poor girl. I don't believe in murder unless it's done for the right reasons, and my friend, this is definitely a good reason," I say as I shrug my shoulders, well aware I have sealed his fate.

Nuclear

The guy swallows hard as Ryker stands behind him and puts his hands on either side of the man's head. He forces the guy to look down as he says, "She doesn't get to be the last thing you see, but just know she is the reason for your death." With those words, Ryker quickly snaps the raider's neck and throws him to the ground.

The man is a broken, mangled, and bloodied mess.

I've never seen someone break someone else's neck before. I've seen it in movies, but in person it's different. First, you hear the loud crack of the spine ripping apart violently. When you look at their eyes, fear is forever ingrained in them, even when they become lifeless. The head is contorted abnormally to the side and almost faces the backside. The image does make me cringe at the thought of how much it must fucking hurt.

Ryker walks over to me and helps me off the ground. Given what he just did, it shocks me how gently he is helping me to my feet. His breathing is heavy as he is coming down from his adrenaline high. The only raiders left are the women, but Cerberus has had a hay day chasing them around. Other than having two bloody mouths, she looks untouched. She goes for the ankles of one, rendering her unable to walk. While that lady is on the ground, Cerberus does a run and jumps onto the upper body of the other one. She rips flesh until that woman's screams dissipate.

The only thing I can muster up is, "Thank you," as I look at him.

He continues toward me, causing me to back up and nearly trip over the dead guy behind me. He's scaring me as no words leave him, and a fire is still burning hot in those bright green eyes.

A funeral pyre of fury and lechery.

I keep backing away until my back rests against the rough bark of an oak tree, and I can't make myself any smaller. He leans forward, resting his right arm above my head. His eyes catch mine.

"Let this serve as a warning, little fox. If another man touches you, he will die. If another man loves you, he will die. If you tell me that I can't love you, can't touch you, or can't be by your side, then be prepared to pull the trigger on your pistol, because if I can't have you, you're going to have to kill me to be free of me."

He leans in deadly close to my lips but stops, waiting for me to return the gesture. As much as I appreciate being rescued, I'm certainly not a damsel in distress, and I refuse to reward him with my body like all the women do in the fairy tales from my childhood.

"Do you understand?" he asks, his gaze boring into my soul, making my heart thrash in my chest.

The rebellious side of me that refuses to be owned or commanded by a man begs me to fight back, but the other part is afraid of the look in his eyes.

Nuclear

Afraid to be burned by the inferno raging in front of me.

It feels like I'm standing too close to the sun, and the heat could burn me to ashes at any moment.

I've never seen a feral beast like the one before me.

"Yes," I whisper, as my eyes hold his.

My insides are feuding because a part of me really wants this, but I think it's because he just tortured a man for me.

If that doesn't get the message of "I want to fuck you more than I want to breathe" across then I don't know what will.

I lean in, and our lips graze.

The feeling of him so close is inebriating.

My panties are soaked from the way this man makes me feel.

"You're a psychopath," I mutter. He laughs, a deep sound that makes me shiver. When I don't kiss him, he leans over to my cheek and lightly kisses it.

"Yeah, but you're falling in love with me anyway. What does that say about you, little fox?" he retorts with a smirk.

He runs his fingers across my now purple neck and kisses it as if to take the pain away. His lips make me shiver and I do my best to ignore his gesture.

"I'm sorry this happened to you," he remarks with shame in his stare. I bring my hand up to my neck.

"It's okay. I should've been more prepared to take on multiple men. It's been a while since I've been in hand-to-hand combat," I respond, trying not to stumble over my words from the desire for him building inside me. To be so crazy, he's so caring and affectionate with me, making hating him so hard.

"Honestly, the cattle whip was the worst part of tonight."

"What do you mean?" he asks.

I motion towards the wound on my arm. It's already stopped bleeding, and only the sting remains.

"Never again," he whispers.

He kisses my hand before pulling himself away, and I can't stand to admit that my heart sinks. The cold air haunts the warmth of where his body was pressed against mine. The way I feel about him solidifies the complexities of human emotions.

I hate him, but God, I want him.

24

MAGGIE:

TEAMWORK

I woke up this morning in a sweat, my shirt clinging uncomfortably to my body. The nightmares haven't improved even after seven months. I head to the bathroom, grab a washcloth, wet it with cold water, and press my face into the dingy fabric. I drag the cloth under my chin and down my throat, until I eventually reach the back of my neck. My neck aches to the touch. Even though the bruises are fading to shades of green and yellow, it still hurts to the touch. I take off my soaking wet clothing and reach for something comfortable and dry.

After lazily donning my attire, I make my way to the kitchen. On the way down the hallway, I can smell the enticing aroma of cheap coffee. I turn the corner and see Ryker sitting at the table, sipping on some.

Goddamn.

He is a beautiful man, and even though I can't decipher how I feel about him, it doesn't change how stunning he is. My eyes trail his body up and down without making it evident that I'm studying his features. Even sitting down, he towers over the table in front of him. He's dressed in a black T-shirt with scattered holes throughout the fabric, and some gray sweatpants. The shirt hugs the muscles of his arms, and I do my best to ignore the way his biceps ripple as he reaches for his coffee.

He smiles lightly at me while I walk to the coffee pot, snapping out of my gawking daydream. I pour a cup and sit at the table as well. Human interaction is pleasant nowadays, especially when the person in question is not trying to kill, rob, or rape you.

Before I can start a conversation, he states, "There's a storm coming today. I can smell it."

"Wait, wait, wait," I reply with confusion. "Did you say you can smell the rain?"

"Yes," he says with a chuckle. "You've never heard of petrichor?" I look at him with perplexity.

The man is like the most beautiful hybrid of a dictionary and an encyclopedia.

"Ummm… I have no idea what that is." I laugh nervously.

"It's defined as a word to describe the unique earthy smell present right before it rains," he replies like he is trying to quote the definition he read somewhere, still holding his smile. "Well, even if you are lying, I wouldn't know. I can't exactly google it." I giggle. "So, I will just have to take your word for it."

I smile as my eyes catch his deep emerald pools. My heart skips, and it feels like thousands of butterflies are desperately trying to escape my body. The way he makes me feel is something that I'm not sure I have ever experienced before.

I realize I'm flirting and I'm trying my best to look away from his eyes, but I can't seem to find the strength to do it.

Something about last night has my insides twisted.

I want to hate him; any normal person would've been disgusted about the torture and the words he professed about me after killing the man.

My mind and heart battle internally.

I don't particularly appreciate being "claimed," but something about a man who will murder anyone who touches me gives me a certain feeling of euphoria that I know isn't normal. In fact, it should give me the ick.

"Can I ask you something?"

"Anything," he responds eagerly.

"I'm at peace with what happened last night, but if I would've asked you to spare that man, would you have?"

Hesitation doesn't even settle on his face as he answers with,

"Absolutely. If last night didn't prove it, I would kill for you, but I would also never use a weapon again if you asked me to. It scares me how much control you have over me, and I feel like your hooks dig deeper into me every day. I would gladly let you rip me to pieces and applaud you as you tore me apart. The question of whether I live, or die does not matter, as long as it's for you."

His words burn into my soul like a curse.

A curse that has solidified feelings that I don't want to have.

A curse that will make my heart ache if I don't get to *need* him like he needs me.

My brain seems to short circuit like a compromised motherboard as it's torn violently between love and hate.

Rational vs. irrational thought become background noise in my mind as they lock horns.

Nothing I can say is a sufficient response to his words, no matter which path I choose.

All I'm able to get out is, "With the rage I saw in you last night, I didn't think anything could change your mind."

He laughs and replies, "I've been told I'm pretty scary when I'm angry, but you are the water that can contain the spread of my flames. You are the only thing that can redirect my mind. That's why I'm so damn obsessed with you. You make me feel."

My mind flashes to the moment where he waited for me to approve the execution of that man. It wasn't a long moment, but it was there. Like driving under a bridge in the pouring rain, there was a break in the storm of his emotions.

Tears start to pool in my eyes, and it takes everything I have not to start sobbing.

Nobody has ever talked about me the way he does. When he looks away, I wipe my eyes quickly and conceal the way I feel.

Like a dog that won't stop barking, something in the back of my brain incessantly reminds me that every time I care for someone, they die. It's safer for him that I don't get attached.

I redirect the conversation.

"I'm planning to head to the lake today before it storms. Cerberus typically goes with me. She likes to get out. Will you be okay by yourself?" He cocks his head to the side, obviously deciding if he should make a smart-ass remark, but he just says, "I would be fine, but I'm coming with you. I'm going stir crazy myself."

I was hoping he would invite himself.

Slowly browning grass crunches under our feet as we make our way to our destination. We make small talk and sarcastic jokes along the way, but the agonizing trepidation that something could emerge from the tangled branches surrounding us never fades from the back of my mind.

"So, did you have any pre-war life plans?" he asks curiously, breaking the silence on our trek.

I sigh before responding,

"Didn't we all?" I remark. He raises his eyebrows encouraging me to open up about pre-war Maggie.

"Yeah, I did. I was just about to graduate with my D.O. Maggie Compton, Doctor of Osteopathic Medicine," I embellish while simultaneously spreading my hands apart in the air and looking straight ahead as if to make my non-existent title sound more dramatic.

"It was such a waste of eight years of medical school. If I knew the world was going to end, I would've done something way cooler." I give a wry laugh.

"Oooooo a doctor. No wonder you are so good at sutures," he teases as he chuckles.

"Was there a special man?" His eyes are wide in anticipation.

"No. There wasn't a man that could put up with my independence... or my work schedule. Honestly, I preferred to be alone. I would find an occasional fuck here and there, but even then, I've never been impressed." I shrug.

Nuclear

"So, what I just heard was that I was the first man to make you cum and I didn't even fuck you." A mischievous smirk curls the end of his lips.

I shove him to the side feeling my cheeks and neck redden. I hide a small smile because he's totally right. I have never had an orgasm from a man, let alone one who didn't even have to use his dick. Every sexual experience I've ever had with a man has been the guys solely interested in getting themselves off or not knowing what a clit is.

"Don't get cocky. These two fingers have done more for me in my entire life than any man has." I raise the index and middle finger of my right hand and kiss them in appreciation. He laughs and retorts, "Once you give me a chance, you'll never have to use those again."

My mouth goes dry and my heart thumps wildly, but I refuse to let him win.

"Yeah, yeah, yeah, you're all talk," I mock. A smile plasters itself on his face, and I give him a sassy stare.

"God, I love your defiance." His gaze lingers on my face.

I redirect to get his attention off me.

"And what about you, pretty boy?" His mouth drops open.

"So, you do think I'm pretty?" he asks as if I just gave him the best compliment anyone could ever give him.

I roll my eyes, knowing damn well that I do think he is absolutely drool worthy.

"I did, in fact, have plans for my life. I had just started my career."

Please don't have a hot job.

Please don't have a hot—

"I had just started my own veterinary clinic back home. I literally only had the doors open for 5 days! I saw 37 patients before the war and then poof— my career— all those years of hard work, gone in an instant. It was devastating, honestly it crushed me. My work was my life."

Well fuck. Of course, he has to be hot *and* take care of animals *and* be passionate about it.

"So that's why Cerberus likes you so much," I declare.

"Yeah... that's most likely it. Animals just know when people are not a threat to them." He lets out a nervous laugh.

"I ran for so long after losing everything that mattered. I got tired of it and just 'volunteered' for the draft," he casually states.

"You did what?!" I probed loudly.

"Are you crazy?" I inquire, shaking my head with disbelief written all over my face.

"Well, I thought that if they didn't force me into it, they wouldn't be afraid of me escaping, which would lead to me having some freedom instead of a short leash. I had no idea they were illegally experimenting on us." It seems to still strike a nerve when he talks about it, but he shrugs and laughs it off.

"You are insane! I bet that was a huge slap in the face. Don't you regret it?"

"I did during the pain of it all, but—." He catches my stare. "Since I found paradise in Appalachia, I wish I would've done it sooner. Getting to be in your presence is worth every experiment I was put through. I regret nothing, little fox." My heart is chaotic, and warmth radiates in my chest. Just as words start to surface in my brain, Cerberus stops in front of us.

Her ears move feverishly listening for something. I shush Ryker with my index finger pressed against my lips as I motion to Cerberus's stance. Very little makes it past her, so if she hears something, it's usually not good.

The forest is silent, but it's not just any kind of silence. It's the silence that you hear after the first snow of winter. It's eerie and haunting. I look to Ryker, and he has already surveyed the area.

He whispers, "Ten o'clock," and motions to his left. The leaves deep in the brush begin to vibrate. We stealthily make our way to the opposite side of the clearing we are in before whatever is coming can emerge. A deafening screech echoes through the forest when we reach the other side from our left. My ears begin to ring as I prep my crossbow. He pulls out a knife with his right hand, and his left hand is on the pistol in his belt.

Just when I feel like I can't breathe from the prospect of danger, a creature comes forth from the dark, desolate greenery. It is large and grossly deformed, but its characteristics make it easy to assume it was a centipede at one point, but now it is close to an elephant's size. It has long spikes protruding from its neck, shoulders, and mid-back. There must be at least one hundred of them. They look like porcupine quills with the way they project from its body, but they are massive in size and could skewer a person like a meat kabob. Its ribs are exposed on one side, and sloughing skin hangs from the bones. In between the ribs is an inky, rotting tissue that pulses with each breath it takes. It has at least one hundred large fuzzy legs, each thin and dirty. At the end of each one are two pinching claws that it uses for balance and… gripping things?

Due to all the gore and carnage I've seen over the last few months, my mind has a tendency to create random scenarios in my head, and in this moment, it chooses to generate an image of how rapidly those claws could squeeze me in half while my eyes bulge out of my head and my organs seep from the safety of my abdominal cavity. Whether it's a fear or safety tactic, I'm unsure, but I refuse to die that way. Not today. Thanks, brain, for the image that I can now add to my growing list of nightmares.

Another blood curdling screech rips from its throat. Upon observing its mouth, there are two rows of endless jagged teeth on the top and bottom of abnormally elongated jaws. Decaying flesh and exoskeleton cover its face, and randomized feelers scatter its cheeks. Four thin, long tongues hang from its black, bottomless pit of a mouth. Twelve bright red eyes burn in anger.

I look at Ryker, trying to hide the fear in my eyes. He is on my left side, and Cerberus is on my right. Cerberus is growling low with her muscles locked and hair standing erect. She is ready to attack at my call.

"Lay low," he says softly. "Maybe we can wait it out." Just as the words leave his lips, the creature goes silent, and it begins to wave two of its tongues in the air as if trying to sniff out prey like a snake would. Loud and harsh gusts of rotten breath circulate in our direction as the thing desperately searches.

Fear slams into my gut, and I can feel the adrenaline coursing through my veins rising to dangerous levels. I aim my crossbow, accordingly, steadying my shaking hands. It turns in our direction and gets unnervingly close. I come to the conclusion we aren't leaving here without a fight. I hold my breath hoping that this thing can't sense movement.

Like it could read my mind, it goes to charge in our direction, its legs moving rhythmically to carry it quickly. It moves like a slinky despite heavy steps beating into the earth. We split off with different destinations. I take a shot with the crossbow and hit the creature in one of its eyes. It lets out a furious squeal, as it swats uselessly at its injured eye capsule.

Angrier than it was, it barrels toward me.

Cerberus is already on its heels, trying to avoid the grip of its claws. She weaves intricately under the creature, until she leaps and bites down on the joint of its front leg. The crack of exoskeleton echoes around us, sickening but satisfying. Its claws curl in pain, and its attention is redirected, trying to locate the source of pain underneath it. I grab the rope from my waist belt and throw it over a high branch on an old, weary maple tree, praying that it can support my weight.

I create a slipknot with quick motions of my hands and turn back to see Ryker ready to strike. I get a running start and use the tree trunks as leverage as I hoist myself up to the top of the creature, landing on the upper part of its neck above the spikes that could've impaled me. It distracts the creature but sends it into a blind rage. I do my best to hold on.

This feels like the most unfair bull ride.

Let's pray I can last at least eight seconds.

Ryker runs under the monster with his knife drawn. Using both hands around the handle of the knife, he stabs the blade into the creature's chest and drags it through its armor as he slides beneath the massive beast.

The creature roars in pain.

It thrashes side to side violently, confused as to where its attacker is. Black goop forms a halo on the ground around the beast as it profusely bleeds out. Throwing its body left and right over and over, it eventually exhausts itself until it collapses. Its legs twitch and wave in erratic patterns as neurons fire uselessly throughout its body.

The force of the monster slamming into the ground launches me sideways. I lose my balance and can't get a grip before falling off it.

I land face-down on a bloodied Ryker. Shock freezes me in place, and my eyes get caught in his gaze.

I never noticed just how beautiful his eyes were until now. They are three shades of green. The outer edges are a deep emerald green, and the middles are an alluring sea foam green. Around his pupils is a viridian green, and like an artist painted them brushstrokes of that color circle toward that shade of bluish green that resides in the middle.

He's truly breathtaking.

I'm so distracted that I don't realize how close my lips are to his. We are both breathing heavily, and I can feel his heart beating in my chest.

I just want to—

"If you want to kiss me, just do it," he encourages as he grips my arms which holds me in place. I think about making a smart-ass remark, but honestly, at this moment, the urge to kiss him is overwhelming, but I just need to listen to my brain for once and not my heart.

I pull away (surprising myself that I had the willpower to) and take one more look at his sexy, bloodied face before rubbing my thumb across his cheek and then standing up.

The sticky tar substance from the creature's insides webs between us as I force my abdomen from his. A disgusting wet squelch sound makes me cringe as I work so hard to get myself off him. I hold back a gag as the smell of rotting decay fills my nose. Shaking my palms in a rhythmic motion, molten tissues flick into the dirt around me. Once my hands are less sticky than they were, I offer my hand down to him to help him up. He takes my hand but stands up with ease, obviously not needing my help.

After standing and getting our bearings, I look for Cerberus. I don't immediately see her, and panic sets in. I get ready to start shouting, and out from under one of the monster's many legs, pop two heads.

"Are you okay, girl?" She makes her way to me, tail wagging. I lean down and pat her side.

"Good girl," I mumble. I look back to Ryker who looks slightly defeated. I assume it's because of the missed kiss opportunity, but he walks over to the beast. He lays a hand on the upper shoulder of the creature.

"I'm sorry," he whispers and pats the creature before walking back to us.

Nuclear

Well, that was hot. To apologize to a creature who was a victim of a bunch of rich men fighting over land, it gives me a new perspective on Ryker. He looks at me, eyes tired, and says, "Time to head home?" I nod. I pat his shoulder, and we head back to the cabin.

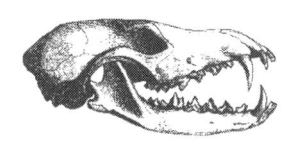

Ryker opens the silent screen door of the cottage, and we make our way inside; all three of us sticky and exhausted. Radiation blood is different than regular blood. It's thicker, darker, and smellier. It does not harbor a metallic smell, just the smell of death, and trust me, if you've smelled it before, you know exactly what I mean. I would compare it to stinky tar mixed with death on a cracker.

I walk Cerberus to the bathtub carefully, making sure not to drip any of the substance on the carpet. I turn the water spigot on to let the temperature rise. I check it to make sure I don't scald her. As I look at my dirty furry pal, I flick my fingers free of residual water.

"Alright, we've got to get that nastiness off of you, especially if you want to sleep in the bed tonight," I say sternly. As if weighing her options, she looks back and forth between me and the door. Finally, she hops into the halfway filled tub, understanding the task. I run my hand over the fur on her back. Her silky coat is matted with the foul black liquid, and when I pull my hand away, liquid strands of sticky tar span the distance between it and her back. I grab the shower head and soak her, watching the inky pigment circulate in the clear water and quickly disperse throughout the tub. I grab some shampoo and work the soap deeper into her coat. The suds are quickly pigmented in shades of gray as the substance begins to release her fur.

Ryker turns the corner. "Can I help?" he asks sweetly.

"Of course, but the princess is pretty particular. Think you can meet her demands?" He looks me over and says, "I know I could meet the demands of every woman in this room." I stutter, speechless; red heat radiates up my cheeks as I blush. He kneels next to me, despite the fact I'm still standing.

The sight of this man on his knees makes a delicious ache pulse between my thighs. It takes my brain a few seconds to process that I'm staring.

A smile appears on his lips as he catches my eyes. "Like what you see?" he inquires, raising his eyebrows before focusing back on Cerberus.

Yes.

Oh my God, yes.

Take me, please, Ryker.

I try to form a response, but my mouth opens and nothing comes out.

Nuclear

I reach forward and pull a blade of grass from his thick, black hair. "Sorry, I just didn't think you'd want to keep this."

"Oh yeah, it'd be an absolute shame for that to go down the drain when I shower." He chuckles and shakes his head seeing right fucking through me.

It takes everything in me to focus on the task rather than the gorgeous man kneeling next to me. He reaches for the shampoo and squirts some on Cerberus's hips and tail. Both heads focus on Ryker and pant, as he scrubs behind her ears. Even Gold Eyes is relaxed around him, which says a lot because she's usually the "tear people to shreds" head, whereas Blue Eyes, is the more lenient one. It gives me a little comfort to know she trusts him too. He aggressively yet gently works the unpleasant substance out of the fur that it clings to, much more graceful than myself. Cerberus stands still and is very patient with us as we scrub her.

It takes about four good scrubs and rinses to get the water to run clear off her. As I'm finishing rinsing her, he reaches down and pats her heads. "Good girl," he says in a way that makes my knees weak, and I can't help but wish he was talking to me.

25

MAGGIE:

EMOTIONS

"Come on, girl!" I dictate to Cerberus as I pat a freshly cleaned and dried towel on the floor in front of the tub. She looks at me hesitantly and paces the tub a few times while contemplating her escape strategy. She leaps gracefully over the tub edge, clearing the acrylic bowl with ease. Before I can wrap the towel around her, she begins to shake back and forth, starting from her heads to her tail. Water from her thick coat soaks Ryker and I instantly. I look at him with my hands held up in a poor attempt to prevent getting soaked further. He looks at me with a surprised expression, and we both burst into laughter. Cerberus stops shaking and looks at us confused as to why we are laughing. I reach down, pick up the towel, and start to dry her further.

Her undercoat holds a lot of water, and I want to ensure that she doesn't soak the sheets if she lays in the bed. Cerberus gets the special treatment of a two-towel job as

Nuclear

Ryker dries her faces and I dry her back. He's so good with her, and I'm almost a little jealous of their relationship.

I rub the towel vigorously through her fur until it no longer glistens in the light. After at least twenty minutes of drying, her fur is returned to its natural glory. I hang the towel over the bathtub edge and wipe my brow.

"That was a workout," I say as the burn of repeated motions dissipates from my arm muscles. I reach out to high-five him, and then I realize that Ryker and I are still covered in filth. Streaks of black goop stream down his face, and they have begun to crack as the air has stimulated coagulation of the rancid blood.

Something about a man with blood covering him is so... Hot.

His arms and torso are splattered with a tarry liquid that streaks as it mixes with sweat. His shirt is torn in several places from the monster's strikes, revealing tiny scratches on his skin beneath the larger rips.

His emerald eyes always seem to be watching me, studying me. Desire flashes through his gaze as he rakes his eyes up and down my body before catching my glare. The way he looks right now is mesmerizing. The butterflies in my stomach turn feral as they brutally beat against my organs. I walk over to him and lick my thumb and begin to wipe the substance from the corner of his mouth. He snaps his hand up and grabs my wrist, and stares at me intently, noticing that he has caught me off guard. His calloused hand is warm against my skin, and his hold on me could bring me to my knees with how good it feels. I stutter and say, "I—I just didn't think you'd want to taste that." He smiles and says nothing, but I know what he wants to say. Something along the lines of, "Maybe not, but I know what I would like to taste." He drops my wrist.

"I think it's your turn to get cleaned up." He motions toward the shower.

"And before the words leave your pretty lips, don't worry, I'm leaving," he confirms. He exits the bathroom, and I must admit I love watching him leave. For a man, he has one hell of an ass. I shake my head as I redirect my thoughts, repeating to myself that I hate him.

I hate him.

I hate him.

I hate him.

Hopefully, the more I say it, the more I'll start to believe it.

He stalked me, claimed me, and I had no say in any of it. He laughs at my attempts to blow him off, but I think it's because he sees through me. I have every reason to dismiss him and the way he feels about me, but my body keeps telling me to go back for one more drag, one more touch, and one more glance.

I take my clothes off and do my best to avoid the sticky goop on them from encountering my skin. I have a feeling this stuff will be hell to get off, so the less I have to scrub, the better. The water immediately runs black from my body, over the shower floor, and down the drain. I use the soap bar from the shelf and generously rub it into a clean washcloth. The scent of lavender and vanilla fills the shower, and as the calming scent overwhelms my senses, my mind begins to wonder.

I do my best to think about anything but him, but he invades every crevice of my mind, even the darkest places where I try to hide.

Why do I feel this way?

Everything about him screams "Danger!" But he is so good with me. The way he listens, the way he speaks to me, and God, the way he looks at me is everything I want.

When I'm next to him, my mind forgets about the pain, the loss, the trauma, and the shithole world we live in. He makes everything disappear for me, but when he's not there, the demons come rushing back, and they drag me back under the violent riptide swirling in my head. He's like a damn drug.

His electric personality, intoxicating voice, dark beauty, and exhilarating touch have me in a choke hold, and his grip keeps getting tighter and tighter leaving me absolutely breathless.

The thoughts make my breathing increase as I picture his hand around my throat. As I raise the washcloth to clean my neck, I find myself sliding my fingers into the same spots his fingers had sat on my flesh.

I stop and snap myself out of my daydream. Rational thoughts and mental clarity bubble back up to the forefront of my mind.

What am I thinking?

I can't fall in love with this man. It is the end of the world; the last thing I need to find is love, if that's even what this is.

Love will get you killed.

Peace of mind goes out the window because all you worry about is the other person.

I lean down, scrub the sticky mess from my ankles, and battle silently with my thoughts, torn between masturbating to my fantasies of him and not letting him take my sanity. I stand back up, letting the water run down my face, and try to just enjoy a relaxing shower without contradicting thoughts.

Sometimes, I wish internal monologues didn't exist. I don't think anxiety would even happen anymore if that were possible. I run my fingers through my hair, ensuring I removed all the shampoo and blood. The water begins to run clear, so I guess I got it all. I reach over and turn the knob off as the last bit of steam rises to the ceiling. Squeezing my hair out, I leave as much water behind as possible. I grab a towel from a rusty hook on the wall and walk over to the sink. Looking in the mirror, I sigh. "You are good enough. There's a purpose for you here. Keep going." I mumbled the same words to myself every night for years. I grab another towel and wrap my hair up in it.

"Ryker, the shower is free!" I yell, wanting him to catch a glimpse of me still in my towel.

There's no rule about teasing him with what he can't have.

Silence fills the room as I wait for a response, holding my breath in anticipation.

Suddenly, muffled footsteps tread closer and closer. The sound of them entering the room brings me comfort. I slowly release the breath, which has been taking up residency in my lungs. Shyness creeps into my demeanor. He whistles when entering the bathroom, followed by saying, "I'm sure you've heard this before, but damn, you are beautiful." I roll my eyes.

"Okay, Romeo. Get yourself cleaned up, and then we can talk," I say with a small smile, before shoving an extra towel into his hands. I walk into the bedroom and then to the closet and grab some pajamas consisting of my shorts, a sports bra, and a loose, long-sleeve shirt that exposes one shoulder since the neck hole is so wide. I'm so glad I fit into the clothes that the closet is filled with.

Someone had great taste.

I sit on the bed "crisscross applesauce," as I used to say when I was a kid.

I smile at that.

M.C. Blackheart

I look out the large cathedral window in the bedroom. The stars are beautiful tonight and solidify why I stay here. More and more stars appear in the sky, and they all seem to twinkle in a rhythmic pattern. I find myself tracing constellations with my eyes and whispering their names to myself.

Something about company at the end of the world makes my surroundings a little less scary.

I hear the water turn off, but I keep staring outside, refusing to give him the satisfaction of me waiting to look at him. I catch brief glimpses of him while he looks down or away from me. He walks out with wet black hair slicked back, but a few strands hang loosely in his face, unable to be tamed. His short beard glistens in the light from the residual moisture in it, but there isn't a single facial hair out of place. The details on his arms are immaculate and make me want to drool. His muscles are well defined, and his veins trail visibly where the water was hot, complimenting his arms' size. Multiple scars are noticeable on all areas of his upper half, varying in severity. Most look like knife fight marks across his torso, short and calculated scars in potentially dangerous places. They are similar in appearance to the singular latitudinal one-inch scar on his left cheek.

Long jagged scars stain the skin across his ribs, down his back, and across his arms and legs. All of them appear to have not been sutured and left to heal on their own as evidenced by the silvery flesh reconnecting his skin. He still has a damp towel wrapped around his lower half, tucked in loosely at his waistline.

Nuclear

It would be so easy to... take off.

Multiple tattoos decorate his brawny exterior, including an intricate sleeve on his left arm, which trails onto his chest. His left leg has patchwork tattoos, which is my kind of style. I have patchwork everywhere. It tells me he has impulsivity, and I can relate to that. On his right side is a large jackalope tattoo. The tattoo is neotraditional and illustrates the front half of the jackalope as if facing it head on. It's head faces toward his abdomen with strong eyes. Small horns are shadowed by tall rabbit ears. The front two paws arch up as if it's going to leap, while the back feet aren't visible. The creature is framed in beautiful black and white dot work greenery.

"Why a jackalope?" I ask. He smiles.

"Oh, so you can look at me." I do my best to keep my blush from filling my cheeks, and raise my eyebrows as if to say, "Keep talking, I'm waiting for an answer."

"My mother used to tell the myth of the jackalope and that if I ever saw one, it would bring good luck. Now more than ever, I need all the luck I can get." He shrugs as he continues walking to his room and returns with a pair of gray sweatpants.

Oh. My. God.

He's huge. Like not human huge.

The outline of his length is visible, and my pussy pulses at the way it would feel. I quickly avert my gaze back to his face, before I let on that I'm screaming internally.

I'm sitting at the head of the bed, and he sits in the middle.

"My mom used to tell me to listen truly, you must master silence. That's how you catch a jackalope. In the position I was in with the military with being expected to perform quietly, I feel that I embrace silence, but I have yet to see a jackalope." I giggle and joke, "Or they just don't exist."

"Yeah, maybe, but I've searched my whole life for one, so it would be a waste of my whole life to give up looking."

He smiles, and it makes me smile at the little bit of childhood innocence he holds onto. We are silent for a beat.

"But then again, I seem to have found my own good luck charm." He stares at me with his grin still lingering. Red heat burns in my cheeks, as I bite on my fingernail. I don't respond, I just look at anything else but him, because honestly, I don't know how to respond.

"The way you catapulted yourself on top of that thing today was amazing. In all seriousness, you moved so gracefully, and it was mesmerizing to watch you defend yourself. We were a good team, if I do say so myself," he says confidently, reading my face to find an emotion, hoping I'll agree.

"Thank you. It was lots of practice, but I couldn't have taken that thing down without you. Thank you for not leaving when it charged me." He looks at me curiously, and his gaze moves to the wolf tattoo on my thigh, shifting back and forth with my eyes.

Nuclear

"I told you, Maggie, anything that touches or threatens you will die at my hands, and this is the second example of that." He takes his finger and softly traces the scars that the tattoo covers. His eyes reveal he desperately wants to ask how I got them, but I can tell that he is hesitant. His touch sends little chills down my leg and all I want to do is give in to him. I know I should pull away to get the message across, but I don't because the warmth from his hand feels right.

Before he can ask or speak at all, I say, "Since you want to ask, I'll tell you about the scars it covers." He nods, intrigued by my words.

"Before I tell the incredibly mundane story of my life, there's something you need to know about me. I've always been on my own. I have only had me, and even in the presence of others all I've ever felt is hollow. I'm a shell of a woman who has given up trying to fill the void inside me because every time I do, it's false hope. The emptiness grows twice the size as I'm trained to love people who leave me…" I wipe away a tear from my cheek, unable to meet his emerald gaze. I look up, hoping to stop the flow, but instead, more tears gather, blurring my vision. "I— I don't know how to love someone who won't hurt me."

The words come out fast and painful like ripping off a band-aid. I sigh, trying to pull myself together.

"Maggie—"

I cut him off, because if I stop now, I'm not going to get through my story.

"When I was eleven, I lost my parents in a car crash. I was put into the system. Foster homes came and went, but each one was worse than the one before. Whether it was utter neglect or creepy and handsy foster dads, it never changed the fact that I was an unwanted orphan." I run my fingers over the tattoo.

"The depression started early. It's like a darkness that slowly and silently consumed my life. It built itself a home inside me until nothing mattered anymore. Dissociation and emptiness dug their hooks in so deep, that I couldn't feel anything anymore. Not love, not happiness, nothing. Every positive feeling I had ever felt was gone. The cutting was enough just to make me feel something, but then, one day, the suicidal ideation started.

"Like a virus that spread so fast, it was all I could think about.

Why was I here?

What purpose could I possibly have?

What was the point anymore?

Nobody would notice if I was gone.

Would anyone care?

"I contemplated different ways: pills, deep cuts bleeding into a bathtub, and even the gun on my bedside table. On the day I was finally ready, a happiness I had never felt before rushed over me. The warmth and light that I found in knowing the end of suffering was so close took so much weight off my heart and mind. I went and did all of my favorite things that day; I got a massage, a manicure, and a pedicure with my foster sister before I went to my favorite place. I mean after all, I wanted to die pretty." I chuckle to myself.

"When I was young, there was a place my parents used to take me. It was like a secret paradise here, in the Appalachian Highlands, called the Cobweb Waterfall. You walk right up on a giant roaring waterfall when you approach the location. The water would stream down the rocks and earth in little trickles. The water resembled veins as it rushed down the mountainside, slowly eroding the earth away one day at a time. There is a very steep hike up to the top of the waterfall, but when you get to the top, the air feels like it's sucked from your lungs as you take in the otherworldly beauty.

"The grass never grows taller than your ankles, but it's the greenest grass I have ever seen in my entire life. Dahlias and day lilies bloom everywhere and display a rainbow of colors all around. The cliff is adjacent to a large valley, and when you look between the giant hillsides, more mountains appear as they fade away in shades of blues and greens. You can see parts of the city from how high you are. The air is always cool and light, making the chore of breathing easy. The scent of spring water and untouched earth surround you when you stand on that ground. It feels like the top of the world."

I stop to look at him to see his reaction to my words; his gaze is locked on me with questions still swirling in his mind.

"I spent my evening picking flowers and enjoying the peace. I reminisced on the memories and the positive energy that that place brought me. The sun began to set, and hues of purples, oranges, reds, and pinks spanned the sky and cast a glow over the land I sat on. I reached into my pocket and pulled out a bottle of Xanax that had been prescribed to me for anxiety. I was only supposed to take one nightly to control the symptom that plagued my mind, but in high doses, I read that the medication would decrease my respiratory effort. At the time, I felt I would get tired, close my eyes, and go peacefully to sleep with no tomorrow to worry about."

I pause before continuing, unable to bring myself to look him in the eye, so I stare at my feet as I swing them slightly over the edge of the bed.

"But then *it* happened. The ground shook beneath me, and birds began to fly out of the trees around me. It was like the world had spiraled into absolute chaos. The explosions became louder and louder, and mushroom clouds became visible. The reds and oranges of the sun setting just beyond the horizon began to melt into the smoke and flames of war.

"In a panic, I ran back down the mountainside, unsure of what was happening. I tripped over a branch and tumbled down the rigid earth. The ground was unforgiving as it gave me blow after blow as I rolled until I suddenly stopped. I found myself at the mouth of a small cave. Disoriented, I crawled into the narrow mouth of it. I stumbled until I got a few feet into it. My vision started to tunnel as I fell to my feet. I laid down on my back with my ears ringing until the world disappeared. I didn't know then that what I had just witnessed was the beginning of World War III. So, looking back, I guess this was my purpose, and if there is a God, he chose one hell of a way to get the point across that it wasn't my time." I smile slightly at that and let out a restricted laugh. I look at him to find him totally enthralled by my words, hanging on each syllable, patiently waiting for the next. Concern fills his emerald pools, and his typical smartass demeanor is gone.

"When I woke up, I realized that fallen rock and debris had closed the cave. I had to dig myself out of my temporary tomb, unsure of how long I had been out. I moved dusty stones and muddy rocks until my fingers bled, and even then, I persisted until a blinding light pierced between them. I strenuously dug harder and harder until every stone was overturned behind me. The daylight was overwhelming, and my corneas burned as I tried to get my eyes to adjust to my surroundings. The desolation was devastating. The earth that was once so beautiful was destroyed before me."

I take a deep breath and sigh as my mind flashes to Stevie, and the heartache that comes with the thought of her. In this moment, I realize that I haven't told a soul of my last few days with her, and how I let her down.

"I had a sister, and her name was Stevie. She and I had been through the last two homes together, and we got close because we were both orphans. As soon as I could afford it, I bought a house and had her move in with me. She's six years younger than I am, but I fought for custody when I was eighteen and won. I was her sister, but I also was her guardian. After years of living together, she announced she was going to move out and go live with her boyfriend of four years. She didn't need me anymore. She was the only person to ever need me, and she didn't need me anymore." I stop as tears sting my eyes, and I try to swallow the lump in my throat.

I control my breathing and continue, "She became my only purpose for living. I just wanted to see her succeed and I was so happy for her and James. He was a good guy, and he wanted nothing more than her happiness. What more could I ask for? I was in my last year of residency, with no time for a personal life, and honestly, I envied her. I made the decision to take my life after she announced their engagement because there was nothing left in this life for me. She had someone else to take care of her." He continues stroking my thigh in a comforting way, and honestly, it helps.

"I went to the bank and signed over the deed to the house, my car, and everything of value I had to her. She'd find out after I was gone, and then she would be set for a while. The government covered my student loans because we were foster kids, so she wouldn't have any extra debt. She had just one more year to go and she would have both her biomedical and chemical engineering degrees as she dual enrolled for them. She was always so damn brilliant. She was staying one last night, the night I went to take my life, and I just couldn't bear to say goodbye. I didn't want to see her cry over me." The tears begin to stream down my face, and I swipe them away with my palm.

"Everything happened and all I could think about was getting to her. When I was finally able to return home after I

Nuclear

got a radiation suit, there was nothing left of the house and not a trace of Stevie. All I can hope for is that she was asleep when the world burned, and that she didn't see it coming. It was at that moment that I vowed to never get attached to someone again because the only thing worse than emptiness is all consuming grief. One of the only things that keeps me going, is that she may still be alive."

    I sigh before more tears rush me and it takes everything I have not to start sobbing.

26

MAGGIE:

I AM BROKEN, TOO

I peer at him through wet lashes.

"And that is how I became the crazy lady who prefers to sit alone in the dark."

Sadness fills his eyes. His hands slide over mine on the mattress,

"Oh, my sweet little fox. You are not crazy to feel cold, dark, and lonely. You've simply learned to live in the dark. It has become your definition of normal. Your trauma, the life you led before has been all consuming darkness, and no one can pull themselves out of that alone no matter how strong you are. All I want is to sit in your darkness with you until you are ready to let me help you find the light, and if we sit in the dark forever, I promise to keep you warm."

Nuclear

He puts his hand on my outer face and wipes a tear that's just begun to fall with his thumb. My heart thunders in my chest and the butterflies in my stomach feel like waves chipping away at a crumbling cliff. His emerald pools swirl with desire. I pull away and lean in the opposite direction.

I don't want his pity; I just want him to know my story and how fucked up I am. I can't let myself get attached like I did with Stevie; it could destroy me this time. I want to scare him off so I don't have to worry about losing someone else, but more importantly *I will dry my own tears*—because I always have.

He sighs with disappointment as I get up from the bed.

"Maggie, wait—" he manages to get out before I cut him off.

"You literally stalked me and made me afraid to go outside for weeks. I can't just let you wipe the tears of my trauma and pretend like none of that happened. I don't even know you!"

It's true, I don't know enough about him, but I do trust him and that scares the hell out of me. I walk towards the hallway, but he catches my wrist.

"You're right. You don't know me but tell me that I don't make you feel safe. Tell me that you don't want me. Tell me you want me to leave, if you are so afraid of me."

"You need to leave, Ryker. I don't want you here anymore," I demand through my teeth, as I pull my hand from his grip and head towards the bedroom door.

The lie tastes bitter on my tongue.

He lunges from the bed and leans over me, slamming the bedroom door shut over my head. Cerberus begins to growl.

"Then why didn't you kill me when you had the chance?" I pause, knowing the answer doesn't help my side of this argument. It's like my skull is made of glass, and he can see straight through to my thoughts.

"I was in your control, you could've ended all of this, but you didn't want to. Admit it. You want me just as much as I want you. You may lie to yourself, but you can't lie to me."

I never have lied to myself about how I feel about him, but I know I shouldn't feel what I feel.

His face is millimeters from mine, and his breathing is heavy with frustration and lust. One more tear trails down my cheek. His hand comes up and wipes the droplet from my face. We both stare at each other, with no others sounds but rapid hearts and labored breathing.

After years of being broken, undesired, and alone, someone wants me.

He wants me. He wants me for my darkness, and to pick up the pieces of the broken shell of a woman I am.

I want to feel my stars align in my galaxy.

I want to be needed. I want to be his.

I want to finally have a life worth living.

Can I finally have something that I want?

In this moment, I surrender the hate I'm supposed to have and embrace the only person who has ever had faith in me.

Fuck it. I lean into him and press my lips to his. He kisses me back until we both have to come up for air.

"Finally," he whispers against my lips.

"Shut up and fucking kiss me," I retort.

He runs his hand through my hair and pulls me in. His kiss is demanding and hungry. It's a hunger I feel could devour me whole if I let it. My back is pushed so hard into the door behind me that I feel I may become a part of it.

His free hand pulls me into his hips by my waist, and I grind into him, embracing every touch he offers, so tipsy on the way his skin feels on mine. I suck his bottom lip between my teeth and pull back slowly. He growls in my mouth as he exhales, which is his only warning before he picks me up. I swirl my tongue with his, savoring the way he tastes. His hands brace my hips around him, before he carries me to the bed and lays me down. He releases my lips.

"Maggie," he purrs at the helix of my ear, while he supports his weight as he hovers above me. The way he says my name makes my nerves tingle under my skin.

"I told you during our first encounter that you were going to have to beg me to fuck you. I meant it. I want to hear how bad you want my dick in that tight little pussy." His lips trail the length of my neck, tortuously teasing. My eyes close and roll back as the heat of his breath sends shivers down my spine. His lips hover just above mine as he stares into my eyes waiting for me to oblige.

"Please," I beg against his mouth. He groans in anticipation.

"Again. Use your words. Tell me what you want," he teases, while hovering his strong hands just out of reach of my skin, waiting patiently to tell him what I want.

I run my fingers across his cheek, never taking my eyes away before I say,

"Please fuck me, Ry."

"It sounds so pretty when you say it," he says as his grip returns to my hips, making me shiver.

"Say it again, you made me wait so long for this," he whispers against my lips.

I lean forward to catch his lips, but he pulls back, and a sexy little chuckle fills the space between us.

"I want you to need this, to crave this as much as I do. I want you to feel the weeks of need that I have felt waiting for you," he whispers as his cock jumps against the apex of my thighs. I moan when I feel how much he's loving this torture.

He smirks, but his eyes stay locked on mine, waiting for the words.

"Please," I whisper as I catch his bottom lip with my teeth. His breath becomes ragged, but he doesn't budge. My hands hold his face as he lingers above me. I stare hard into those gemstone eyes that make me lose control.

"Ryker, I *need* you to fuck me, please, please," I plead.

Truthfully, I may die if he doesn't appease this ache between my thighs.

He lifts me just long enough to take my shirt off. His hands quickly grip both cups of my sports bra as he pulls it in either direction, ripping the middle seam until the straps slide off my shoulders.

Passion soaks my soul and my panties. He tosses it to the side and looks me up and down as he takes me in.

"Goddammit, Maggie, you are beautiful." I try my best to hold down the red heat threatening to flush my face and neck and run my hands over his chest, realizing that I did a shitty job suppressing my blush. He sits on his knees between my legs as I lay bare on my back.

I breathe deep as I take him in.

His green eyes watch me closely as I study his features. His abs and lats ripple as he breathes shallow, hungry breaths, and his biceps pulse with intention as if he is deciding where to touch me first. His face is dark, but that damn jawline of his is still prominent even in dim lighting.

I open my mouth to comment on his beauty, but before I can manifest words, he leans his head down and kisses my chest, making me forget how to speak. His touch sends electricity through me, and I can't help but shudder under him.

The curiosity of what he wants to do to me have me almost gasping for air.

He gently sucks my left nipple into his mouth as he explores my body with his hands. I can't control my movements or moans.

I'm just a hopeless horny mess.

He uses his tongue so skillfully as he drags it across my chest to my right nipple, which is already pebbled and waiting for him. He swirls it in his mouth and uses his teeth to bite down just enough to give that perfect mix of pleasure and pain that makes me shake. I arch my back and let out a little sigh.

If only he knew how wet I was for him. He slides his hands down my hips, taking my shorts and underwear with them. His lips burn sweet heat into my skin as they drift down my abdomen. My thighs are already wet from my arousal, and I'm slightly embarrassed by how easy it was for him to make me so drenched. He branches off to each thigh, kissing every part of me he can. I can feel him smile as he feels the wetness on my thighs. My hands tangle in his hair as excitement coils inside my abdomen. He drags his teeth across my skin and bites down, marking me. He makes his way back to my center and kisses my pubic bone. His siren eyes stare up at me as he whispers,

"Say it again, sweet little fox." I'm so lust drunk that it takes me a few seconds to find the words.

"Ry, please. Please fuck me," I beg, not caring how pathetic I sound. He breathes against my sensitive skin as he descends further down. He licks my clit one time and meets my gaze again.

"You taste so fucking good," he says so damn seductively. He slides his tongue over my clit, starting slow and quickly increasing his pace, and I do my best to control my involuntary movements and noises. He moves his tongue from my clit to my opening and forces it inside me, lapping at my arousal. His pace remains strong and steady despite my incessant squirming. My hands tangle in his hair.

"Ryker... Ryker," I moan as he brings his index finger up to my entrance, teasing the tender flesh. He stops licking to glance up at me. "You are so pretty when you want me. So pretty when you beg for my cock. I wonder how pretty you'll be when you *take* me." The words send my mind spiraling in thoughts of how he'll feel inside me.

Would he even fit? Doubtful, after seeing the outline of his cock in those gray sweatpants.

Before I can resurface, he slides his finger into me.

I let out a needy whimper.

Another finger makes its way in as he tastes me and curls his fingers in that one spot that makes the world fade away. The consistency of pressure he can keep with his tongue while finger fucking me and hitting all the right places amazes me. After a few minutes, I get the sensation of needing to empty my bladder. I can feel an orgasm forming low in my abdomen. As if he can feel it, he eats me more desperately and fingers me faster and harder.

It sends me over the edge.

The room starts to spin, and my extremities go numb.

My thoughts dissipate and the only thing I can see is stars.

I feel myself release on him.

He doesn't slow down, though; he keeps going at the same pace through it all, letting me experience a mind-blowing orgasm. My thighs clamp tightly around his head.

Is it bad that I want him to drown in my pussy?

He deserves it with talent like that.

My hands grip his hair harder as I rock my hips against his face.

He comes up for air, absolutely soaked. Droplets of me drip from the untamable strands of his hair that fall into his face.

Flames of desire flare wildly in his eyes as a wicked smirk tugs at his lips. Every inch of his face glistens in the dim light.

"Did I just...?"

I can't even finish the question. Embarrassment paints me in a blush of crimson.

"Yes, you did," he confirms with a mischievous smile.

"And I'm going to make you do it again all over my cock."

He is so fucking hot.

He licks me slowly from my pussy to my abdomen and up my chest.

As he breathes against me, I feel little chills and delicious goosebumps on my skin.

He kisses me like he is drowning, and I'm the oxygen he needs.

The taste of myself bleeds onto my tongue, and my pussy pulses for him.

I break away from our kiss to slide his sweatpants down. His cock slaps my thigh as it falls from the towel, hot and throbbing. I let out an extended gasp as panic sets in when I comprehend just how huge it is. An additional ridge sits behind his massive head. Thick veins trail the sides of his girth, and I'm beginning to wonder if he's even human. He smirks and says,

"Don't worry, my sweet fox, I know you can take it."

He makes his way back to my lips, smiling against them as he feels me tense from the sensation of his cock sliding through my arousal, up my thigh, and then his broad head lining up with my entrance. He teases me for a moment as he moves his cock over my clit.

"Look at me," he commands. I do and I notice how his pupils are so dilated with excitement that only slim rings of green are visible in his eyes.

"Say it again. Tell me what you want, what you need from me." His voice is rough as he makes himself wait.

I run my hands through his hair on the back of his head. I make my eyes as sultry as shadows casted by flickering candlelight.

"Ryker, I need you to fuck me. I need to be so full of you that the only thought I have is your name. Please, please, please give me every inch of you," I whisper the plea, but never drop my gaze as he forces his huge cock into me.

The friction is so unbearably intense that I'm practically panting. I do my best to keep eye contact for as long as I can, but it feels so good that my eyes roll back. It takes the breath from my lungs, and a depraved moan escapes my mouth.

The way it stretches me is what I'd imagine it feels like to be torn in two, but in the most delectable way.

The veins on his cock seem to work in his favor adding even more pleasure to his strokes. He pulses his cock inside me stretching me wider.

I whine with each pulse he makes.

His tongue licks up the curve of my ear and he growls, "Mmm, that's my good girl."

My pussy clenches around his cock, and I know he can feel it because he becomes untamed after. His strokes become ravenous as he tears me to pieces, but he continues with little whispers of affirmation.

"You feel fucking amazing," he says through shaky breaths, followed by, "You are doing such a good job taking this cock. It's like you were made for me." I moan as heat rises in my body.

The praise he gives me makes me absolutely feral.

His hand makes its way up to my throat, and he squeezes tight enough to where my breathing becomes little squeaks, making euphoria escape into my veins. Breathing feels like it's no longer a necessity.

"Eyes on me, baby girl."

My eyes pierce into his with unfiltered desire.

"Squeeze a little harder, Ry, it's the only way I learn."

His tongue glides slowly across his dark smile, and he lets out a raspy curse.

"Fuck, baby, it sounds so good when you say shit like that."

He tightens his grip on the sides of my neck.

"Ryker..." I say breathily. My hands explore his well-defined shoulders, feeling them ripple with each of his thrusts, and I can't help but sink my nails into them. I dig and trail them down his back, making sure to leaves marks behind. He hisses through his teeth and whispers,

"If you wanted it harder, little fox, all you had to do was ask."

A mischievous smile appears on his face as he slams his lips to mine. I quickly react and nip at his lip again, dragging my teeth forcefully across the soft tissue. I draw blood, uncaring of the consequences. The metallic taste creeps across my tongue, and I can't help but moan at the taste, knowing that he will have a bruise in the morning. Instead of an audible threat, he clamps down on the lower left side of my neck. I scream from being startled but also the pain, as he physically marks me again. When he pulls up from his bite, he whispers,

"Mine." Before I can do anything in response, he latches on to my chest, roughly sucking my skin until another bruise begins to form. He remains hovered over me with his body between my thighs. He watches me and studies my face. My thoughts are formed, but no words escape, just moans of pleasure. He nips my ear lobe and whispers, "You are mine. Say it." I ignore his command, and he withdraws himself from me.

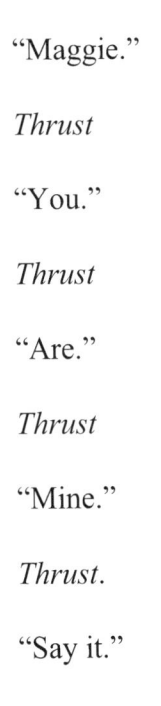

"Maggie."

Thrust

"You."

Thrust

"Are."

Thrust

"Mine."

Thrust.

"Say it."

His thrusts are deep and brutal until he withdraws entirely. He lets his cock rest just outside my pussy, refusing to give anymore until I acknowledge that he has claimed me. I need more, I need him.

One word escapes my lips,

"Yours."

"That's my perfect girl," he whispers, gripping my throat again. He slams back into me. My noises are involuntary and shaky at this point as he continues his pace. I'm so full when he's inside me, but I want more. *I want him so deep in me that I can feel his cock ever so slowly push the air out of my lungs.*

"Fuck, Maggie, you feel so fucking good," he says, interlocking his fingers with mine as he presses the backs of my hands into the pillow on either side of my head. The world starts to go black again, and I can feel the same sensation I had while he was eating me.

"Ry, I'm going to—" I can't find the words, as his thrusts make basic English difficult to speak. He smirks, feeling me tighten around his length, and says, "I know, baby, I know," as my body tenses under him.

My release rips through me, stealing every bit of composure I have. My extremities tingle as purple sparks emit from my hands. His eyes widen as he watches me, but he doesn't ask questions and I'm so grateful. I don't care if I turn blue, I never want him to stop.

He slows his hips to let me enjoy the orgasm in its entirety, but the sheer size of his cock keeps it going. I let out a loud scream. I feel like I'm levitating off the bed, but his hands hold me down like a weight on a balloon full of helium.

My breathing is heavy as I return to earth. His eyes meet mine, and his lips curl into a smile. He whispers, "That's my good girl," before patting my cheek. He puts his lips to mine and leans up.

He withdraws himself and flips me over.

It happened so fast.

The physical emptiness I feel from the absence of his cock is haunting.

He bites my left ass cheek, before he enters me again. Stone hands lock my hips in a bruising grip, as I bury my screams of pleasure in my pillow.

"Baby girl..." he moans. The words make me come undone.

I didn't think I could be anymore turned on, but that fucking did me in.

My hands are gripping the sheets so hard I feel my fingernails rip a small hole in the thin fabric. The spots that his dick finds inside me are places that I didn't even know existed. A sting sets in on my right ass cheek as he spanks me. It makes me wetter, and I can't help but want more.

"Harder," I demand. He not only spanks me harder, but he thrusts harder inside me. He runs one hand up my back, up the nape of my neck, and fists my hair, pulling back just enough to make my head tilt toward him. He finds my ear with his mouth. "You are mine. You belong to me, Maggie." The words feel as soft as cashmere as they roll from his mouth effortlessly.

"Do you want me to use you, little fox? I want to come so deep in your sweet pussy and fill you like the cum dump you are."

My breath hitches and the words scratch a kink I didn't know I had.

I assume that it doesn't matter if he fills me because I haven't had a period since I was injected with chemical 1837. I would be willing to bet that the substance burnt up every egg that my ovaries had.

"Use me, Ry," I order back. He lightly licks the helix of my left ear before he drops my hair and pushes my face back into the pillow. He holds me there while his other hand steadies back on my hip. His hips stutter against my ass as he keeps every inch of himself inside me. A raw moan echoes through the room as he finds his release. It's a sound that makes me shiver. I want to hear him do it again and again. Every pulse of his dick stretches me as I revel in the way his cum fills me. He softly kisses the small of my back as he slowly pumps in and out of me, making sure I get every drop of him like I asked for.

Feeling him pull out of me, he collapses beside me. I roll over to where my head rests on his chest. My fingers trail across his skin, seeming to sizzle against the inferno of his flesh. Before he can say anything, I catch his lips between mine and say, "I never wanted you to leave." He leans in to kiss me.

"I know," he says as he smiles against my maw.

I melt at that and melt into him.

27

RYKER:

REDEMPTION

I did not think I was capable of experiencing love, but Maggie's head on my chest is the closest I imagine I've ever been to it. I've wanted her so badly for what feels like years, but it's only been weeks. How she looked at me last night made me want to beg to love her. To be next to her, to feel her breathe, to kiss her feels like pure divinity.

Even if our broken and missing pieces don't fit, I will make them fit. We will never be apart again. I have nothing and no one to return to, but I may have a fresh start here. I have never wanted something as much as I crave Maggie's love. Given the current state of the world, finding a glimmer of hope for happiness is worth holding onto.

Last night replays in my mind. She turns primal and selfish when she's wet, and I want to spend eternity chasing that side of her.

As far as I'm concerned, my life's purpose is her, even if I never get to touch her again.

As I brush the hair out of her face and behind her ear, I come to terms with the fact that Maggie is my home, my heaven, and I will do everything I can to protect her from our cruel world.

Her eyes flutter open, and I do my best to hide the boner I've gotten thinking about her last night. She looks up at me and whispers, "Good morning," followed by a smile and burying her face back in my chest. I can see the medium-sized purple hickey I created last night. I run my finger over my lip and feel the soreness from her bites. She wanted to show me she could be the big bad wolf, too. She's not close to that, but I'll let her think that for now.

I think she's afraid of losing control. She doesn't realize that she will never lose power in our relationship. If anything, she now has all the control over me and my actions.

Her soft lips graze against mine as if to tease me. She goes to pull away, but I grab her face and kiss her hard.

I need her like I need to fucking breathe.

I slide into some sweatpants after I wake, as there is a slight draft in the cabin this morning.

I round the corner making my way into the kitchen. Maggie's onyx hair cascades across the table as she leans in toward her little book. She nips at the inside of her cheek as she concentrates on every stroke of her pencil. Her cup of coffee steams next to her, but it looks untouched as her eyes never leave her illustration.

How have men looked at her in the past, and not seen everything they could ever want? She's intelligent, cunning, adventurous, talented, and she's so damn gorgeous. I would do anything for her, to have her, to be hers.

"And just what will you plan to name that one?" I inquire walking over to pour myself a cup of coffee.

She jumps at the sound of my voice as it breaks her unwavering attentiveness.

"What did you say?" she asks as she tucks her hair behind her ear.

"I asked you what you plan to name the beast you're drawing." I respond.

"How do you know what I'm doing?" she queries, confusion writing itself into her facial features.

I perch myself behind her so I can get a glimpse at her work from over her shoulder. My fingers caress her hair as I move it to expose her neck. I lean in to hover over the shell of her ear and whisper, "Now what kind of stalker would I be if I didn't know?" She shivers as I place a kiss gently behind her ear. I continue as heat flushes her neck, leaning away slightly, returning my tone to a less provocative one, "Are you drawing that centipede thing from yesterday?"

She nods before responding, "I'm torn between Terror treads or Slinkspine." My head tilts from side to side as I contemplate the names.

"I think Slinkspine just sounds like a creepy crawly thing, so that has my vote." She nods as she writes the name underneath the almost finished sketch.

"Slinkspine it is then."

A calm silence begins to form between us but is swiftly broken by a loud crash and growl reverberating from the fire pit area on the backside of the house. Cerberus beats us both to the window. Peering through it, I see a familiar beast.

It has four front legs, each with rotting flesh hanging from them, exposed bone on multiple places on its body, and webbed skin melting off. Tufts of black fur cling to ill-fitting facial bones.

What I see next, stops me in my tracks.

Breath comes hard as anger and fear tense my muscles. Antlers like a deer's protrude from its head, and a scar runs from the left antler through its eye and down its face, sending adrenaline surging beneath my skin. This is the same beast that attacked my fellow soldiers and I a few weeks ago.

Without hesitation, I enter my bedroom, put my equipment on, and slide my mask in position over my face. The mask is a necessity for me, and honestly, I haven't taken on an opponent without it since I have been in the military, other than the creature Maggie and I took on yesterday.

But today is different. This is a battle I must win to not only avenge my squadron but also protect other people who could get lost in these woods.

Maggie meets me at the front door, confused.

"Why all the attire? We can just wait it out. It's likely just passing through," she says as she tries to reassure me.

"That's what took out my entire team when we first arrived here. I have to prevent it from killing anyone else."

I slide my hand up the side of her face and gently tuck her hair behind her ear.

"I can't have it coming after you. I finally have you." I smile lightly before continuing.

"I also can't have this thing killing innocent people who get lost out here. I was lucky, but no one else was, and I won't risk it again." As a man who has studied animals for years, I know animals are not evil. They are trying to survive just like humans, but this one poses a danger to the ones I love, and I must protect the things that matter most to me.

Where my hand rests on her neck, I can feel her pulse increase. Her eyes lock on mine, and like a damn mind reader, I can see her thoughts.

"I'm coming with you."

"No, it's too dangerous," I warn without hesitation. She stares at me, refusing to back down.

"Ummm, are we just going to pretend like I wasn't a total bad ass yesterday? I don't know if you've realized this, but I can take care of myself. I did it for a long time before you came along." She raises an eyebrow, and I realize her rebellious characteristics will prevent me from winning this argument.

"Fine, but you do what I say when I say it. Do you understand me?"

"We'll see," she teases with a wink as she goes to put her gear on. She comes back dressed in a black low-cut tank top. Her nipples show through just enough, and it takes everything I have not to throw her down and show her what it's like to not be in control. She has camouflage cargo pants that compliment her ass, and her tank top is tucked into a belt around her hips, holstering her favorite weapons. I assume she has fingerless gloves on for holding onto rope, as she did yesterday. And finally, my favorite part is that she has a beautiful pair of Doc Martens on. They are black leather, with the words "skull crusher" displayed along the side. The sight of her makes me want to fucking tear her apart.

She sparks something in me. Something that makes me ravenous and unhinged, but also controlled and calm.

She makes me as unpredictable as the ocean. I have to work so hard to control myself when she is next to me.

"Skull crusher, huh?"

She giggles. "Yeah, I've only crushed skulls once or twice, but I thought it sounded intimidating, so I stitched the words with a needle and some white thread I found in my nightstand." I laugh. "You're just a jack of all trades, aren't you? Any other talents I need to know about?"

"Not at the moment, but I'm sure you'll see that I definitely have other… skills," she answers tauntingly. I smile and can only imagine the possibilities of what she's hinting at.

We walk outside to the same eerie silence I experienced during the first encounter with this creature. Her footsteps are calculated and totally in sync with mine. My pace is fast and light. Cerberus follows by our side, intensely focusing on the beast before us.

I look at Maggie and whisper, "My first rendezvous with this creature revealed that it's blind. However, its hearing is impeccable, so do your best to stay quiet." She nods in understanding and motions to the left side of the thing. Cerberus and her exchange a glance and she holds her finger up to her lips to signal Cerberus to remain as quiet as possible. She and Cerberus split up from me, and I cover the beast's right side. Maggie understands this is my fight, but she is here for support and assistance if needed.

I fucking love her for that.

I look over to see Maggie in position and loading her crossbow. Cerberus is in a stance that indicates she is ready for attack at Maggie's call. I remove my pistol from my belt, click off the safety, load a bullet from the mag into the chamber, and prepare for the war that I'm about to wage. Sweat starts to bead on my forehead, and I try to suppress the images creeping their way into my head of Cairo's body at the feet of this monster. I nod to Maggie and take a deep breath before pulling the trigger twice, aiming at the creature's chest. The gunshots ring throughout the clearing, followed by a vicious roar.

The creature's demeanor changes quickly, becoming uncontrollable, destroying everything in its path. Its face scrunches in pain as it barrels around in a rage. Its guttural growls make unease settle in my gut.

I grab my blade with my opposite hand, ready for the fight ahead. I dodge large paws and sharp teeth. I pull the trigger of the gun again, aiming for a head shot. It moves before the bullet reaches its target. It hits the creature in the neck, and black goop begins to seep from the entrance wound.

All I've done is severely piss it off.

It perks up as it determines which direction the bullet came from. Loud stomps pound into the earth as it storms in my direction. I trip over a tree root and lose my balance. A large paw smacks me across my leg, and its sharp claws tear through my flesh, leaving long, wide, and jagged wounds. I dodge more and more angry swats until the creature leans over me completely. It stills and sniffs the air around me. Silence ensues before a howl rips through the air as it prepares to bite through me.

Nuclear

I brace for impact, but as quickly as fear comes over me, it dissipates when an arrow pierces through the creature's eye.

Maggie.

It screeches and rears back, shaking its head side to side, trying to shake the arrow out of its face. I get out of its way just before I get trampled. I briskly regain footing, limping slightly due to the pain, and missing muscle tissue. The creature charges, and by happenstance, it's headed in Maggie's direction.

Cerberus weaves through its legs, biting and gnawing at its ankles, avoiding the wrath of its claws. Maggie wraps the rope around a tall tree branch and takes off for a running start as she attempts to rebound off another tree and onto the creature's back.

My heart wretches in my chest as the branch that held her leverage breaks, and she begins to lose balance during her rebound. Before she can recover, a giant paw slaps her out of the air and onto the ground harshly. It rips through the flesh on her stomach and chest. Blood seeps through her tank top almost instantly and begins to drip to the ground. Even with the black fabric, the crimson color is prominent in the daylight. It pins her despite Cerberus trying her best to distract the beast.

No, no, no!

Not again.

I'll be damned if I lose someone else to this thing.

Rage burns through me as I slide under the beast and lift. The beast is confused and thrashing as I raise it off Maggie and toss it across the clearing. It hits two trees and causes one to uproot from the ground.

As it lays there, trying to shake off its daze, I expeditiously rush behind the tree that's close to collapsing. I push the tree toward the beast. The roots rip from the ground one by one until the weathered oak descends over the monster. Once pinned, I walk towards its head. The creature is no longer struggling under the tree but whimpering instead.

A small part of me still finds pity for the beast despite the animosity fuming inside me from all it has taken from me. It doesn't understand what it's done, it's just an animal in a very unfortunate situation. I grab my knife hard until my knuckles turn white with fury and approach the monster.

"I'm sorry, but I can't let you hurt anyone else."

I swiftly thrust the blade through the creature's skull. The dagger sinks right through the rotted bone. Bloody tar gushes and covers me. The scent of metal and decay attacks me, making nausea tumble through my stomach. When the creature stops moving completely, I remove my knife. The blade slides out of bone and tissue as easily as it went in. I wipe the dagger across my pants, and once it's somewhat clean, I place it back in its holster. I turn to find Maggie standing behind me. Gnarly, deep, jagged wounds continue to bleed, and her shirt drips blood to the ground. She needs stitches.

Nuclear

She is a mesmerizing site with the crimson color staining her clothes, chest, and cheeks. Her eyes are glazed as if her adrenaline high is starting to wear off and the pain is becoming more real. My heart throbs in my throat, and I find myself falling to my knees in front of her.

28

MAGGIE:

LOVE AND BLOOD

My chest aches as blood coats my body in thin waterfalls. I get up to see Ryker has slain his beast. A look of relief washes over his face as he has just killed the demon that has been haunting his nightmares for the last few weeks. When I get to my feet, I find myself to be unbalanced and stumbling slightly as I try to shake off the weight of sensory overload. The blood loss still makes me a little dizzy. I walk over to him, letting him have his moment of triumph. Something about that damn mask and the blood splattered on his body makes my pussy throb for him.

I want him.

His eyes meet mine, and he is visibly relieved that I'm able to walk away with my injuries. The longer I gaze into his emerald pools, relief turns to need.

Nuclear

Need for me.

Before words can leave my mouth, his lips are already crashing into mine, creating a kiss full of words when there aren't any. My mouth is slightly parted, and he slides his tongue past the threshold of my lips, swirling it in sync with mine. His mask rubs my nose slightly, while his stubble tickles my face. I can feel the blood on both of our faces smear as neither one of us breaks away from this kiss. I moan into his mouth, and his kiss gets harder, like he is trying to suck the air from my lungs.

All the hate, love, and passion surge as my nails dig into his muscular arms, leaving crescent-shaped marks. Without breaking our kiss, he swiftly undoes my belt and pulls my pants to my ankles, which I kick aside. I reach down to unbutton his pants, freeing his cock.

Honestly, I don't think I'll ever get used to the size of it or how it feels between my thighs.

He lifts me and wraps my legs around his waist. His cock rests right below my pussy and I brace for an aggressive thrust into me, but instead, he slams me abruptly against a tree, forcing me to exhale. My arms wrap around his neck, and a small purple aura glows from behind him. It comes in a flash and only lasts for a second before it's gone. His warm muscles house strong metal, as he presses himself into me, leaving no space between our bodies. His eyes lock onto mine as he pulls away from our kiss, and I forget how to inhale. He places his hand on my face so his thumb rests on my cheek and his fingers rest on my neck. His thumb slowly makes its way to my lower lip as he sensually pulls it downward. He tries to move it away, but I grab his hand. I stare intensely into his deep eyes as I spiral my tongue around the tip of his thumb.

    Enthralled, he watches as I slip his digit further into my mouth. His eyes roll back as I suck his finger before pulling it out of my mouth. He squeezes my cheeks with the same hand and purrs, "I can't wait to see what that pretty little mouth can do. You, looking up at me with my cock buried in that throat, is a scene I'm sure only angels could paint." He bites his lip obviously letting his imagination run wild.

    My blood from my wounds coats his shirt as he presses against me. The pressure of his chest makes the injuries throb, but I don't care. I know if I told him that they hurt, he'd stop, and I really don't want that. I want the wild creature in his eyes, and the dark need begging for me there.

    He continues to hold my face as he waits to watch me take his cock. He pushes it in slow, letting me feel every inch. His eyes never leave my face as he watches me take the first couple of strokes while he stretches me. Once he is all the way inside, he leans to my ear and snarls, "Good fucking girl." His deep, raspy voice makes my pussy tighten around him. He nips my bottom lip as if to make mine match his. My swollen lips ache as he refuses to let them recover from the bruising power of his mouth. As he forces himself deeper, I realize that this is more primal than making love. This is raw and rough. This isn't just rough, this is hate. This is pure passion and need.

Sheer fire consumes my thoughts, burning away all the negative emotions I feel for him, only leaving behind one thing.

Dark devotion.

All I want is for him to have me. Any way his heart desires.

The rough bark of the tree scratches my back as I try to decide whether to grip onto it or lose my hands in his anatomy. I moan feverishly in between his name breathlessly leaving my lips. My body is sore from my bleeding wounds, but the overwhelming need to be devoured by him is the only thing that matters. His fingers trail down to my clit, where he rubs me with just enough pressure to make the world start to blur.

"Ryker..." I whisper and feel his grip and thrusts become harder.

"Yes, baby, say my name," he pants into my ear. My nails tear through the flesh and scars on his back, and he hisses through his teeth in pleasure. An orgasm starts to build inside me as he continues to hit that spot that sends tingles through my body. His lips trail my neck, and he bites sharply down on my shoulder. The sensations of pleasure and pain are too much for me. His lips return to my ear, and he says, "I want you to cum on me, little fox."

His cock is too much, but not enough at the same time. I want more even though I don't think more could fit. He gives another thrust all the way to the hilt, and all I can feel is intense pleasure burning me from the inside out.

"Please, baby girl," he says, sending me toppling over the edge, into the abyss known as ecstasy.

My orgasm begins to tear through me as his fingers leave my clit and wrap firmly around my throat. His grip secures me to the tree behind me, and he tightens it as screams try to escape. High pitched snuffed squeals of satisfaction are the only things that leave my throat.

His hand is a necklace that I want to wear forever.

The endorphins I feel are otherworldly as he continues his thrusts at an unrelenting pace. Stars cloud my vision as it blackens around the edges while I peak in my climax.

As I come back down, his grasp on my throat doesn't give. He pounds into me harder and faster, and his hold on my thigh and my throat become aggressive as black threatens the edges of my vision. Small whimpers escape me in little breaths as the oxygen in my body is replaced by the biggest cock I've ever seen. His hips stutter as his body gets impossibly closer. His seed streams inside me in waves as he continues to flex his cock. He lets go of my throat and leans his forehead to mine, breathing heavily.

"My sweet little fox, you drive me mad." He adorns as he lets out a sexy, dark chuckle. He kisses my forehead and changes my position in his arms to where he is carrying me with one arm under my upper back, and the other in the pit of my knees. The coppery smell of my blood lingers between us from the open wounds on my chest. It should make me sick, but it doesn't. Weirdly enough I find it hot that it's smudged across our bodies and staining both of our shirts. A morbid reminder of the passion that just ripped through us both.

His release begins to trickle out of me, and I try to hide how aroused it makes me. Being used for his pleasure is something that makes me want to combust.

He grabs both sets of our pants and I say, "Cerberus, come on," over his shoulder in a breathy tone as we head inside.

He turns the shower on and sets me on my feet, ensuring I have my balance before letting go. My legs shake from exhaustion and euphoria as feeling starts to come back to them. He helps me undress my top half, avoiding my injuries to the best of his abilities. Once the water is warm, he encourages me to get into the shower, not far behind in getting in himself.

The water stings my wounds, and I suck in a breath through barred teeth. He looks up in concern before bringing himself into the shower.

"Are you okay, love?" he asks wrapping his arms around me slowly from behind, trying to be mindful of the rips in my skin. I feel him crane his neck over my shoulder to make sure his grip doesn't rest on them. Trails of black and crimson swirl in the bottom of the shower as they travel down the drain.

"I've had worse," I confirm with a shrug, while he gets a washcloth. He lathers it with soap and ever so gently begins to scrub the blood from my body. I bar my teeth hard as to not let on just how much it hurts.

"Unclench your jaw, baby girl. There's no shame in showing pain. You'll give yourself a headache with how tense your jaw is."

I release my tight facial muscles and squeeze my fist instead.

"Those are probably going to need stitches, Maggie. They are still bleeding," he observes with empathy. I turn and look at him before asking, "How good is your suturing? Not to brag, but mine is pretty great." I laugh and reference the scar on my face as I trail my fingers across it. As if he can feel my insecurity, he kisses the permanent reminder.

"I'm pretty good, but knowing you and your independent ass, you'll do it yourself."

I roll my eyes; even though he's right, I probably will.

I'm not used to anyone caring for me, so why start now?

How would I let him even if I wanted to?

I look down at his calf and notice a couple of deep gashes that are still oozing blood.

"I don't think I'm the only one who needs stitches," I say. He smiles and replies, "I can't wait for my favorite nurse to doctor me up then." My chest feels warm; he has a knack of causing that to happen. "I could never be a nurse. My bedside manner would be terrible," I joke. I take the washcloth from him and begin to clean my blood from his chest.

Nuclear

"What can I say, I like my bedside manner rough."

I shake my head with a small smile that turns my lips up at the edges. His muscles don't give even a little when I press into him. The man has to be some kind of cyborg with metal that tough under his skin. Since I physically have so much metal in my body, I can't help but wonder which parts of him are real or robotic. He watches me as I scrub his upper half.

I love the way he's always watching me as weird as that may sound.

"Let me see that calf," I lightly demand as I get more soap and form a healthy lather on the cloth.

"I can get that, love—"

Before he can finish that thought, I'm already on my knees in the shower. I study the wounds closely, recounting how the claws tore through his flesh. I begin to clean around the wounds as best I can, trying to not hurt him.

He never winced.

"While you're down there..." he purposefully trails off, looking down at me with a mischievous smile. I laugh, but don't dismiss him. I look up at him and kiss the head of his penis. He lets out a small sigh, followed by, "I was joking, but don't you dare tease me like that. I will tear you apart." He's obviously holding back from touching me, I assume because of the wounds and the rough sex we just had, otherwise I know his hand would have been in my hair. I stand up and rinse the washcloth before I respond, "But Ry, you make it so easy to tease you." I bite my bottom lip.

"I want to watch you come undone," I say as I push him back against the wall with my hands on his iron chest. Our bodies rest half in water and half out.

"Bite that lip again, I fucking dare you," he threatens with dark eyes.

My eyes wonder the expanse of his body, while I fold my lip between my teeth.

He grabs my face and squishes my cheeks. "You're playing a dangerous game, love."

"I guess it's a good thing I know how to win," I remark, breathing confidence on his lips.

I kiss him with heat that could solder even the toughest metals together. My tongue ventures into his mouth, and I feel like a teenager with how much I don't want this make-out session to end. His hands trace the curves of my body, and that alone keeps me warm. His touch is static, leaving sensations on my skin that make me shiver. Abruptly, he pulls my waist into him, never dropping our kiss.

I move my lips to his cheek, chin, neck, and chest, leaving little bites in between. He watches me closely, unsure of my next move, but I want control this time. I trail my fingers down his abdomen as I kneel before him. I find myself eye level with his monstrous cock. A bead of pre-cum shines on his tip. I look up at him, and he stares at me, watching and waiting. I lick his tip savoring the salty, bitter, and sweet taste of him. I swirl my tongue on his head before taking him deeper and deeper. His head kicks back and the moans he lets out make me drip for him. I stroke him faster until he is squirming with pleasure. His hand tangles in the hair at the nape of my neck. He pulls himself out of my mouth, holding me in place. Saliva webs the gap between my lips and his broad head.

"Do you like that? Do you like being in control?" he asks, pure seduction clinging to his words. I nod with what little range of motion I have.

"It's too bad that you chose to bite that lip, otherwise, I'd let you have the control you're too afraid to ask for." Before I can object, he thrusts deep into my mouth, face-fucking me hard enough that I have to time my breaths. The loud smacking echoes in the shower as he maintains a brutal pace, making tears sting my eyes. The tears that fall vanish almost immediately into the water that cascades over my face. His eyes roll back as he swoons. "Fuck, baby girl, you feel like fucking Eden." The words make me quiver, as he pushes his cock so far down my throat that I gag. He holds himself there and pulses it, making me drool. My pussy screams for him again as he uses me. As he goes to withdrawal himself from blocking my airway, I drag my teeth just slightly, not enough to hurt, but enough to remind him that I can be a brat. He lets out a dark laugh before grabbing my throat, leaning down, and raking his teeth across my mess of a bottom lip.

"That wasn't very nice," he taunts. "Just trying to win the game to let you know who's actually in control," I whisper with a smirk.

Instead of challenging me further, he slides down onto the tile bench in the shower. His eyes catch on the tattoo on my wrist with an emotion I can't discern before quickly focusing back on me. I pull away from his heat with protest from him and reach over to the small knife in my pants pocket, just outside the shower. I spread my thighs and sit on his bare lap, our most intimate parts resting against each other. I kiss him firmly when I return, and he sucks my lips and tongue in ways that could make anyone blush. I feel his cock harden to steel between my legs as I rock into him. I open the knife and lay the blade on his chest.

"Would you bleed for me, Ry?"

His eyes widen in almost disbelief, but he doesn't hesitate to respond.

"Of course, I would," he marvels with sincerity. He grabs the side of my face and wraps the other hand around my grip on the knife. Without breaking eye contact with me, he presses the blade into his flesh and guides my hand over his heart. We guide the knife like a Ouija planchette, unsure who is actually moving the blade but already certain of what the marks will be. Together, we carve four lines in his skin, and he never once flinches at the pain.

When he pulls my hand away, I drop the bloodied knife to the shower floor. There, on his chest, is a perfectly carved "M." Little rivers of red flow over his skin and to the floor as the water rushes over the new wound, and I lean down to kiss it. He groans in response and lifts my hips slightly so he can position his cock perfectly for me to sit on. I hesitate and stare at him. The metallic taste of blood starts to become prominent across my taste buds, which is becoming a familiar taste of intoxicating poison, drawing me back to him.

"Sit down, Maggie," he commands. I slowly begin to sit on his length, easing him inside me. His head penetrates me, and I swirl my hips on it as I begin to descend inch by inch. He hisses as I slide down him. It takes me a few strokes before I'm able to take all of him. After I'm fully seated, I try and steady my breathing from the sensation of his cock stretching my tight cunt. He opens his mouth to release another demand, but I raise up quickly, making his eyes close. "Shh... Let me take care of you," I whisper. I work his cock inside me, riding it at a faster pace, supporting my weight with my hands planted firmly on his chest. I bounce my ass on him over and over again, feeling his cock pulse inside me. I grind my clit hard into his length as I continue my pattern.

"Oh my God!" I shout as I take him deeper.

"God isn't here," he reminds me through gritted teeth.

The response makes my body feel hot and sends shock waves through my chest. The growing wetness between my thighs isn't just from the water in the shower.

"Ryker," I continue to moan. He follows suit with, "Maggie."

The way he says my name makes me brave. I reach up and wrap my hand around his throat with an uncertain grip. He looks at me in surprise but also with need before he leans into my hand, encouraging me to squeeze and take control.

I ride harder and faster until an orgasm starts to build low in my stomach. He smacks my ass hard. It makes me jump, and I loosen my grip on his throat. He does it again sharply, and the sting, mixed with the pleasure from my clit, puts me over the edge. My hands grip his pec muscles, and my nails dig into his skin, leaving behind small crescent moon imprints. He grips my wrists helping support my weight as my orgasm explodes through me. It sends me into an alternate universe of lights and leaves my ears ringing. He snarls, a low guttural sound, and takes over from beneath me, thrusting hungrily to maintain my orgasm. He pulls a nipple between his teeth, and I whimper from the sensation.

After my moment of pure bliss, he pauses. He looks me up and down before reaching to the floor to pick up my knife. The blade is now free of pigment as the water droplets glisten on it.

"Maggie." His tone is seductive and prideful like I imagine a predator would sound when it corners its prey. He presses the flat side of the blade to the skin on the left side of my chest, right over my heart, just above where the upper laceration ends.

"Would you die for me?"

"I—" I stutter, not expecting the question. I center myself and respond,

"I have nothing else to live for."

He nods, smirking as if he knew what I was going to say.

"That's my good fucking girl," he praises. He then presses the blade to my chest, hard enough to make me gasp but not hard enough to break the skin.

"Show me how pretty you can be while you bleed for me."

I hold his wrist as his hand curves around the blade, guiding him to carve his mark. He thrusts inside me, rocking his hips in a steady rhythm that makes my head fall back as he begins etching into my flesh. The blade slices through in a few different lines, as my mind tries to process the sensations and over stimulation. The wounds sting as water rushes over them, and I pant in sweet agony, no longer able to catch my breath. When he pulls the knife away, I look down to see his masterpiece. Over my heart lies an expertly carved "R." Ropes of scarlet stream down my abdomen and onto his, swirling with clear water where we are connected. He leans forward and kisses my wound just as I did him.

"So fucking pretty," he whispers as he drives deep into me, catching me by surprise. Our chests collide and in conjunction with the water falling from above us, our wounds touch mixing our blood as if creating a pact.

His hands grip my hips as hard as a vice. He speeds his pace, not letting me come up for air, and preventing me from maintaining the control that I've so desperately tried to keep. I grind my clit against him, letting him do most of the work. His hips slow as he pants and growls, "Fuck... Maggie." It makes my pussy tighten, and he sucks in a breath, indicating that he feels me.

Feels what he does to me.

He fills me once again, and I never want him to stop. I want all of his love, hate, sex, pain, and cum. Anything he has to offer, I want it. I want to be so full of him that it's indiscernible where I end and he begins. The noises he makes are incredible, and make the hollow feeling of lust come creeping back in.

I gasp at the emptiness I feel as he pulls out of me, feeling so cold and meaningless. He tangles his fingers in my hair and rests his forehead against mine.

"I love you," he murmurs as he turns the water off. It shakes me to my core, and my mind is spinning from what just happened. He wraps a towel around my shoulders, and quickly sweeps me off my feet. My mind is trying so hard to say three simple words.

Eight letters.

But the words don't come out. Not because I don't want them to, but because I'm terrified of the way I feel about him. My eyes catch on our blood mingling as it circles the drain.

"Alright, ready?" Ryker asks as he undoes the lid on the aged vodka bottle. It's not isopropyl, but it's better than nothing.

"I don't think I'll ever be ready for the burn I'm about to feel, but it probably won't even compare to the pain I felt when they injected those chemicals in me." I let out a weak chuckle following the statement. I have a towel held just above my nipple line to catch the excess vodka as he cleans the wounds.

"Let's get this over with," I say, already holding my breath.

"1, 2—" he counts as he skips three and quickly pours a generous amount of the alcohol over the four long wounds that span almost the entire length of my chest. I grind my teeth and do my best to stay composed. My muscles tense at feeling of my heart being on fire. A bead of sweat forms on my brow as the pain raises my body temperature.

"You okay, baby girl?" Ryker asks concerned. I smile lightly at him and respond, "Yeah, I'm okay, but what happened to three?" He shakes his head and laughs as he asks, "Does anyone ever say three?" I roll my eyes. He grabs a suture kit from my pack from the aircraft and pulls out a hooked needle and a braided nylon cord from its packaging.

"I'll do my best to prevent these from scarring," he reassures me.

"Ry, I'm covered in scars; I'm not afraid of a few more."

"And if I could kill every person who scarred your skin I would."

"Well, then I guess you'd have to kill yourself, too." I laugh as I playfully say the joke.

"Touche." He shakes his head.

"I think only two of these will need stitches," he reports as he manipulates the skin between each wound.

"The top and bottom ones have already started to scab over."

"Ready?" he inquires, more anxious than I am.

"Yes," I blurt out and close my eyes as he grips the frayed edges of the first laceration. I feel the needle pierce through the bottom of the wound, through my muscle, and back out above the wound. I open my eyes to make sure his square knot is good because if mine is better than his, I have to give him shit about it. He grabs the hemostats from the bag and skillfully wraps the nylon around them, pulling and securing that loop to the tail of the nylon cord on the opposite side of the wound. After performing and tightening the knot, he snips the end of the nylon close to the edge, and I have to say the suture is perfect. "Well…?" Ryker asks, waiting for my approval until he continues with the other stitches. I'm almost disappointed that they are as good as they are because I was looking forward to the jokes I had already planned.

"Eh, it's okay..." I say with a smile and a loose shrug. He looks at me and raises a brow.

"Okay, okay, it's perfect," I admit reluctantly.

"I know," he taunts, grinning from ear to ear.

"I'm going to finish you up, okay? Just let me know if you need a break."

"Yes, sir," I respond.

I place my hands behind me and lean on them, squeezing my eyes shut as he preps for the next stitch.

"Alright, here we go."

After finishing the first wound, he quickly moves to the second. He is deep in concentration, biting the side of his cheek as he meticulously maneuvers the needle.

"Ry?" He pauses, and glances up from his work.

"Yes, little fox?"

"How do you know you love me? That's such a big word for only knowing me of me for a few weeks, but actually knowing me as a person for a few days." He sighs but continues suturing, making eye contact frequently. His concentration and accuracy of stitching never falters as he says, "I think you can fall in love with someone for all the right reasons, but that's not the type of love that lasts. My demons find refuge in you, and just the sight of you calms the angry seas that rage in me. To truly love someone means embracing their darkest parts. You could never push me away; I recognize your darkness, and I wouldn't want you any differently. I crave for you to love me back, but I just need you to exist to give my beating heart a purpose. My love for you owns my bones, and when my time on earth is done, my soul is yours to take." He finishes a stitch, and lets the needle hang from the cord entangled in my skin. His hands hold my face tightly as he stares into my eyes. I feel like he is reaching for my soul as his dilated pupils bore into mine. His lips rest close enough to graze mine, but not close enough to kiss me.

"I'll give you the fucking world. All of it," he whispers against my lips.

"Whatever you ask for is yours. I'll hold your hand and set the world ablaze to help you find your peace. That's how I know I love you."

Tears fill my eyes, and slowly drift down my flushed cheeks. At a loss for words, I press my lips to his so hard that my swollen, bruised lips throb. The man has a way of stealing my breath and my words. I pull away and rest my head against his breathing heavily, trying not to bawl.

I've never felt so *alive*.

He kisses my forehead before returning to my ravaged chest. The wounds no longer seep blood, but instead have begun to coagulate. He grips the needle and hemostats and resumes his intricate work. To see such a large man, maneuver such a gentle and delicate process is an odd sight, but it's comforting. His large and well-muscled hands are something you'd expect to see on a man in the construction industry, but he manages such dexterous work as if he's done it a million times. He continues his stitching just as feverishly as a spider rebuilding its web.

"Finished!" he exclaims as he snips the last stitch with the scissors.

"Honestly, that wasn't that bad," I remark. He picks up the towel and soaks a little vodka into the edge of it, and runs the disintegrating fabric around the wounds, cleaning the rest of the dried blood from my skin.

"Thank you."

"You're welcome, my little vixen."

"Well, let's take a look at that calf, Ry." He lays face down on the bed.

"Damn, if you weren't wounded, I could take advantage of you in that position," I joke.

"It wouldn't be taking advantage of me if I asked you to do it."

He replies without skipping a beat. My heart races and I smile but don't respond. He turns to look back at me. "Ah, I knew that would make you blush." He smiles to himself.

"You got me," I acknowledge as I start prepping the braided nylon.

"Won't be the last time." He winks at me as he settles his head back on the pillow.

"Okay, okay. You ready?"

"Yes, just move quickly, and I'll let you know if I need a break." He breathes in slow and controlled breaths as if preparing himself for how painful this is going to be.

"Yes, sir," I mumble with a sarcastic salute. I grab a towel and place it under his calf to catch the runoff of vodka, while having another towel handy to dry his wounds if needed. I pour the cheap liquor over his lacerations, trying to focus on the deepest parts of them. He only has three, but all of them need stitches. They are gouged and still slowly oozing blood. Clear liquid trails down his leg as it mixes with dry, cracked maroon blood stains on his skin. I let the vodka sit for a minute before starting to fit the jagged edges of them back together. I grab the needle and force it through his tissue. The needle pops through easily, making this process much faster for us both. I close the first part of the wound with a square knot, and clip the nylon cord, moving to the second stitch. I repeated this process on all three wounds thirty-nine times. We sit in blissful silence, just enjoying each other's company.

"Finished," I announce as I wipe his skin clean, just as he did for me.

We have *literally* sat on this bed together and sutured each other's wounds.

Not only has this random man walked into my life and started to pick up my pieces, but I'm realizing he is broken in all the same ways I am. I can't help but think that I'm fixing

Nuclear

something in him the way he is fixing something in me. I never thought I could love someone or find some kind of happiness again, but I may have found something close. I breathe deeply, enjoying these moments as we heal each other physically, emotionally, and mentally.

I guess the apocalypse is the best time to catch feelings for your stalker.

My mind replays our self-inflicted wounds touching and our blood mixing as it circled the drain. He's gotten into my bloodstream, and I'm not sure I'll ever be able to shake him.

29

RYKER:

STRANGE GLOW

I feel so guilty as I hold her tonight. Her body curves into mine, and her warmth radiates against my skin like a roaring furnace. When we showered earlier, I noticed the tattoo on her wrist. Honestly, I hadn't even thought to look for it because that number means nothing to me.

She's Maggie to me, and that's all she ever will be.

But the number on her wrist is 416.

My last mission was to obtain target 416.

My little fox was my target all along.

It's eating me alive knowing that the military is actively coming for her, *hunting her* like persistent poachers, and she has no idea.

Nuclear

I couldn't tell her after everything we've been through today. I brush her hair from her face and solemnly come to the conclusion that I owe her the truth.

She deserves to know.

They sent me, and I pose no threat to her; however, I can't say the same for the next soldiers sent out. Initially, I intended not to find target 416 and find myself, but it's my luck that I would fall in love with the target. All I can do is hope that she doesn't feel betrayed if I tell her.

It's my responsibility to protect her now.

When she wakes, I have a cup of coffee ready for her, as well as an improvised version of venison sausage. She sits at the table, one foot resting on the chair, wrapping her hands around the warm cup. Her oversized shirt drapes over her palms, and her adorable quirkiness fills me with warmth.

Cerberus lies lazily on the floor, and I rub her belly with my foot. Both of her tongues flop to the side as she rolls onto her back and sticks both front paws in the air. What's that saying? Pets look like their owners? Cerberus and Maggie look nothing alike, however, their personalities and actions mimic each other. Both are all bite and no bark until you get through their tough exteriors only to find the sweetest and most loyal beings.

"Where are we going?" she asks, curiosity heightening in her voice.

"If I told you, it wouldn't be a surprise, would it?" She sticks her tongue out at me and says, "I guess that's true."

"We have to arrive around sunset, so we have the day to ourselves." I smile, hinting at the possibilities. She stands and walks over to my chair. Her thighs spread across my lap as she seats herself. She wraps her arms around my neck before kissing me.

I pull away slightly and joke, "Now hang on a second, I slaved over that stove this morning to make you breakfast and you didn't even touch it." A smirk tugs at the sides of my lips. She laughs before purring, "I think there's another sausage that needs my attention this morning." I roll my eyes and smile as she intertwines her fingers with mine and encourages me toward her bedroom. I eagerly follow her like a moth into the flame. I just want her love, her heart, and her soul. The animal in me wants to take, and take, and take from her, and she will always have something to give. She will be my demise, but I'll be damned if I ever turn away from her.

"Go get ready, and we will head that way."

She sighs, frustrated that I won't break on telling her the surprise, and treads back to the bedroom to change and get dressed. She returns with her hair in two long braids framing either side of her face. Her raven hair pops the bright colors from her eyes. She is dressed in her usual attire; honestly, I never need to see her in anything else.

Nuclear

She is breathtaking as my little Skull Crusher.

"Ready!" she exclaims excitedly as she loads her crossbow and arrows on her back. Cerberus perks up when Maggie grabs the weapon. Her loyalty to Maggie is impressive. She is ready to go wherever Maggie goes and will protect her until the end, and for that I am grateful.

We travel through the thick woods, and a cool breeze blows through the forest causing chills to tease my skin. The leaves on the trees are beginning to turn all shades of reds, oranges, and yellows. The bright colors light up the forest despite the thick canopies. The leaves haven't begun to fall yet, indicating that we are still in the early stages of autumn in Appalachia. I see goosebumps creeping up Maggie's arms, and I reach forward to rub my hands up them, calming the chill with the warmth of my palms.

"Thanks," she mumbles as desire mixed with gratefulness swirl in her eyes as they catch mine.

"Oh God, don't look at me like that," I contend, biting back the passion threatening to boil over.

"Like what?" she asks confused.

"Like you need me. I can't fucking handle it," I answer, stepping closer to her. My hand trails her cheek.

"It makes me want to beg for you," I whisper, feeling lust in my chest. Her cheeks flush but not from embarrassment. Before she can respond, a loud whooshing sound from our right echoes through the trees, and I look at Maggie as my fight or flight kicks in. My hand finds my pistol within a second as I my gaze locks on her. She looks unconcerned and smiles.

"Stay calm. Just watch, Ry." The way she says my name makes my heart wild under my ribs.

Three giant Luna moths, each the length of a basketball court, fly out of the trees.

"They have very short lives because they don't have mouths, and usually only live for a week. I've only seen them one other time here. They are one of the only beautiful things left I think."

If only she knew that she falls into that category as well.

They are immaculate as they float through the air seeming to weigh nothing. Large pale green wings with dark edging fill the sky around us. Their lower wings have long tails that intertwine with one another much like her fingers do with mine. Their wings are so powerful the wind from under them makes the leaves dance on the trees as some fall carelessly to the ground. If dragons were real, the moths would probably be the same size. Cerberus whines as she sits beside an enthralled Maggie. I feel so small in this moment. The amount of color and grace that fills the clearing before us is mesmerizing, and the atmosphere makes the whole world disappear for a few minutes. They weave and twist above us as if they know they are putting on a show. They are a sight that most people probably only get to see once in a lifetime, if at all.

Nuclear

The beautiful massive insects disappear back into the lush tree canopies, making a part of me feel empty.

"Well?" she asks, a large smile spanning the entirety of her face.

"There aren't words to describe them," I marvel.

"It's all bad at this time of my life, so it's nice to have something like that to look forward to." I nod in agreement with her but respond, "That's how I feel about you, little fox." She smiles softly and kisses my cheek.

"It's my turn," I state as we approach the exit of the overbearing greenery around us, concealing the clearing directly on the other side of it. I pull back the thick branches before us, and her eyes light up as the scene comes into focus. In front of us are thousands of passionflowers of all shapes and sizes. Hues and shades of purple and blues span for miles. She walks into the flowers, hands by her sides, running her fingers through the lush petals.

"This is… Amazing." She breathes with wonderment. I follow behind her, watching her take in the scene. I pluck one of a smaller size and tuck the stem behind her ear. She looks down and digs the toe of her boot into the dirt like a schoolgirl who just got a compliment from her crush.

"You are magnificent," I purr.

"Thank you," she responds playfully. Cerberus takes off from beside her to run through the clearing, enjoying the exercise.

The sun has almost set on the horizon. Darkness grows through the clearing, and the flowers begin to glow around us as it spreads. The glow is a radioactive green and contrasts beautifully with the darkening sky. Her eyes widen and she looks at me.

"How...?" she asks, not finishing her full question and patting my shoulder in excitement. Her mismatched eyes spark emotions in me, and the craving for her begins to eat at my soul as her hand runs the expanse of my arm. The flower nestled behind her ear begins to light her face making her look of divinity.

"Radiation exposure has its perks, I guess." I shrug and smile at her trying to contain the monster creeping under my skin. I curl her back to my chest and wrap my arms around her. I breathe her in and feel her pulse race under my touch. She looks up at me with her whole body lit in the best places from the strange glow elicited by the blooms. I lean down and kiss her, soft at first, but as my need for her grows, so does the roughness of our kiss. She meets my lips with the same desire, and I feel my sanity start to come apart.

As we move and try to step into each other's skin, pollen from the flowers floats into the air and surrounds us like little stars, glowing brighter and brighter like fireflies on a warm summer night. I would be more concerned for Maggie and I's safety around such radioactive material had we both not been experimented on to resist such exposure. Although, it would probably be smart to avoid directly inhaling contaminated pollen as regular pollen is enough of an allergic nuisance on its own. There's no telling what radioactive pollen would do to our sinuses. We pull away and look around at the little galaxy we have created.

For the first time in a very long time, I can breathe and be present in this moment. My heart pounds like a blacksmith's hammer against vulnerable metal as her icy hot eyes meet mine, and my entire being rips at the seams. I lift her with ease and wrap her legs around me.

"Just feeling your eyes on me makes me so fucking wet," she murmurs against my cheek. I grasp her hair and glide my tongue into her mouth, finding hers and intertwining them. Her hands explore my shoulders and arms making a ravenous hunger for her grow inside my chest. I lay her down gently to the ground under me, in a small clearing among the flowers.

With one hand, I support my weight, and with the other, I undo the button of her pants. I trail kisses down her neck and bite down harshly, resulting in a breathy moan. My cock twitches in my pants from the way she breathes in anticipation, the way her body begs for me. I look up at her and take her shirt off slowly as I kiss down her chest and run my hands around her torso to unclasp her bra.

She's so fucking perfect.

She slides my shirt over my head, and I pin her to the ground by her throat as I lean into her ear. She breathes in sharply from surprise.

"Little fox, you have some rules tonight. I'm going to limit your vocabulary to very few words," I say. She smirks and asks in a hushed tone, "And what might those be?" I smile and respond with pure seduction against her mouth,

"Faster, slower, harder, and softer."

She bites her lower lip, and stares at me before she remarks,

"You forgot about deeper."

"That's my girl," I praise as I squeeze in on the sides of her neck. I slide her pants down, and she does the same to mine, almost in sync. My length rests against her thighs as I grind into her. A begging whimper leaves her pouty lips. Her arousal coats the apex of her thighs and glistens in the odd glow around us as I line up to her entrance. I hover my lips just above hers and watch her take my cock. I force my thick length inside her, feeling her tight pussy cling to it as I struggle to slide in and out of her. She whines as I roll my body against hers. I run my fingers down her chest, her stomach, and stop when I reach her clit. I rub with just enough pressure and a steady pace to help her edge her orgasm. She clenches around my cock, and I groan in response. She smiles, knowing what she did to me. I lean down to her ear, and whisper,

"You look so pretty with my hand around your throat."

Her eyes roll back as she wraps her hand around my wrist. Her pussy clenches tighter around me as I feel her nearing her orgasm. I thrust harder and deeper until I hit that spot that makes her back arch. Her body writhes as her release tears through her. Little hums escape her mouth and escalate into hushed screams.

"Ryker," she begs over and over through restricted whispers as she preserves her air under my relentless grip around her throat, digging her nails into my back. I can feel blood pooling in the shallow wounds. When she comes back down, I release her and pull out of her. She looks at me with confusion and disappointment.

"All in due time, little fox." I wink and roll over to my back. I fist her hair and growl,

"I want you to taste yourself."

Her eyes widen as I pull her on top of me and encourage her towards my pelvis. She licks down my stomach, her tongue searing into my flesh, and bites down on my hip, making sure to leave a bruise. I hiss through my teeth as she looks up and winks at me.

The glow of the flowers accentuates her bone structure and produces a glow in her eyes that lingers. She looks dangerous and seductive like a starving succubus ready to eat me alive.

And God, do I want her to eat me alive.

She circles my head with her tongue slowly, and my head falls back because of how good her mouth feels. She runs her tongue over my slit with just enough pressure to open it. A small groan escapes me as euphoria rushes through my veins. She swirls her tongue down my shaft and licks from base to tip before devouring me. She starts with slow strokes and quickens her pace as she takes my cock deeper. Tears build in her eyes from the size of it, but she acts unfazed. I keep a firm grip on her hair as I ask, "How do you taste, little fox?" Instead of a verbal answer, she looks up at me before stroking me faster. Spit coats me as smacking noises leave her mouth, while she milks pre-cum from me.

"You're so fucking pretty when you suck me," I rasp in affirmation. She is doing so well that she has me close to an orgasm within minutes.

I withdraw myself from her mouth, and with my thumb, I wipe the saliva off her chin and kiss her one more time. I look at her and command,

"Hands and knees, baby girl. I want to watch that pretty ass bounce on me."

She does what I say with no question. I bite her ass cheek making her jump at the sensation, before lapping at her tight ass hole. She roughly breathes out not expecting it. I kiss up to the small of her back before lining up with her sweet pussy. My cock forces its way into her cunt once again. Her breathing turns to panting as she tries to catch her breath.

"Ryker," she pants.

"Yes, baby. Say it again," I beg, loving the way my name sounds on her tongue.

Nuclear

"Ryker." My cock pulses inside her from her voice repeating my name almost in sync with the pulsing glow of the flowers. My hands squeeze her hips as I thrust myself in and out of her. "Maggie, you feel so fucking good." I reach one hand around and rub her clit intensely.

"Give me one more, please, little fox," I plead as I stimulate her from every angle possible.

"You like that, don't you?" I ask sensually from behind her.

"Yes." She breathes through gritted teeth, trying to keep herself together.

"Harder," she commands. I oblige and her whimpers become louder. Her pussy tightens, and her arousal drips down my shaft. Shaking, she screams,

"Deeper, baby, deeper."

I submerge myself until my balls slap her clit. I repeat the motion over and over until her body quivers from her orgasm. I work with her, grinding in her to maintain it as long as possible. Her legs shake, and she falls to her elbows as her arms can't support her weight any longer from the pleasure. I lay my body on top of hers, hook my arms under her trembling elbows, and wrap both of my hands around her throat. Her sounds become higher pitched as her breathing becomes shallower. I drive my cock harder and deeper into her pussy as it grips me in all the right places. My grasp tightens on her throat as I snarl her name, "Maggie," I repeat until she follows with,

"Ry, deeper, please."

With that, my hips slow, and I spill inside her. Her tight walls make me dissolve into pleasure. I pump in and out of her feeling my release drip out of her pussy. I slide out of her and let her roll to her back. She's gasping as she gestures for me to lie down next to her. I shake my head and respond with the question,

"Did I say I was done?"

Her mouth drops open as I slide my face between her thighs. I keep my eyes held to hers as I slowly lick her clit.

"Ry…" She breathes as I tease her sensitive sweet spot. She runs her hand from her breast to her stomach, to her pelvis, and then softly into my hair. I growl in response and speed up. Her head kicks back. I slide one finger into her quickly. She is soaked from the mix of her arousal and my release. It begins to pour from her as I slide in and out. I find her G-spot and curl my fingers into it, watching as her back arch from the sensation. I pull my drenched fingers from her and slide them down to her asshole. I begin to circle it teasingly. She gasps. "Wh—what are you doing?" I pull away and say, "I want all of you."

I glide my index finger slowly into her, stretching her until I'm able to ease my middle finger in as well. She sucks in a sharp breath.

"Tell me it doesn't feel good," I insist, watching her closely. She whimpers in response, and I return to licking her to make the stretching easier for her to adjust to. I can tell she's edging close to an orgasm, so I pull my fingers out quickly and kiss her pubic bone.

She looks down at me with disappointment.

"I was so close…"

"Baby, I know, but I want to watch you cum while I'm inside you. I want to feel you."

Her look changes to confusion until she feels my thick head touch her asshole.

"Ry… wait… I—I don't think I can take it."

She starts to panic, but I don't give her time to overthink it. I make sure I'm wet enough not to hurt her as I spit on the head of my cock, mixing her dampness and my saliva as I stroke it from head to hilt. I push forward, slowly stretching her, feeling her resist the urge to tighten as my head pops through her threshold.

"Baby, you take me so well. I know you can take it," I encourage. I work slowly with small, short strokes until I get past the threshold. She lets out a loud moan and clenches her jaw, while I take my time, trying to stretch her without hurting her. Once she's less tense, I continue to slide in.

Inch by inch.

"It's too much... I can't. I'm so full."

"Baby girl, I know, but you are doing so well. You're such a good girl." She lets me advance on until she completely consumes me.

"I'm so proud of you,"

I murmur as I begin to thrust back and forth. Her eyes are squeezed shut, trying to get through the pleasure soaked pain.

"Maggie." I grab her face in my hand and direct her eyes to me. "Look at me."

Her eyes open and meet mine. Blown pupils hide the majority of color in her eyes as she's overtaken by anxiety and pleasure.

"You're taking it so well. You're so pretty when you take me. Just listen to my voice. Let me talk you through it." She starts to relax as she adjusts to my length inside her. I start to increase my pace, and her breathing becomes erratic.

"How does it feel?" she asks in my ear. "Like fucking paradise," I whisper as I nip at her earlobe.

Before I can ask her how she's feeling, she begins to shriek louder, and her nails cling to my shoulders, telling me she's close to her release. Her hole grips me so well, and I can feel her stretching around me as I give her a consistent grind from my hips. Like a tightly coiled spring breaking, she explodes into a rippling orgasm. Her back arches, and she yelps as she rides out her release.

She gets so tight that I near a release myself.

As she starts to come down from hers, I bury myself deeper into her until I fall straight into pure euphoria. She runs her fingers through my hair as she lets me fill her again.

I lean down and kiss her forehead and then kiss her lips.

"I told you. I knew you could do it," I tease with a smile. She just rolls her eyes, but I know she enjoyed that too. When I pull out of her, we both lie next to each other, trying to catch our breath. It's so surreal under the stars and being illuminated with the odd glow from the flowers.

"That was amazing." She sighs, satisfied from beside me. I fit my fingers between hers and lift her hand to my lips, kissing it gently. "You are amazing. Everything about you makes this life worth living."

She blushes and cuddles into my chest before we talk for hours, watching the sky and Cerberus jump through the flowers.

I was planning to tell her everything tonight, but I want her and myself to remember this night as a positive experience, as there aren't a lot of those left anymore. I'm terrified that telling her what I now know is going to ruin things between us.

Something always ruins the good things.

I run my fingers through her hair and watch her eyes flutter in happiness.

If only I could keep my little fox this happy forever.

"Maggie, I need to talk to you about something, and I need you to hear me out before jumping to conclusions." She cocks her head to the side in confusion but sits down on the bed next to me. I reach for her hand and run my thumb over the experiment number on her wrist. She reflexively tries to pull away, and come to think of it, she always pulls away when I grab this wrist as if trying to bury the trauma displayed on it. I sigh and start to explain my epiphany.

"My squadron and I were deployed to obtain target 416. They gave us no other details except coordinates and a target number. They did not describe the target as male, female, or even human." Her eyes widen, and unfiltered panic fills them as she tries to pull her hand from mine. I don't let her remove herself from my hold yet.

"We were told that the target would be in the general location and not to return to base until we retrieved it. Maggie, I swear I didn't put it together until the other night in the shower when I saw your tattoo. I'm in love with you, and I'd do anything to protect you. I promise my intentions are pure with you. I had no idea who you were, and I was solely drawn

Nuclear

to you for your beauty, independence, and how you carry yourself." She stays silent, and her face drops.

"So, you knew two days ago and kept it from me?"

The question and the hurt look in her glassy eyes brings my heart to its knees, and she quickly rips her hand from mine.

"I wanted you to enjoy the simplicity of not worrying about running for one more day. You deserve that. I want you to know that you need to start prepping yourself. They are coming for you, and it's just a matter of time until they find us. Please tell me you removed your tracker when you ran."

"Of course I did," she snaps back at me.

"I destroyed it, too. How do they know I'm still alive?"

She looks to me for answers that I don't have.

"I don't know. As I said, I knew the coordinates and your experiment number. I do know they have a high bounty on your head, too. You are one of the only experiments that retained multiple skills from experimentation. You are also the only female I have seen who survived everything. I truly didn't suspect you to be 416 because I have not seen a female soldier since before I was in that hell hole myself. Knowing what they did to me, they probably want to study you to duplicate your results in other people, especially women." She sucks in a sorrowful breath, tears well in her eyes, and my heart feels like it's going to explode from her anguish.

She looks away from me, trying to conceal her fear. I reach down and lift her chin to look at me as tears begin to trail down her cheeks. She tries to flinch away from my touch as my thumb strokes her face.

"Don't hide from me," I whisper, wanting her to know she's safe to show her emotions. She leans into my hand after I say the words.

"Baby girl, I escaped, too. I have no plans of returning. You and Cerberus are my life now. I will never leave you. I will do everything I can to protect you, even if that means sacrificing my life." Her tears stream faster, and sobs begin to escape her.

"I refuse to go back there and endure more torture, Ry. They will have to kill me because I am never going back." Dread covers her face. Rightfully so, too.

The scientists and military are cruel, brutal, and unforgiving. She reaches her hand to my wrist and points to my experiment number.

"830," she mumbles. "This number means nothing. You are Ryker to me—" I cut her off, and my hand caresses her face.

"You are Maggie. A strong, independent, stubborn, and beautiful woman who holds my heart in her hands. I love you." She hesitates but leans into the heat of my hand. She doesn't say it back, and that's okay for now. She didn't say it back in the shower either, but I would do anything just to hear those

Nuclear

words leave her lips. She doesn't want her heart to get hurt, and I understand.

She'll say it when she's ready.

The thing about Maggie is that when she's hurt, she's dangerous to herself. She could easily set the world on fire, but instead, she internalizes her pain and wages war on herself. Love is a new aspect of her life, and I have to respect how much pain she has endured in the past.

I know she loves me, but how can she truly love me until she loves herself? Based on our conversation of her time in the military, she seems to harbor a lot of shame and horror from being experimented on and used, making it hard for her to be comfortable in her own skin.

I will patiently wait for her to say it back.

After all, we have all the time in the world.

I pull her in close, and she collapses against me, sobbing so hard that my heart starts to physically break leaving a hollow sensation behind.

"I'm scared." I lean to her lips and kiss her softly. Her salty tears stain my lips when I pull away.

"I know, baby girl, but I will find you. If they come for you and take you from me, I will kill everyone who ever laid a hand on you. I will rip their heads from their bodies and stomp their corpses. There will be nothing left of them. In a thousand lifetimes, I will always find you. There is no where you can hide or be hidden that I won't find you," I remark, leaning my forehead against hers.

Why can't we just stay like this forever?

Just us in the wreckage of a broken world.

30

MAGGIE:

PREPARATION

"Maggie?" Ry asks from across the table.

"You've been swirling your spoon in your coffee for five minutes while staring at the wall. Where is your mind, love?"

Great question: where is my mind?

The weight of impending doom crushes the rest of my thoughts. It's as if the reaper holds my hourglass, and he's patiently awaiting the last grain of sand. No matter what I do, I can't seem to escape capture.

I'm afraid I'll always be running. The good only seems to be temporary for me.

I can't seem to stop obsessing over the negative.

"Honestly, Ry, I can't stop thinking about what will happen if they take me again. They will be tougher on me and make sure I conform this time. My freedom feels like an hourglass teetering to the end of its contents." He's silent for a beat and then responds, "I know it's impossible not to think about it, but Maggie, it has been a week since we talked about this. I don't want you to live in fear of the slight possibility the government will find you out here. It's going to cause you to have a nervous breakdown." He sighs.

"I'll tell you what: let's plan to set up traps around the premises to ensure we at least get a warning before they sneak up on us. Does that sound okay to you?" I contemplate the plan he's putting forward.

"That may be the only thing that will help me relax a little," I mutter, not making eye contact with him, continuing to fidget with the spoon in my morning coffee.

"I noticed when I started living here that there are traps and hunting equipment in the cellar. That's where my infamous crossbow came from." I smile. He laughs and beams,

"There's my little fox. It's nice to see you smile. We will lay traps at dusk when the temperature starts to cool off. Is that okay?" I nod.

"Thank you," I respond with sincerity.

"You're welcome, love. I'm only happy if you're happy," he promises, making me smile even bigger. He walks over and leans down to kiss me. He softly brushes my lips, sending electricity through me. He presses his lips into mine before pulling away and looking at me. His green eyes swirl with concern and an emotion that I think is love. He runs his thumb down my cheek and nods, confirming that he is looking out for me.

"Come on, Cerberus," he chimes, grabbing the tennis ball from the counter.

"Let's go play." She hurries behind him, prancing with excitement.

Dusk arrives swiftly, a reminder of the borrowed time I'm on; the days slip by faster than I can keep up. We head down to the cellar, where a musty smell hits me as we open the door. The concrete room is dimly lit by a single pull light.

Cracks trail along the walls, indicating its age. The air is cooler than it is outside. The lighting is a dim pale yellow and only spans through the middle of the room. The corners of the cellar are still dark, seeming to conceal secrets in their expanse. It looks like monsters will crawl out of the darkness at any moment. The great thing is that I have night vision, so I can rule out monsters as I descend the cobblestone stairs.

Cerberus stays at the door to keep guard while Ryker and I gather several weapons, traps, etc.

"Damn, these people were ready to catch anything," he marvels, looking around like a kid in a candy store.

I reach for some netting and rope to make spring traps like you used to see in the cartoons.

You know what I mean, right? A person steps on the net under a pile of leaves, and the net swallows them as the rope cinches the net closed, and they dangle like a fish being pulled out of the ocean by an excited fisherman.

"Mags! Look!"

He grabs three bear traps and eagerly shows them to me.

"If any of those idiots step on these, well, needless to say, it'll fulfill our intentions." He winks.

"You're right, and I'm glad you are strong enough to set those."

He chuckles. "And don't you forget it. I'm not doubting you, but you won't be coming near these bad boys."

"That's ironic because I was very tempted to set those up to catch my stalker out in the woods." I wink and crack a wide smile.

"You're so cute acting like I wouldn't have been watching you set those up," he retorts shaking his head as a one-sided smirk pulls at his lips.

I roll my eyes and stick out my tongue at him before I grab everything I can fit into a sack and have the super-strong man carry it up. I could do it, but it's good to stroke a man's ego every now and again.

We start by setting a trap every ten feet, ensuring they're varied enough that no two identical traps are next to each other. As we move into the tree line, we place traps about fifteen feet from the edge of the lush greenery. I set the first one, laying down netting with a rope threaded through the border of the net. I hang the rope close to a tree trunk to make it not so noticeable, and when everything is in place, I begin to disguise the trap, so you don't recognize it at first glance. Once I'm happy with how it looks, I set the spring that will trigger the trap.

"Nice job, little fox," he booms with pride.

"Thanks. You're the best cheerleader."

I laugh because he is a huge man who was definitely never on a cheer team. He makes a mocking face to me and turns to begin the next trap. He grabs a bear trap and anchors it to the ground with stakes. He wiggles his fingers into the crevice between the teeth of the rusted metal, pulls, and easily retracts the trap as he lays it in position. The trap is camouflaged well by tall blades of grass. Before he walks away, the trap snaps closed, making him jump. I can't help but snicker after making sure he's okay.

"Something about a big man getting scared and jumping out of his skin is comical to me."

He sticks his tongue out at me and responds with,

"Something about a scared girl who's powerless from her stalker makes my cock hard."

He guffaws as heat rises in my face.

I don't have a comeback for that one.

He looks down and adjusts the trap one more time, once again exhibiting no struggle. "Only twenty more traps," he says sarcastically.

I skip ahead of him, trying to return my cheeks to their previous non-reddened state.

The next trap involves a little bit more rigging.

I set a trigger wire attached to two arrows that will release simultaneously. I make sure to set the arrows a couple of feet apart vertically. That way, it increases the chance of a head shot and an ankle shot. Ryker helps me decide the best arrowheads for the most damage. We decided to use up all the mechanical broad heads before switching to another type. I have quite a few, so these should be in the majority of our traps. The mechanical broad heads are typically used for large game-like bears and are meant to pierce through flesh and bone. When the arrowhead lodges in the tissue, two securement pieces deploy from the sides of it, ensuring that it will need to be removed surgically if it doesn't create an exit wound.

Our next trap was courtesy of Ryker's mind. I don't know how many of these he and I can make, but it's pretty damn devious. I chose twenty sturdy branches from the healthy, young oak trees around us, and now I'm sharpening them to jagged points. Ryker grabs a shovel and begins to dig a giant pit. It must be the super strength, but it only takes him about thirty minutes to dig the hole. His strength allows him to uproot an insane amount of soil at each shovel scoop. He tosses each over his shoulder as if throwing a handful of sand each time. When he's happy with his work, he ushers me into it with my newly created spears. I lay the freshly whittled wood down when I reach the bottom.

Before decorating our spike pit with the weapons I created, I ask Ryker,

"How deep is this?" He smiles and responds,

"I thought it was only fitting that if this is someone's grave, that it be six feet deep."

I smile as morbid thoughts cross my mind. I walk over to him and wrap my arms around his neck.

"It's ironic because, at the end of my days, I want to be six feet under with you." He watches me carefully, licking his teeth as I continue.

"Would you fuck me in a grave? Would you spend all eternity in the dirt with me?" I ask, biting my bottom lip.

"Death is inevitable, so I might as well get comfortable, right?" His face gets serious for a second as he replies,

"When you die, we die together. I will not do this life without you, and I won't allow you to die at the hands of the people coming for you, either. A grave for you is a long time away. I can promise you that." I lean forward and glide my tongue over his lips, my dark thoughts consuming me. He snarls, slamming me against the cold muddy wall, gripping my throat until the only sound I can make is a squeak as sharp as a rusty door hinge being forced to open. Fear and excitement make my eyes dilate.

"Do I scare you, little fox?"

"Yes," I whisper breathlessly, trying to conserve my air.

"Good," he says, breathing against my ear. "Don't tease me unless you mean it," he warns quietly, never leaving my ear. He releases the tight grip around my throat but doesn't move his hand. I move my hand up to his and slide it slowly up my mouth before sliding his index finger between my lips and sucking it slowly. He lets me have this control, watching me as I drag my teeth across his finger. I pull his finger out of my mouth and let his fingers pull my bottom lip down. He leans forward to my cheek, so close that his warm breath raises goosebumps on my skin.

"I would spend all eternity chasing you and pleasing you whether we spend it buried six feet deep or through a million lifetimes. You are mine, little fox, and you will never be able to escape me. Not by running from me and not in death. I will haunt you anywhere you are."

At the last word, he nips my ear and grips my waist so hard that my legs begin to tremble.

"I fucking love it when I make you shake."

His words feel like velvet as he whispers them across my skin. He roughly tugs my pants down as he stares into my eyes, kissing me passionately as he moves my underwear to the side and glides two fingers over my slit.

"My morbid little fox, you do want this. You are so wet that your arousal is dripping down your thighs." I smile and breathe against his lips.

"I guess you could say that I'm a little fucked up." With that, he slides his fingers inside me while hungrily kissing me, refusing to let me come up for air. I moan as he curls his digits into that spot that makes me breathless. My sounds become faster and high-pitched as he keeps a merciless rhythm. An orgasm teases me as he explores my most sensitive area. It makes me slightly upset that he doesn't even have to try to make me come.

He is just so damn good with my anatomy.

The cool dirt flakes off the pit wall as I ride this man's fingers with sheer pleasure coursing through my body. My body nearly convulses as my orgasm tears through me. He continues rubbing me until I stop moving underneath his touch. "That's my girl," he praises, before pulling away from me leaving me cold and empty.

"Kneel," he demands, undoing his belt. I listen and do as I'm told. His muscular arms ripple as he messes with his buckle, making the veins in his forearms pop out from under his skin. His cock springs out of his pants as he lowers them. I reach forward to wrap my hand around his length, but he smacks my hand to the side.

"Not so fast, little fox. I didn't say I was ready for you."

I sit on my knees confused but patient despite how bad I want to taste him. He pulls his belt off from the buckle side and creates a makeshift leash by sliding the end through the buckle but not engaging the securement mechanism. My heart quakes in my chest as fear tunnels through me like a termite in fresh wood.

"Do you trust me?" he asks.

"Yes," I whisper, unsure of what to expect. The adrenaline of fear and anticipation of arousal make my heart a runaway train, thundering down wobbly tracks with unhindered force. The sensations become inextricable from one another in this moment. He puts the slipknot belt over my head and gently tugs the worn leather until it's snug around my flesh. I swallow hard, feeling the material rub against my throat as my trachea moves.

"Open your mouth," he orders. Sweat beads on my palms as my mind tries to form a thought.

Something, anything to say.

I drop my jaw slightly, leaving my mouth parted. He grabs my face with his hand and squishes my cheeks before he leans down closer to my lips and slowly drops his spit into my mouth. The warm liquid mixes with my own saliva as the taste of him becomes abundant on my tongue. I hold it in my mouth while I stare up at him.

He lets go of my face abruptly and wraps his hand around the base of his cock. Without waiting for his next command, I lean forward and run my tongue along his shaft.

"Maggie, I didn't—" I take him deeper before he can finish. Tension binds my throat from the stiff leather noose. He maintains constant traction on it, and it tightens and loosens slightly with each stroke of him. Hot tears well in my eyes as I do my best to avoid my gag reflex. I stroke him fast and deep-throat as much of him as I can. He hisses in pleasure and fists my hair, releasing his grasp on his cock. He pulls my hair as his fingers tangle in it, sending pinpricks across my scalp. Almost in punishment for not following his command, he stops my head and fucks my mouth, tightening the belt. Harder and deeper, he sinks his length into my throat until I reach the base. His soft balls graze my chin. Tears stream down my cheeks in mass amounts, and saliva drips down my chin and onto my chest as he completely takes control of me.

And I let him.

My pussy throbs from the sight of him breathing heavy and looking at the stars above us while forcing himself into me.

Enjoying me so much that he can't focus on anything else. He may have me by the throat, but I am in control of him and I fucking love it.

He moans, "Fuck, you feel so fucking good."

Unable to stop and unable to breathe, I let him find his pleasure.

I let him use me.

"You're such a good girl. You take my cock so well."

He pulls himself out of my mouth to let me catch my breath. I take in a deep breath. Before words can form in my thoughts, he's already forcing himself back in. He holds a steady grip on the leash to hold me in place as he fucks my mouth hard and fast until my vision starts to blacken around the edges. My whole body quivers as I wait to swallow him. His hips slow as he moans, "Fuck, Maggie." His salty release fills my mouth as he glides himself in and out of me. His cock pulses, as he drowns me in his orgasm. His grip on my hair lessens, and he strokes it lightly. He pulls himself out of me and helps me to my feet as I gasp for air. Sliding the leather belt through the buckle, he removes it from my neck. He tucks his cock back in his pants, and I pull mine up as well, trying to hide how much wetter I am. He leans down and kisses me softly. I totally forgot about the mascara I had put on that I had found in the top drawer of my nightstand, until he whispered,

"You're so fucking pretty with makeup running down your face." My cheeks redden as he wipes them with his thumb.

"Come on, babe, we have work to do," he says like he didn't just bruise my throat.

31

MAGGIE:

CAT AND MOUSE

"Dammit, Ry, you know I'm not stronger than you," I sneer in frustration.

He currently has me pinned to a wall with his large hands gripping both my wrists in one and my throat with the other, sounds sexy, but when you're competitive, and we've been sparring for hours, it loses its sex appeal.

"It's not about strength; it's about technique and being able to escape. Try using your legs more next time. It doesn't matter how you get out, just as long as you do."

He releases me.

"I'm getting frustrated with myself, and it's making me uninterested. Let's take a break for a while. I'll get some lunch ready, and then we can focus on different skills. We can revisit sparring tomorrow." I say, exhausted from the hours of intense fight training he has put me through. We are stronger than each other in different ways, but he has superhuman strength in this case, so I don't stand a chance once he gets me in his hands. I know for a fact he could lift a mutated bear that weighs at least a ton, so it's really not a fair fight. He sighs. "That sounds like a plan." Discontentment is all over his face. He isn't even trying to hide it.

"Go ahead and say what you're thinking," I insist, ready for an argument. It's just better to get it over with. We've been at each other's throats over the last week. We are both overwhelmed with so many emotions as we prepare for the fight of our lives. "I don't want to fight with you today," he responds.

"Then stop getting frustrated with me. We've been practicing my fighting skills and honing my senses for the last week. I can't be the best super soldier in a week. It takes time."

"We don't have time!" he thunders, anger boiling under his skin. The statement brings tears to my eyes, but not because he raised his voice at me.

It's because he's right.

They are coming for me whether I'm ready or not. Fear hits me like a derailed train. I do my best to swipe the tear trailing my cheek before he notices, but I'm too late. He sighs. "I'm sorry, I shouldn't have raised my voice at you. Unfortunately, the chemicals inside me make my anger hard to regulate. I'm working on it." He pauses a beat when I don't respond.

Nuclear

"Maggie, they are coming for you." His left hand holds his weight against the wall while his right hand balls up in a fist. "And—and I can't lose you." He takes a deep exasperated breath and continues,

"You have become the sole reason for my existence. If there is no you, then there is no point for me to be alive. You've sparked something inside me that I haven't experienced in a very long time. Hope. You give me hope, and it outweighs the fears and doubts that plague me. I love you."

Tears well faster in my eyes when I realize his internal struggle. He really does love me, and I'm pretty sure I love him.

I don't even love myself, so I need him to help me define a path to how I do that. He leans forward and places his forehead softly against mine.

"I know you are dealing with an internal battle, but I'd like to think you love me, too. Let me correct that; I'm not giving you a choice— you do love me, and one day, you will give me the satisfaction of hearing you saying it. That said, though, I don't want you to say it until you genuinely mean and believe it. Until then, I'll take your silence as confirmation." I lean up, peck his lips gently, and pat his chest.

"Thank you," I whisper in appreciation of him understanding that I'm not ready to go there yet.

"Let's get some lunch." I redirect grabbing his hand and interlocking his fingers with mine.

As I pick at my lunch, my mind drifts to what might have been if my aircraft hadn't crashed that day. I like to think I would've done everything in my power to avoid kidnapping people and forcing them into this life. The thought of someone losing their freedom because of me is unbearable. I want to think that I would've hidden people and explained to them the ways to avoid capture, but is it really better anywhere else? Severe radiation mutation, becoming a government experiment, or becoming a raider… that's really the only options, and they all suck. Still, at least people can make their own fucking decisions and not be forced into a painful lifestyle. A lifestyle that destroys everything about you. Every injection chips away at you until you are depleted of the physical, emotional, and mental capacity to fight for yourself. You become a shell, no longer harboring the person you used to be.

"Mags? Are you okay?" Ryker is looking at me concerned, which has become a look I'm familiar with nowadays.

He reaches across the table and lays his palm over my hand resting on the table. I look at him, guilt and sorrow heavy in my chest.

"I almost put people into the life that has broken me. They sent me on my first mission to recruit people, and somehow, the aircraft just happened to crash. I can't help but think about what I would've done to those people. I'd like to think I would have helped them avoid this fate, but what if others had been there with me? They would've reported my insubordination, and I would've been tortured into submission—" I trail off but return to my statement, "but at least no one would've suffered at my hands."

I poke a bite of venison on my plate with no intention of eating it. Before he responds, I say, "I know you must have been deployed on some missions; hell, you were sent after me. Please tell me you weren't one of the bad guys."

He sits back in his chair, obviously caught off guard by my question as he folds his arms across his chest.

"It depends on your definition of a bad guy."

Seeming to contemplate his response, he replies, "I tried my best to save who I could, but unfortunately, given our situation, it didn't work out for everyone I was sent to kidnap." My eyes widen as I comprehend what he's implying.

"So people suffered because you feared what would happen to you?"

Anger starts to settle in my bones as I circle and stand behind my chair before resting my hands on the back of it.

"That's not fair. You know what they are capable of."

"You just played God and decided who got to keep their freedom and who was to be thrown into the pound and experimented on like cosmetic rats?"

The question comes through my gritted teeth with malice.

"I thought you were one of the good guys. I really thought that of all people, you would be someone who would fight for everyone and take the beating. How do you live with yourself?" I spit with a bite of rage and betrayal. He stands up and slams his chair into the table so hard that one of the back support bars falls off. Anger seethes in his eyes as he steps toward me. He backs me into the corner of the room. He's scaring me, but I refuse to show him my fear. I meet his eyes, ready for the war I have started. His tone is calm, but his eyes are on fire as they pierce into me. A sliver of control holds steady in his emerald pools, but it's waning.

"First of all, I never claimed to be a good man. I have my fair share of sins. The only thing I've ever promised you is that I would worship you like the goddess you are. Look around, Maggie; in case you haven't noticed, our world is not black and white anymore. It's grey. Morals are no longer clearly defined, and I have to do what I must to survive. If I could help everyone avoid what I went through, don't you think I would? Those choices are not a luxury I have anymore."

He slams his hand next to my head, and I try to hide my wince as I fully prepare for his fist to hit me. My trauma shows in that moment.

"Secondly, I remember all eight people I had to give up to the government. The way I operated was to save as many people as I could, but if I was exposed for helping people escape, the torture I would've endured would've been so severe I couldn't guarantee that they wouldn't flip my humanity switch. You and I know that if that happened, everyone I was sent to get would return to the compound with me." His voice never wavers as he calmly explains the type of man he is, but anger and hurt rage in his eyes as he never looks away from me, but my eyes look at anything but his.

His other hand slams beside my head as I try to avoid his gaze.

"If I'm going to explain myself, then you are going to fucking look at me," he growls at me. I look up at him with a scowl.

"I did what I had to do to survive, and you, of all people, should understand that 416."

Anger seeps into my veins.

The number brings back a flood of flashbacks.

"You don't understand what I went through. I thought I was just Maggie to you. I thought the number doesn't matter," I hiss back at him.

"Oh, I don't? Last time I checked, I also have a number I'm forced to wear. We can deny it all we want, but it happened to us, and we have to deal with it." He motions toward his wrist.

"You're just mad because you want to be better than me, and maybe you are, but when I look at you, all I see are the scars that match mine. Face it, you would've made the same fucking decisions I did. You would've done anything to avoid the high levels of torture. You're mad at me because you know I'm right.

"You want to live on this moral compass, but unfortunately, baby girl, we live in a world where you only get murdered if you don't fend for yourself. You can sit here and keep lying to yourself, but it'll only get you killed, and that may not bother you, but it doesn't sit well with me. I will not let you put yourself at risk because you can't figure out where your morals sit in a world without morals. Face it, Maggie, you and I are the same."

I try to push him back to get free of the cage he created with his body.

He doesn't budge.

Damn, superhuman strength is killing my independent woman rage.

He laughs at my attempt to escape him.

"Haven't you learned yet? You are mine, and now there are two things that you can't escape."

"Oh yeah, and what are those?" I snap back sardonically.

"The truth and me."

A cold chill crawls up my spine with the way his words sound.

"We'll see about that." I slip out of his hold and knee him in the stomach. He launches back slightly, just enough to be stunned by my sudden aggression.

Nuclear

He lunges for me, but I dodge him. He stops himself against the wall before turning to chase me down the hall. I've already taken off and am out of his sight before he bounces from the wall.

"You better hide well, little fox, because when I find you, I'll fuck you."

I can hear the smile in his voice. Something about this cat-and-mouse game has my panties dampening, but I refuse to let him have me this time.

I meant what I said, but is he wrong in his accusations of me?

Would I have made the same decision?

I'm definitely no saint, but in this world we are in, would my sins outweigh the good in me?

There's a closet in the bedroom with a doorway in the ceiling leading up to the attic. I haven't made a trip up here yet because, let's be honest, attics are usually creepy, but I have a furious and horny man after me, so I'm desperate.

I pull the hatch and quickly climb the ladder, making sure to pull it up when I reach the top. I sit on the attic floor and I slow my breathing, holding as still as I can. The cabin is old and creaky, and it would take one squeak of ancient wood to give away my location. If I have super hearing, I'd be willing to bet that he does too. I hear his loud, angry footsteps cross into the bedroom.

"Come out, little fox; you couldn't have gotten far from me." I swallow hard as he opens the closet but does not find me. Coat hangers slide side to side as he frantically searches. He lets out a frustrated sigh before he closes the door with a slam and exits the room. I breathe a silent sigh. Since I've evaded him for the moment, I decide to look around.

Quietly, I tiptoe, investigating all the things up here. Most of the boxes contain clothing and small antiques. Nothing interesting; they remind me of things a grandma would hoard. I stumble across a chest labeled "MISC." I dig through it quietly, making sure not to move too much at a time.

The box reflects the label well. It's full of all kinds of stuff. There are a lot of tattered papers, including newspapers from when the war began. There are at least eleven back-to-back stories advising the public to avoid radiation exposure and how much potassium iodide you can safely ingest to avoid cardiac arrhythmias. Some articles discuss how to shield yourself with lead sheets and how to protect your home from contamination using heavy metals.

It's ironic because we have spent so much time trying not to expose ourselves to heavy metal, only to find ourselves scrunching to collect them.

I find a thick rope and use it to my advantage. It'll piss Ryker off when he trips over it, but hey, I'm already in for a pounding; I can't make it much worse on myself. I secure both ends of the rope to either side of the attic walls just above the ladder entrance. I returned to the box I was digging through and

Nuclear

pull out a few bottles of potassium iodide and polaroids that have been untouched. The pictures are mushroom clouds of explosions that appear to have occurred close to the area we are in. Someone was really invested in the war and trying to avoid being found. I discovered some folded paper on the bottom of the chest, and unfold it gently, finding a few different things.

The first is a map. It is hand-drawn, but it's not a location map. It looks to be an airway duct map. It's labeled "Fort Hamby Ventilation Map."

Holy shit.

This person has drawn an elaborate map of one of the biggest government facilities in the area. Ryker and I both came from there. The second page is a note describing how the power is generated in the lab. Whoever made this was going to save someone, but without any context, I'm unsure of the story line. I hear Ryker return to the bedroom and reopen the closet door. He pulls the attic door and realize I've been caught.

"Little fox, I know you're up there," he teases as he ascends the ladder. Stepping onto the attic floor, he trips over the rope I laid out. I am oh so grateful at the moment that I set my trap. He falls forward, and I come from behind him, straddling his back and firmly pulling his arm behind him.

"Gotcha."

I shout snidely with a sense of pride. I roll him to his back and pin him by his throat.

"That was too easy, fox," I say, mocking him.

"Is that so?" he asks, grabbing my wrist. Fear washes over me when I discern he won't just let me win. He reverses our position, and now he is on top of me. He has my wrists pinned with his hands. "I've been looking everywhere for you. You've been such a bad girl."

Oh fuck. He's never called me that.

"Ry, pause for like two seconds; I have to show you something."

"Sorry, we are way past stopping. Something about how you run from me makes me crave you more." He leans down and kisses me hard as he starts ripping my clothes off.

No seriously.

He grabs my top right between my breasts and rips it off me, right down the middle of my shirt. It pulls something primal from my core, and I bite down on his neck, leaving a mark, not caring about what it'll look like later. He growls low and rough, but never stops moving his hands over me.

I listen to the anger pulse through his veins as he tugs roughly at my pants. He doesn't let me have control of anything, he is too blind with the rage sprouted from my venomous words. He arches up just enough to undo his pants with one hand. His huge cock rests against my stomach as it's freed. He catches my gaze and looks me in my eyes before he slams inside me, and I come to the realization that he isn't planning on giving me an ounce of mercy.

Nuclear

Thank God the chase turned me on, too; otherwise, that probably would've hurt more. He is relentless with his thrusts, ensuring I take every inch of him with each stroke. Abruptly, he grabs my throat, stealing the air from my lungs. Dust swirls in the attic as we wrestle, thickening the atmosphere around us. My moans are dampened by the lack of air, and small squeaks are the only sounds I can manage. I grip his shoulders hard, steadying my shaking body against him. He leans down and sinks his teeth into the flesh of my breast. His bite brings the perfect mix of pleasure and pain that he's so good at finding. I close my eyes and begin to feel an orgasm pulling at my insides. I do my best to focus on my fast-approaching release, but my mind is distracted by how forcefully he's thrusting in and out of me.

I really pissed him off.

A sharp sting radiates across my cheek. I feel the heat start to rise in my face. He doesn't use all of his force for the smack, but just enough to bite my skin. Before I can protest the slap he just gave me, he grips my cheeks in one large, calloused hand.

"Eyes on me, baby girl. This is what you wanted, isn't it? You're going to watch me wreck you."

His words are absolutely filthy, and they edge me closer to drowning in sensual bliss.

An overwhelming mix of emotions floods me. That was a first for me. I've never been slapped during sex, but I think I liked it.

Thinking about anything is too hard right now.

I try to push him back, but he slams my wrists into the tattered wooden floor of the attic, and the aged boards crack in protest to the force applied to it. He grinds his hips hard into me.

"Ry—Ry," I moan as my orgasm almost overtakes me. He hastily pulls himself out but keeps me pinned.

I feel the flames in my eyes.

Hateful words threaten to spew, but he looks at me with no sympathy.

"You can't finish until I say you can." He growls the words as he brushes his lips against mine.

"I'm going to edge you to an orgasm over and over again until you've learned how painful your words can be. When I feel like you've learned your lesson, I may let you have what you want."

He smiles maliciously as he drives his thick cock back inside me. He leans down, catches my bottom lip between his teeth, and harshly pulls back on my flesh. The familiar taste of blood creeps into my mouth. I arch my back at the sensation of every inch of him. He watches me revel in the way he feels.

"If you're mad at me, you are doing a horrible job showing it," he whispers with a laugh as he slides his cock out of me all the way to the tip and then presses it back in.

Little whimpers escape me, as I begin to understand the afternoon I'm in for. His lips are mere centimeters from mine as he watches me take his cock. Another orgasm begins to creep inside me, and I do my best to hide it from him so he won't be able to stop me from my release. He quickens his pace and kisses me hard. His tongue makes its way past my lips, and the electricity trailing through my skin makes me shiver under him. He releases one of my wrists and begins to tease my nipples. It is just enough to push me until I teeter the cliff of absolute ecstasy, but Ryker quickly pulls himself from me, obviously seeing through my plan.

"Motherfucker," I mutter under my breath.

"I'm a patient man. I could do this all day."

He chuckles as he watches anger paint my cheeks.

"Maybe if you beg for it, I'll let you have what you want." He smirks as the hurt begins to seep away from his eyes.

He slides back inside me, and groans in response at how tight I am for him as he sets a moderate pace and doesn't take his eyes off me.

He's waiting for me to beg.

His kiss is punishing and angry, and his hips mimic his harsh demanding lips and the way he stretches me becomes overwhelming. My orgasm builds, as it never completely leaves the pit of my stomach.

"Ry—Ry, please let me finish. Please let me show you what you do to me."

He lets out a guttural howl as he fucks me harder.

"Please... Please," I beg incessantly.

He doesn't stop this time as I near the lake of pleasure I so desperately want to drown in. My orgasm rips through me, and stars start to cloud my vision. He continues his merciless rhythm until his hips stutter as my orgasm comes to an end. He finishes inside me, filling me with hot streams of his seed. He kisses my forehead and then reaches my lips holding them for a beat, catches the helix of my ear and whispers,

"I love you even when you fucking hate me."

The statement makes my pussy tighten around his cock, and he laughs in response. It's at this moment I discern that I have him wrapped around my finger. He would do anything to please me, but all he wants from me is love. He's helping me get closer to finding that word's definition.

32

MAGGIE:

LILY

"Ry, look at all this stuff," I say practically bouncing up and down with excitement. I motion towards the "MISC" box, and I show him the hand-drawn map of the lab's air duct system. His eyebrows raise, as he stares at the wrinkled paper.

"What would someone be planning to do with this?" he asks, perplexed. Before I answer, I keep digging. I hand him all the newspapers I had found earlier in the large tote box. His eyes study each paper, analyzing them for clues or helpful information. My eyes catch on a journal as I reach the bottom of the box.

The book is leather-bound, raggedy, and worn. The wear on it does not suggest age, but rather heavy use. I run my fingers across the cracking leather. There's a woven cord wrapped around the journal, securing it closed. Ryker must notice that I'm intrigued by something because he looks at me and inquires, "Well, you got quiet. What did you find, love?"

I'm unsure what I've found so I raise it for him to see. I carefully unwrap the braided twine binding the journal together as clumps of dust fall from the pages and onto the ground. Ryker perches himself to where he can read the pages over my shoulder.

Before I get to the first page, a wallet-sized photo drops from the worn pages. I pick it up and study it closely. It's a portrait photo of a girl with bright blue eyes and warm ebony skin. Her hair is voluminous and curly, resting just above her shoulders. She's wearing a modest but complimenting red dress. Genuine happiness fills her oceanic eyes. I flip the picture over, and the backside reads: "Lily, 2103." I lay the picture down gently as I open to the first page, which reads:

August 13th, 2105

The war has grown and festered into worldly demise. Lily and I have moved to the cabin to live off the grid for a while. They are after her. The government has been stealing our loved ones, and unfortunately, my daughter falls under the age guideline for "recruitment." The greed of our politicians and government officials has led to them needing my little girl to fight their war.

I won't let this happen.

Nuclear

My sweet Lily will not fall victim to a losing game. Self-preservation is all I have left to offer for us.

Everyone who gets taken by the military never returns home. We are unsure of what happens to them from this side of things, but I'm sure they fight until they die. The government's resources are dwindling, and it's just a matter of time until everyone is dead anyway.

Part of me aches to have my sweet Sarah with me.

Being a single parent all these years only to lead up to this.

Having to hide my daughter and watch her be stripped of a future.

She'll never get married, she'll never have kids, and she'll never be safe again. The other part of me is grateful that Sarah doesn't have to watch or be a part of this. I don't think her sensitive heart could handle the sadness in this situation, and I couldn't make a promise to my beloved wife that I don't think I can keep. When they track us down and come for her, they will send many soldiers, and being as feeble as I am, I wouldn't stand a chance of saving her.

This is the only gift I can give her. I can help her run. I will gladly give my life if it means her safety, but I'm unsure my death will mean anything. I love her so much; how am I supposed to accept that we are on borrowed time? Have I failed as a father?

-Sam

M.C. Blackheart

Tears pool in my eyes as I realize what happened here without needing to finish the journal. I look up at Ryker, and he squeezes me into him as I continue to turn the pages.

September 1st, 2105

Today, I went into a small town around five miles out. Lily stayed behind to avoid someone seeing her. There were a couple of tiny shops that looked aged and empty, but untouched. A few stores still had grocery items and pieces of clothing. I found a half-full piece of luggage in the back of one of the shops. I grabbed everything I could that may be useful, including survival supplies, food, coffee, toilet paper, and different outfits for us both. I even managed to grab a couple of pairs of boots.

On my trek back, I had my first run-in with a creature. The radiation had mutated it to the point that it had begun to rot. I'm guessing it was previously an opossum, but it was something else now. Its teeth were disproportionate to its mouth, causing its upper jaw to hang to the side. Its fur was falling out, and the skin underneath was scarred and burned. I snuck around it as I was unsure how violent it could be, and my goal was to avoid using my gun as much as I could to prevent attracting God only knows what to the loud sound. I would kill to have a silencer.

-Sam

November 29th, 2105

Nuclear

They came during the night. Raiders, I believe, is what they are calling themselves. There were eight of them. They were large, burly men with weapons I had only seen in the movies. Lily and I put up the best fight we could. I was able to kill three of them, and Lily was able to take out one on her own.

I was so proud of her.

Unfortunately, I was shot in the right shoulder, which hindered me from fighting for her.

They took her from me.

My chest burns with fear of what will happen to her.

I tried.

I tried so hard.

My heart is physically breaking. I would be lying if I said I hadn't been contemplating suicide tonight, but if I die, who will fight for her?

I am all she has left.

No one else cares if she lives or dies in this netherworld.

She wouldn't give up on me, so I can't give up on her. I will likely die in this fight to free her, but at least I can say I did everything I could.

Where do we begin? Probably stitching this bullet wound.

-Sam

I look at Ryker over my shoulder; he has been reading just as intently as I have. This poor father and daughter were brutally torn apart. It's no different than just about everyone else right now, but it still hurts me to know that this keeps happening and is the story for so many people. We are all victims of the same assailant.

December 1st, 2105

I've spent the last week hiking and venturing through the cold and rigid forest, looking for any sign of her or them.

I've come up empty physically, mentally, and emotionally. However, I stumbled upon a place just north of the cabin called Ft. Hamby this morning. It's very secretive and secluded.

I think it's a lab.

There's no telling what they are experimenting on in there. I overheard a conversation between two men in white coats at the front entrance. To sum it up, they stated that the raiders had been supplying the people (the victims) in exchange for supplies, food, and money. Not sure what good money would do you in times like these, but they must have their reasons. Anger surged through me when I realized that Lily might be in here, but I had to maintain a level head until I could devise a plan. After all, my right arm is still out of commission for now.

Hang on, my sweet Lily, I'm coming for you.

-Sam

Nuclear

December 30th, 2105

I befriended a guard outside the building by acting like a raider who needed supplies. He has a tablet device, and just as fate would have it, he had a map of the air duct system through the facility pulled up due to a possible breach. I stood beside him glancing at the screen as he focused on it, not watching my wondering eyes. I studied the map as well as I could, making sure to remember every turn and location, praying for a photographic memory. He turned his tablet off within fifteen seconds and said he had to investigate the issue. He advised me to only return with collateral if I wanted anything, as other guards weren't so lovely and would not entertain my requests. I nodded and thanked him generously for the snacks he gave me. After disappearing into the trees, I immediately began to draw the map. I drew two copies just in case, placing one in this journal, and one in my shirt pocket.

After sunset, just as dusk crept in, I walked the perimeter of the building, searching for the entrance vent. It didn't take me long to find what I was looking for.

It's located on the right side, about six feet off the ground. There is a sensor just above the vent, which looks motion activated. That must be how it detects a breach. Now, I have to devise a plan to get in, grab Lily, and leave without being noticed. Easier said than done, but I have nothing else to live for.

-Sam

January 10th, 2106

M.C. Blackheart

This will be my last entry. This journal still has so many empty pages, but my time to fill them has come to an end. I have devised a plan and do not plan on returning to this quaint cabin even if I get Lily out. They will come looking for her here.

If someone finds this place and finds sanctuary here, please know that you are welcome. I hope you find what you need and what you're looking for.

I always loved this place, as no one could ever find me here.

Well, that was until people started hunting other people anyway. I hope you keep your loved ones safe and make sure to always stay one step ahead of your enemies. I'm leaving an extra copy of my airway duct map just in case you find yourself in the same situation as me. I'm leaving this picture of Lily so she will live on and so she becomes more real to you. Besides, when she's back in my arms, I won't need a picture anyway. The cabin used to be used for hunting, so I hope you find everything you need. Take care of yourself and be safe in this messed-up world.

If you find this and Ft. Hamby is your next stop, please kill every one of those sons of bitches you can.

-Sam

It's hard to breathe for a second after finishing the journal passages.

"Ryker, I think we have a plan B," I state confidently.

Nuclear

"What do you mean, love?" he responds.

"Sam left us everything we need to take the fight to them, but I'm only doing that if they come after us first." Ryker nods in agreement.

We neatly pack everything back into the box but not before discovering a larger-than-usual metal compass. Its body measures about five inches in diameter, featuring a gold faceplate and a black-and-green arrow that wobbles slightly as I turn it. The letters symbolizing the cardinal directions lay slightly lower in the face plate than everything else. An odd decoration tactic, but I also don't design compasses. I look at Ryker. "That may be useful one day. Don't forget that if we have to leave here."

"Wait a second, there's an inscription on that. What does it say on the top piece?" he asks. I pop the lid of the compass open and notice the very faint etching of letters. They honestly just looked like scratches on worn metal. A couple letters were distinguishable, however not in a sequence that made sense.

"I can fade the tarnish, give me just a minute." I'm already halfway down the ladder before Ryker says, "Of course you can. What can you not do?"

"I can't pee standing up." I shrug and giggle. He rolls his eyes.

"And I'm grateful for that."

I come back with a bowl lined with aluminum foil, baking soda, and a cup of warm water. He looks perplexed. "I didn't know we were having a science fair! I would've brought my vinegar and baking soda volcano."

"Very funny. You can make fun of me all you want, but just remember that my useless knowledge is going to help answer our questions," I remark sardonically. "What would you do without me?"

"I'd be lost, little fox, I would be totally and utterly lost."

He tucks my hair behind my ear. The fight we had earlier seems to no longer be relevant.

I pour a hefty amount of baking soda over the noisy foil in the container, before placing the compass lid in the bowl as well. Filling the container with water just over the lid of the compass and holding the main face out of the water, excitement builds as I wait. I feel like a true crime investigator who just discovered fingerprints at a crime scene for the first time.

"So how long do we wait?" he queries from beside me.

"At least twenty minutes, but I'll check it as we go."

The minutes pass swiftly, and I pull the compass from the water after science has done its job.

"The moment of truth," Ryker announces as I begin to rub the lid with my shirt. The tarnish begins to vanish without harsh scrubbing. Once I can see all the letters, I raise it to eye level and read aloud,

"I'm the beginning of eternity, the end of time and space, the beginning of every end, and the end of every place. What am I?"

Really?

A fucking riddle?

I did all this hard work for a riddle?

He begins to laugh as I sigh, but it's so contagious that I find myself chuckling too.

"Wow, all that for a riddle that I probably won't ever figure out," he states.

"I know, right? It's literally the apocalypse and here we are trying to solve a riddle without any prize," I respond.

I place the compass back in the box but continue to let the riddle reside in the back of my mind.

I place the lid back on the box and then lay my head on Ryker's shoulder. I think our findings settle the anxiety in both of us.

33

RYKER:

THE RECKONING

Fall came and went expeditiously. The leaves fell from the trees, and cold temperatures began to creep in slowly like vines climbing old wood. The air grew crisp and foggy, and the woods became silent as the temperatures dropped.

I guess animals still hibernate?

Thankfully, the heat in the house is still functioning well. We check the traps daily as the anticipation and anxiety of an attack have Maggie and I on our toes, just waiting for the day.

"Ry?"

Maggie looks up from my chest. She just woke up, her eyes still sleepy and calm like light rain on a tin roof, but

Nuclear

I've been awake for a while, watching her sleep and taking in every ounce of her.

"Yes, my sweet vixen?" I whisper, trying not to pull her totally out of her sleep. She pushes herself up to my lips and kisses me once softly. I return the kiss but grab her neck gently to hold her on my lips for a little longer. I just need to soak in the taste of her lips. She pulls away and murmurs,

"I know you would, but promise me, if the military comes for me, you won't die for me."

I clench my teeth and my face drops.

"You have given me purpose and are the only thing that matters to me. Without you, there is no reason to live—"

"And you expect me to live without you?" she inquires sweetly but sternly. I smile and hold her face in my hand. "How about neither one of us dies, and we tear down a tyranny of assholes together?"

She smiles and follows with, "Deal."

I look outside and see snow starting to fall. A white flake lands on the window and quickly vanishes, leaving a tiny water droplet in its place. The drop trails down the window, and more flakes join and melt beside it. Maggie's head snaps to the window.

"Have you ever seen snow?" she asks with a wide smile spanning her face. Her childlike excitement makes me grin.

"No, I haven't. We didn't get much snow in Arizona," I remark.

"We get at least one heavy snow every year in Tennessee. I look forward to it."

She walks over to the window and traces the paths of the melted flakes with her eyes. I can see the flight of thoughts behind them as she jumps from one to the next.

Sliding her boots on she expresses, "I need to stand in it. I need to feel it. What if I never get to feel the snow again?" She smiles and looks down with uneasiness in her gaze.

"I promise you will have a long life and see the snow, the sea, the mountains, and whatever else your heart desires."

I've been thinking over the last couple weeks that we should probably consider moving locations. We've been here too long. As nice as it is here, it's not safe. The military is coming for her, and it would be hard to pinpoint our location if we never have a consistent one. Plus, I'd love to see her eyes light up when she sees the sunset over the ocean, the Grand Prismatic Spring, and the rock formations in Utah. I can't wait for her to see it all with her fingers entangled between mine.

She stands to her feet without responding to my statement.

She's obviously not getting her hopes up for winning this battle.

"Let's go." She pats my shoulder and walks down the hall.

Nuclear

"Come on, Cerberus!" I hear her call from the living room. I get ready speedily and follow behind them.

A cold sting splinters from my left shoulder.

"Gotcha!" Maggie says while running away and laughing. We have spent the day in the snow, and dusk is starting to settle on the horizon. I reach down to pack my snowball, but she's already pelted me with another. I throw mine with a direct blow to her chest. The snow bursts into smaller clumps as it hits her skin, like a fluffy cloud breaking into a million pieces.

"Oh no, you've shot me. I'm going to die," she announces dramatically as she falls to the ground and lays in the snow.

"If only I had a big strong man to give me mouth to mouth and save me." I roll my eyes and walk over to her.

"I heard you needed a big, strong man." I kneel beside her. She sticks her tongue out to the side, pretending, very badly, that she's dead.

"Oh no, I think this woman needs mouth-to-mouth."

I lean down and kiss her cheek, and she retracts her tongue, waiting patiently for me to kiss her, but I don't. After about ten seconds, she cracks her eyes, peeking to ensure I'm still here. I can't help but smile. I lean down and kiss her before sitting her up. I run my fingers through her hair, twirling through the jet-black strands as cool snow clumps dance along my hand, melting against my body heat.

I pull away and whisper, "I love you, Maggie." Her hand grips my cheek, pulling me back to her. Time seems to slow in this moment as her eyes stare into mine. Her thumb strokes over my cheek.

"Ry, I lo—" she starts, but her gaze darts from mine to the tree line. The fear in her body language makes me freeze.

"What's wrong?" I ask, shaken by her sudden change in demeanor.

She is off the ground within seconds and heads straight for her bedroom. Panicked hands grab her knives, crossbow, and pistol. She starts to holster all of it.

"Maggie?"

"They're here. It's happening, Ry."

"How do you know?"

"You can't hear them? They are just beyond the trees. There's at least ten of them."

I grab my gear and weapons just as she does. Cerberus can feel Maggie's panic, and she's already waiting by the front door.

Nuclear

We walk outside, and I hear nothing but the silence of the first snow of the year. The silence of snow is creepy as no sound reverberates.

"I don't hear anything," I whisper to her.

"Close your eyes and concentrate. Tune out every other sense but your hearing," she whispers back. I do as she says, and she's right; multiple footsteps approach through the trees and snow. The snow crunches under the weight of our enemy's feet, and it's the only sound that gives them away.

I nod in agreement, confirming her suspicion.

We all stand back-to-back, ready for the fight we have been prepping for.

Maggie loads her crossbow just before throwing her arrow bags over her shoulder, and I load both of my pistols, ensuring my other magazines are ready to go. My breathing is painfully labored with anticipation, and my heart feels like it's coming up my throat. We listen to our eerie surroundings until the "shink" of a metal trap and a scream fills the air. Painful howls echo in every direction erratically, as every trap we set is activated. I lose track of how many traps have gone off after I get to twelve.

They weren't fucking around; they brought a shit ton of soldiers. There's at least thirty total.

A man pops up from the brush, and Maggie nails him between the eyes before he can pull the trigger on his weapon.

A single trail of blood forms from the arrow's entrance wound and makes its way down his face as he falls backward.

She reloads within five seconds.

I fucking love this woman.

Another soldier emerges from the brush, and I discharge my weapon before he completely crosses the threshold of the tree line. He falls backward, only his feet visible in the brush.

One by one, Maggie and I pop them off.

Another one emerges, avoiding my shot.

He's fast, like abnormal superhero fast.

It seems like the government has been improving their experimentation with someone having speed like that. Are we outdated experiments? Can we keep up with these people?

He gets about five feet from Maggie, but she lands the arrow in his chest. He hits the ground with a loud thud.

His body shakes in agony as he lays on the ground, fighting to stay alive, and his eyes beg Maggie to spare him, but she doesn't.

She grabs the arrow, twisting it in his chest with ease watching intently as the life leaves his eyes. After his chest stops heaving, she rips the arrow from the puncture wound and she reloads her crossbow with it. The crimson dipped arrow awaits its next victim, and a sense of pride washes over me.

My little fox is so brave and cruel.

I just saw a side of her I've never seen before and want to watch her do it again.

To watch her take a life is extraordinary.

To see the flames flicker in her eyes without faltering, is a sight that ignites my soul.

My little skull crusher.

The fascination of the cold beast under her skin makes me have to adjust my cock in my jeans.

Two more soldiers come forward just as fast as the one before, snapping me back to reality. Their plan seems to be to staggering the number of soldiers we face at a time. I'm unsure if it's to study our fighting techniques or if it's to make how many there are unclear.

Cerberus speeds off, taking one down and ripping him to pieces within seconds, while I popped two rounds into the other one, unsure of what I hit but aiming to kill. He falls forward, landing on his face. They seem to always approach as if they think they can beat us.

Underestimation can be just as deadly as curiosity.

The pure white blanket of snow that was underneath our feet begins to slowly ombre into a deep red slushy mess.

More soldiers appear in a pack of five, and one gets to Maggie, grabbing her wrist before she can get a good shot. I raise my pistol and release the bullet into the back of his neck. It enters and exits as blood spouts from both wounds. The realization of how close together we are becomes apparent when the bullet entered the guy's chest directly behind him.

What's that saying?

Oh yeah, two birds with one stone.

Maggie kneels in front of me, grabbing a hand with a large knife in it. With the flick of her wrist, she shatters the guy's extremity, takes the knife, and stabs it into his chest. The act is clean as if it had been rehearsed many times.

"Thanks," I say, smiling. The chills I get from seeing her this way make my soul ache for her. "You're welcome. Thanks for the help a second ago," she responds, smiling and wiping sweat off her brow.

"Anything for my little fox," I promise without ever dropping my grin. We direct our attention back to the trees. I raise my weapon with my finger stiff on the trigger.

What emerges next has me in udder disbelief. My digit hesitates to fire the weapon as a tall man walks out from the trees. He has dark curly hair and olive skin. His eyes are two angry blue pools. He has a mechanical right arm and a bionic right leg. Something is illuminating from under his shirt on his chest. My heart sinks with realization.

"Cairo?"

I whisper, the question making my mouth dry. A flood of emotions sends my mind into a spiral, destroying all rational thought. Maggie draws up her crossbow, ready to attack.

"Stop. Don't shoot yet."

She looks at me, confused, but I don't have time to explain.

"Cairo!" He looks at me but isn't really "looking" at me. He's looking through me.

How is this possible? I watched him die. The scene haunts me every day, but here he is, standing right before me. I walk toward him, gun still drawn.

"Cairo, man, it's me, Ryker."

He stares at me, studying my features slowly with no emotion. I approach him, starting to lower my gun.

He takes advantage of my attempt at kindness, balls his metal fist up, and delivers a right hook so hard it sends me into a nearby tree.

"Ryker!" Maggie screams.

The impact knocks the wind from my lungs, and it takes every bit of effort I have to remember to breathe. My left cheek throbs as blood begins to fill my mouth. I reach my hand up to my face, finding a split along my cheek bone from the hit. I look back to him, dazed and reeling.

Is this real?

If this is a nightmare, it's beyond time for me to wake up. I get up with my palms raised, easing my way toward him, but his sights are already locked back on Maggie.

The next series of events shocks me as I try to regain my footing. Cerberus comes to me to help me toward Maggie. Cairo's arm begins to transform into a bionic ray gun. The sounds of grinding metal echoes through the clearing. The gun appears within seconds.

Before he gets within twenty feet of her, he launches a blast in her direction. Yellow gamma rays rip through the air, lighting up the darkness until they hit her in the chest. It sends her flying backward; before she can return to her feet, he does it again, knocking her back down. He walks closer to her to deliver a final blow, smiling as the ray gun powers up. I try to rush to her but I'm being attacked by more soldiers. As fate would have it, something I have never seen happens.

Maggie begins to glow.

Her veins begin to radiate a neon purple light from under her skin. She is focused on Cairo, and her attention doesn't even waiver to me. She looks down at her skin in shock and fear but doesn't dwell on it. It's like she knows how to use whatever is happening. The colors of her mismatched eyes start to illuminate, as purple electricity ignites from her fingertips. The snow below her has almost completely melted because she radiates so much heat. She holds her hands parallel and contains flashes of lightening between them. It grows into a chaotic ball of temperamental energy, and she launches it at Cairo.

The electricity overwhelms his bionic parts as purple sparks erupt from the mechanical makeup.

A single drop of blood drips from Maggie's right nostril and trails down her upper lip. Unfazed by her bloody nose, she looks at her hands as Cairo still stands, preparing for another launch at her. She lifts her palm to him, and electricity shoots from her and wraps around his bionic arm allowing her to control him like a fish on a hook.

The beautiful strands of electricity appear to short out his robotic makeup and his bionic parts begins to twitch and malfunction. The shock brings him to his knees as she approaches him, using her stream of electricity as a leash for him. Despite his strength and cyborg enhancements, he cannot break her hold. He squirms and clenches his teeth, desperate to free himself. Without lowering her outward-facing palm, she raises her other hand toward his face as she stands over him. She wraps her hand around his jaw and looks him in the eyes.

"Remember," she whispers, never looking away. She sends electricity through his face, which glows purple as it travels through his body. The dim glow under his skin is fluid like as it moves smoothly throughout him. She closes her eyes as more blood runs from her nose and ears.

More men sneak from the tree line, and Cerberus and I do our best to hold them off, but we are severely outnumbered. One of the speedy guys emerges from the tree line behind Maggie. His movements are so fast my eyes can hardly keep up with him. He gets to her within three seconds, beating me by a few feet.

A gunshot flies, and Cerberus lets out a whimper. Maggie's concentration breaks to look for Cerberus and the fast guy injects Maggie with something before she can figure out what's happening.

"Maggie!" Fear makes the scream guttural as I cry out for her.

She crashes to the ground, and I try to run for her, but there are too many of them. They carry her away, and all I can feel is rage. I begin using my strength and throw men like rag dolls through the clearing.

Cairo becomes limp, but he is conscious. He makes eye contact, and in an exasperated voice, he asks, "Ryker?"

"Cairo! No, no, no! Cai!" I scream, nearly releasing the sob forming in my throat. Soldiers grab Cairo before I can reach him, pulling him into the darkness of the thick brush.

The last soldier in my path lunges for me with his knife drawn. I try to throw a punch, but like he was expecting it, he manages to grab my hand midair. He thrusts the knife forward at my torso but misses by mere millimeters. His hand wraps around my throat, squeezing so hard that I can feel my windpipe bruise.

It would be impossible for air to move in or out of my lungs at this point. I claw at his wrist, trying desperately to break free, but it's no use, his grip is stronger than mine.

The scientists perfected my super strength.

My chest heaves as blackness threatens my vision. I fall to my knees, and he lets out an evil laugh.

Only one thought flashes through my mind.

Maggie.

As the knife nears my right eye, I throw myself forward, knowing I have no other option, and slam him hard into a tree. The knife goes off course, and punctures deep just below my cheekbone.

The blade scrapes my teeth and facial bones, and it is a sensation that will haunt my nightmares for eternity. A rageful scream bellows from my throat.

No more. I'm done with this.

The guy is disoriented, and his grip waivers. I take the opportunity to free myself, but the knife runs up my face, until I can get a grip on it. The weapon is so close to my eye that I'm sure I will lose it, but thankfully, the blade never sinks into my cornea. The pain of the wound doesn't even register in my brain with the anger flooding through me.

Blood pools in my eye, turning my vision crimson and blurry. I use the knife blindly and sever the man's Achilles tendons, reveling in his scream of agony. I flip him over in one swift motion and pin him beneath me. I raise my hand with the knife grasped tightly and stab the man in the chest over and over, putting every emotion I have into my thrusts.

Rage blinds me as I sink the knife through flesh and bone. The man's skin filets easily, and his bones crack under my strength. Blood gushes from my repetitive motions and covers me from head to toe. The warm liquid sprays my face on my final blow to his chest. My breathing is heavy as sorrow tears through me, brutal as it rips apart my sanity.

Tears fill my eyes as the reality that I have failed my girl squeezes my heart. I lift myself off the man, kicking him with force and gathering all the saliva I can muster to spit on his pathetic corpse before running to the tree line.

It's too late.

They have my heart and my best friend. Every last one of them will wish they had died tonight, because the next time we meet, their deaths will be slow. They borrowed time tonight, but rest assured, they are already dead.

The reaper ALWAYS comes to collect debts owed to him.

I can't wait to feel their blood coat my hands, as I tear them limb from limb. Anyone who lays a hand on my little fox will die.

Nuclear

They took everything from me, and I plan to set the world on fire, watching as they all fucking burn.

I drop to my knees with my face tilted up to the sky. Blood pours down my face, rapidly soaking my clothes. The icy, winter air bites against my cheeks as I scream, a raw, primal sound echoing into the dimming sky.

"*MAGGIE!*"

MAGGIE:

EPILOGUE

My body bounces as the car I'm in obviously doesn't have good suspension. My head is pounding, my body aches like the end stages of a fever, and fear begins to settle into my bones. I blink my eyes open, bracing for bright light, but instead, I feel a burlap sack over my head. I stay calm, trying not to alert the person in the car that I'm awake.

Talk about déjà vu.

Everything is still blurry, and I try to put the pieces together.

Ryker.

Oh my god, Ryker.

Is he dead?

Is Cerberus dead?

The thoughts and concerns fill my head, and tears well in my eyes.

Nuclear

The worst happened.

We lost.

There were so many of them, and then the biggest bombshell sabotaged our defense. Cairo is alive, and I could see the shock in Ry's eyes. My heart hurt for him when he realized his friend wasn't inside the shell of the man we just fought.

Oh my God, he's dead, and I didn't tell him that I loved him.

The thoughts and regrets battle in my head, and tears stream down my cheeks. I try to collect myself and take in my surroundings, but my heart is too heavy to let my mind think clearly.

"Take another left and an immediate right, and we will be there," a deep voice says from beside me.

I discern now that I'm handcuffed as well.

Fucking great.

The car drives for three more minutes exactly and then abruptly stops. Two car doors open, and a firm grip yanks me from inside the vehicle.

"Wake up, princess, we are home," a familiar husky voice states. My body protests in pain, but they don't give me a choice. Four hands harshly guide me forward, two rest on one of my arms, and the other two rest on the other arm. As I enter the building, bright white light pierces through the holes of the burlap sack, and it is blinding. I blink and squint, trying to clear my vision through the hot tears that don't stop coming. The sterile smell of rubbing alcohol makes all the vicious memories of this place come back in overwhelming flashbacks. I try to keep from hyperventilating as my mind spirals out of control.

I refuse to show them fear and will do whatever it takes to survive this place. I cling to the hope that Ry might still be alive—and if he is, he's coming for me.

All of these people will die when he finds me. They should be terrified of the monster he will become if he's alive. A cold sheet of metal is placed behind me. Someone undoes my handcuffs, and my hands are quickly put into leather straps simultaneously. A belt is secured around my waist. It's just like the table from my initial encounter with this place, but this time, I'm standing. The only belt I ever want wrapped around me is Ry's. The thought of him hurts so much.

The bag is ripped off my head, and my eyes struggle to adjust to the room I'm in. My retinas feel like they are screaming from the intensity of the light.

When my eyes finally take in my surroundings, the clear image of Dr. Hyde stands before me.

"Ahh, 416, it's so good to have you back. I have big plans for you, my dear."

My heart drops, and I swallow hard as I come to terms with the fact that I've returned to hell.

ACKNOWLEDGMENTS

TO MY HUSBAND, GAVIN, THANK YOU FOR SUPPORTING MY WRITING DREAM, HELPING WITH THE STORY LINE, ALL THE WAR REFERENCES, PLAYING FALLOUT WITH ME, AND LISTENING TO MY FIRST READ THROUGH. I COULDN'T HAVE DONE THIS WITHOUT YOU. THE INTENSE LOVE THAT RYKER HAS FOR MAGGIE WAS INSPIRED BY THE LOVE WE SHARE. YOU HAVE ALWAYS BEEN MY BIGGEST SUPPORTER, HELD ME DURING MY LOWEST LOWS, AND CELEBRATED MY HIGHEST HIGHS. I TRULY COULD NOT HAVE A BETTER LIFE PARTNER. THANK YOU FOR BUILDING ME A PC WHEN MY LAPTOP ALMOST DIED DURING WRITING, SO I DIDN'T HAVE TO STOP. THANK YOU FOR HAVING FAITH IN ME. AND THANK YOU FOR THE INPUT ON THE SPICY SCENES AS WELL, YOU HAVE A FANTASTIC IMAGINATION. I LOVE YOU. IT'S ALWAYS BEEN YOU AND IT WILL ALWAYS BE YOU.

TO MY FRIENDS HANNAH, AMANDA, AND JADA, YOUR ONGOING SUPPORT AND EXCITEMENT HAS MADE THIS SUCH A FUN PROJECT AND THANK YOU FOR TAKING THE TIME TO BE MY BIGGEST CHEERLEADERS. THANK YOU FOR BRINGING SUCH JOY AND HAPPINESS INTO MY LIFE AND HELPING ME CREATE THE GNARLIEST OF MONSTERS.

TO MY EDITORS LILLIAN AND RAMONA, WHAT A WILD RIDE! THANK YOU FOR HELPING MAKE THIS BOOK AS STRONG AS POSSIBLE, BUT ALSO HELPING ME GROW. THANK YOU FOR

TAKING THE TIME TO EXAMINE MY MANUSCRIPT AND MAKE THIS BOOK RELEASE POSSIBLE. I'M ETERNALLY GRATEFUL.

TO MY ONLINE BLACKHEART BOOK CLUB WHO HAVE LISTENED TO ME TALK AND SHARED MANY LAUGHS WITH ME, I'M GRATEFUL FOR THE LOVE AND SUPPORT. I HOPE THIS BOOK MAKES YOU PROUD.

FINALLY, TO EVERY READER, BLOGGER, AND CREATOR WHO TOOK THE TIME TO READ THIS STORY AND SUPPORT A TINY INDIE AUTHOR, THANK YOU. THANK YOU FOR THE THOUGHTFUL REVIEWS, THE INCREDIBLE POSTS, AND ANY SUPPORT YOU CAN GIVE. I AM SO GRATEFUL. THE FACT THAT I AM WRITING AND WILL BE ABLE TO CONTINUE TO WRITE IS ALL THANKS TO YOU!!! THERE AREN'T ENOUGH WORDS TO DESCRIBE HOW THANKFUL I AM FOR ALL OF YOU.

UNTIL BOOK TWO,

M.C. BLACKHEART